# Shadow

# Shadow

## IAN ENTERS

WEIDENFELD AND NICOLSON
LONDON

First published in 1989 by
George Weidenfeld & Nicolson Ltd
91 Clapham High Street, London SW4 7TA

British Library Cataloguing in Publication Data

Enters, Ian
Shadow
I. Title
823′.914 [F]

ISBN 0–297–79506–6

Photoset by Deltatype Ltd, Ellesmere Port
Printed in Great Britain by
Butler & Tanner Ltd
Frome and London

to Michal

# Part One

# CHAPTER ONE

'Will you come here and clear this mess immediately! I won't ask you again.'

Mother, firm and angry, strong on rules and ready with her inimitable thumb for every action of his as a child. Peter limped into his room. Joan, his mother, stood amidst his precious collection of cardboard boxes all glued and stiffened by old grey slivers of wood smuggled in from the yard fencing to make a ship.

'How can I keep this place tidy if you don't clear away your mess? You must sort it out or throw it out.'

Peter could not speak. He had a cleft palate, but emotion stifled him so often that no words came anyway. He looked up at his ship, the boxes he'd ferried up from the kitchen, the smeared pot of flour paste he'd mixed and then allowed to set in the enamel saucer, the stiff yellow brush like Dad's smoking finger and the scrapings of curled and crisped brown card stuck like his sister Claire's curls when Mum pinned them into place with tortoiseshell clips. He shuffled towards the door. He liked his ship. His Mum caught him by the arm, round the elbow, where it hurt.

'You're not daft and you're not just walking off. At nine years old, you're old enough.'

Peter wriggled in her grasp silently, his mouth tight, the hare-lip bleached like a scar, but Joan held him harder until he stood still, sullen and rigid, staring at the floorboards. She wanted to put up her hand and bring it ringing down across the back of his head. She almost did so, her arms flexing and pulling the boy towards her but something in his stillness, in the crouched and sullen expectancy of his shoulders, stayed her. With a sigh she released her son and he scuttled out of the room.

Joan moved heavily across to the small attic window, propped her head in her hands and looked out over the empty fields to Barham Village. This same view had greeted her for the last ten years; it was totally familiar and with that familiarity had come a stale recognition of failure every time she stood absorbed, unconsciously registering that outside world of Norfolk, that part of England to which she'd come after the Second World War with such hopes, with a husband suddenly met and quickly married after the armistice.

She peered inside her memory and peopled Brook Street, Clapham, her original home, with the celebrants of peace on the day she met Paul – street-party time, noise, brass band, banners, red, white and blue, Winston Churchill, jelly and cakes. Yes, her mother was there, faintly disapproving, standing outside the grocer's shop, their shop, talking with the minister of the congregational church they attended. He was interested in her; her mother had encouraged him, but he was old, at least fifty. What would life have been like with him, Joan wondered, rubbing her thumb against the window-frame where the old paint bubbled and cracked away to show some more of the dark green over which she'd slapped the white ten years ago. She flicked the piece of white from under the nail. No, not for her the quiet certainty of faith and the wondering dismay at the obvious catalogue of worldly wrongs. This was the day that Paul, in khaki and smiles, with wide shoulders and conquering hero stride, had visited his parents' corner sweet shop, now a shell and parents dead from the blast, and been asked to join the party.

'We've all to be neighbourly now. The lad has nowhere else but his old street,' Mum had explained, putting him next to her as if he were still the little boy Joan had gone to school with.

'This will never do,' Joan muttered. 'There's still the beds to be made and the meal to be cooked.'

She put her reddened hands on to the window sill, pushed herself up and mechanically cut a swathe through her chores, bundling up Peter's contraption and stuffing it into her hessian rubbish sack, before starting on the tangled blankets on the bed.

Her son was outside by now. His younger sister Claire had called plaintively after him as he'd scrambled down the stairs but he had ignored her, left her rummaging through mother's sewing basket, picking out the reels and lining them up across her doorway. She never seemed to be in trouble, never seemed to annoy his mother.

He disappeared inside the decaying shell of a tiny outhouse, its timbers smelling of over-sweet fungal rot, its roof a patchwork of holes and its wall shivering in the easterly wind. At the back and along one side were five hutches, all individual, made out of various off-cuts of wood and furniture. Peter picked up a biscuit tin and perched it on top of the largest hutch, the remains of a sideboard with its main door removed and mesh firmly stapled in its place, and peered into the dark corner of the sleeping area whistling gently through his lip. It made a funny squeaking sound like blowing through grass between the thumbs. There was a loud thump in the darkness and then a velvet nose and twitching whiskers followed by a huge rounded back emerged.

Gently Peter opened up the hutch, unclipping the wood struts at the top and sides of the mesh from the rusty nails, and slid his arm across the sawdust towards the bowl. He was too late, too noisy or Floater, the buck rabbit, was just being awkward. Floater flashed in a whirl of dust and droppings towards the bowl, landed on it, scrabbled, scoring deep lines in the wood of the floor, and Peter hastily withdrew his hand.

'Same old game, Floater. Can't you think of something else?'

That's what his Dad always said and then he'd push the rabbit to one side, ignoring the long claws as if they didn't exist, and pull out the bowl with his other hand, pinning Floater against the wall of his cage as he did so and laughing at the rabbit's futile kicking, but although Peter mouthed the same words, he didn't match the action. Instead he pushed a stalk of old cabbage through the mesh and started tickling Floater's nose with it.

'Come on, Floaty, have a nibble.' Floater launched his front paws at the mesh and seized the food with a tug. As he munched, drawing on the pulpy stick like a smoker dragging at the first fag of the day, Peter stealthily flattened his hand between mesh and surround and shuffled it cautiously down and round towards the upturned bowl. Floater thumped and jumped back towards it. Peter flinched, giggling, but this time he kept his hand on the bowl. He looked admiringly at the buck.

'Don't let the bastards get you down. That's right, isn't it?' His father's words again.

Quickly Peter finished feeding the other rabbits. They were for the pot, not for stud – no names for them. He put the tin back in its place, top pushed firmly on for fear of the rats, and then, hunch-shouldered, hands in pockets, he made his way back to the house. He should have cleaned the rabbits out as well as fed them. A week's droppings had accumulated, but he didn't like spading out the wet orange and brown mouldy remains and left the job undone too often for his mother's liking.

'You cleaned those rabbits out then?' she'd say, wiping her hands down her apron as if preparing her palms for action. There were advantages in having a cleft palate. A mumble could mean anything. His mother would look suspiciously at him and, very very occasionally, she'd bustle out of the kitchen and march across the yard, the wind flicking her skirt petulantly, to inspect the job, but she didn't like going there, preferring to leave the rabbits to Dad and even if they hadn't been cleaned, she'd be the one who'd have to do it. Peter couldn't see the point of cleaning out the rabbit-pie hutches, as Dad called them. He looked after Floater all right. Floater was the important one.

Today his mother said nothing; she was still caught wondering what she'd seen in her husband and why he'd become as he was, a shambling morose figure. When they'd come to the farm they'd brought such hope with them. They'd been lucky with the sale of Paul's parents' corner shop site, and the proceeds had just about provided enough capital to buy the buildings and part of the acreage. He had been so adamant against staying in London.

'It's no place for kids. You're trapped, closed in. It's space I need.'

Maybe the tanks had given him a fear of confined spaces. One night, a few months after their marriage, Joan had been thrown bodily from the bed with Paul landing on top of her like a sack of potatoes, crushing the breath from her and bruising her side so she could hardly walk next day. He'd said he was dreaming about emergency drill for leaving the tank and Joan had stroked his cheek as if she wasn't hurt at all and cuddled him until he went back to sleep.

Then, when he talked about the farm, she could understand his dreams. He seemed so convincing, strong, optimistic, confident, but now the dreams were nightmares and every day was a drab battle for survival with her husband refusing the fight, just pottering from one make-weight task to another. Well, she couldn't do it all and wouldn't do it all, she thought, but the broken latch on the back door rankled, the cracked windowpane in the toilet irritated and the weeds sprouting in the fields unchecked by thistle-docking left her raging inside.

She heard his footsteps crunching across the patchwork of old bricks that acted as the path from yard gate to back door. It was time for the midday meal and he was probably shambling in from the Anchor in Barham. He could throw his fine hopes and life away, but she wouldn't, and nor would she throw away her children's hopes. She put plates on the table, told her son to wash his hands of all that rabbit muck and lifted Claire to her chair with a quick swing from her hips.

'Upsidaisy lovey – time for lunch.'

Her husband stamped across the floor.

'Talking to me then?'

'Take it or leave it,' muttered Joan, pushing bread and cheese towards Claire.

'Lunch . . . lunch . . . lunch. Who do you think we are anyway? Lord and Lady Muck? Dinner did for me and'll do for you too.'

Peter slid into the kitchen like a shadow and slipped to his place, eyeing his father. Dad's voice could go either way at the moment – into sullen anger or sudden surprising laughter – but there was an undercurrent of secret excitement in his voice that Peter found unusual. His father, tall and awkward, buckled himself onto his chair.

'Aren't you even going to take your coat off then?'

Dad pulled his formless blue overcoat closer round him.

'It's keeping us warm, isn't it?' He winked at Peter and stretched out a long arm to the cheese. As he did so, he surreptitiously opened his coat so that Peter could see a pert billiard-ball head and bright bead eyes. A sudden squirm beneath the coat and it had disappeared. Claire had seen it too. Joan was turned to the sink, straining off potatoes in a cloud of steam. Peter's eyes opened wide and he stayed silent. He always stayed silent. Besides, it was a secret.

'What's Daddy got? What's Daddy got?' Claire cried excitedly.

'Can it, kid!' drawled her father, imitating Cagney, but Peter could tell he was angry with her and this pleased him. Joan, arms on hips, faced her husband.

'Not another bloody animal, is it?' Peter wriggled in his seat. When his Mum swore it was serious.

'No farm's complete without livestock, dear, and this little lass will keep the pot boiling.'

He drew a long sinuous white fur stole out from under his armpit like a shamefaced conjuror with a shop-soiled rabbit, and produced an albino jill ferret that hung momentarily, then writhed and flashed to the floor. Joan screamed, clinging to the sink, ramming her legs together.

'Get that thing out of here. Get it out! You know I hate 'em. Get it out!'

Dad casually leaned over and lifted the ferret towards his wife. He smiled.

'It's only a ferret, Joan. Don't get all upset about a harmless ferret.'

There was a rancid musk in the room that made Peter's nose wrinkle up. Claire started to cry, her round face screwing up and mottled patches appearing on her cheeks. Joan took her courage into her hands and patted her daughter stiffly on the shoulder, her eyes still fixed on the ferret. It wasn't her fault she didn't like animals and couldn't cope with gutting and preparing the rabbits and chickens. She liked the cows and looked after them, did everything a farmer's wife should do with the milk and cheese, but it was just little creatures she couldn't manage, the way they jerked as if still alive after Paul killed them, the way they scurried full of fear and making her afraid.

'Will you please get that thing out of here? You're frightening the child.'

'Peter's not frightened, are you mate?' He waved the ferret in front of the boy. Peter was frightened, petrified, his eyes riveted to the demonic head of the ferret, but he was fascinated and he tried not to show fear. He shook his head slowly from side. Joan hoisted Claire from her chair and rushed out of the kitchen. Her husband leaned back, the front legs of the chair lifting from the stone floor, and laughed loudly. He looked at his son but Peter stayed quiet, serious, looking at the ferret. His father's laughter changed to sudden silence, then a stare.

'Please yourself then. I'm off to the hutches. The rabbits'll drive Josie here wild but the spare caging'll do for now and at least it's safe. These things would wriggle through the ars'ole of a constipated miser.'

Peter followed his father to the outhouse. He didn't want to, knowing the state of the cages, but there was no alternative as he watched the long creamy lines of the ferret hanging in his father's red fist, still from the clench on her scruff, all her speed and ferocity latent.

One of the side hutches was empty – last week's rabbit. The old sawdust and droppings were still piled there. Dad fetched his son a clip round the ear.

'Should'er been cleared out by now, lazy little sod.' He scooped out the gunge with a rusty old grate shovel, still clutching the ferret in his other hand.

'Here – cop 'old of Josie, will you?' He thrust the ferret at Peter, who tentatively put out a hand as she arched towards him, quivering, smelling the leavings of her natural food all around her.

'Not like that, you stupid halfwit! Behind the head and watch her teeth. They're not there for decoration. She's not a bleeding pussy cat.'

Peter steeled himself and took the beast. His head still rang from his father's blow. The ferret seemed an extension of Dad's temper,

6

another means of ensuring Peter did as he was told when he was told.

Luckily the ferret didn't bite. Peter's small fingers clutched the neck and froze there, fearful lest she twist in his hand and direct a blow at his face. But she was looking intently at the nearest hutch where Floater was sitting, his dark fur pressed up against the mesh and his ears flicking backwards and forwards.

'That'll hold all right. I knew there'd be a use for that old fireguard. Now pop her in.'

Peter thrust his hand into the gloom of the cage, jerked his hand open and pulled it out with frantic speed. His finger joints ached with the holding of her.

'The more she's handled, the better she'll be, but she's had an upsetting time of it and could do with some peace and quiet, so we'll leave her to snuffle round and sort out the furniture. Wait on though . . . it's not too soon to show her where grub comes from. I'll give her some.'

Peter went to pick up the biscuit tin, but Dad started to laugh. 'You must be joking! I don't know what I did to deserve a lump like you. It's meat she needs, not that old crunch and munch.'

He reached across to one of the other hutches where a doe had recently dropped kits. Dad rummaged among the litter while the doe made mock rushes at his hand in her fright.

'Where's that runt then?'

He forked out a scrawny scrabbler of a rabbit, a tiny under-developed creature with its first fur scarcely covering it. He slid back the ferret's grid slightly and slipped the rabbit in.

'Watch this then, Peter. That ferret'll find her own food. It's not too soon to start her.'

Even as he spoke the little rabbit bounded at the grille and bounced back. It rushed into a corner and hunched bottom out against the white streak of malignity that first scored black blood lines across its narrow and shivering hindquarters and then, as the rabbit squealed and bottled itself further into the corner, twisted like a corkscrew under, round and between the rabbit and the hutch walls. There was a high-pitched tiny shrill, like air squeezing out of a punched balloon. The rabbit seemed to leap up and then fall almost at once, the ferret's teeth locked in its neck.

Peter's mouth was dry and a lump of bile heaved up at the back of his throat. His eyes couldn't leave the feeding ferret.

'That's why jills are better than hobs, girls are better than boys,' explained his father. 'Jills are more manoeuvrable, can skedaddle round a rabbit in a corner or blind run. Quick, wasn't she?' Dad plunged his hands into the huge pockets of his old coat and leaned against the outhouse wall, looking across at his new acquisition with a satisfied smile. He stayed there a moment or two and then approached the cage again.

'Still,' he said, his hands leaping out of the pockets like claws, 'we can't have her learning to kill and then lie up on the meat. We'll spend all our time digging her out. She's got to learn that she kills, we take and then she feeds on what we choose to give her.'

Once again the cage was opened and the man cautiously but steadily put out his hand for the jill's neck. She bottled-brushed her tail, spitting viciously, threatening to attack but unwilling to leave her kill. Suddenly the hand creeping towards her became intolerable and she leaped at it and fangs sank in. Then she was away, but Peter's father took the rabbit carcass anyway. He held it at the front of the cage and whispered.

'Come on Josie. Come and get it. Food is here.'

Josie crawled forward low to the floor, her head lifting and scenting the meat while Dad took it away and then brought it back. Eventually he released the rabbit and Josie again sank her head into its throat.

'She'll learn,' he muttered, apparently oblivious to the blood on his hand. 'Joe said she'd do that at first, but he reckoned it better to feed like this in the run than lose her down the first rabbit hole.'

Peter left the outhouse. It had suddenly become unbearably hot in there. His stomach heaved and he retched, his head against the icy cold of the grey stone wall. Slowly his stomach righted itself and he shivered. Then he felt his father's hand on the back of his neck, propelling him along the wall to the back door.

'One's a runt and the other's a Mummy too-good, but the runt'll have to do me. Now get inside. It's nature, that's all.'

But it wasn't nature, and Joe at the pub had not told Paul the right way to train a ferret. Peter's father lacked the patience for it, and the early feeding system bred mistrust. Josie would skulk in her cage rather than leap towards the hand that fed. She became as her owner made her – subject to moods, untrustworthy and increasingly vicious on the kill. Peter would not touch her unless his father forced her to his hand, and he was bitten a couple of times. Joan tried to keep her son away from the creature, but her husband pushed protests aside. As time passed and Joan continued to insist that the ferret be only her husband's concern Josie was left longer and longer in her hutch, in worse and worse conditions.

# CHAPTER
# TWO

A cold late spring left the cattle short of feed, but a dry hot sun rose in the sky towards the end of June and stayed there, bleaching the grass of its lushness and baking the clay to a solid crust so the pasture could not recover to make good silage. When the rains came in early September, the Norfolk farmers found their yields dramatically reduced and Paul Townsend had to fall back on his tiny safety margin of capital to buy in feed for the winter. He raged about his misfortune and talked about selling up, but nobody except a fool would want to buy the small and inconvenient farm. It wouldn't even fit easily into another's acreage.

The sun returned in October. The woods on Barham Estate glowed like fire and the good land seemed to sigh with regret that it was fining up too late. Pheasants strutted blindly along the lanes and verges. Dad took to taking Peter out for a walk, as he called it, and he grew used to the large coat and the occasional pheasant plucked out of its stupidity into oblivion.

Barham Estate had suffered over recent years, and was just getting sorted out after the war. The Frobisher family was gone and a manager had been appointed to rejuvenate the land. Meanwhile, there were better pickings further afield, and Sandringham was only three miles away. Peter walked there with his father, limping along a few yards in the rear, scuttling the first tree-fall of leaves. His father kept beside the beeches while Peter tramped the wide green verges. The light shone with a pure and fragile clarity.

The dark woods were full of twitchy windy rustlings and the grass Peter trod was a rich clear emerald patched with gold.

'This weather won't last much longer,' Dad had said that morning. 'Better make the most of it.' And they'd set off very early, Dad ignoring his wife's pursed disapproval of his activities.

Dad already had a pheasant under his coat, driven into his arms by Peter's rush along the outside verge. He was on the lookout for no more. It was time to turn and trudge back home, but Paul walked on. Peter watched the bobbing halo of tobacco mist caught by the sun, smelt the whiff of old crushed-down woodbines, heard the hiss of black boots through whispering bracken and the hum of his father when he was happy. The further their walks took them from the farm, the happier his father seemed.

Dad was singing a round – he always sang in rounds, as if to pause was anathema to him, as if wherever and whenever his wife joined in she could not disturb the circle of his own sound. Not that Peter could remember the family singing together, but some vague feeling inside assured him that his parents must have done once. Now it was a father's sound, far removed from his normal harshness, not even one of his army songs.

'Ah poor bird! Take your flight, far above the sorrows of this sad night.'

He'd started too high and had to adjust to reach the later notes. He stopped and knocked his pipe against a tree. The ash flakes flew and he put the pipe to his lips and blew to clear any clogging threads of spittled tobacco. Satisfied the stem was clean, he stuffed the pipe into a pocket; it clicked against the round tin and nestled with the Swan Vestas. He walked as if he would never stop patrolling the wood edge.

It was then that Peter saw the pheasant, a large cock bird, jewelled and sequined. Dad saw it too, for he was suddenly still, a dark shadow melting into bracken. There are so many pheasants and they are all so rare with the flash of wings, the poke of tail, the strut of legs and the jolt of head. Shot with sun like a bluebottle's body, the cock watched over its brood of females with anxious pride. It stood by a clay and sand bank ten yards from the road and looked anxiously back towards the trees, towards the shadow, where its haven should be.

Peter did not want to see his father's directions, but he had to watch, pick up the right-handed gesture that he should walk quietly along the verge while Dad reached the cover of the bank, to lie in ambush there for the pheasants' distraught and flurried clatter as Peter suddenly rushed the panicked birds towards him. There was more luck than judgement in the system. For every bird caught, twenty escaped, but Dad seemed to be able to gauge with some skill the possible scurrying route of the birds and used his coat as a net, tossing the great blue mass over the creature and then seizing the whole bundle in one quick movement.

Peter began to run his up-and-down, hopalong gait. His left shoulder looped to the side to compensate for his shorter left leg and his narrow head bobbled from the uneven steps. Although his father had told him to shout, yell anything he liked, his approach was clumsily noisy in movement, silent in voice.

The pheasants took fright, scattering and charging back towards the wood behind the bank, but some instinct warned the cock, perhaps the scent of tobacco or just a perverse kink in its nature, and it doubled back, flapping for the other side of the road. Suddenly all was panic, a loud whirring undignified smashing of wings, while the hen birds melted into the safety of the trees. The cock pheasant veered away from the boy and flew directly into the side wing of a silent silver ghost of a car. Peter turned, thinking it had escaped, pleased that it should have done so and next moment he was struck across the chest and staggered back, flailing his arms but unable to stop himself falling to the ground.

Peter heard footsteps thunder, saw his father's coat thrown on the earth beside him, felt the draught as it billowed and then settled.

'My God – he's been hit!' He was swirled up and round by his father, and stood wobbling on his feet, not certain what had happened.

'That's right, you bastards – drive on! Don't worry about knocking over my son, will you?'

Peter looked at his feet and green, blue blood seeped down his old duffle coat, darkening the brown to black.

'You all right, boy? Did you run on the road? How many times have I told you to keep on the grass?'

Peter stared at the blood and wondered whether it belonged to him and whether he could be dead.

'Did you see the car? Rolls Royce it was – could have been the Queen for all I know.'

His father's hands were roughly patting him, turning him round, inspecting him for damage.

'Not a mark on you – all the blood's from the bird – must've been thrown against you by the car – present from the Queen. Pity she didn't stop – could've thanked her properly.'

The hands went away and then swooped down to pick up the broken body of the pheasant, checking for injuries, just as they had done to his son moments before.

'It's a miracle,' he said, smoothing back the plumage. 'He's unmarked really, just a bit bloody under this wing.' Dad held the bird in front of Peter's face and then whisked it away. 'What a weight! That's got some meat on it.'

Dad started to chuckle half way home. 'I don't see why I should hide this one away,' he said. 'We came by this one fair and handsome. Here, catch hold. You caught it. You carry it.'

The bird was laid into Peter's hands and its head lolled away from him. Its weight seemed to increase with every step, as Peter dogged his father home. The light began to fade rapidly as clouds built from the north and still Dad chortled.

'Would you believe it? A poaching party with the Queen. Would you bloody well believe it? Coronation a couple of years ago and introductions to yours truly this year with a free pheasant thrown in. What a story for the pub! What a tale for Joe! He's not the only one with a story. Could be worth selling this bird at the Anchor, keeping the other for food. Townsends – by licence of Her Majesty – provider of fresh royal pheasants! It must have been her. Who else would float about Sandringham in a Rolls? Even if it wasn't, it had to be one of the family.'

He laughed again, turning back towards Peter, but, as ever, all he saw was a pinched face and the raw wound of the hare-lip in a white surround.

'Here, give us that pheasant. You're trailing it on the ground. Tired, are you?' Peter nodded.

Dad marched triumphantly into the house, full of immediate pride, and slammed the bird onto the kitchen table. Joan was washing Claire's hair at the sink, rubbing the green soap over her head. Interrupted, she snapped at Paul.

'Shut the door then. Claire'll catch her death.'

Peter, arriving well to the rear of his father, shut the door. Claire started to wail. 'Soap in eyes. Soap in eyes.'

Hastily Joan wrapped a towel round her daughter's hair, glancing surreptitiously at her husband who stood, arms folded, over his afternoon spoils. Normally he had the grace to hang his proceeds in the outhouses, and pretend they were legitimate fare. She quickly rubbed her hands on Claire's towel and turned to Paul.

'What happened then? We're all desperate to know, aren't we? Stop picking your nose, Peter.'

'Good job you didn't do that earlier my lad, eh?' Dad winked, shoving a sharp elbow into the boy's side, but Peter didn't respond.

'Oh, one of those moods?' Joan half laughed, relieved, wondering what had caused this unlikely event.

'Present for you,' he nodded towards the table. 'And this one,' he forked out his first capture of the day, 'is just a little taster.'

'Oh yes, by courtesy of which kind landowner this time? I've told you I don't like thieves and I won't have my children stealing.'

Paul raised his eyebrows, pursed his lips and whistled tunelessly. Joan kept going.

'I never understood why my mother, God bless her, made me learn the Ten Commandments by heart, but now I do. Thou shalt not steal.'

'I told you,' said Paul, sounding hard done by and aggrieved. 'I told you she'd automatically think the worst of me. Well when you've finished accusing me right left and centre, I didn't steal it, did I Peter?'

Peter shook his head because that was the response Dad obviously expected. Joan took no notice, turning back to pour cold water into the enamel jug, before adding hot from the copper.

'Needs to be bloody well stuffed and framed that bird. It does, you know.'

Joan put her little finger into the water, shook off the droplets, folded her arms and settled her bottom against the wooden draining board.

'All right. Tell us what happened.'

With many sidelong winks and interrupted by disbelief from Joan, Paul recounted how they'd been innocently walking along the road when a huge Rolls Royce had slid by, knocking the pheasant into the verge right at their feet, and how the Queen had waved from the window saying, 'You might as well have that, my good man.'

'And you expect me to believe that?' said Joan, quickly standing up and unwinding the towel from Claire's head, putting her by the sink and rinsing off with a splashing stream from the jug.

'Don't care one way or the other,' retorted Paul. 'Just don't go calling me a liar and a thief, that's all. I'm off – get a better audience in Cleethorpes on a wet Monday.'

'Since when were you in Cleethorpes then?'

Paul grunted angrily, swung away towards the door, plucking up the great cock pheasant on the way.

'You can't give me credit for a thing, can you? Ask the boy. Go on. There's a splash of blood on his coat where the bird hit him.'

'Needn't have come like that,' said Joan stubbornly as she rubbed the towel roughly over Claire's head. 'He'll tell us a lot, anyway. The day we get words out of him will be the Day of Judgement.'

Dad caught Peter by the arm and tugged him over in front of his mother.

'It's true what happened, isn't it? All you've to say is yes. It won't hurt you.'

'Don't bully him, Paul. You know what they said at the hospital. He'd speak in his own time.'

'Hospitals don't know everything. He needs a bit of a shock to stir it out of him.' He returned to the boy. 'Now come on' – but his voice was a trifle kinder – 'just say that one little word. Yes. It won't kill you.'

13

Peter stared at his mother. Slowly his head moved from side to side.

'There you are,' mocked Joan. 'He said "No".'

Paul glared furiously at his wife and then threw Peter's arm down as if it were contaminated.

'I'm off out!' he repeated, all his good spirits evaporating. There was a warning in his voice and Joan knew she should heed it. An evening's drinking on top of anger often brought violence.

'All right,' she said quickly. 'I believe you. I was just joking.'

'That's more like it,' he grunted, still dissatisfied, and walked out.

Joan shrugged. Perhaps she should have accepted his story, but it wasn't right to involve Peter in his poaching and excuses. She looked at the front of his coat. Yes, there was a stain there. She pulled him to the sink and sponged it down with an old cloth.

'That won't come out too easily and you need it for school as well,' she sighed. 'But it'll have to do, I suppose.' She undid the peg buttons and slid the coat from his narrow shoulders. 'Sit yourself down and I'll get you a bite to eat when I've finished Claire off.' The little girl's hair was as straight as twine, but Joan liked to make a little row of curls along the fringe in the hope that early training would lead to wavy hair. There was no sign of success yet.

'He's had a lot to put up with, your father,' she said now, as she stuck a hair-grip into her mouth, teasing its end open. The trouble was, she thought, he always harped on about how he was rooked by the previous owner, how the land was solid clay and he couldn't afford the machinery to break it up; there was no drainage; the field size and shape were hopelessly inconvenient. All the signs of a run-down, infertile homestead stared him in the face when he'd come to look, but optimism and sheer ignorance had led him into the purchase and she'd been as bad, carried away by her husband, the ex-soldier, the one who seemed to know.

'He's no farmer, no countryman, no more than me, but will he be told? Will he listen? The pub doesn't open for an hour, so he'll knock around with old Joe, pretending he is one of them and that'll lead to more trouble.'

Joan finished her daughter's hair and mumbled round the kitchen finding food. There were boiled eggs and soldiers and a cup of milk each. The two children sat quietly, listening, watching her intently. She pulled herself up short. She hadn't realized she was talking to herself.

'Yes, he's had a lot to put up with, and that includes you two.' She had to be loyal; she didn't want her children having no respect for their father. 'Now hurry up and eat. You're to have a good stand-up wash, Peter, before bed, so don't run away, and remember, it's school tomorrow.' Peter nodded almost eagerly, and Joan sat down next to him.

'You like school, don't you? Well, most of the time. Lessons anyway, and you like Mrs Gribbons.' She smiled encouragingly at the boy. 'How about a nice "Yes Mummy" just to show you know what I'm on about?' The momentary flicker in Peter's eyes died. Joan looked down at the table, traced her fingernail round a knot, wondering how to go on. Perhaps it was futile even attempting to raise a response.

'You know you had a little operation for your mouth when you were young. Well the doctor said you could speak quite well but you had to try more. How about saying your name?'

Peter lowered his head and refused to make a sound.

'Peter says things to me,' said Claire, preening herself.

'Yes, I know, dear, but not proper words. He should use proper words.'

Peter shot a look of fire at his sister. She grinned.

'Peter said naughty words.'

Joan wished she hadn't started trying again. Mrs Gribbons had talked to her about language coming from the home and had given her some cards with pictures and sounds, but Peter had ignored them.

'No, not naughty, just jumbled up because of his mouth.' Joan got up. She should have remembered not to start with Claire there. Claire always liked to speak.

'Go and get your school-bag, Peter, and you, young madam, can hold your tongue.' She drifted back to the sink carrying the crushed eggshells.

Claire suddenly screeched in pain and Peter scrabbled out of the room.

'As soon as my back is turned! Shut up, Claire – you're not dead yet.' Joan pulled the girl off her stool and rubbed the red pinch mark on her leg angrily. Claire subsided.

Joan took out the large grey metal tub from behind the door into the passage and began to pour hot water from the hissing old copper. Then she pulled a worn velveteen curtain across the back door, lit the lamp and raked up the solid fuel stove. She enjoyed wash night; so did the children. Peter returned to her call and she scrubbed him down as he stood naked in the tub. He became like a great baby on these occasions, content to be washed and towelled, to be inspected behind the ears, to have his short leg massaged warmly. Joan had always done that as if some superstitious belief could bring that inch or two of extra growth.

'Was there any little accident while you were pregnant, Mrs Townsend?' the doctor had said. 'It's not much, you know – hardly anything to worry about. Lots of people have one leg slightly shorter than the other, but we must do something about his mouth. That's first priority.'

She'd never mentioned how her husband had thrown her out of bed and landed on top of her, but she sometimes thought that could be the reason for Peter's little trouble, as she called it. Damaged goods – that's what Paul called him, half jokingly – but she'd never suggested that he might have done the damage. It's just being a war baby, she'd thought. Could've been much worse.

Eventually, wrapped and warm, clean and comfortable, Joan read to the children, pointing at each word in turn. She knew Peter could read; he could certainly write, after a fashion, with letters back to front and with no awareness of size or regularity. If only he would talk as well. *Black Beauty* was the choice tonight, Joan's choice. The horse was going through the tribulations of cruelty. When it was time for prayers before bed, Joan added, 'God bless all animals everywhere.'

Peter didn't understand.

# CHAPTER
# THREE

Paul was drunk, not obviously, but deeply so. He'd arrived at the Anchor on the dot of opening time and George, the landlord, had scoffed at his story but bought the pheasant for a fair price, no questions asked. Now the pub was full of steamy heat, long glasses in small puddles and about fifteen men trying to forget it was Monday next day. It was only nine o'clock and that by the accelerated pub clock, but Paul had downed five pints on an empty stomach and bought Joe and a couple of other pub acquaintants a few. They all sat round a small table by the darts and Joe, the time-honoured seer of the group, the countryman of vast experience, began to recount an exploit when out ratting with his two terriers. He had a natural gift for storytelling, unlike Paul, and held his audience, although Paul became increasingly uneasy, befuddled and angry.

'I mind the time because it was just before that freeze couple of year ago.'

'More like ten,' chipped in Johnny, a young man of twenty-three. 'I were still at school — couldn't get in for a month.'

'As long ago as that were it?' mused Joe, sipping a little beer. 'Before your time then, Paul?'

There'd been a World War on, thought Paul bitterly, and they measure time in cold weather. He'd been shivering in a tank across Normandy and they'd been tucked in their cosy homes, able to enjoy a few pints.

'We'd worked the old quarry just alonger your place Paul, and cleared a few rabbits,' Joe continued, now the early skirmishes were out of the way. 'But the rats was lying low. I had this feeling that they was having an underground party that night round by the — what do you call it — all that old tackle at far end. Well I netted a few holes, slipped Fitchy Ferret in, but would he go? Would he hell! He'd yellowed, so I shoved him in and stood on the hole. You should've felt the ground squirm and the noise — enough to waken the graveyard . . .'

17

'I reckon there be rats along the wall there too – flesh eaters,' said Denis, a round, serious-faced man with goggle glasses hooked over squashed ears. He studiously rolled a narrow cigarette between nicotine-stained fingers. Joe didn't like the interruption.

'I've bin alonger there – some big rats but not like at the quarry. Well I took my foot off and all was quiet, not a sound. Then out shot the biggest rat I ever seen and I seen a few, you know that.' He paused, took a sup, holding his audience.

'Pink elephants an' all I wouldn't wonder,' grunted Paul, shifting his buttocks in his chair and leaning back. But Joe couldn't be put off his stride.

'My bleeding terriers was at another hole by now and I didn't have no gun so I thought he'd got away, but no. This rat weren't about to run. He'd come out spoiling for a fight – went straight for my leg, up the trousers . . .'

'He bloody didn't.'

'He did an' all – straight up the hool intent on nipping my precious off. I had those trousies off so fast – quicker'n if that film star had spread her legs for me, you know, Jean Harlow.'

'Seen those pictures of that blonde piece, Joe – new she is – an eyeful she's got. Marilyn Monroe.'

Joe looked with a withering and pitying eye at Johnny.

'You're young yet Johnny, don't know what experience is, wouldn't know the difference between a woman and a shop's dummy, you wouldn't. You want to hear this story?'

'Doubt if the rat found anything worth bothering his teeth over.' Paul spoke heavily. 'Or do you keep squeaking now because you lost 'em?'

The three other men looked over at Paul. They recognized the signs. Joe didn't take offence, and went on in a suddenly deep voice that had the others laughing.

'There I was, no trousies and this rat leaping about, so I swung my spade, cut off the big bastard's head – blood everywhere, bloody everywhere.'

Paul heaved himself up and the table lurched, slopping beer.

'Easy on mate, easy on.'

'I tell you the bloody Queen gave me that pheasant.' The men looked at each other.

'Course she did – you told us, didn't you?' Denis murmured, fumbling in his pocket for matches. His tiny stump of a cigarette had gone out.

'Well, just you bloody well remember that. That's all.' Paul

lurched past the table and out of the door. He needed a slash out at
the back. The three others looked relieved.

'What's bitten him, then?' Johnny said.

'Then I dug down for my ferret, terriers at the ready . . .' Joe had
lost his audience. He downed another sup and picked up Johnny's
packet of cigarettes. 'Can you spare one, lad?' He pushed the inside
box up and pulled out a filtered cigarette. 'Makes a change from
roll-me-ups,' he grinned at Denis, who was placidly stretching a thin
line of tobacco into another cigarette paper.

Paul returned. The cool air in the open privy had steadied him a
bit. The conversation turned to desultory chat, then Joe ventured to
bring Paul into the limelight again. After all, the man had bought
most of the beer.

'How's your ferret doing then, Paul?'

Paul looked at him sideways, but the question seemed innocent.

'Josie – violent. She wouldn't back off a fight.'

'Rats is different,' murmured Joe appeasingly. 'Ferrets'll suddenly
lose heart with them. They're best with rabbits.'

Paul nodded, but in his mind he saw Floater in his cage. He'd
shown no fear of the ferret, and had recently taken to lashing at the
hutch front with his rear legs. He took another mouthful of beer.
This was a chance to show these labourers. At least he owned his
land. They'd treated his story as if he were beneath them. He'd
fought in the war as well. Joe was too old, Johnny too young and
whatisname had something wrong with him – chest or something –
didn't stop him coughing back twenty fags a day though. With a
steady pull Paul drained off his pint, put the empty glass firmly on
the table and leaned forward.

'I'd bet a rabbit against that ferret of yours, Joe.'

Joe smiled ruefully and shook his head. The man was clearly mad
with more than drink, stupidity as well.

'No chance of that, old mate,' he said gently, while he raised his
straggling grey eyebrows at the other men as if to say, 'Humour him,
lads.'

'Oh?' said Paul, ready to take offence again. 'Why's that then?'

'She's dead, just like the one in my story, killed by a rat protecting
her young. I told you earlier, Paul, when you come round with that
fine pheasant from the Queen.'

Johnny snorted into his glass. Paul glared at him.

'Anything funny?'

Johnny blew his nose on an old rag and kept a straight face.

'I'll make a book on it,' Paul shouted. 'Rabbit against *my* ferret.
Put your money where your mouth is, Joe.'

Paul widened his audience. People were listening to him at last. He stood up, shaking his head to clear it.

'A little bet, lads, at my place – fair fight between my ferret and my rabbit.' Laughter greeted his words and Joe gently pulled at his sleeve.

'Ease off, Paul. Don't make a fool of yourself.'

But Paul was beyond recalling and some fierce spark of conviction in Floater's aggression carried weight.

'What are the odds then?' came a shout from the corner.

'Million to one against the rabbit,' sneered one of the darts players. The men had crowded round the table, stopping his throw.

Paul stared round and a scarcely held silence fell.

'I'll bet that in a fair and open fight between my ferret, Josie, and one of my rabbits, the rabbit will win. I'll give half a crown to any man who wants to bet on the ferret, if the ferret wins. Half a crown to me, if the rabbit wins.' His words were jumbling up inside his head, crowding to get out, but the men seemed to understand.

'It'll be a fix,' sneered the darts player. 'Let's finish the game. I've just a double top to get.'

'It's no fix,' said Paul, whirling round. 'Joe's seen the rabbit. Ask him.'

'What do you say then, Joe?' prompted a fat squat man who used to work on the same farm.

'Well I've seen the rabbit and the ferret,' said Joe judiciously, scratching his deeply creased chin. 'Rabbit's a fine buck – no doubt about it – but ferrets eat rabbits and that's about the long and the short of it.'

'But is the ferret hungry?' George, the landlord, leaned over the bar, worried about the beer money leaving, trying to joke his way into pockets.

'Ferret's hungry all right,' Paul said firmly. 'I'm going up home now. Any lads fancying a little bet can come along, but bring your money.' Paul swayed towards the door, pushing aside Johnny, and swung through into the night.

'What you going to do, Joe?' asked Johnny. Joe smiled again, his tobacco-stained teeth yellow against his grey face.

'He's only a comer-in when all's said and done,' he grunted, 'and I've got a half a crown that'll breed another. I think I'll go along. It'll be a change at any rate.'

Most of the men went with him, loudly laughing in the darkness. A bit of a wind had come up and rain swept them along. Two had lanterns and the twin patches of yellow light bobbled along behind the long-legged stride of Paul, who marched in silence, keeping a little way ahead.

Peter's attic bedroom faced the yard at the back of the house, and he was a light sleeper. Subconsciously he heard heavy boots, restless squawking from the few hens in the run. He opened his eyes. There were no curtains at his window and the lantern gleams flecked the grimy glass. The gate banged and then banged again, unfastened and caught by the wind. The wooden slats would be off by morning, he thought. It's got to be closed. Dad had only patched it together again a week or so back. He'd be angry if it were broken and somebody would get the blame. Peter yawned, but knew he'd have to close the gate. His bleary mind did not connect the sounds of men with the gate banging. The hens were quiet now, tucked in the dark corner of their roost, and there were no voices and no lights. He slipped out of bed, the worn linoleum by his bed striking a damp chill into his feet. He felt around for shoes and slipped them on. The leather was like cold cardboard at his ankles and the laces were long on the floor. When he walked, he consciously lifted his toes to keep the shoes on and his limp was heightened. Eyes screwed up, still clutching the sleep that he wanted to keep warm within him, he soldiered down the black stairs – two bare tread flights and the clumpity clop would raise the house, he thought. But nobody woke.
     Peter reached the passage to the kitchen and fumbled to the door. Here a little warmth from the recumbent stove touched him. He stretched up to pull back the kitchen door curtain and reached down in the dark to find the bolt. It was not shot across. Dad could not be home yet. Because of the darkness Peter had thought it was the middle of the night. Perhaps it was early and there was no need to secure the gate. Dad would do it when he came back.
     Peter pulled open the back door anyway and shivered, peering out across a gleaming yard, hearing the hiss of rain in the holed guttering. He wanted to cower back inside, but the gate banged above the noise of the rain and he quickly snatched a waterproof from the hook by the door and shuffled out across the uneven ground.
     The wind caught him at the house corner, belching out the coat and catching his face with chilly rain. The last vestiges of sleep were swept away cruelly and Peter grappled with the gate, forcing its latch firmly into position. As he turned back, he noticed lights in the outhouse and distorted shadows thrown against one of the walls. The wind was taking sound away from him, but loud voices, angry maybe, swelled in his ears, carried across the yard in a brief lull.

21

What should he do? His first thought was that thieves were rifling the rabbits and he should call his mother, but there was no telephone in the house. The village exchange was two miles away and Bates, the local policeman, the same distance. Then he remembered that Dad was still out. He'd probably come back soon. Should he wait up for him? Warn him at the gate about the thieves? He didn't think of his father being with the men, one of the group. Perhaps the men were smugglers or wreckers off the Broads. He'd heard about people like that at school: 'Watch the wall my darling when the gentlemen go by.' Perhaps he should slip back to bed, pretend he'd seen nothing. Curiosity was great in him, but so was fear, particularly of his father after a night in the pub. He felt very cold now as well as frightened and began to hobble back to the house when sudden shouting behind him made him think he'd been spotted and he broke into a stumbling run.

Next moment he was on his face in the wet. He hauled himself up and clattered into the house, ramming home the bottom bolt, dragging a stool across the screeching floor, standing on it and forcing the top bolt across as far as it would go into its socket. The door was warped and Dad rarely bothered with the top bolt, it being so stiff. Then he clambered upstairs, regardless of noise, but still nobody seemed to wake. Mum was used to pretending to sleep when Dad came home from the pub.

Peter kicked off his shoes and hurtled into bed where he curled up in a fetal position, eyes tight closed, but the picture he had glimpsed flickered still. There was a horde of men charging across the yard towards him. He'd heard the shout of 'Stop the blighter!' He'd been seen; he must have been seen and now they would batter at the door to stop his mouth. He should have watched the wall my darling like Mrs Gribbons said.

Through the hunched blankets and muffled ears came more noises from the yard. The hens were squawking and screeching and there was more shouting. Peter buried himself further into the bed. They were stealing the hens now or they were bringing the old tree trunk they used as a perch to work as a battering ram against the back door and then, sure enough, there was a great banging on the door, echoing through the old house right to the rattling roof slates, and more shouting. He heard movement on the stairs and bolted out of bed, dragging his blankets with him. He toppled inside his clothes cupboard and pulled the door to, swallowing himself up in blankets and utter blackness, the tangible blackness of total blindness after searing light. It was absolutely silent. He didn't want to hear, but his ears strained, and all that seeped through was the hum in his brain. The door was thick and the clothes around him were dense.

In his attitude of strained watching and listening Peter crouched for what seemed hours, and in this attitude he eventually fell asleep.

Mum found him next morning. A brilliant shaft of light dazzled him, hurt his aching head, cut through the immense lethargy of a night spent in stuffiness. Joan pulled him out gently and carried him to the bed. This was not the first time he'd huddled into the cupboard. Whenever Dad was violent Peter'd be found there.

'Come along, Peter. Everything's all right. Wake yourself up.'

Joan went over to an old chipped jug by the wooden chair and wet the corner of her apron with cold water. She bathed Peter's temples and slowly he began to focus on the world.

'I don't know what you were up to last night, my lad.' Mum's voice held an underlying grimness that caught Peter's attention and then he saw his mother's face. There was a weal of red across her left eye and her lip was split, puffy. She gently put her fingers to the boy's patched-up hare-lip and smoothed it.

'That's all your father seems to know about lately,' she murmured to herself. 'He never used to be like it.' She turned away abruptly.

'School for you today.' Her voice was thick, stumbling out of her lips like speech after the dentist's injection. 'That'll be best for you, but you'll have to go by yourself.'

Peter nodded, watching her move over to his chest of drawers and wrench at the middle drawer that always stuck. He felt angry inside now and embarrassed, angry at his mother as if she was responsible for his life. Her flabby voice, so unlike her normal speech, irritated him. She went on piecing her words together painfully, almost dreamily.

'Claire's still asleep and he'll be dead to the world for a bit. You'd be better off out of it. I didn't tell him you locked him out last night, but your Dad will brood on it. He thought I'd done it.'

Why was his mother talking on and on like this? She didn't normally. She hardly ever spoke to him really, except to tell him what to do.

'I didn't tell on you, Peter, but you shouldn't have, you know.'

Joan turned towards him again, whispering as if they were fellow conspirators with a common enemy. 'It makes things worse later.' She pointed to her face ruefully. 'He was angry enough already – no need to lock him out.'

Peter started to cry. She didn't understand and he couldn't cope. He twisted on to his stomach to hide his face and then felt her hand warm on his shoulder. He was revolted by it, its implicit understanding that was not understanding, its shared suffering that was not shared, could never be shared. He lay there rigid and unaccepting. Slowly the hand was withdrawn.

'You're overwrought. That's what it is. Perhaps you'd better stay here in bed for a bit. I'll bring you up some breakfast.'

No, that wasn't what he wanted. He wanted out, away from this cloying closeness and responsibility. He slid off the bed, shaking his head. Joan tried to resume her normal attitude.

'Well, get your clothes on and downstairs with you. You'll have to hurry. It's late.'

Ten minutes later, a hunk of bread and jam in his fist, satchel over his back, Peter scampered down the lane towards a haven. His mother trudged across to the cows, looking at her feet all the way. The udders were full. She left Claire sitting at the table under strict instructions to stay there and keep her mouth shut. Upstairs was a looming threat made only too tangible by the rumbling thunder of snores that seemed to slide through the floorboards and invade even the closed door of the kitchen.

# CHAPTER
# FOUR

Most of the children of Barham attended the village school when their parents had no need for them in farm labouring or jobs around the house. There were times of the year when the schoolroom was almost empty. Harvest, potato picking, chicken plucking all came in their seasons. It was a question of custom and economics. Despite the convulsions of war, little change of political or social attitude was visible, and the deaths of young males made it even more urgent to use the children well.

Mrs Gribbons, the teacher, was a comer-in and she brought with her opinions and approaches of a revolutionary nature to Barham. Immediately after the war the government set up a one-year emergency training scheme for teachers. Mrs Gribbons, her husband a casualty at Dunkirk, with no children of that marriage, with few qualifications but of proven worth – she had been in Sheffield during the blitz and had become the first and last woman to run the billet room of a major munitions steel works – had taken advantage of the training and had come to Barham in 1947. Now, in 1955, she was still regarded as strange by the village, but she had won a grudging respect and attendance figures were improving annually.

Little events become legendary in small villages and stories of how the new teacher told old Westby, the gamekeeper at Barham Estate, that his children had to be at school or they'd be as good as trapped in one of his wicked gins and how old Westby had told her to mind her own business and he'd mind his and then how she had asked him who was minding the children's business, provided gossip material for weeks. Still, nothing could change Westby and his children wandered the fields learning the lore of the land, not the learning of books. When they did come, they cramped themselves into the corner of the room and, by the end of the day, glowered with enforced restrictions on their bodies as if she held them to the desks with iron clamps. If she sent them on errands or took them out, they'd disappear like as not and all they'd talk about was gamekeeping.

Mrs Gribbons saw change all around her in the expansion of communications, the emancipation of women – she felt bitter about how she'd lost her job at the steel mill after the war when the men came home. Her immediate solution to losing her husband and job was to become a teacher, use the position she'd reached as a ladder to another task where she could foster other people's aspirations, help to bring about a new society. With these ideals, Barham had appeared barren ground; but she would treasure small successes. Peter could become one of those successes.

Mrs Gribbons, a bunched and brown woman, was in the school early. She filled the inkwells from the brown pots, one for red and the other for blue, and then in painstaking copperplate handwriting listed the spellings for the day on the board. They all formed words within a theme and the older children were expected to write a piece of their own, using the day's words. Today the theme was 'In the City'. She put various pictures up on the front wall and found a short piece of writing to read aloud.

She smiled grimly at her preparations. The children knew little about city life and she'd long ago decided that her themes should be about what children didn't know as often as about what they did. She could initiate any amount of work about villages, farms, winter in the countryside, cows, sheep, carrots, and she took a perverse delight in conjuring unusual topics for consideration. Many of the youngsters hated the day's theme writing. Nobody was allowed home without finishing the task, and she'd stand quietly watching the last stragglers of each day tumble off her conveyor belt.

Peter would be one of the last to finish, not from lack of desire to work but from the extent of his ideas caught up in a world beyond his own, and from the difficulty he had in writing words down. He didn't seem able to order letters into sequences nor shape them properly, but Mrs Gribbons persevered, figuring out his meaning and praising his sentences.

Mrs Gribbons rarely left her schoolhouse except to attend meetings of the school managers and to play the organ at the congregational church. Every night she would prepare her materials painstakingly so that the children would have their requirements to hand and there'd be no fuss in the classroom of having to collect this or find that, a chaos of children out of desks. She valued order and a system. Now, she put on each pock-marked desk necessary paper, pencil and rubber, a list of sums for each child, and a reader. She was ready.

There were thirty-eight children officially on roll at her school; about thirty attended regularly and she tried to present individual work for each child at some time during the week. Her methods were her own; her results generally good, although lack of variety in the routine – the discipline of the billet mill lay in repeated programmes – produced competence but rarely excited the children. It was a security that Peter craved, a time when life was ordered for him in such a way that his emotions could normally be kept at bay.

'Good morning, boys and girls' – forced, bright voice.

'Good morning, Mrs Gribbons. Good morning, everybody' – sing-song rhythm, monotonous delivery tailing away into a mutter.

'Sit down, children.' Scraping of chairs, nudged desks and gradual hush. 'Hurry up, Michael. There's no need to scrabble on the floor.'

'Please Miss, I can't find my pencil.' A few giggles.

'I can give you five minutes searching-time after school today, if you like.' Mrs Gribbons flicked open a little red book on her desk. She kept a running total of time wasted by individual children and exacted repayment. Michael sat down, the pencil grubbed up from the floor, its neat sharp point still intact.

'Michael couldn't find his pencil. He was looking for it but couldn't find it.' Mrs Gribbons dwelt on the words 'find' and 'look for'. 'Can you think of anything that you have to find sometimes, that you have to look for?'

Silence greeted the question and then a couple of hands almost reluctantly went up. Teacher's guessing game had started. Mrs Gribbons obviously knew the answer.

'Yes, Elsie.'

'My shoes,' she lisped.

'Good, Elsie,' but the tone of the 'good' suggested that there was more to come. It was only a start.

A few more hands went up.

'Socks.'

'Screwdriver from the shed when my Dad was . . .' But Mrs Gribbons was pointing to the next hand.

'If I want a hanky, I can't find one for looking, Mum says.'

'Some taties out the bag.'

All these remarks were met by the bland 'Good' but everybody knew that not one of them was the answer. Mrs Gribbons slowly gathered all eyes to her; she would tell them. 'We must try to find and look for more than just "things" in the world. There are ideas to find, ways of doing things and there is God to try to find. You'd have to look very hard in your drawers for God, wouldn't you?' Mrs Gribbons smiled and so did the children, uneasily. 'Now I'll give you a clue for something that is looked for and found. All of these things were looked for and found and so they all have a special name:

railway engines, aeroplanes, radiograms, television – has anybody seen one of those?' There was an immediate stir round the classroom, but Mrs Gribbons didn't wait for the chat to grow. 'There are lots of other things and more are looked for and found every day. Now then,' she beamed round the class, 'can anybody tell me what all these things are? Yes, Joseph?'

Joe's grandson spluttered with excitement.

'You see pictures on televisions and . . .' Mrs Gribbons stopped him.

'You do see pictures on televisions,' she said, with great weariness in her voice. 'We want to know what all these things are, all together.'

Silence fell. The sound of an axe thudding against the old plum tree in Mrs Rose's garden along the road beat like a heart within the room. The children sat with their heads bowed, embarrassed. Mrs Gribbons turned to Peter.

'Well, Peter – do you know a word for all these things that are looked for and found to help us, or perhaps the word for somebody who does the looking and finding?'

There was a sudden scuffle at the side of the room.

'Margaret, don't pinch Elsie. It's not nice. Well, Peter?'

Peter wrote on the scrap of paper Mrs Gribbons gave him every day for his answers. He handed it to her. There was a pause and then Mrs Gribbons smiled at him benignly.

'Well done, Peter. The word is invention. You haven't spelled it correctly but you've got it right. An *invention*, children, is something looked for and found to do a job for us all.'

While the children puzzled about how 'taties out the bag' could be an invention, Mrs Gribbons turned to the word list for the day. The city seemed to abound with man's invention and it became clear that the countryside in comparison was a bleak place for this particular search-and-spot exercise. Eventually those children capable of writing started to link the words of invention into sentences.

So Mrs Gribbons, with well-meant preparation and concentrated effort, taught the children that there were right answers in the world, that there were experts and that very few children could ever achieve those answers. The rest were doomed to failure in her eyes, in parents' eyes and in the outside world's perceptions. The few who could answer or who, by chance, fell upon the expected responses were resented by the others. Peter was no exception. Unusually, however, he was not teased and bullied. He carried a circle of privacy around him. His silence baffled the others, and his cleft palate and limp somehow scared them. The only challenge to Peter's cocoon came when the Westby boys were in school. They had little time for stricken creatures, and physical deformation in nature was an invitation for natural selection. When they came, Peter stayed in the schoolroom during break and scurried home before the others were let out of school. Mrs Gribbons was aware of and worried by Peter's isolation, but could find no way in which to break it down. Maybe she even revelled in this one child of unusual capacity and distinct problems.

Today the Westby boys – the name had the ring of American gangster or cowboy films – were not in school. Bill and Dan Westby were out with their father preparing a shoot for the next weekend; they were learning about cover, sightlines, breeding pens, beating and shooting. By early afternoon, however, they'd whipped off back to their cottage and then had wandered with subconscious instinct across to the other side of the village and out on to the road leading to the ramshackle Townsend farm. As Peter lurched up the road from school, Bill and Dan were working the field edge by it, spotting the tracks, droppings and scrapes of their customary prey. Bill, the older of the two, a short-cropped, dark-haired, stocky ten-year-old, noticed Peter first. Dan was scrabbling down a bit of banking with a long stick.

'Ere – there's that thingy with a limp.'

Dan, younger at eight, thinner, but longer than his brother, with the same head of rounded bone, peered through the base of the hedge.

'So it is,' he grinned up at his brother, expectant. Peter's distinctive gait brought him steadily nearer. His face was down and his satchel bumped on the small of his back with a reassuring rhythm, patting him along.

Peter drew alongside the hedge without noticing his hunters. Bill eased himself through a gap and suddenly stood in his way. Dan wriggled through a thin track like an eel and slipped behind him, still managing to hold on to his stick. Their victim, with his chin tucked to his chest, almost walked straight into Bill, froze and then took in his adversary. A flicker of panic crossed his eyes and he twitched, fighting for control. Bill noted the reaction and was pleased. He said nothing, standing there grinning, arms folded, one leg crossed over the other in a miniature parody of his father when he caught a lad on the estate.

Peter shuffled to the right to skirt him and walk on. Bill hopped like a nosy crow across with him, imitating his lurch, still grinning. Peter froze again.

'Nice satchel that,' Bill broke the silence. Peter didn't respond.

Suddenly the boy in front of him clutched at his stomach and doubled up in great retching laughter. Dan had carefully and quietly poked his stick between Peter's legs and was waggling it up and down obscenely. Bill pointed behind him, gasping with mock laughter, and Peter swung round. His leg caught on the stick. He tripped and the stick snapped.

'Ere!' said Dan, aggrieved, holding the stump under Peter's nose and then tossing it over his shoulder to lie with the remains, 'the little bleeder's broken my stick.'

'So he has,' agreed his brother with the air of a judge. 'He really doesn't know his own strength, does he?'

Peter recovered and went to walk forward. His lip was white now and his hands were trembling.

'Not going anywhere, are you?' asked Bill. 'Not after you broke my brother's stick. What you going to do about it?'

A red flush touched Peter's cheekbones and his head was beaded with sweat. Terror and aggression fused. He knelt down and picked up the two pieces of wood, pointed to one and put up one finger, pointed to the other and put up a second finger in an unmistakeable gesture of hatred. Bill burst out laughing again.

'Very good,' he invited his brother to join in, but Dan stood and glowered. 'But Dan doesn't think it's funny, squirt. He wants a fight, don't you Dan?' Dan nodded; he wasn't having any cripple putting two fingers up at him.

'Well, it looks as though you're going to have to fight him, squirt – that, or you can fight me if you'd rather.'

Once again Peter tried to walk forward, but this time Dan contemptuously pushed him back with the palm of his hand on his chest. Peter staggered again, and almost fell. Dan rushed him, fists flailing, and Peter fell to the floor, squirmed and wriggled to one side. Dan paused. He hadn't even touched him.

'Get up, custard face,' he hissed. Peter pushed himself up unwillingly and Dan attacked again. This time Peter hunched, turning his back on the blows that rained down on him. Bill pulled his brother off. This was no fight. It was a boring massacre.

'You're a teacher's pet, Townsend, a yellow-bellied wormy slime. You're a greasy mushy squashed slug.'

He pushed his face down and under Peter's arm, staring his scorn into Peter's eyes. The cowering figure was transfixed. He shrank away from the older boy and Bill followed him, sneering. Suddenly Peter slashed the stick in his right hand across Bill's face. There was a scream. Bill clutched his face, bending double. Dan ran to his brother and Peter pushed through the hedge and started off across the field towards home.

Bill pulled himself up. The stick had passed underneath his eye by a whisker and traced a red line over his cheek. Bill fetched a grey cloth out of his pocket, shoved it against the blood, looked at the thin oozings and then swung round.

'You're bloody dead!' he screamed after Peter and barged his brother to one side.

'Let me after him!' Bill sailed through the hedge in pursuit, his hurt pride burning far more than the brand on his face. Dan helter-skeltered behind.

Peter, despite his disability, had flown. He stumbled towards the ridge where the field dropped away to the left and the back of the farm. Once there, he'd be in sight of home and safe, but he had another fifty yards to run and the two boys behind were scrambling through the old furrows of last year's ploughing at vindictive speed. Peter's chest felt like a furnace, his lungs bellowing flames instead of air. His legs dot and carried him in a hip-swerving, grinding agony.

Just before the comparative safety of the top of the slope, just when Peter expected Bill's hand to land on his shoulders, a large black shape ballooned out of the track in front of him, whisked past his legs and down the slope towards the boys. Peter recognized Floater and, in the same instant realized that the pounding feet had stopped beating ever closer to him. Heaving for breath, Peter twisted round. Floater, his buck rabbit, was sitting ten yards down the track, about five yards from Bill and Dan. He rubbed his nose with his paws casually and looked as fine and relaxed as if he were out for an afternoon stroll.

'Look at the size of that rabbit,' Dan gawped. Bill went to run on after Peter, but he too stopped.

'It's a bloody monster that is,' continued Dan, using his father's words when confronted by a large victim. Bill transferred his attention to the rabbit and began to creep up on Floater, who sat, twitching whiskers, oblivious to his danger. Dan quickly and stealthily flicked off his jacket, passed it to his brother.

Peter realized they meant to catch Floater for food. They didn't know it was Peter's rabbit, his Floater. They just knew it was rabbit, and big rabbit pie at that. Bill raised the coat steadily just like Dad with a pheasant, ready to throw it over Floater and jump on him all in one movement. Then his intention was baffled by a howl.

'Naaaah!'

Peter, flailing with the sticks still clenched in his hands, came crashing down towards them. Floater took off like a possessed spirit, leaping to one side and tacking across towards the scrub away to the right. Dan and Bill chased him, whooping and whirling the

31

coat and Peter, pulling up short, turned and ran the short distance to safety. He watched anxiously as Floater disappeared in the coarse grass and reeds of the rough ground. Surely his tormentors would give up now, but they paused at the edge and then began to move with stealthy black shadows into the hideaway.

# CHAPTER
# FIVE

His heart pounding within his ribcage, his mouth working in panicky spasms, Peter arrived at the outhouse. He normally fed Floater on coming home from school. It couldn't have been his rabbit out in the field, or, if it was, it was like an image or spirit rabbit which appeared in order to divert the Westby boys. Floater had rescued him, but he couldn't have escaped from his hutch.

Peter's eyes adjusted to the dimness and he made his way over to the hutch, almost convinced that Floater would be there, ready with his raking claws and great mounded back to protect his food bowl in their game. The mesh door was swinging wide. He trod on the bowl, which had rolled onto the ground. Still Peter looked inside the hutch, poked into the sleeping quarters. But there could no longer be any doubt. Peter's rabbit was out, at large, hunted by the Westby boys, fleeing through the scrub and with none of the field sense and survival techniques of the wild within him. Peter saw his father's hands on a rabbit snatched from a hutch, saw the momentarily stretched body, the chop of the neck and the sudden stillness. That could be Floater now.

So far he had had eyes only for Floater's hutch, but now he looked slowly round, took in the rest of the outhouse. This was where the men had come. Were all the rabbits gone? Had they all been stolen by thieves? That idea was dispiriting enough, but he needed to confirm the loss of Floater with further objective evidence. He checked through the hutches. Only Floater was gone. Then he reached Josie's cage. He normally kept well clear of it, having come to fear her shape, movement, musk and teeth. Today he winced back as he saw the front grid lying on the floor, but, more and more puzzled, he moved across to the dim corner.

Stillness and an odd musty smell greeted him. He peered inside cautiously and then jerked back his head. Josie was there, a lurking predator, but there was no movement in the cage. Peter edged back towards it and his eyes took in the long off-white body as it lay in a distorted, ungainly posture, the tail slack and the smooth body mottled and blotched with rust. Josie lay there all higgledy-piggledy, yet stiff. She looked as though she'd been thrown. Peter warily put out his hand to touch. The pelt was like dandelion fluff on his forefinger and underneath there seemed to be hard bone, inflexible and frozen.

Slowly now Peter moved out of the old shelter. In a state of shock, he stumbled towards the back door past the chicken run. His eyes passed over scattered feathers lifting and falling in the slight wind; he saw, without registering, two hens lying in a curious sculpture, twin legs intertwined and bald plucked patches amongst the plumage; dark splashes of brown had been dropped around them. Another hen seemed to have toppled off its perch and crushed its head on the stone flagstone. There was life here, however. Another hen, trailing torn tail-feathers, was pecking for food and grit, blood and bonemeal around the fallen bird. Yet another hen clucked busily over the run, up and over the two frozen chickens. Peter changed direction again and made his way towards the cowshed.

The previous night's rain still filled the holes in the yard and khaki green moisture oozed around the cowshed. Peter, in school shoes, limped straight through the water and the manure. The farm had six cows; they were inestimably valuable and Mum looked after their milking and care.

Inside the shed all was peaceful. The cows leaned over the rail. Gertie stood, as always, back to the world, flicking her paintbrush tail at Peter's face as he walked past, counting each patient. Yes, they were all there; yes, they'd been milked by his Mum – there was no distension of the udders and no discomfort; yes, they'd been fed a little cake and been watered down. They were ready to be returned to the small field. Peter normally did that task but today he hadn't exchanged his shoes for the old gumboots. He smeared mud across the stone-flagged kitchen floor as he trailed inside.

The house seemed quiet, as if uninhabited. Mum was not in the kitchen, but a few pots on the table suggested she had been there shortly before. Peter slumped at the table, leaned his head on his hands and stared vacantly ahead of him. A late bluebottle battered at the window; a door creaked in a draught; a chip of wood cracked in the stove and a pale, primrose pale, sunlight filtered through the dull pane on the back door. Peter observed that all the boots were lined up by the chipped blue wall next to the door and the newspaper beneath was freshly laid. All the tiny things he saw and noted came to him from a great distance, like deeply significant clues to a mystery belonging to somebody else, living at a different time in a different place.

Slowly Peter looked down his body as if it didn't belong to him and then shuddered, his whole frame twitching with suppressed tears; his hands clenched paw-like at his chest like a squirrel tense before the barrels of a shotgun and then slowly, very slowly his body relaxed, shoulders falling, head dropping, back curving. Peter brought his hand to his forehead and stroked two fingers up and down his brow as if soothing a massive headache that beat behind his temples and as his body relaxed, so the visible pulse flickering at the veined sides of his head diminished and disappeared. With immense decision, he scraped back his wooden chair and worked off his shoes, kicking them on to the newspaper. One of the shoes knocked against his father's size tens. A boot toppled and fresh mud fell off its sole. It would be too late to find Floater now –better to wait until the Westby boys had given up. Peter prayed they would give up and that Floater would stay hidden.

No use sitting here, he thought. Claire and Mum must be somewhere about. Dad too, from the look of things. He padded over to the teapot in his socks. It was warm. He inspected the room more consciously, beginning to feel curious about the situation. Mum's apron was hanging from the old clothes-peg by the sink – that only ever came off on special occasions. Dad's shotgun, normally hanging over the stove, was missing, but its licence was on the table instead of in the dresser drawer; the drawer itself was bulging out of its slot as if it had been hastily searched through and its contents stuffed back hurriedly, any old how.

He shuffled across to the door to the passage, opened it and listened intently. Yes, he could hear a muffled voice. He passed on down the narrow way, intending to go upstairs where he assumed the family was, but as he passed the door to the front room he realized that the noise came from there. He froze. They never used that room except for best and best never seemed to arrive.

He pushed down the handle firmly, remembering it sometimes stuck from lack of use, then peered round the door.

'Ah, there you are, Peter. Come on in and be introduced.' His mother was pink in the cheeks, her eyes brighter than he'd seen them for a long time. She was wearing powder. He could smell its sweet dusting from the door. Claire was sitting on the old best carpet of dark blue and red at the foot of Dad's chair. Her thumb was stuck firmly in her mouth and she was staring up at the sofa opposite. Mum skirted the little side table on which stood a tray of special teacups and saucers and took him by the hand, bringing him reluctantly over to her chair by the china cabinet so that he could see the man sitting with a cup of tea on his lap. Peter noticed that his father was staring out of the window.

'This is Mr Eldon, Peter.' Peter nodded towards the chair, his eyes lowered. Mum stage-whispered, 'I told you about Peter, didn't I?'

'Yes, indeed you did.' A firm voice, a voice that listened to itself as it spoke. A cool hand slipped under Peter's chin and his head was lifted. 'It's a pleasure to meet you.'

It was an old man, thought Peter. The eyes were pale blue, veined with threads of red, set in a smooth white face. Hair was wispy white. He was wearing a black suit and his shoes – Peter was looking down again – were shining two windows at him, but he didn't know who he was.

'Mr Eldon is a friend from a very long time ago,' Joan smiled archly.

'Oh not so long, not so long in an old man's life!' chuckled Mr Eldon musically, weighing the notes. 'But it is a great coincidence, maybe, I may say, a providence that I should come here to serve.'

'Mr Eldon is coming as the new minister to Barham, Peter. I used to know him when I wasn't married in London.'

Only the other day she'd been thinking of this man, this person that her parents, or her mother at least, had hoped she'd marry and now he had arrived, old enough to be her grandfather, almost sixty by now, yet a very comforting visitor to receive when so much seemed desperate around her. She'd always thought of him as a small man, but he seemed even tinier than she remembered.

'And I have been drinking your tea long enough, keeping you from your farming duties, no doubt.' Mr Eldon pulled himself up from his sofa and Paul rose as well, towering above his wife's visitor. Dad's pleased he's going, thought Peter.

'But don't you go walking into any more doors, Mrs Townsend – but perhaps an old friend may call you Joan.'

Mum shook her head breathlessly. Although her face was well powdered, the previous night's marks were still evident. 'It was the wind,' she explained, obviously for the second time. 'You try carrying logs through a swinging door some time.' Joan smiled brightly round at her husband.

'I'd leave such heavy work to the more sprightly ones amongst us.'

Paul turned back from the door as if the comment could have been levelled at him.

'Oh, Paul is very good normally,' explained Joan. 'But when he's so busy outside, I have to get along as best I can inside, and of course you must call me Joan. It wouldn't sound at all right being Mrs Townsend when we've known each other so long.'

'You're very kind. It's a pleasure to meet a face from the past in a new territory for me. I do hope I may see you in chapel occasionally. I should appreciate that feeling of continuity.'

There was an uneasy pause before Paul said, 'I'll fetch your coat then.'

Amidst cheerful thanks for calling and frantic waving from Claire, Peter returned to the kitchen. He cleared away his school shoes before Mum found them, put on his boots and went out to field the cows. He avoided looking at the dead hens and only cast a brief fearful glance towards the rough scrub where Floater had run. There was no sign of movement there, but Peter knew he would have to look, and he couldn't go alone.

Later, over the tea table, conversation about Mr Eldon returned, but there was a taut restraint in Joan's and Paul's words. Peter sensed undercurrents of feelings and there were mysterious references he did not understand, but then there were so many things he did not follow that additional mysteries just seemed normal, the customary maze through which he tentatively moved.

'It's been a long time – that's what people, say, isn't it?' said Mum, still smiling as if the grin had been cut upon her face along with the split in her lip. 'Better Mr Eldon than the visitor you brought home with you.' There was a note of scorn and fearful triumph in her voice that Peter could not remember hearing before and he quickly flinched, looking at his Dad for the anger to flare, but Dad seemed to burn into himself and no words came.

'You'd better clear up outside as well. I'm not having Claire going out the back with that mess there.'

Paul nodded grumpily. 'I was owed that money,' he said thinly and distinctly. 'I tell you, they cheated me last night.'

Joan spooned watery poached eggs on to slices of her home-baked, rather flat bread and presented them to the children.

'You won't get away with it though, will you?' Once again there was that note of cheerful triumphant fear, the sort of sound made by a young child just as he launches himself down a steep slide.

'Leave it alone, will you Joan?' the man muttered. 'Let the children have their tea.'

Claire pushed her egg away with her blunt knife. It skated off the toast and the runny centre slid on to the table top. She started to cry, 'Nasty egg – don't want.' Paul nodded as if the girl had confirmed his inmost thoughts. He heaved himself up, grabbed a dishcloth, wiped the table and then went to clean Claire's face with the same cloth. Joan seized the dirty cloth indignantly.

Claire, unaccustomed to her father helping in any way, stopped yelling and stared. Peter tugged at his mother's sleeve. She tried to ignore him, but he tugged even harder. Since coming home, he'd been in a shocked trance, but now he knew what he wanted and had to do.

'Try talking, Peter,' said Joan eventually.

'Leave the lad alone, Joan. He's got enough on his plate.'

Peter looked at his plate and then gazed at his mother. He swallowed, the adam's apple bobbing in his thin neck. He pointed out towards the yard.

'He's seen the hens.' Joan glared at her husband. Paul went to protest again, but, amazingly, Joan overrode him. 'You've done enough for one day, haven't you?'

'Don't you talk to me like that.' A dark flush filled his unshaven cheeks, but the reddening held guilt more than anger.

'Come on, Peter, you tell your Mum. What is it?' Joan knelt down beside the boy and put her arm across his shoulder protectively. Claire started again, 'Nastyegg! Nastyegg!' Joan took no notice. She still murmured, 'Come on, Peter. You tell your Mum.'

Peter pointed again at the window but this time his mouth was filled with a huge blind sound of unhappiness, almost a wail, but something more besides.

'Floater!' The unintelligible sound carried such an intensity of loss and sorrow that it pierced into Joan like a needle. Suddenly Peter was sobbing. Joan didn't know whether she'd had a success or not. Was the boy crying from the shock of seeing the dead hens? She had meant to clear them earlier but she couldn't bring herself to it when the wind made their feathers look alive still. Had he been into the outhouse and seen the empty hutch and dead ferret? She had meant to meet him from school, spare him that sight, but her guest had prevented her. Were his tears a combination of last night and today? Probably, she felt, and went to cuddle him, but Peter wriggled from his chair, put on his boots and pointed Mum's boots towards her. There was no denying the message. Joan went with him out past the outhouse, through the gate, up the slope and across the scrub. Peter stared around him and Joan, sick at heart, followed.

There was no sign of life of any sort, no movement in the brambles, no sound at the top of the quarry, no fresh tracks through it. Eventually Joan took the boy's arm and gradually the two made their way back to the farmhouse. When they reached the yard, Peter broke away again, hobbled into the outhouse back to Floater's cage. Maybe he'd come home by himself, but the hutch was still empty except for a few hardy flies that lifted and settled again on the cold dung pellets. Joan left him there after he'd shrugged aside her attempts at comfort and when, half an hour later, he returned, his face was cold, pinched and grey.

# CHAPTER
## SIX

Later that evening, with the children in bed for the night, Joan confronted her husband.

'Not going to the pub then?' She pulled a pile of ironing to the table. Paul merely shook his head. She flicked the ironing board up and placed a bowl of cold water by the side. Her pair of irons stood on the hot range. Joan found her old oven gloves and rummaged through the pile of clothing for the roll of damp hankies and tea towels. It saved sprinkling them with water and they were flat and easy to do. She always followed this routine, using one of the tea towels as a pressing cloth for her best skirt and, if her husband bothered to put them out, his jacket and trousers. When they'd first been married, Paul had insisted on pressing his own trousers because the way he'd been taught in the army was the only way to obtain a knife crease, he said, but now he didn't care. The two of them never seemed to go out for an evening's entertainment and Joan had liked nothing more than a dance. Paul had been a good dancer, she thought, but Thurriton was the closest place for dancing, at Roxy Hall, and it all seemed a long way away after the cows had been finished and the children settled.

She glanced over at the big wireless on the shelf Paul had put up for it when they'd first moved in. She normally listened to the play on Monday evening but Paul was usually out at the pub and, tonight, Joan steeled herself to find out from him what had happened.

'It's not very nice to be brought home by a policeman, is it?' Joan pursed her lips primly, leaning into the iron. Paul picked up an elastic band and sat down. From a pocket he produced a stub of candle, a matchbox and a used cotton reel. With his penknife he began to score wedges in the reel.

'I think I've a right to know what you've been up to – a court case like as not – that's what Bates said.'

Paul struck a match and blew out the flame immediately.

'If you'd only explain, I'd try to understand. At the moment all I know is you split Joe's head open because he wouldn't give you half a crown and when Bates checked your shotgun licence it was out of date.'

Paul started to smooth a section of candle, slivering off shreds of wax and then running a burning match over the surface.

'It didn't happen like Bates said.' Paul looked intently at what he was doing. Joan switched irons and sprinkled water over a dry and wrinkled shirt.

Gradually Paul began to explain. His voice became more animated and Joan didn't interrupt, although the iron thudding and the cloth swishing made an unspoken commentary of disapproval.

'The two with lanterns stood either side of the shed and we cleared a ring in the middle, for the fight. I took out Floater first. He was scrabbling like fury. Look at my arms.' Paul hoisted the sleeves of his grey pullover and showed the ridges of claw marks along his wrists. 'I gave him to Joe and he held him in his coat. The others went a bit quiet-like then, seeing the size of the rabbit. Then I took out Josie, she was already dancing up and down, spitting and glaring. Well, we crouched round and I put her into the ring at the same time as Joe dumped Floater in. Josie started walking towards Floater waiting for the rabbit to cringe, but Floater thumped and humped back. He didn't run. Josie didn't know what to do – you could tell that – she just sort of stopped, with her nose lifting and dropping. Then she moved on, but then Floater hurtled at her, lashing his legs at her. I tell you that ferret looked amazed – not frightened, just amazed. She could have taken that rabbit – course she could – but she didn't understand it. She threw in the towel and slid out of the circle without so much as a by your leave. Johnny should've stopped her. Next minute I was after her, with all the rest, but she'd bloody well found the chickens, hadn't she? Not daft, that ferret. I grabbed the mucking-out spade, jumped in and tried to catch her – didn't want to kill her – but she'd gone mad. I was lucky really in the dark there with all them chickens. I caught a flash of white and swung the spade.' Paul paused, remembering, reliving the crunch of spade on flesh, feeling the churning of his beer-laden stomach, hearing the jeers and shouts. He glanced towards his wife but she went on ironing.

'Well, we went back to the shed – me with the ferret – but no rabbit in sight. "Well lads," I said, "let's see the colour of your money – half a crown each, wasn't it?" But would they hand over?' His face went dark with anger and he began to score the edge of the table with his penknife. 'Would they hell! It was Joe started it. He said there hadn't been a fight, that both animals had run off, that nobody owed me nothing. I was bloody angry, I can tell you that, Joan, but there was eight of them and they just left and then I found you'd locked me out . . .' He stopped talking, tossed his penknife to the tabletop and rubbed his fingers together, embarrassed. 'Well, I'm sorry for what I did. It was everything on top of me suddenly. But you shouldn't've locked me out, you know.'

'What do you expect me to do with a crowd of drunken men smashing up the place?' Joan stopped ironing for a moment and stared at her husband. He was quelled. He took up the band and threaded it carefully through the candle piece where the wick had been removed and then on through the reel, fixing it in place with a matchstick at either side.

'Doesn't explain today though, does it?'

'What doesn't?' Now that the first part of the story was over, Paul felt marginally more confident. Joan forked another shirt out of the basket. She had thought she was past caring what her husband did, past feeling anything for or against him. Suddenly she was deeply angry at the man. He thought he could blether through a childish tale of two animals having a fight for a bet, one of them his son's only friend, and then feel justified beating up his wife and attacking a man.

She spread the shirt-tail down the board and put the iron back on the heat. Then she turned towards him.

'Being charged with assault causing grievous bodily harm to a sixty-year-old man, let alone your wife, who I quite understand doesn't count and isn't thought of by anybody, least of all the police, as needing protection from the likes of you – that's what your story doesn't explain, doesn't even try to explain.' She grabbed the iron and brought it hissing down on the shirt. Paul winced.

'All right – I've said I'm sorry, haven't I?'

Joan sighed and sprinkled more water. He wouldn't change, except for the worse. Paul tried to gather his thoughts and continued.

'I woke up late. You know that. I didn't feel too good.'

'Hangover,' Joan stated.

'Well whatever it was, I still felt angry. Floater had beaten Josie whichever way you looked at it and I was owed money, cash we could do with at the moment.' He appealed to his wife's fears over the housekeeping, but she didn't respond. 'So I thought I'd go round debt-collecting.'

'Is that why you took the shotgun?'

'Bloody hell, woman, you're worse than the police. No, I took the gun for the crows over by the quarry woods. You heard me tell Bates that.'

'With a hangover? We have to walk round on tiptoe feeding you black coffee because your head aches something rotten and then you go off to blast crows out of trees? Likely, isn't it?' Joan finished buttoning a shirt, tucking the arms neatly behind and folding it into a rectangle. She took out the last one and attacked the collar, cuffs and inside seams.

'By the time I got to Joe's place he wasn't in, so I went on down the pub. Joe was scrounging a pint as normal, having a big joke at my expense I can tell you. George, the landlord, you know, asked if I was going into big fight promotions. Well I pulled up the shotgun – a sort of joke like – covered Joe with it. He was leaning back in his chair, laughing at his own bloody joke again. I'd bought that old soak about five pints last night and he couldn't even give me what I was owed. "Mine's half a crown," I say to him. "I don't want no bloody drink, just my money." He went white then I can tell you.' A trace of mulish pride stained his voice. 'And he says not to be so stupid. "Stupid?" I says. "Who's stupid? You're the stupid one – now, hand over," and I waggled the gun a bit. George went to put his paw on the gun. "Get off it," I says, pulling away, but I must have fired off a barrel – didn't mean to – and the shot went flying up into the ceiling – nowhere near anybody. Next moment Joe was lying on the floor – chairlegs had slipped from under him I suppose and he'd hit his head on that jutting timber by the window. "Look what you've bloody done," shouts Johnny, all fired up and taking it all wrong. Well I told him I didn't touch Joe, but they said I shot at him. He was lying still but there wasn't much wrong with him. Johnny got hold of his coat and Denis lifted his head as if he was a corpse. I've seen corpses in the war and they don't sit blubbing in a chair after being shot, I can tell you. What would bloody England have done if we'd all started crying when bloody Hitler started dropping bombs?'

Joan intervened. 'You don't have to swear,' she said. 'Poor old man – you frightened him near to death, I shouldn't wonder. And you're sure you didn't hit him or shoot him?'

'Course I'm sure. George needn't have called in Bates. It was all an accident.'

Joan shook her head, not certain whether to believe his story or not, not certain whether it mattered much either way. Her husband had behaved terribly. Why couldn't he see that his violence bred violence?

'Look, do you think I'd be here now if I'd really shot him? I'd be inside on an attempted murder charge. I tell you it was an accident. Even George finally said it was.'

43

'And that's the whole story?' asked Joan, full of doubt.

Paul nodded heavily. 'How many times do I have to tell you? It was an accident.'

Joan's mouth tightened. 'At least you're banned from the pub,' she said. 'Small mercies. Perhaps you'll start thinking of your family a bit more.'

Paul returned to his contraption, twisted the band round and round until the matchsticks were taut against the wax and reel. Then he placed the machine on the table and the unwinding matchsticks took the reel over the table and half way up the pile of finished ironing until the slope became too steep and it toppled off backwards. Joan breathed in deeply and pushed it back to her husband.

'You're just a big child. I don't know what I saw in you.'

Paul tried to laugh it off and took the reel.

'Last tank in the regiment,' he said. 'I'll give it to Peter tomorrow.'

'Not much of a replacement for a rabbit.' Joan said bitterly and in silence she put away the ironing board and carried the pile of laundry upstairs.

In bed that night Paul lay on his own side, not touching his wife. He wanted to lean over, ask for forgiveness, but it was not in his nature, nor, he knew, would Joan bend towards him. He lay there baffled, feeling trapped and hurt. He'd thought Joe was a friend, but he'd been betrayed and cheated. Of course he shouldn't have reacted as he did, but he was a man, not a weakling like that Eldon. He'd fought for England, been a good soldier, had decorations to prove it. What did they expect him to do when cheated, smile and say never mind?

Joan also lay with her eyes open, looking out to the lighter grey of her curtained window. She thought about the arrival of Mr Eldon. Perhaps he'd be able to help the children and her. It was such a coincidence for him to arrive in Barham that she felt some good would come of it. With a little shock she realized she wouldn't mind at all if Paul were to be put into prison, as long as she could have her children and give them food and clothing. Yes, she would take them to chapel in the village. She should have gone before now but Paul had scoffed, saying he didn't believe in that rubbish. When you were dead you were dead and that was that, and when she'd asked him about his mates in the army he'd just said that they'd had a job to do and that was about the size of it. There wasn't much point in putting haloes on them. Joan didn't know what she thought, but maybe she'd meet other people in the village if she went. Despite her long years in Barham, she had few acquaintances and no friends. Joan decided to try to leave her isolation. If Paul would only work steadily, they'd manage all right. Perhaps the latest shock would bring him to his senses. She fell asleep with Mr Eldon's face twinkling at her over a cup of tea. You couldn't leave go of hope, she thought.

# CHAPTER SEVEN

By the time of the magistrate's hearing, Paul had convinced himself that he was being badly used and only needed to explain as he had done to Joan and he would be released with a caution. He resurrected his charcoal grey wedding suit and sponged, then knifed the creases. He found his only pair of decent black shoes, worked at their uppers until they were sparkling and polished the insteps until they shone. Joan trimmed his hair and he shaved with strop and open razor meticulously. His suit was, if anything, slightly too big for him now. He'd lost weight since the war, except round the waist where a small belly of beer forced him to breathe in to fix the clip. He was ready for the hearing, a smart ex-soldier, one of England's heroes.

He marched the five miles to Thurriton, telling Joan she needn't bother with food for him. He'd sort himself out, and, as she followed his straight back down the front path, he could have been the same man she'd married, although she'd noticed with a pang that there was a bald patch the size of a half crown on his head when she'd trimmed him. His jaunty grey trilby covered it now.

'Good luck,' she called from the front door and he waved his right arm without looking back and stepped behind the line of poplars that took him round along the quarry track. Joan started her day, not expecting to see Paul until late afternoon.

She'd just finished feeding Claire at one o'clock when the back door burst open. Paul's face was pale but wet with sweat and his tie was loose around his neck. At first, she thought he was drunk, but he wasn't.

'What is it?' She started away from the sink, hastily rubbing her dripping hands on her apron. 'We didn't expect you so soon.'

He stomped to the table and sat, glowering.

'All that bloody way for nothing,' he grunted. 'They didn't even let me explain what happened.'

Joan set a cup of tea in front of him, stirring in three sugars. 'I walked in – name, age, occupation and all that. How do I plead?

Not guilty, of course. Then this smooth lawyer stands up and says the case should be referred to the Crown Court because of its serious nature. He presents a piece of paper to the magistrate, that Farmer Blagstock over Priory Whelk would you believe, and he looks it over and then says to me "You will hear in due course of the time of sessions at the Crown Court. Case adjourned." And that was it. I was in and out in less than five minutes.'

'Didn't you say anything then?' Joan asked incredulously.

'Well, I said I was a busy man, being a farmer, and couldn't it be sorted there and then? But this lawyer stood up and said that "the accused" obviously didn't realize the seriousness of the charge and for his own good he should go to the Crown Court and Blagstock agreed.' He supped his tea noisily and stood up.

'Well, I've done my bit, haven't I? I went to explain and all that happens is I'm supposed to go to another court. They should get it right, shouldn't they? It wouldn't happen in the army. If they want me again, they'll find me here. I'm not traipsing all over the countryside just for a measly little accident.' He slammed his cup down on the draining board. 'I've got things to do, can't stand around all day.'

'Change your clothes, Paul,' Joan called helplessly. 'Don't go spoiling your suit.'

Paul stopped by the door and looked at his clothes, his shoes now filmed with dirt from walking ten miles. He shuffled his jacket from his shoulders and unlaced his shoes. Without another word he walked up to the bedroom and when he came down he was dressed in his dirty baggy corduroys and his maroon pullover with holes at the elbows. He didn't mention the hearing again.

For the next two months or so, Paul, banned from the pub and isolated from his previous companions, worked hard, preparing the back fields with manure from the cows, a long and difficult task with the ancient Massey-Ferguson tractor that had come with the farm waiting for a spare part that Paul could not afford, and only a large handcart and shovel as a replacement. Before a fortnight was out, his clothes and body were impregnated with the sourness of splashed cow dung. He turned in a frenzy of banging and sawing to the backyard, rebuilt the hen run, repaired the outhouse and, using an unusual spell of bright dry weather in November, splashed whitewash over all his constructions. His hands, caught by a prevailing cold easterly, became rough, red and sore so that he could hardly bear to pick up the paintbrush, but he persevered, smearing great gobbets of dripping over his fists to protect them and incurring the anger of his wife when she found the food missing.

Paul hardly ever left his land except when he went out setting snares for rabbits at night and collecting them in the early morning, during the false dawn. Necessity drove him hard and he was adept at finding the rabbit trails, looping the neck nooses at just the right height, knowing when to leave a trail for a day or two and when to return to it. He refused to go and ask Bates for the return of his shotgun. 'The magistrate said I couldn't have it,' he said briefly when Joan wondered whether, being innocent until proved guilty, he shouldn't have his shotgun back. Without it he had to work hard to provide meat for the family and Joan stopped enquiring about where the food came from. Of course it was poached. Where else could they find food? Yet he didn't get himself another ferret, nor did he try to buy another stud rabbit for breeding. He told Peter, when striding the rabbit paths one early morning, that he'd finish sorting out the outhouse first and then decide, but Peter wasn't really listening because he lived in dread that they'd turn a corner and find Floater choked in a wire noose.

Joan escorted Peter to and from school, Claire trotting along with them. She sensed his fear of the journey. Mrs Gribbons knew of her husband's brush with the law – the whole village knew, of course – and she felt even more protective of Peter, keeping him inside most of the day, feeding his isolation and sense of difference. She felt sorry for Joan, pleased to see her in church on a couple of Sundays and anxious to help her strange little son.

Peter worked with ever-increasing fervour, and the Westby boys steered well clear of him. The story of his Dad shooting a man worked on them and they didn't dare touch the man's son, the boy that had charged at them flailing sticks and screaming like a mad thing. Besides, they felt guilty. They'd cornered Floater in the scrub and they'd killed him and taken him home for the pot, not knowing the special nature of the rabbit. When their Dad had seen it he'd laughed. He didn't often laugh and when it came it was a thin dry creaking sound. He'd given both lads a friendly clip round the head because he'd heard all about Townsend's loss of rabbit and ferret.

'He's poaching enough off the estate, I reckon. It's time we was paid back,' Westby said, and Floater became a tasty stew. But Dan had his own rabbits, including a fine buck, and he began to have an inkling of why Peter had screamed at them. Bill told his parents that he'd caught his face on a bramble, a common enough occurrence anyway, and the event was soon forgotten by the adults. It was just that the brothers didn't follow up their threat of revenge and for this Peter was grateful.

Paul became a rare figure in the village, a tall frowning man to be avoided by adults and to be feared by children.

In early December the official envelope arrived. Paul was outside putting the finishing touches to a huge cold frame he had been working on, using timbers he'd dragged from the old quarry track and a number of old windows in their frames that he'd 'found' still miraculously intact in a disused cottage on the Barham Estate. Joan called him inside the kitchen, a knot of worry winding up inside her.

'It's come then,' she said, handing the letter over. Every week of grace since the magistrate's hearing had distanced the affair, made it seem as though it was all over, and Joan did not want the fragile peace destroyed, certainly not before Christmas. She'd already had to tell the children that there would be very little in the way of presents, but they'd try to enjoy themselves with good food and a few little odds and ends. Now, with the letter in her hand, she imagined it to be the first step towards imprisonment for her husband, something she could look at with equanimity when he was displaying the worst side of his character, but still a frightening possibility for the family.

Paul turned the letter over in his cracked, chapped fingers. Slowly he realized what it was. He had steeped himself in hard physical labour for weeks and gradually his drunkenness and violence had become to him as a dream. He was already doing time for his crime, he felt. He tried to slide a nail under the flap but couldn't, so he tore the top of the envelope straight off, inadvertently slitting away part of the letter. He looked at the contents but did not absorb them. He had never been one to read much and these words were long, important-sounding and very involved.

'What does it say, Paul?'

'Just a load of twaddle,' he said, flapping it away from him as if it were contaminated.

Joan took the form from his hand and scanned it quickly.

'You're to appear in court on December 15th – that's a fortnight's time.'

'They can stuff that,' said Paul, taking his customary angry attitude to anything that worried him or which he didn't understand.

'You'll have to go.' Joan waved the paper towards him, but Paul brushed it to one side.

'It was an accident. If I've said it once, I've said it a hundred times – it's all over and done with and whoever heard of going to court for not having a shotgun licence? They didn't give me a licence for my 303 and they were pleased enough for me to use it. No, they can stuff it.'

'It's in Norwich,' explained Joan as if the city could act as a magnet for the man.

'Don't care where it is. That Bates didn't have any right to take it further. It was an accident and I've paid for it, haven't I?'

Joan felt an unusual rush of sympathy for her husband. He imagined that if he kept on saying 'accident' enough times, the whole problem would disappear. He sat down at the table, running his hand through his thinning hair and then picking at some flaking dead skin on his finger. Flecks of white crumbled on the tabletop.

'Where's Daddy go?' asked Claire, trotting over from a pile of cushions and old clothes she'd been making into a home for a doll.

'Never you mind – it's not for little girls to worry their heads over.' Joan picked her up, put her back on the heap. 'There you are. You finish your game.'

'Where's Daddy go?' Claire insisted, not to be diverted. Paul looked over towards his daughter.

'Oh, I'm not going anywhere, love. Don't you worry about that.' He stood up, his dark eyes looking inwards and then staring out at his wife defiantly. 'They'll have to come and get me. That's what they'll have to do.' He started to walk about the room, shifting a mug on the dresser, rattling the penny tin and putting it back, kicking an ill-fitting cupboard door into its place and then watching it swing open again as if it were committing a deliberate act of sabotage.

'That's no answer, is it?' Joan spoke softly, winningly but urgently. She put out her arm to check him as he walked past, but withdrew it quickly, observing the expression on his face.

'It's the only answer they'll get from me,' he said. 'They can't push people around like this. I'm not going.' He went over to the window, a black shadow against the light, then he swung round and marched to the door, turning there to deliver his parting shot.

'Not that you're bothered, are you? Probably want me out of the way for all the time o' day you give me.'

Paul left, strode past his cold frame, didn't glance at the new hen run, left his freshly painted and fitted gate open and started off towards the village. Joan hurried over to the window, watched him go, then grabbed the old Oxo tin from the shelf and looked inside. There should have been three pounds and two ten-shilling notes there. The ten-shilling notes had gone. She ran back to the door, looking out across the yard. Her husband was already a hundred yards off.

'And that's no answer either, is it?' she yelled at the retreating back, but Paul didn't hear.

Paul was not going to the pub, however. He cut across fields on the south side of the church a quarter of a mile outside Barham and now one of the relics of bygone prosperity, skirted its silent chancel wall where the graveyard used to be and leaned against the edge of one of the flying buttresses, looking out over the Estate which stretched to the copses where Westby lived. It was typical Norfolk December weather with a high but uniformly grey sky, wind cutting across from the coast bleaching the fenceposts white with cold and salt. There was an underlying threat of squalls, either of thin rain or flecks of gritty snow, building away to the north.

Paul pulled his coat around him, plunged his hands further into the deep pockets, found his old cap in one of them and tugged it on to his head. Then he set off down through the disused church lane, a wide footpath set between what must have been a parade of charcoal-stick poplars. Now the brambles, nettles and thistles ruled the path and the trees were choking with thick ivy. Even though the vegetation was in abeyance with winter, the path seemed closed in, sunk between two fields, and the trees, a later addition to this Saxon walk, were being attacked from the high banking on either side. There was welcome relief from the wind here, though, and Paul stretched his legs, straightened his shoulders, finding release in the regular tramping through the customary path. There were times in summer when it was virtually impossible to pass through this way, but Paul frequently used the route and a narrow track had evolved over the thirty years it had been out of use as a church thoroughfare.

He dipped down past the cottage where he'd found the windows. It used to be lived in by the church caretaker, one of the Estate properties, now so out of sight that the managers didn't bother with its upkeep, leaving it to moulder into the greenery until its doors turned mossy green and mildew crept up the grey stone, tingeing it with decay. The garden was marked by a single gatepost with a rusty hook hanging from it, but the gate and fence had long since gone for firewood. The managers tended to keep the farm-workers on the cluster of houses to the south-west of Barham on the road where the bright green paintwork proclaimed their livery.

Paul paused by the gatepost, scanning the cottage frontage. For a moment he saw it as a place to hide, somewhere he could rest up away from trouble, if the worst came to the worst. Then he swung round to the east and came out of the sheltered path into the wind and the traditional deceitful flatness of Norfolk. He'd sometimes wondered why the Norfolk people all seemed so short and round. He was six foot and felt a giant in Barham. Joan said it was because little people keep warmer and there was something in that, he felt.

That Eldon should feel at home. Ever since he'd visited the farm Joan had been off down to the church of a Sunday and her talk was laced with references to the old man. Paul didn't like the influence he seemed to have over her from the past.

Along the side of the acreage ran an access path which turned into a narrow rutted way past a small broken wall that seemed to sprout from the earth with no visible purpose. Beyond stood Westby's cottage. Paul leaned against the wall, rummaged in another pocket, found his pipe, scraped around its bowl with a small knife, patted each pocket in turn for his tobacco collection and matches and then carefully assembled the dried-up shreds of old tobacco into a wedge between forefinger and thumb. There were greenish strands among the brown – Aaron's rod, a weed spiking up behind the cowshed in Paul's backyard. Joe had recommended using it for tobacco, saying it helped the throat. Having filled the bowl with scrupulous economy, holding his left hand cupped around the operation of filling with his right to prevent the wind whisking away fragments of his precious mixture, he thrust the pipe back into his pocket and walked forward to the cottage.

He pushed through a gap between house wall and fence and turned into the back to be met by a crescendo of yapping, yelping, snarling and growling. Inside a high-sided pen to his right, four or five terriers raced up and down the fence, stopping only to scrabble at the ground or leap towards the barrier. They sounded continuously, trying to match each other for high-pitched volume. The back door opened and old Westby with his shotgun on his arm came out, followed by an ancient shambling black labrador cross. Two- or four-footed visitors were rare unless eager to steal from the pullet run.

'What do you want then?' The question was curt. Westby knew his visitor. He had suspicions that he was a poacher and he knew about the attack on Joe. He knew no more, though. He hadn't heard the details from the witnesses who were still talking about it down at the Anchor. Westby kept himself to himself, a bit like Paul over the last couple of months. Gamekeepers aren't popular figures, and Westby's reputation for sourness was deserved. He was a short man, slightly rounded in the shoulder but with a large head and face. He always wore a cap and his clothes were a tattered parody of the official garb of the estate.

Paul pulled himself up from his haunches where he'd been inspecting the terriers at close quarters, a scrutiny that sent the dogs into paroxysms.

'Gi' over you bleeders!' Westby bellowed – a big voice from a small frame. Slowly the barking died away. Westby stood waiting. He wasn't one for words.

'I'm looking for a dog,' said Paul.

Westby merely spat on the ground and grunted.

'I heard you had some pups,' continued Paul, nodding towards a lean-to by the side of the pen, guessing the litter might be there. Joan had mentioned the pups a while before; she'd been telling Claire about them.

Still Westby didn't speak. Paul was explaining his business, and didn't need anybody else jibber-jabbering on. Paul, brought up to London talk, found this silence difficult to cope with. He preferred spoken responses; it helped the conversation on. He attempted a joke.

'I've come to see a man about a dog.' He grinned but Westby took the statement at face value, seemed to chew it over and then walked past Paul towards the lean-to. There was a small access door from outside the pen and Westby freed the wooden peg, holding it in place with one hand while he leaned his shotgun against the wall. He pointed to the gun and the labrador waddled over to it and sank down by its side. Westby jerked his head and Paul came over to him, peering into the blackness. There were three pups, Lakelands, same as the terriers in the pen. Westby leaned over a small wire fence across the door and lifted them out one by one, putting them on the ground with a certain gentleness.

'How many were there?' asked Paul. Stupid question; there were three now and that was all there was to it. Westby grudgingly answered, 'Six.'

Paul nodded but Westby didn't go on, so he squatted down to look at the pups who were skittering about, investigating, poking, rolling, nipping and suddenly stopping totally still as a new experience touched them. One was worrying the labrador's great paws with little pins of teeth. The big dog seemed oblivious and then eased away, knocking the pup gently to one side. Immediately, the pup seized a stick and started shaking it – the inimitable terrier rats'-neck breaker. The other two pups stayed close together by the wire. There was a discarded rusty kettle near them and the smallest terrier put its front feet and head into the gaping top and then backed out, dragging the kettle along a foot before freeing itself. It squeaked, tiptoed round the kettle as if it might bite and then whirled across to its friend by the wire.

'Terrier pups always look like little old men,' said Paul. 'It's their tiny whiskers sprouting – should've shaved by now!' He picked up the pup by scooping the stick under its belly. It was male, marginally bigger than the others. 'This'll do,' he said. Westby nodded slowly. It was the dog he'd have chosen, but he already had two of the pups inside the house for his own use and the sixth he'd drowned, a useless specimen.

'How much?' asked Paul, but Westby shrugged, not naming a price. Paul was in a quandary. He had no idea how much a Lakeland terrier pup was worth. He handled the pup, inspecting its mouth and gums, feeling carefully round the base of its ears, looking at the eyes by pulling up the terrier's natural frown. The pup didn't seem to resent his enquiry – another point in its favour. Westby suddenly spoke.

'Want to try him?'

Paul didn't understand what the gamekeeper meant, but he was beckoned along to another corner of the yard. As Westby moved off he whistled the labrador to the two other pups. The old dog stiffly stood, stretched his back legs individually, and with great care, almost as if he were afraid his legs would break if he pushed too hard, staggered over to the pups and flopped down beside them, his nose falling watchfully over his front paws.

'Good old dog that,' said Paul. Westby twisted a bunch of keys tied to his belt with twine and fiddled open the padlock of another shed. Inside, the gamekeeper's equipment was all neatly shelved and racked. The stone floor in the middle was swept out and the tools greased. A wooden trough along one wall was full of black sand and a line of what Paul presumed were spades and forks were plunged into it. In another corner behind a square fisherman's basket were a couple of old ammunition boxes, solid and reinforced with metal lining. Paul had seen thousands of them during the war. Westby reached under a shelf and dragged one of the boxes out until it stood in the middle of the shed.

'Bill!' Westby bellowed back down the yard. 'Bring Slasher.'

The two men stood in the shed silently for a couple of minutes, Paul wondering what was happening, and then Bill trotted up with one of the adult Lakelands tugging him along on a line of tarred thick rope. Westby nodded and pointed Bill to the trough side of the shed where he drew out a length of hardboard and stood with it in front of him, his fingers clenched over the top and his eyes shining. Westby closed the shed door, slipping a long masonry nail into the eye. Light still spilled in through a side window but the sides became dim, shadowy. A tiny whimper of expectation spilled out of the adult dog.

'Father,' explained Westby with sudden talkativeness. Paul nodded, bemused but slowly realizing that something alive was in the ammo box because Slasher's intent gaze never shifted from it. Westby took the pup from Paul's hands and put him near his sire. Slasher took no notice of him but Westby forced the terrier round and pointed him at the excited little black nose of the pup. He then cuffed Slasher round the ear none too gently. 'Gerroff him then, won't yer?' He grunted and Slasher faced the box again.

'What's going on then?' asked Paul, curiosity getting the better of his wish not to appear ignorant. Bill answered him. With his Dad there he wasn't afraid of this tall man, with his threatening reputation.

'A few rats in the box,' he explained. 'Slasher'll see them off but watch the littl'un. Slasher sometimes gets a bit excited and might snap up the pup when he's had the rats.'

Paul understood that this was a test of the pup's courage in the face of life's greatest enemy. If the pup ran away, he'd be no good in the eyes of the Westbys. The pup could easily be caught by a rat's fangs or the adult dog could mistake pup for rat in the excitement, but Westby's system was marginally more humane than pitting pup against rat with a big boot and a spade ready to stop the carnage when the pup had proved itself or tried to run.

Paul remembered the last animal fight he'd watched and some of his old anger bubbled inside him. Westby bent over the ammo box to spring back the catches.

'Keep that board between rats and that trough. I don't want any bolting behind there.'

Bill nodded. A shiver of excitement ran through Paul and he noted, with a thrill of pride, that the pup had taken up a miniature reflection of his father's stance. Generations of breeding were working their genes through the dog and his tail, the hair on his neck and every whisker were taut, trembling with pent-up readiness.

Westby eased up the clamps and then he pulled himself up, took a spade from the trough and kicked up the fastening, knocked off the lid with the spade and booted the box over almost in the same movement. From darkness into light rats leaped, and returned to never-ending darkness with the economically swift bites of Slasher, who seemed caught in a thousand frozen exposures of a film in the act of snatch and neck-break.

Now stillness, and there were six rats neatly killed and lying on the shed floor, not much blood, not a mark on Slasher and the pup was the only creature still moving. Westby had collared Slasher. The three humans watched as the pup kept grabbing at the rats' necks with his tiny mouth and his head kept shaking imaginary rat. Westby nodded, pleased. He even allowed a smile to touch his set face as he bent down and plucked the pup from the corpses. Pup continued to worry the heavy gloves on his hands. Westby passed it to Paul.

'Two greens and cheap at that,' Westby said.

Paul nodded. He was certainly worth it, he thought, but he only had the one pound on him. He brought out the two ten-bob notes.

'I'll bring the other tomorrow,' he said, hoping that Westby would agree, a slight flush pinking his cheeks.

'You better,' Westby said, taking the notes and folding them into his inside jacket pocket.

'I pay my debts,' Paul muttered grimly. He nodded at Westby and walked out of the shed with his purchase. Mrs Westby was standing at the doorway, Dan peering round from behind her.

'Cheerio then,' he called to them, but they didn't reply. The wife rubbed tired hands on a faded apron and turned back into the house.

As Paul walked along he kept his hand on the pup, now curled in a pocket. Weary from exertion, it slept, but not before scrabbling at Paul's hand a little and squirting pee.

Paul rummaged through his coat and found his prepared pipe, paused by the entry to the Saxon lane, cautiously took his hand away from the pup to light up and then set off in high spirits with his trophy in his pocket. Joan had gone on and on at him about that rabbit of Peter's. The boy had spent his time gazing around as if Floater would emerge from nowhere. Now he'd have a pup for an early Christmas present – a darn sight better than a rabbit any day. Paul resolutely refused to allow the letter summoning him to court to cloud his thoughts.

# CHAPTER
# EIGHT

The small community of Barham lost its huge church when the family estate passed into managerial hands. The church commissioners decided that the faithful should travel five miles to Thurriton or six miles to Priory Whelk and one priest should serve the three parishes. Of these, Barham was the least accessible, least prestigious and least wealthy. Thurriton had a small boat-repair and boat-building industry and an electrics firm had recently set up there, creating about fifty jobs and a small housing development on the Norwich side. Priory Whelk was gentleman farmer territory, not short of a penny or two to rub together. It was natural for Barham to lose its church. In addition there was a strong Nonconformist tradition in the village, and the chapel occupied a site near the village green with a small manse house next to it. It was not a rich living and was used as a pre-retirement retreat for elderly ministers and, therefore, regular changes occurred, most caused by the death of the incumbent.

Mr Eldon was the replacement for Mr Rogers, who had died during the previous August after preaching the Sunday service. The new minister differed from the others in that he had private means. The frugal living at Barham was largely immaterial to him, for his father had been a wealthy shipping merchant plying out of the docks near Southwark in London. He was an only child and despite his father's anguish when he decided to enter the Church, and the Nonconformist Church at that, eventually the estate had come to him on his parents' death, leaving him free to preach and free to serve without the noose of financial hardship round his neck.

Joan's mother had, of course, been aware of Eldon's hidden wealth but her plans for Joan had disappeared with her daughter's marriage to Paul. Only later, when it was too late, did she upbraid Joan for missing her chance. Not that she could have done anything, thought Joan sadly. How many girls would exchange their youth and their quickening bodies for a slow descent to a quiet comfortable middle age with an elderly man? No, it had been inevitable that

Paul, bronzed from Africa, heroic from Normandy, tall and full of war tales, should take his prize. Nevertheless, 'if only' are powerful words and they occurred often as Joan whisked along to the village.

The minister was not in his house. Fresh paint, a neatly dug garden and a trim hedge showed a new occupant. The previous tenant had hardly coped with the grass and weeds had covered the borders. Because it was December the garden was bare, but it seemed to hold a promise as Joan wheeled Claire's pushchair up the tidy path to the front door.

She knocked, and a sudden sinking and trepidation filled her heart. She wasn't one to bleat of her troubles to others. She'd smiled bravely at solicitous enquiries after her health from various members of the congregation. Now she didn't know whether to feel disappointed or relieved when nobody opened the door.

She looked up and down the narrow path crossing the village green, but all was still. Frost lay in the dip down by the elms and there was little colour in nature. She looked back at the manse. The door was a bright orange, detail picked out in white. Window frames sparkled with white and the ivy that had clad one side of the building had been ripped away. Here the old stonework had been refurbished and repointed. Even the roof slates had been replaced. A small trail of smoke snaked out of the chimney and the windows shone, newly cleaned. Compared to her house it looked so tidy, so assured and clean-cut although she didn't like the orange. It's too glaring, she thought. A quiet dark blue would have been more in keeping.

Joan pushed Claire round the corner of the cottage to the chapel. Perhaps Mr Eldon was there, and having come so far it would be foolish not to check.

'Where going?' asked Claire for the fifth time.

'Ask no questions, you'll be told no lies,' answered Joan perfunctorily.

'Ever seen a da di da di doing up his flies,' Claire chanted. Joan stopped.

'Where did you pick that up, young madam?' Claire grinned at her. Joan shook her head and walked on. She skirted the mud surrounding the chapel carefully. Repairs were going on here but had not yet been completed. The arched doorway was open, and she hoisted Claire out of the pushchair and slipped inside.

It was dark and chilly. Black hymnbooks, backs splitting and leaves spilling, were piled as neatly as possible on the shelves by the entrance. It was musty and damp, seeming far worse than on a Sunday when the coming and going of the congregation and the spill from the yellow lights seemed to take away the drabness. Joan had never been in the church when it was empty before. Could do with a good airing, she thought. The wooden seating was bare and functional. Some attempt had been made to polish the rows. A threadbare blue carpet passed between the pews and led to a dais ringed by a rail, with a lectern placed inside. Above the dais a plain wooden cross hung against the wall. Joan looked back at the entrance. A gallery coming from beside the main door held the organ. She'd never been up there and so she moved across to the steps leading up to it. The treads were worn in the middle and grey with dust at the sides. She mounted carefully, Claire tucked to her hip. The organ side faced her and set into the brown wood was a small plaque announcing that the organ had been installed by Waite Brothers in 1921 and purchased by charitable subscription. She edged round to the seat and was able to look out over the main body of the chapel.

Suddenly Joan heard loud voices and firm footsteps approaching. She, realizing the absurdity of the feeling even as she stepped backwards away from the gallery rail, wanted to remain unnoticed as if she were an intruder. Claire was a lump in her arms. She put her on the stool.

'Sssh!' Joan hushed her urgently as she began to wriggle her feet down to the narrow ridged pedals. 'Just sit still.' Then she remembered that the pushchair was outside the main door. Whoever was coming would be bound to see it and, after all, she had come for the purpose of talking to the minister. She had every right to be in the church; she just felt concerned lest the organ gallery was somehow private territory.

Two men came into the chapel, one short, white-haired, quick-footed; the other taller, clutching a cap at his side, big-booted and long-stepping, following the older man with deference. Mr Eldon peered quickly round and then glanced up to the gallery. Joan stepped forward into the light, feeling as she had once done as a girl when she'd slipped some biscuits from the barrel of broken ones her mother kept on the side of the counter and her mother had caught her, pushing through the beaded curtain at the back in the very moment of theft.

'Ah, I thought somebody was lurking in God's house, and where better for a little lurk?' Joan smiled down at the little man with the big voice, blushing pink.

'I can see him!' shrieked Claire. 'Look!' There was a mirror above the organ and Claire could see the floor of the chapel in its tiny reflection.

'Two of you, eh? It is a little dark upstairs there, so please excuse my lack of recognition. Besides,' Mr Eldon turned confidentially towards his companion, 'my eyes are not very good beyond three or four yards. It can be most embarrassing. I tend to see the world in rather hazy generalities and happy clouds of colour, but people don't always understand. They think I've cut them dead in the street.'

Joan came down the steps, her shoes seeming far too big for the narrow treads. The minister peered straight at her. They were much the same height.

'Joan, how good to see you. I do hope we didn't disturb your thoughts charging in like this. To tell the truth, as a good minister should unfailingly try to do but often doesn't, John here and I were discussing those major matters of repair and renovation I mentioned in my sermon a week or so ago, and forgetting the precious and proper function of our chapel as a place of peace.' John looked down at his size ten boots and the minister smiled apologetically.

'I came, hoping to see you.' She caught at Claire's hand as she scampered away down the aisle, missed and covered her confusion by calling, 'Now you just behave yourself, Claire.'

'Well, I shall just be a minute or two with John here. He has kindly agreed to manage the mending of the roof and some internal decoration for us. Maybe you could give admirable advice on colour and other essentials, Mrs Townsend.'

He used her last name as a sort of introduction to John. He, being of the village, knew who she was without it, but Joan appreciated the courtesy. Mr Eldon led the way down the central aisle.

'This blue is drab – once a good carpet, but now tired, definitely tired – like an old minister, much of the use gone from him.'

'I wouldn't say that, sir.' John's interjection was expected.

'Oh, I can buy things, yes, but money isn't the heart of the Church, you know.'

'It's very good what you're doing for the village.' John's voice held sturdy recognition and respect.

'Well, thank you, John, and I'm sure that if you can remove that touch of dry rot in the far wall – I pray it has not spread too far – give a general lick of top-quality varnish to all wood panelling and pews – naturally stripping the old top layer off first – I think this chapel will look something like welcoming. What do you think, Joan?'

'It smells a bit musty as well,' said Joan. 'Is the heating all right?'

'There you are,' laughed Mr Eldon. 'What did I tell you, John? Trust a lady to touch on essentials.'

John interposed seriously. 'The smell is because of the rot but the lack of heating doesn't help. There'll be some damp there too and it keeps people away on cold Sundays.'

'We shall look to the heating,' continued Mr Eldon flamboyantly. He bent down to where Claire was sitting on the step smoothing her finger over the carpet pile, her thumb in her mouth. 'Kneeses and toeses shall be warm as our noses and we won't need clotheses to keep ourselves snug,' he chanted triumphantly, poking his little white finger at the various parts of Claire's body. Claire's eyes gazed seriously back at him.

'Now I will trot along to the manse and put the kettle on. Follow just as soon as you like. We might as well have our little talk in comfort.'

Although she'd already spent longer than she'd intended in the village, Joan could hardly refuse the minister's tea and the letter from the court burned in her handbag. Besides, Paul would not be back from whichever pub would serve him yet and she could always meet Peter straight from the village. Paul could manage for himself with food – a liquid lunch as like as not. It'd be better to keep out of his way until the alcohol wore off.

The minister had changed into maroon carpet slippers when he ushered Joan and Claire into an immaculate sitting room.

'Tea first, then business,' he twinkled at Joan, pouring two cups of tea into delicate china from delicate china and popping a tea cosy over the pot. 'Another one for later maybe, or perhaps you would like to share a little lunch?'

'Oh no. Tea is lovely.'

'A biscuit for Claire?' Claire took a chocolate-coated shortcake from the proffered plate.

'You be careful with that chocolate, Claire,' said Joan, conscious of the cleanliness about her. The minister passed Claire a very large white napkin, spreading it out across her lap as she squatted on the carpet.

'Ready for all eventualities, young Claire – crumbs on the napkin, chocolate on the mouth and no mess on the furniture. All sticky fingers to be made into chocolate finger-biscuits!' Mr Eldon laughed but Claire, once again, just stared at him.

'Lovely to be able to return the compliment of tea,' continued Mr Eldon, unabashed by Claire's lack of response, 'or is there an ulterior motive, another reason for knocking on my door than the search for Earl Grey?'

Joan put her cup down. The tea was a bit weak and had that church mustiness about it. Perhaps it should have been left to stand a bit longer.

'I hardly like to bother you, Mr Eldon, and I'm not in the habit of talking about my troubles to all and sundry, but I do have a little problem I thought you might be able to advise me on.'

Well that wasn't so bad, she thought. Mr Eldon nodded sympathetically. He too had heard the village gossip, had noticed her eye and lip when he'd visited and not been convinced by the swinging door, but he hadn't done more than smile and shake her hand.

'Anything I can do to help, I will,' he said and his voice was serious. Joan took a deep breath. Suddenly the words caught in the back of her throat. She felt like crying and was furious with herself for the swelling in her eyes.

'Take your time, Joan,' Mr Eldon murmured.

She fished into her handbag instead of speaking, covering up her anxiety. She thrust the letter into the minister's hands. As he meticulously pieced the paper together and read, Joan began to speak. She explained how much better her husband had been recently, but how they'd been through a bad time. She described how the letter had arrived and her husband had said he wouldn't go to court, that he'd stormed off to the pub refusing to listen. As Mr Eldon continued to look at the letter, she found herself talking about how the summons to court occurred and why she felt so alone at the farm, how Paul could fall into such black moods and how scared she was he would revert to his old ways. Slowly, having said far more than she'd intended, she came to a halt, drained and quiet.

'How is Joe then?' asked Mr Eldon tentatively, as if embarrassed by Joan's sudden wealth of feeling.

'He is perfectly all right, so Paul says. I haven't seen him since what happened, but Paul knew he was all right. He says Joe just goes into the Anchor to scrounge pints off people and then he tells them about what happened as if he were the hero sticking up for all the lads that Paul was trying to cheat.'

'You only have your husband's side of the case, Joan.' She tried to interrupt but the minister spoke on. 'You must, of course, believe your husband to be innocent, but we also need to see how he will appear in court. I shall see the policeman – Bates, isn't it? – and find out a little more. I think you'll find your husband will recognize that he must do as the law demands. Leave him alone about it for a little. He'll come round and we shall see what we shall see, won't we?'

Something in the minister's jauntiness, the reassurance of his voice, carried weight. Joan thanked him.

'Oh, there's nothing to thank me for, my dear, and now you must let me drive you back to the farm in my new little runaround. That is, if Claire has finished with the chocolate biscuit?' There was a stain of irritation in his tone.

Claire had wiped her hands on the beige carpet, giving it a few darker marks. Joan apologized profusely and the minister found a sponge as if from nowhere with which he cleared the stains despite Joan's offers to do the job. She felt strange watching the elderly man on his knees rubbing intently while she stood, holding Claire's hand firmly. She'd always believed him such a silly fussy man when she was younger, the butt of children's jokes. But there was a certain dignity about him, she saw now, even when scrubbing at his precious carpet.

'There,' said Mr Eldon, leaning back on his heels. 'I think that will do very nicely – clean as a cat's whisker and no harm done. Shall we collect Peter from school on the way?'

# CHAPTER NINE

It was sums time in the schoolroom. The four round globe lights lit patches of desks and the sky outside was darkening almost visibly. Early flurries of snow were intensifying and the children could hardly take their eyes from the whiskery wisps of snow whipping across the high windows. It was the first snow of the year and all the children, except perhaps Peter, were on the edge of their seats.

Mrs Gribbons turned on the table lamp by her side. Its light shone forwards on the teacher's desk, enabling her to observe the work of the children as she called them individually to sit at a high-seated chair next to her. To the pupils gazing up at the desk, she became slightly silhouetted by the light and her shadow was cast up against the blackboard like a watchful monster. Now, as fidgeting increased with the snow, she coughed warningly and the youngsters subsided, bowing their heads to their books but inwardly cherishing knots of anticipation and excitement. Mrs Gribbons turned her head so her bun looked like the monster's nose with a few hairs sticking out of its nostrils and looked thoughtfully out of the window. No, she decided, these thin flakes would come to nothing. It was too early in the year and the clouds were without that deep yellowish bruising. In Sheffield she had never been able to tell, the sky there habitually taking on a sulphurous colour, but here, in clean Norfolk, she prided herself on gauging the weather accurately.

'Elsie, bring out your work please.'

Elsie, a freckled thin girl, whom Mrs Gribbons had called Elspeth until her mother had come in and told her she was Elsie and that was all, pushed back her chair noisily, was told to move quietly, and came up to the teacher's desk. Hush returned to the room as Mrs Gribbons scanned the rows of simple arithmetic, then she began to speak to Elsie in a deep whisper which all the class could hear. It acted as a dark backcloth for their silence. 'Carrying one' was a stumbling block. Elsie returned to her seat and Peter replaced her. This time there were no words of correction, but Mrs Gribbons shaped Peter's numbers along a line and asked Peter to copy the figures. This he did slowly, with fair competence, stopping to distinguish six from nine, but still reversing his three. Mrs Gribbons wrote out the numbers again and sent Peter back to copy them out ten times. Just as he sat down, the door to the schoolroom opened and Mr Eldon popped his head around it.

Mrs Gribbons looked up swiftly; she'd heard the children stir rather than the door opening. She felt mildly irritated by the disturbance. A knock would not have come amiss, she thought, but she smiled towards the minister, who, with exaggerated tiptoes and a finger fleetingly put to his lips, came across to her desk. He left the door open, perhaps expecting Joan and Claire to follow, but they stayed outside, not wishing to intrude. Peter saw them there, his mother shifting from foot to foot as if needing the toilet.

The teacher stood up and her shadow ballooned and touched the ceiling. She crossed to the door, a good six inches above Mr Eldon.

'Do please come in, Mrs Townsend,' she said brightly. 'There's quite a draught today, isn't there?' She turned back to the class, pushing the door firmly shut with her foot, a habit born of carrying piles of exercise-books and readers. 'Continue with your work, children. I'm sure you all know Mr Eldon by now. We have private business to discuss.' Her face implied that she couldn't understand why the minister's private business should interrupt her public duty. People didn't drop into factories for little chats.

'We are sorry to intrude, Mrs Gibbons, particularly when everyone is so busy, busy as the proverbial bee.' Mr Eldon's voice had a warmth and vibrancy that caught the children's attention. They turned from their books, pens poised but still.

'I think I spotted a hive round in the garden. Is that so?' The children gazed at the visitors, all pretence of work disappearing.

'Yes, Mr Eldon. We do have a hive and we make a little honey in the summer. It is one of our practical rural projects, but hardly the weather for it at the moment.'

Really, the man was impossible. How could she maintain discipline with the children? This was at least the third arrival in the last two months and he always left the children excited and without concentration. Yet he didn't seem to feel her disapproval. Even now he was skipping down the aisle talking to individual children, beaming all the time. Mrs Gribbons turned to Peter's mother.

'Were you with Mr Eldon?' she asked.

'Oh, in a way, yes, but I'm sorry we interrupted. I've only come to collect Peter.'

The teacher frowned. She greatly valued a peaceful end to the day and parents were expected to wait outside for their children. There was little room in the school – just a small cloakroom area off the schoolroom – and often seven or eight mothers collecting offspring.

'I wouldn't have come in,' apologized Joan, 'but Mr Eldon said you wouldn't mind, just this once. He said you wanted a word about Peter.'

It was true. She had mentioned Peter's unusual qualities to the minister and indicated that a word with parents wouldn't come amiss, but for him to bring Mrs Townsend along was impertinent, in her opinion. There was a burst of laughter from the back of the room. She looked across quickly. Mr Eldon was holding up Michael's arm and counting off his fingers for him and then pointing at his exercise-book.

'I've heard of arithmetic with fingers,' he said with mock severity, 'but muddy fingerprints in the book show muckiness not mathematics.'

'Mr Eldon!' called the teacher, her voice tight and angry.

'Oh, don't you worry about me, Mrs Gribbons,' he called back. 'I'm just sorting out young Michael here.'

Mrs Gribbons turned very pale; her lips pinched together. She clapped her hands twice, sharp cracks for immediate attention.

'Well, children, you may put your books away quietly. It is a few minutes early but the weather is poor and some have quite a distance to travel. If you know your mother is coming, wait in the cloakroom. Don't go home alone, thinking you'll meet her on the way. Chairs on tables. Lead on.'

Mr Eldon bustled back to the front as the children poured out around him, noise already erupting. His face beamed at Mrs Gribbons.

'So thoughtful of you, Mrs Gribbons. It is certainly an unpleasant afternoon.'

'Very,' agreed Mrs Gribbons, not thinking of the weather.

'Now what about young Peter here?' The minister rubbed his hands together and they all looked at Peter, who was slowly packing his satchel, wondering what was happening. He hated being picked out as different like this, resented his mother coming into the room and now the new minister, every time he'd come, had looked at his work, rubbed his hands, just as he was doing now, and smiled all the time. He made Peter's flesh crawl and when he patted him on the head before trotting off, it felt as if he had nits for the rest of the day. Claire didn't like him either. He knew that. He didn't know how, but he knew. She was standing with her legs crossed and her fingers up the side of her skirt, fiddling with the knicker elastic. No, she didn't like Mr Eldon and neither did Mrs Gribbons. She had her 'I've told you once and I'm not telling you again' face on. Mum was smiling at him. She liked him, liked him a lot. What had his Dad called him when Peter shouldn't have been listening? 'A poor old queen!'

'Perhaps you would wait in the cloakroom for your mother, Peter. She won't be long. Why not take Claire with you? You can show her the pictures on the cloak pegs,' said the minister.

Peter trailed out of the room, his sister following, her thumb stuck in her mouth. Dad said that when an officer wanted you to do something particularly nasty he'd talk all nice to you – 'an order in fancy dress'. That's how Mr Eldon asked them to leave the room and, anyway, it was Mrs Gribbons's room. She'd looked even angrier, but why didn't she say something?

When, a few minutes later, Mr Eldon, Joan, Peter and Claire had left, that was the very question Mrs Gribbons asked herself. Why had she allowed the man to come in and run the place on the pretext of helping with the Nativity play? It was not a church school and he had no right to drop in whenever he wished, but somehow he was very hard to put down and very knowledgeable, undeniably so. If he could arrange for Peter to sit scholarship papers for Greelham School in the spring he would be doing the boy a service, even if Mrs Gribbons would miss her silent protégé. Next time, Mrs Gribbons decided, she would ask Mr Eldon to wait outside.

'Where is he then?' A tall dark man lurched through the door aggressively. Mrs Gribbons faced him, yet another hiccup in her daily routine.

'Where is who?' Her words rang with the resolution of a moment before.

'Peter – my lad.' Paul Townsend looked round the schoolroom somewhat wildly, as if the boy could be hiding behind a desk. 'It's only three thirty now,' he went on, 'but there's nobody outside.'

Mrs Gribbons breathed in deeply. She felt sorely tried, but she could deal with men like Paul. He was rather like some of the steel men in Sheffield, all right as long as they knew exactly what to do, when to do it and to whom to complain when they did it wrongly.

'We finished a little early today because of the poor weather, but every child has been collected. I believe that Mr Eldon, the new minister, gave your family a lift back to the farm. You'll find them all safe and sound on your return.'

'Almost ran me down, that car did. It's a narrow road at the best of times. Bloody thing went sailing past. Why didn't it stop?'

'It's a dim evening, Mr Townsend.'

'And I take a dim view of my son going off with that man.' Paul nodded curtly to Mrs Gribbons and left as quickly as he'd come. The door banged and then swung open again. Mrs Gribbons closed it firmly, feeling marginally happier than she had before Paul had arrived.

Paul stormed back along the bare cold road. He'd come into the house with the terrier ready to make amends for his temper, to bring a little Christmas cheer with him, and found a silent shell, no food ready, Joan's normal chores undone. He'd dug out a large cardboard box from inside the pantry, lining up tins of corned beef and peaches along the stone floor to empty it, and snuggled the pup inside the high walls in an old piece of blanket. Then he'd grabbed a bite to eat. Still nobody returned. He'd pottered about in the yard and eventually decided to go and meet Peter with the pup in his pocket. He'd bought the pup for the boy, he thought, and, by God, he'd give it to the lad himself. It was twenty minutes later and still no wife, no children and the long walk back after watching a car almost knock him over and then to hear that the minister, Eldon, was driving them about the countryside. Well, he couldn't afford a bloody car.

With every step back, Paul stoked his anger to a blaze. When the car whisked by him, back towards the village, he brandished his fist at it, but Mr Eldon did not see him standing by the side of the hedge. The minister's eyesight was poor and he held his driving licence from a time when a test was not required.

Mr Eldon had dropped the others off at the end of the track up to the farm, not wishing his car to be spattered by mud from potholes, and concerned lest a deep rut should break a spring or axle. Peter was impressed by the car, a new Morris in two-tone green. Most cars were black, very occasionally maroon. Peter liked all things mechanical and Mr Eldon talked incessantly about erudite matters of clutch, brake and accelerator, ignition and distributor, the function of petrol and the need for brake pads. The minister knew little about cars, but his vocabulary was impressive and Peter listened with increasing if grudging admiration. It was a novelty to be flying through the countryside peering out into grey and inhospitable land. He saw his Dad as they pulled away out of the village and waved frantically out of the back window, but his Mum said they should get themselves back home quickly, so they didn't stop.

Joan was filled with almost guilty excitement. Right from the time of packing the pushchair away into the neat little boot at the back to being tucked into the front seat with a rug round her legs, she'd revelled in the attentions of the minister, who seemed to show such awareness of small creature comforts and concern for her feelings. She couldn't fail to respond after years of rough and ready hand-to-mouth existence with Paul. She'd seen her husband, but he'd been walking in the opposite direction, had probably been drinking until closing time at three o'clock. She didn't want him to be put next to Mr Eldon. The minister was such a sweet little man and she felt no fear nor threat from him. He might be a bit nosy, a bit fussy, but he made her feel important and reassured her.

How she winced on entering her own home again! A pile of greasy washing-up left on the side, a pervasive smell of some animal or other and a soggy patch of grey newspaper, cupboards gaping open with ill-fitting handleless doors and broken hinges and battered table and chairs. What a contrast to Mr Eldon's house! No, she couldn't call him Arnold, not yet anyway.

She dumped her handbag on the table and moved over to the stove. At least that was still alight, although very low on fuel. She riddled the grate and added precious coal, willing it to blaze and quickly heat the draughty old kitchen. Then she lit the oil lamp, pinching the wick into shape and wiping her blackened thumb and finger on her hastily assumed apron. She resented the lack of generator and electricity. The whole of Barham now was on the national grid, but their farmhouse was outside the area as yet, although promises of installation were frequently made and as frequently broken. Still, she would make every effort to improve the house and how she managed it. She owed it to the children, but where could she start? She sighed heavily. Food for the children had to come first, then milking and swilling out. House-cleaning would have to wait until later, but she'd work through the washing-up before going to bed. She couldn't leave that mound of crockery and pans another day. She remembered with a pang how Mr Eldon had looked briefly into the kitchen on his first visit before being taken to the front room. She hadn't seen his house then and now wondered what he could possibly have thought of her.

Joan quickly buttered bread and put a pot of jam on the table. She added some cold custard to two bowls of stewed apple left over from the day before, and looked in dissatisfaction at the spread. Then, with some self-consciousness, she put Mr Eldon's gift of the remains of a flan and a sponge cream cake next to her more barren fare. The children sat up at the table and Joan added tea to her large brown enamel pot. At least the tea would have a bite to it, she thought.

The children were just settling to eat when Paul arrived. Joan had not really thought about him since seeing him in the village. Now, when he walked through the door, there was no ignoring him. The back door rattled in its frame, the curtain was ripped to one side and the house shuddered when Paul slammed the wood behind him and stood glaring across the kitchen.

His violent walk, making about twelve miles in one day, had heightened his colour to bright beetroot and anger was threading his forehead with deeply ploughed furrows. His eyes seemed to be all pupils, set back deep in their sockets and sparking with a cold flame. Even before he started to speak, Claire was whimpering, her thumb firmly fixed in her mouth.

'And where the bloody hell do you think you've been?' he demanded, pushing one of the wooden chairs out of his way as he barged towards his wife. She stood her ground, holding the teapot, suddenly surprised from her thoughts about Mr Eldon and plans for a better future.

'I could ask you that,' she said jauntily, but her voice trembled.

'Shut up!' He shoved Joan on the shoulder so she staggered against the sink. Hot tea spewed through the spout and steamed to the floor. She almost dropped the pot, but managed to twist and put it on the draining board. Claire began to cry in earnest and Peter turned white, shivering in his chair.

'You've been leading me a bugger of a dance all day, you and that old fool. Even got him to drive you home in his smart little Toytown motor. He's nothing but a little noddy man with bloody bells for balls.'

Joan felt sick inside. Mr Eldon's kindness would always be transmuted by Paul into dirt.

'Don't be revolting, Paul,' she pleaded, 'and think of the children.'

Paul laughed, a nasty harsh sound. 'I am thinking of the children,' he said. 'That little man is nothing but a pervert and I don't want you having anything to do with him. Understand?'

'He's a minister of religion, an old friend and only wants to help,' Joan mouthed desperately.

'And that's what he says,' Paul jeered. 'Do you understand?'

Joan didn't reply. Paul did not stink of beer and his voice was not slurred by alcohol, yet he was behaving as viciously as when he was drunk. Suddenly, his face was thrust right into hers, his breath hot on her.

'Do you bloody well understand?'

Joan decided to turn away wrath with gentle words. There was not much else she could do. 'I understand,' she whispered.

Paul turned away from her brusquely, a point of honour satisfied.

'I've been all over today,' he said loudly. 'Over to Westby's, down the village, back again and no wife at home with a bit of grub. I hope if you ever marry,' looking at Peter, who winced away from him, 'I say I hope if you ever marry – not likely with your looks, lad, but never mind, you're not missing much – just make sure your woman isn't one of those stuck-up bitches with one mouth always open and the other one as tight as a duck's arse.'

'Paul!' interrupted Joan, shocked to the core.

'Well?' Paul wheeled back to her, challenging her again. She wilted back. 'If the cap fits wear it, not that you need one or any other kind of protection.'

Joan rushed over to the children and began to hustle them out of the room.

'Come along children. Daddy's just having a joke.' Paul roared with mirthless laughter.

'Don't take them away. Leave 'em be. They need their tea.'

Joan continued to push them to the door but Paul intervened physically.

'I told you to let them have their tea.' He shoved Joan back into the kitchen. 'Besides, I haven't finished yet. I haven't reached the important bit.'

All the time Paul had been in the room, even in the height of his rage, he'd kept one hand in his pocket. Now he pointed mysteriously at his pocket with his free hand and winked at Peter.

'Now let's all sit down, tuck into a lovely-looking tea and then we'll see what I've bought for you, Peter. It's Christmas soon, isn't it? I thought you might like your present early.'

He smiled broadly at his son but Peter stood frozen by the door, and it was Joan who brought him trembling back to his chair. The boy creaked down on to it, unable to take his eyes away from his father. Dad had been so much better lately and the boy had not had to scrabble into his cupboard or hide in the outhouses for a couple of months, but now, today, he was frightened to the marrow. Claire huddled in Mum's arms as she stood at the sink, her face pale and compressed, as expressionless as she could make it, not wishing to provoke further wrath.

'Come on, son. I'll not bite you. You've done nothing to be ashamed of. There's this lovely pie and cake your Mum's made. She's good for something after all. Have a nibble.'

Paul helped himself to a large slice of flan and then divided it down the middle with his fingers, putting the halves on to the children's plates. Joan sidled to the table, hushing Claire and sitting her on her lap. Peter didn't eat, didn't even look at the food, just stared like a transfixed rabbit. What could be in his father's pocket? Last time it had been Josie who had emerged with her fangs and musk.

'Oh,' said Paul nodding round knowingly, 'he wants his treat already, can't wait to find out what his Dad's bought him. Well, for once, we'll have treats first and eats after.'

His left hand withdrew from his pocket and the little terrier, half asleep, half suffocated by long submersion in the fluff of the pocket, blearily and wearily blinked, stood and then tottered on the tabletop.

'Here he is,' said Paul triumphantly. 'A lovely young Lakeland for you, Peter, to replace that rabbit of yours. He'll be a good little ratter. Westby sold him to me and he knows a good dog even if he is a miserable old sod.'

Paul gazed round the table, smiling broadly, willing the others to smile too, but his family sat like statues around him, only their eyes flickering nervously towards the pup and away again.

The pup, as sleepy young animals will, slumped hindquarters down and puddled on the tablecloth that Joan had put on as a token gesture of a more civilized society. Paul picked him up and put him onto Peter's lap. Peter's fingers almost instinctively began to rub the terrier's fur beside his ears.

'That's the way, lad. That's the way. He'll need a bit of training, but you and me together'll sort him out, won't we?'

Joan silently fetched a dishcloth, soaked up the puppy's urine and rubbed the patch with a splash of disinfectant. The smell of damp reminded her of baby's napkins and she felt like crying, but stifled the impulse. She would give her husband no such satisfaction. Later, when the children were in bed, she would give him his answer.

Claire peeked at the pup from her mother's hip and wriggled until Joan put her into a chair next to Peter where she began to try to touch the little animal. The terrier was beginning to recover, found her little white sausage stuck on his side and with his tiny teeth worried it. Claire squealed in mock fear and snatched her hand away before gradually stretching it out towards the pup again. Peter took no notice, just sat caressing the pup, using it as a baby uses a furry stuffed bear for consolation and security.

'Well at least you can cook, Joan – good pie.' Paul took another bite of flan, chewed and swallowed appreciatively. Joan nodded wrily. Cooking had to be what a wife would do. He would not envisage a man producing domestic food.

'Will you bring the churns round for the milk lorry tomorrow morning?' she asked diffidently. 'They're all ready for the cart.' Paul sniffed, presumably agreeing. 'I've still to do the afternoon's milking,' she went on, 'so if you'll excuse me.' She got up and went over to her boots.

'No, Joan,' Paul hastily smeared his mouth free from crumbs and pushed his chair back. 'I'll milk 'em this evening – save you a bit. I'll sort 'em out.'

Joan knew her husband was a clumsy milker, but she didn't refuse his offer. How quickly his temper cooled, she thought, and how he could just push his words and violence into the past as if they'd never happened. He didn't think his treatment of her was anything other than normal, as he, the male, established dominance over his female. Once he'd done that, he would deign to help her.

'Come on, Peter,' Paul called to his son. 'Bring that pup. He can find out about the cowshed.'

Peter twitched to his feet and carried the terrier across to his boots, shoved his feet into them without putting the pup down and then followed out the door. Joan caught him as he was leaving and levered his arms into his old duffle coat. As soon as the coat was on he grabbed back the pup.

'It's cold out there, love,' she explained, soothing him, and she kissed the top of his head before pulling the hood up and over his thin brown hair. He looks as if he's going to his execution, she thought, and with the departure of Paul and her son, she slumped at the table and wept scalding tears.

She allowed herself a couple of minutes and then set about the kitchen with sudden vigour, getting Claire to put away dried pots and pans, scrubbing the tabletop, sweeping the floor and resolving to buy some cardinal red for the slabs by the stove. She didn't know how she'd manage Paul, but she would not be beaten inside even if he beat her physically. Mr Eldon had assumed she wanted to support her husband; she had spoken words of loyalty about him, putting his crime in the best possible light. Now, not for the first time, she thought it would be a blessing if he were in prison.

Meanwhile, in the cowshed, Paul milked the cows roughly and quickly. Spurts of valuable creamy milk were wasted and Gertie, not liking his impatient hard hands, stood tight, giving grudgingly. Every now and then, Paul stopped pulling the teats and leaned over to nudge the terrier or tickle its stomach. Joan always observed scrupulous cleanliness when milking, but Paul hadn't washed his hands, nor done more than quickly sluice the udders. The only regular source of income to the farm was from clear and uncontaminated milk sold direct to the board, but Paul found milking tedious and slow.

He stood up from Gertie in mid-milk and sat his son on the stool. Peter often helped his mother milk. He enjoyed the firm pull and rhythm. He pushed confidently into Gertie's flank and she, recognizing his hands, relaxed and began to flow well.

'Need to buy a milking machine for these cows,' said Paul. 'Perhaps the bank will help us out.' He turned to the pup and happily teased the little dog, while Peter steadily worked his way through the milking. Occasionally Paul would carry out a brimming bucket and siphon it into a churn before returning to the pup.

'What'll we call him?' asked Paul, but Peter didn't answer. 'I thought something like Nipper would suit him.'

And so Nipper was named.

Paul returned to the house after milking, the anger forgotten and his excitement in the pup strong. Peter and Claire were packed off to bed. Paul sat over a mug of tea listening to the wireless. When Joan returned downstairs, she ignored Paul and attacked the cleaning. The clatter of brush and pan interrupted a programme about Dick Turpin's boxing career, his famous victory and then defeat by the legendary Sugar Ray Robinson, and his return to the ring to fight Alex Buxton for the light-heavyweight title. Paul refrained from hushing his wife and bent over to the set, seeing the fights unfold in his mind's eye. He had always supported Turpin – the underdog with the highwayman's name – and when Buxton was despatched, he slammed his fist on the table and said 'That's my boy' as if he had had a part in the victory and knew Turpin well.

Upstairs, he pulled on his old striped pyjamas and slid into his side of the bed. Joan had hunched herself away from him as normal, but, as he stretched himself out into the icy regions at the foot of the bed, she, with lips clenched, willed herself to speak.

'I saw the minister today about the letter.'

The room became very still.

'Which letter?' Paul asked, choosing to misunderstand.

'He said he would try to help.'

Paul snorted. 'Not much he can do, is there?'

'He's going to see Bates. Find out what happened.'

Paul leaned up on his elbow.

'You know what happened,' he said, a warning note in his voice. Joan stayed still, waiting for Paul to settle, but still he stared at the blackness of his wife beside him. 'You've been blabbing your mouth off to him then?' he said, baldly and harshly.

'No. But you need someone to find witnesses, that sort of thing.'

Paul lay back on the bed, hands behind his head, not wanting his brain attacked in this way. There was nothing to be done and nothing useful could be said, but Joan would keep harping on, bringing up the same old evil in him.

'You may not think much of him, but he was very kind to me today.'

'I'm sure he was. He's not likely to be banged up in the nick, is he? He can afford to be pleasant.'

'And you can't afford not to be. I don't know what came over you today. You'd throw away all your work over the last month or so and what for? I don't know.'

'Stop whingein' on! Some people have been stomping all over Norfolk all day. I need some sleep.'

'And then you come in and push me about the kitchen. What sort of example is that for the children?'

Paul laughed curtly. 'A bloody good one, I should say.'

'You don't know what being decent is, do you? You don't know how to make someone happy. All you can do is play games with your little animals and then go off in a sulk when things go wrong – that, or throw your weight around. When are you going to think of your children? Don't worry about me – I don't expect anything from you, but what about Peter and Claire? Don't they mean something to you?'

'I got Peter that dog, didn't I?'

'Did you?' asked Joan bitterly. 'You pretended it was for Peter because that made it all right, but you got it for yourself really, so you could have a ratting dog, pretend you're a real countryman.'

'Oh, I'm a real countryman all right,' muttered Paul. 'I'm married to one at any rate.'

Joan's mouth closed like a clamp. Perhaps underneath there was a gentle man and all this outward show was built on fear and some strange image of how a man should behave, but she couldn't reach him. Once she'd found his aggressiveness attractive, even exciting. Now she winced from him.

Suddenly Paul rolled over onto his wife. He rammed his knees between her legs, brutally forcing them apart. Joan tried to resist, to fight back, but she defeated the need to scratch and bite. She willed herself to lie still, not to react. His penis burnt into her dry vaginal passage and his rough hand massaged her left breast, teasing at the nipple there, trying to drag it to erection. Joan tried to think of other things. She pictured Mr Eldon offering her the flan and smiling at her, but Paul's hands abruptly seized the flan and started pulling it into pieces and then Paul's mouth started to swallow the portions one by one, without chewing. She was fighting for breath under a heaving pushing mass. The initial pain decreased, but suddenly Paul's hand plunged down into her pubic hair and he started to rub at her with his fingers. Desperately Joan simulated a slight movement of response and immediately Paul groaned; he buried his head in her breast, his flanks quivering and his spent sex shrivelling until it slipped away in a slither of sperm.

For a few minutes Paul lay motionless on his wife. Slowly she brought her hands beneath his shoulders and pushed at his inert frame. With a shudder Paul rolled off her and she eased her legs together, shivering with disgust at the wetness. In the blackness of the room, the two lay motionless and then sobbing broke the silence, a dry racking sob. It was Paul. Joan continued to stare dry-eyed and cold in every limb and every pulse out into the dark recesses, while Paul sobbed his guilt away.

'I'm sorry, Joan,' he finally blurted out, but she didn't reply, just hunched herself over on to her side and pretended to sleep.

She had thought of divorce before when rape occurred, but she had been brought up to struggle on, to accept the man's right as a necessary evil. Besides, how would other people think of her deserting her husband in his time of need, with a court case in the offing? She could put up with the privacy of rape, she decided, but she would take the children away if he started using violence when they were there, as he'd done today. What she couldn't bear were his bitter recriminations against herself afterwards and then the pretence that all was well the next day. Sometimes he'd bring her a cup of tea in bed the next morning and grin at her like a shy but proud bridegroom who'd done his bit and shown his manhood.

Up from the kitchen came the plaintive whine and yip-yapping of the pup. She'd heard it before, but only noticed it now. Paul snuffled and snored as he lay flat on his back. The pup's distress intensified. Best to ignore him, Joan thought, but the noise was as demanding as the cry of a child. Slowly she inched from the bed and threw her old camel dressing gown round her shoulders, but by the time she'd reached the head of the stairs, the noise had stopped. Joan decided to go down anyway to wash.

In the kitchen she found Peter kneeling by the puppy, stroking it and rolling it on to its back, rubbing its tummy and then picking it up, holding its nose against his face. He was dressed only in his pyjamas and was trembling with cold, yet he seemed oblivious to the icy wind blowing beneath the back door. Paul had forgotten to pull across the curtain. Peter sensed her presence behind him, looked up and smiled warily at her.

'You'll spoil Nipper if you come every time he decides to whimper, Peter.'

Peter pointed at the box and then towards the stairs.

'We've already had that out with Claire. You're not going to have that pup in your bedroom. He'll mess the place.'

The boy shook his head, picking up newspaper, his eyes pleading. Joan raised her gaze to the ceiling, praying for inspiration. Without much expectation, she said, 'If you ask me properly, Peter, you can take Nipper upstairs with you but he must stay in the box by the door and you must take him out if he wants to go. Only if you ask me properly.'

Peter stared at her and then at Nipper. 'Come on, hurry up,' Joan continued. 'You'll die of pneumonia if you stay here much longer and I know you can speak when you want to. Claire doesn't pick up all her sayings from me and your father.'

Peter slowly opened his mouth and then, rather blurred but quite understandably, he spoke.

'Can I take Nipper up please?' He hesitated and stammered at the start of the words, but succeeded and Joan's desolation of a few minutes before was changed to a radiant joy. She put out her arms to her son and pulled him to her, the pup caught between.

'That's right, Peter. You just talk to your Mum, won't you? She'll look after you. She'll care for you.' Her eyes filled with tears. Then she pushed Peter away from her, holding him at arm's length, smiling at him through shining pupils. 'Say it once more Peter, just once more. Now I know you can.'

'Can I take Nipper up please?' Peter asked.

Once again he was pulled into her brown dressing gown and his face rubbed against the warmth of her.

'I'll help you with the box,' she said, her hand stroking his hair at the nape. 'What do a few puddles matter between friends?'

When, eventually, Joan returned to her bed and squeezed into her side – Paul had flung his legs across the bed – she was still happy. She even wanted to wake up Paul for a moment and share the news with him. She remembered when Peter had first walked and how they'd sat on either side of the kitchen with the boy toddling between them, backwards and forwards, with his father catching him up under the arms and whirling him round back on the path to his mother. He'd seemed so proud of the boy, but now she couldn't predict his reaction. Paul was a millstone around her neck. She pushed her icy feet against her husband's hot legs. Even in the midst of domestic uproar and hatred, she would have to find a use for him and a hot-water bottle was about all he could manage. With relief, Joan realized she could still giggle at herself. If he brings me a cup of tea in the morning, I'll throw it at him.

It snowed in the night, not heavily, just enough to highlight the swell in the fields and any exposed ridges by quarry edge and the old church mound. Frost, coming later, flecked all the darkened world with eerie white and, as early morning by imperceptible degrees edged grey into the sky and silhouettes out of blackness, so a freezing mist, solidifying as it drifted on from the coast twenty miles away, spread frozen droplets along hedge twigs, fenceposts and even inside barns and outhouses. The trees, sparse along by the quarry, disappeared and down from the small height of the Townsends' farmhouse, the hollows in the fields were filled with white, making the sky and earth look as though rinsed in diluted milk.

Habit opened Joan's reluctant eyes, and bitter experience that to delay snug under blankets only brought trouble launched her out of bed. She was still in her dressing gown. Blearily she crossed to the window and rubbed her elbow against the silvered pane, crumbling off the ice. She crouched down to spy through the gap at the chilly sight. She had no time for contemplating the vision nor desire to do so. It was a day for action, for keeping warm and for holding close to the house and kitchen. She plucked up courage and tumbled out of her night clothes. For a second or two, she stood naked, the same colour as the window, and sky behind her, and then she wriggled into layers of bra, vest, shirt, jumper and cardigan. She scrabbled into knickers and woollen stockings, fixing them in place with plain grey elastic garters. She then pulled on baggy drawers of her own making and topped them with her working skirt and an extra pair of socks. She did not look at her reflection in the thin wardrobe mirror. She looked at her husband instead. He was still asleep, but he needed to be up and about. There was the mucking-out to do, the hens to be sorted out and he had said a few weeks earlier that he would mend the old fencing along the side of the quarry, but that was still undone.

She crossed to the bedside and inspected the snoring face. His chin was tucked under the blankets and his hair flopped on to the bolster like a child's. The frown lines were only traced in place, hardly visible in the cold dawn light. She shook her head slowly and then, with no smile touching her eyes but a grim lift to her lips, she wrenched back the blankets and was out of the room before the anguished shout had even started.

# CHAPTER
# TEN

'No, you can't take Nipper to school, Peter. You're there to work, not mess about with animals.' Nipper scampered under the kitchen table, between Joan's feet, landed in his box and then hurtled out again.

'Shh-sh-ow t-t-teacher,' stammered Peter. The stutter seemed to increase the attention his mother gave him.

'Now, don't be silly about it, Peter. He'll charge about all over the place and Mrs Gribbons won't want messes, will she?'

Claire began to cough loudly. A bit of crust appeared to have gone down the wrong way.

'Cough up, chicken,' Joan said, perfunctorily patting Claire on the back, still looking at Peter. Claire continued to cough.

'You c-can br-br-bring him h-h-home.'

'He's rather young to be gallivanting about the countryside.'

Peter's face went dark and sullen. His mouth tightened and his hare-lip whitened.

'You see what I mean, don't you, Peter?' Peter did not reply, would not reply. Claire knocked her cup of water over and dabbled in the rivulet as it trickled off the table.

'Oh Claire, can't you be more careful!' Joan hastily mopped up and turned back to Peter. She suddenly felt afraid that Peter would revert, become dumb again. Rationally she knew she should not give way, but all her feelings pushed her on to do so. It wouldn't hurt this once, she felt. He'd only started speaking last night and she didn't want him going backwards. She looked severely at Peter, frowning judiciously, not wanting to appear soft.

'All right, Peter,' she said. 'Just this once, you can take him and I'll bring him back home. You've never taken anything to show Mrs Gribbons before, have you?'

'Just this w-w-once,' mouthed Peter, smiling.

Claire finished crumbling her bread on the table and started to dab her wet fingers into it.

Paul wandered into the kitchen. As a matter of dignity, he had pulled the covers back over himself rather than get up at the beck and call of his wife, but now he needed some breakfast. Claire's fingers froze in their puddling and Joan's back stiffened as she spooned porridge into a bowl. He said nothing, walked to his chair, the one with arms, and sat waiting. Joan placed the bowl in front of him and broke the news.

'Peter's speaking,' she said proudly, gazing at the lad. Paul put his spoon back down and looked across at the boy, who put his head down.

'Is he now?' Paul nodded approvingly. 'Good for you – only about six years late – but better late than never. What can he say?' Paul turned to Joan.

'Anything he likes, can't you love?' Joan smiled warmly at Peter, encouraging him, but the boy sat still, refusing to look up. Paul started on his porridge, blurting through a mouthful, 'In his own time, love, in his own time. I've waited long enough. Another ten minutes won't hurt.'

Paul's mouth slurped on his spoon and the kettle hissed. Joan scraped off the warty skin of porridge from the pan bottom with a wooden spoon and squelched it into the hens' dish, glancing up at Peter as she did so. Paul continued spooning but he didn't look at his food, keeping his gaze fixed on his son until some porridge dripped on his chin. Then he wiped it away with his sleeve. Claire looked from Peter to parents and back again, trying to catch their eyes. She screamed, pushing her plate away violently. It fell to the floor, smashing on the stone.

Joan fetched the pan and brush, squatted on her haunches and scraped the fragments up. 'That was naughty of Claire, wasn't it?' She turned to Peter, pleading for a response. Peter looked up, glanced towards his sister and then to his father. The audience was ready to listen.

'V-v-v-ery n-n-naughty,' he agreed.

Paul stood up, leaned over the table and tousled Peter's hair. 'That's the way, lad. That's the way. We won't be able to stop you nattering on now, will we?' He beamed round at the family.

'It was Nipper that did it, wasn't it Peter?' Joan smiled again, but Peter didn't respond this time. She turned to her husband to give praise where praise was due. 'It was a good idea of yours, Paul.'

Peter didn't like the thought that he was speaking because of his father's forethought. He stayed silent for the rest of the meal, but enjoyed the surreptitious glances and comments designed to evoke further speech. It was a rare and special pleasure to feel their eyes upon him, to be surrounded by overt attention and concern, to have his father looking at him as an interesting person, someone with an identity. The power thrilled him.

When Peter arrived at school, he watched his mother take Claire by the hand and march purposefully, without hesitation, into the schoolroom towards Mrs Gribbons. Although he could not hear what was said, gestures and faces spoke. Mum nodded and smiled towards him and Old Gibbon, as the children called her, looked thoughtfully in his direction so that he bent down, fumbling through his satchel. When he next raised his head, the teacher was smiling as well. Claire started pulling on Mum's hand, swinging out away from her and running at the end of each swing back into her mother's skirt. Joan held the pup in her free hand where he wriggled, almost fell and was clutched to her coat front.

Although Peter enjoyed the attention at home, this concentrated interest began to make him feel like an item on display in a zoo or the shop. He was receiving a battery of vaguely hostile, incurious looks from other children as they arrived chattering, whirling, dodging in and out of the lines of desks. Bill and Dan Westby, in today because of the cold, put their hands into their armpits and started bounding up and down the aisle making ape noises. Whenever another child went to join in, the two stopped, stared at the interloper and said, 'What's the matter with you then? Are you a gibbon or something?' And then they'd laugh raucously, slapping each other on the back, before starting off on the routine again through the gangways. Peter tried to stare through them, but they stuck their tongues out and blurted hooting noises into his face and so he turned his back, swivelling his chair on its back legs until he faced the back of the class. The two boys, taking his evasion as success, followed him round gleefully.

'What do you think you are doing, boys?' Mrs Gribbons's voice cut through the high-pitched squeals of the classroom. 'Go and sit at your desks.' Quickly Mrs Gribbons apologized to Joan and began to usher her from the room. Peter pushed out of his place and scurried over to his Mum. She stopped, surprised. Peter put out his hand towards Nipper. He wanted to say goodbye to the pup, Joan assumed.

'You just say goodbye for now, Peter. You'll find Nipper safe and sound when you come home.'

Mum's bright voice could be heard right round the classroom, inviting him to speak, to show the teacher and all the children that he was no longer dumb. Peter partly wanted to please her and see the expectant smiles around him broaden, but he also wanted Nipper to stay with him, not return home. He wouldn't just say 'goodbye for now' in that silly sing-song way. He wasn't a ventriloquist's dummy.

'N-n-nipper s-stay w-w-with me.'

He felt the stir behind him, knew the children were whispering at each other, nudging and nodding towards him because they'd heard him say words. He saw out of the corner of his eye Mrs Gribbons bring her hands up to her mouth in surprised delight. His spine tingled.

'Oh no, Peter,' Joan said. 'Nipper can't stay with you now. We've shown him to Mrs Gribbons and now he must go home. That was the agreement.'

Peter stiffened, his face reddening. Sometimes he looks just like his father, thought Joan, but felt no pride. The class grew very still, watching live theatre with unlikely Peter Townsend as the leading actor, once mute, now with a speaking part. Once again Peter stretched out to take Nipper, but this time Claire intervened. She suddenly swung round Mum's legs and kicked her brother viciously on the shin. Peter doubled over, clutching his leg, hopping ludicrously up and down in silence.

His hushed frenzy had the desperation of Harold Lloyd. The children began to laugh. Joan tried to seize the chance of leaving and pulled Claire to the door, but suddenly Peter grabbed at her sleeve. People shouldn't laugh at him, he thought. Mum shouldn't take away his dog. The teacher pushed between.

'Now come along, Peter,' murmured Mrs Gribbons reassuringly, but Peter ignored her, pinching his fingers into the stiff cloth of Mum's coat. Joan released Claire, pulled off his pincering fingers one by one and opened the door to leave. Peter snatched at Nipper and hobbled rapidly back to his seat with the puppy. A huge cheer went up from the class.

Peter stared round triumphantly. The children, even the Westby boys, were standing up and cheering him on. They could well understand his desire to keep the pup – it was special – and they were so accustomed to Peter representing all that Mrs Gribbons seemed to approve of that this reversal surprised them into acclamation. Peter had never received such attention, such adulation. His chest swelled and he forgot the pain in his shin. He did not hear his mother marching over to his desk, but he felt her arm pull him around and then her hand rang against his cheek. Totally unprepared for the blow, Peter was flung sideways to the floor. In the shocked pause, Nipper squealed and then squealed again, a tiny bleating that seared through the silence.

Peter pulled himself up. He'd landed on the pup's hind legs. Nipper was swinging round, trying to bite at the pain, but one leg hung useless behind him, broken in the fall. Peter started to scream.

It was Mrs Gribbons who brought a semblance of order. She firmly ushered Joan, Claire and Peter out of the room, calling Dan and Bill to come too. She picked up Nipper and Peter, now silent, stared at the pup with horrified eyes, refusing to touch it. After a stunned minute whispers began to hiss between the children.

Outside the classroom she entrusted Nipper to Bill and Dan. 'Take him to your father, boys. He knows more about injuries than most for he traps enough animals. See whether he can splint the pup's legs. If one of you could bring back news later, I'd be grateful.'

'He's one of our pups, Miss,' said Bill, taking the mewing pup in gentle competent hands, as Peter howled protest and tried to wriggle back, but Joan held him in a clasp like a vice. She didn't know Bill and Dan had killed Floater. They'd probably kill Nipper, thought Peter, beyond reason now. Dan ran to the big black door of the school, wrenched it open and then held it there while his brother carried the patient out.

'I'll put my coat over him,' said Dan, and the door slid shut with the image of Dan wrenching off his jacket in the freezing mist.

'You'd better take Peter home, Mrs Townsend. I'll try to send news before the end of the day.'

Letting Claire run on ahead, Joan pulled Peter along the road. By the time they were half-way home, he'd stopped dragging behind, but walked head down, feet trailing, utterly silent to all her attempts to bring him round. Meanwhile, Joan wondered why such things seemed to happen to her, whether Peter would speak again, whether she should have hit the boy. Showing her up in public like that. But the guilt ate into her and she was in tears by the time they reached home. Peter noticed her crying and felt slightly compensated and when Claire ran to Joan, put her arms round her Mum's legs saying, 'Don't cry Mummy,' he found himself saying, 'It was your b-b-bloody f-fault.'

Joan didn't know whether to feel relieved to hear him speak again or appalled at what he said, so she said nothing, but the boy noticed the relief in her eyes and then how she winced. Once again he welcomed his power to influence people around him and, instinctively, he realized the need to maintain the rarity of his speech. He knew words as weapons. He should have been overwhelmed by Nipper's broken leg and for a few moments back in the school, his head had whirled with fear, guilt and pity. Then, when the boys had taken Nipper, rage had possessed him. Now, there was a kernel of calm inside him as if whatever happened to the puppy had been preordained, inevitable. Perhaps all of his creatures were doomed; perhaps he was an instrument in their doom.

His mind couldn't crystallize these thoughts into words, but Peter was beginning to build a means of protection against the wounds inflicted on him, and this core became a little bigger with every occasion of hurt and his heart became a little more impervious to pain. His own disability, his own hare-lip, were outward signs of his strangeness. Now he could speak, perhaps he could unleash those elements that made him strange, and in their expression he would obtain a position and a status. He would return to the fold of normality.

It was only ten o'clock when the three reached the farmhouse. Joan had thought it much later. Paul was sitting in the old carver chair, whittling at a stick of wood, trying to fashion a stoat. Old Joe made lots of creatures out of bits of wood, smoothing them off with sandpaper and then coating them with varnish. Some of them looked really good, Paul thought. He wondered whether he could have a go, perhaps sell them in Norwich. Perhaps he should have been a sculptor. He would fix the quarry fence later.

Joan pushed Peter none too gently into the kitchen and told Claire to go and play. She began to wail, but Joan spanked her backside and she scuttled crying up the stairs to her room. Paul stopped whittling, watched Claire leave and shook his head. The house had been quiet and he'd had his dreams. Now her squawking disturbed him.

'What's he doing back then?' He saw Peter's pinched face, the hands plunged into pockets and the defiant shoulders. 'What's happened now?'

'Never mind what's happened now. What are you doing here? That's more to the point.' She'd reminded Paul about the quarry fence before leaving for school but she just didn't want him there when she got back. She wanted time to talk with Peter, build a few bridges into his unhappiness if she could.

Paul returned to his stick, nicking away at the natural curve instead of shaving with the grain and shape. Joan sighed. She was always sighing recently, sighing with frustration, impotence, unhappiness and sheer drudgery. She pulled herself together. Where was her resolution of yesterday? The bundle of dirty washing was heaped ready for her return by the old sink. It would be best just to get on with that, explain what had happened as she went along, try to ignore Paul's failure to start on the fencing, hope that Peter would understand what he'd done wrong as she told the story. She didn't want Paul exploding at the boy.

She began to sort out the washing and as she tossed underwear into the sink, sheets into pillowcases and other clothes on the pile, she explained what had happened at school. When Joan reached the errand of the Westby boys, Paul started. He'd nicked his finger.

'But I still owe Westby for that pup. Here, get out of the way.' Paul pushed his finger under the tap. 'I'll have to take him the money today. I'll collect Nipper while I'm about it. Don't see why that teacher sent him off with the Westby boys in the first place. You shouldn't've allowed it. Typical bloody teacher – all nose and mouth.'

Paul whacked Peter round the head with the flapping sleeve of his coat. Buttons at the cuff clipped him hard. The boy shrank into the seat by the range.

'And you can come too, you stupid little runt.'

Paul yanked him clear and the chair clattered to the floor. Peter stumbled – his foot had been tucked into one of the leg struts. He pulled against his father's arm. Suddenly Paul let go and the lad staggered back against the wireless shelf. 'Please yourself then. Stay here if you like, stupid little bugger.' Paul marched out of the door, pleased to be going. Then he charged back in. 'I need another pound,' he said half pleading, half demanding. Joan nodded at the tin wearily.

Peter pulled himself up off the floor. The shelf had caught him just on the shoulder. Dad stopped at the door again, looked back at the boy.

'Are you coming then or not?' he asked. Peter shuffled out of the door.

Joan began to fill her old dustbin-like copper with buckets of water. She shouldn't have let the washing mount up so much. Her thoughts returned to the day before and Mr Eldon. He was such a kind little man. Her eyes blurred with tears and she brushed them impatiently away with her cold wet hands. That too seemed to be happening a lot lately, she thought, and then realized that she had thought that thought a lot lately. As the gas popped and spluttered under the copper, she leaned against the sink edge and Mr Eldon's face filled her fantasy. He'd have a smooth little body and would be very gentle all the time. She wondered whether he'd stop talking ever and decided he would, overcome by her love for him. She imagined going out to a no-ration dinner with him, enjoying immaculately prepared food, red roses on the table and the devotions of one of those Italian waiters you sometimes found in Norwich. She shivered. She shouldn't think such things. Mr Eldon is a minister and twice my age, she thought. It's not respectful, but, as she prodded and turned the simmering sheets with the long wooden laundry stick, she dwelt on the day before and fed her empty heart with dreams.

As the steam hissed from the water, clouding the windows,

coating the walls and dripping from the ceiling, the dank smell of washday percolated through the house, into every corner and on up the stairs. It reached Claire and she, snuffing the inimitable smell of soap, steamed cloth and dirty water, trotted downstairs to join her mother. In the kitchen, the two figures became shadows in a ghost world. Mum bending, lifting, leaning into the old mangle, extruded yards of squeezed linen which Claire bundled up into a huge enamel bowl. All the time, the cauldron steamed and water dripped, splashed, splattered and turned into condensation at the touch of a surface. The two became bedraggled and wet.

'Oh, couldn't I just do with one of those twin tubs!' said Joan, wiping her forehead with the back of her hand. 'A bit of electricity would do wonders for this place.'

Claire nodded wisely.

'Mr Eldon has his own little washing machine. Did you see that? Not that you'd have known what it was, but it wouldn't be big enough to handle all our stuff, would it? I don't know where it all comes from, I really don't. Peter stuffs his dirty pants down the side of his bed every day and then wonders why there aren't any clean until I rake them all out. Your father's as bad with his socks and I don't know what you do with your pinafores, young lady.'

Claire grinned sheepishly, feeling warm inside with all the activity, with Mum talking on as normal again, with a job shared and the kitchen transfigured into a warm and mysterious haven.

'If we can get this lot done today and dried on the Dutch airer – there may be a wind blowing up out there but it'd turn the sheets into paving stones – we'll be able to start polishing up the table. Mr Eldon says it's a very nice pine and would look lovely sanded and polished. Dad's still got some of that varnish he used for the chicken run. It's probably in the paint shed.'

Claire chuckled happily and beat down a soggy pile of sheets with her little fists, pushing all those clogged folds and creases into the bowl before the next sausage of cloth squealed and squeaked through the grinding rollers.

'I hope that little Nipper's all right though, don't you? Get yourself out of the bowl, Claire. There's no need to sit in it. You'll have wet knick-knacks.'

Joan picked her daughter up and held her close before returning to her work.

She loosened the rope holding the pulley in the ceiling and let down the airer, like the upturned hull of a skeleton boat sinking through a sea of mist, until she could reach and start draping wrung clothes on it. When it was full she strained on the rope, hoisting the rack and clothes up until only the sheets caused her to duck across the kitchen.

Paul arrived at Westby's again. The walk took longer with Peter in tow and, although the man tried to shorten his stride, he drew ahead over the last stretch and then waited impatiently for his son by the stone wall where he'd stacked his pipe the day before. Now seemed an age since then and the contours of the land, the look of the cottage appeared warped, caught in another moment. The snow and mist, instead of lightening the landscape, seemed to darken its lines and dull the vision. The wind, bitter before, was sharpening its edge still further, stropping on the bald fields and knifing the hedgerows.

'Come on Peter. Hurry yourself. If I hang on much longer I'll freeze my bum to the wall.'

Peter swivelled out of the lane into the full slice of the wind. His body shrank inside his ballooning coat and the blast distorted his face and crippled his approach still further. To Paul, he appeared like an extension of the twisted hedgerow and then a separate malignant creature, a dwarf, hobbling like a picture he'd seen once in a fairy-tale book. Given half the chance, he thought, you'd expect the boy to stay at home in the warm, but he follows me even when I tell him off. Peter panted to the lee of the wall and looked up at his father, flinching as he did so.

'What I have to suffer from you, I don't know,' said Paul, taking the pinched creature's hand and pulling him on. 'I try to give you a bit of help with that pup and I'm kicked in the head for it. If that Eldon's God is really up there, I think he's a bloody sadist watching us scrabble around murdering each other in the War and then, just when we're supposed to be free and happy, he sends a runt like you along to keep him laughing.'

Pushing the boy round the side of the cottage, Paul followed. Here in the yard there was a blessed lull from the wind, but the gale of barking and yapping rose unabated. The back door remained unopened this time.

Paul strode over to it and rapped with his knuckles. The door was locked – unusual in the country. Peter sheltered behind his father now, peering round at the door. There was no answer so Paul banged again, this time using a rounded stone with a hole through its middle hanging on a rope and acting as an improvised door-knocker. The wood of the door was dented like the face of an old cricket bat where the natural swing of the stone had marked it through the years. There was still no answer, despite the increased fury of the terriers at every bang.

'Even if the old man is on his rounds, the wife should be there. Once more for luck.' Paul swung the stone with a mighty crack against the door, splintering into the wood.

'There's no call to go knocking us door in. He's not here and that's the end of it.' Mrs Westby began to close the upstairs window from which she had called, but Paul shouted back.

'Hold on love. The lad here is worried about the pup. Can't you come down?' The woman's arm, all that now could be seen, stopped its pull and then continued until the cottage was shuttered and still.

'Well, I'll be damned,' muttered Paul. 'It's my bloody pup, when all's said and done.'

He went to pick up the stone again, but didn't need to use it for the door opened a crack and the old labrador pushed through his frosted muzzle, snarling. Above the door, Mrs Westby's grey thin face appeared looking like an old mare ready for the knackers and scared of the prospect.

'He says you're not to touch the pup. Here you are.' She shoved something into Paul's hand and shut the door. Paul looked down into his fist, which had automatically clenched. Two ten-bob notes were folded in a wedge.

'What the hell is this?' Paul's voice mounted from incredulity to fury. 'What the hell is this?' He yanked up the stone and crashed it repeatedly into the door. 'That's my bloody dog that is!' The upstairs window creaked open again.

'He didn't think you should have your money even – after what's been done. I'll set the dog on you if you smash up my door.'

Paul's anger flared even higher. 'And I'll kick its bleedin' head in if you do! Now give us that pup.'

Suddenly Mrs Westby's face went pasty, doughlike and her mouth dropped open. The window shut with an emphatic click. Something prodded Paul in the back and he whirled round. Westby stood there, his shotgun trained at Paul's stomach. Dan and Bill stood behind him, their eyes wide. Westby jerked the barrels towards the gate and then held them unwaveringly at Paul's stomach.

'Git.'

'But that's my pup,' Paul blustered. Westby's finger closed over the trigger with unmistakeable intention.

'Trespassin'. Now git!'

Even in the blindness of futile rage, Paul understood that there was no alternative. He put his arm slowly out to one side and put it round Peter's shoulders, drawing him away. Westby followed, his boys behind him, and the terriers spat.

'You haven't heard the last of this,' Paul threw over his shoulder. Implacable silence answered him. 'Load of thieves round here,' he continued. 'Don't you worry, Peter. You'll have your dog back. There is a law in this country.'

The two reached the mildewed remains of the stone wall and the brunt of the wind. Paul turned back slowly to face the gun.

'And you can have your money.' He casually flipped the ten-bob notes into the wind, which took them and plastered them back and away into a tangled web of old bramble and hawthorn. Bill and Dan scampered after them. Westby's eyes flickered away towards his sons and Paul suddenly leaped into the gamekeeper. It was over in a second. Paul held the shotgun; Westby lay on the ground with the muzzles screwing into his temple.

'I didn't fight for this godforsaken bleeding country for nothing, you bastard. You're bloody lucky I don't blow your brains out.'

Westby stayed still, his face a skull, almost unafraid, although his skin was frozen white.

'Git off my land,' he grunted.

'*Your* land. It's not *your* land. You don't own it – you're a bloody slave, not a landowner like me. You've probably heard in the village that I go around shooting little old men – a sort of hobby of mine – so don't come the dead hero on me!' Paul called to the two boys, statues by the hawthorn. 'Go and get Nipper and don't be stupid or I'll blow your Dad's brains out. Understand?'

Bill and Dan understood. Paul's reputation ran before him. But Dan was too frightened to move, and stood rigid while Bill scurried to the house.

'You shouldn't move the puppy. It'd hurt his leg,' mumbled Dan and his eyes welled over.

'He'll have to take his chance,' said Paul as Bill came back round the house, cradling the pup. His mother ghosted him, her hand to her mouth and the labrador waddling behind her.

Silently Bill put the pup into Peter's arms. Nipper was lying still, swaddled in an old blue cloth. Only his black nose and whiskered eyes showed. Paul fumbled in his overcoat pocket with one hand and drew out the pound note he still owed. With a quick movement he bent down and shoved it into the gamekeeper's coat. 'So it's all paid for as agreed. I keep my word.'

Westby was shaking with the ice in the ground, but he said nothing. His eyes stayed fixed on the tall man above him. Paul broke and threw the gun in a black arc towards the house. It crashed into a half-broken bit of old garden wall, bounced back and fell, lodging between some lumps of stone. Its barrels leered emptily into concrete.

'Come on, Peter.'

Paul swung out in a long stride and Peter followed, tiptoeing stiffly, gingerly. Just before the turn in the lane, Paul looked back, found his son already straggling and put his hands on his hips in annoyance. He could see Westby slowly dragging himself to his feet, pushing his wife away as she came to help, and Bill lugging at the shotgun, waving his fist at Paul, his mouth working, but no sound reached them. Peter's eyes were riveted on the pup in the blue cloth.

'They'll have more twelve-bore shot in the cottage. You'll have to step out a bit, but I doubt if they'll do much anyway now. That shotgun might be rather dented. I'll take the pup.'

Paul went to take the bundle, but Peter held the pup to him, staring at his father with an intense horror so that Paul shrugged in assumed indifference and continued along the lane, leaving his son to follow. Paul was triumphant for the moment. His feet marched to the beat of a regimental march and his heart kept time. Perhaps he should have stayed in the army, he thought.

There were no sounds of pursuit. The skeleton trees rattled their bones, the deep-rooted foot-tripping brambles chickered like scraping glass and autumn's leftovers crunched underfoot. Peter hunched himself into his coat, fearful of a touch on the shoulder, lead in his back and more fearful still of the chill little Nipper in his care. He remembered the touch of Josie when she lay dead.

# CHAPTER
# ELEVEN

Paul returned to the farm as if he were a conquering hero, letting Peter rush through the mist still shrouding the kitchen to place Nipper tenderly in his box.

'Shut that door!' yelled Joan from across the room. The wind struck ice into the comfortable steamy heat. Paul kicked the door closed with his boot.

'What a fug! Can't see a thing.'

Peter, half wincing at the task, picked up the tiniest corner of blanket and eased it gently away from Nipper like skimming a plaster off inch by inch, flinching at every hair tugged by the adhesive, frightened of what he might find beneath. Nipper lay inert. The boy put his hand under the pup's belly, lifted tentatively and drew out the blanket, revealing hindquarters swathed in white linen. A smell of embrocation wafted into his nostrils. Two slivers of pea-stick were wrapped against one of the legs.

Peter's hand registered a faint beating inside the frame and the body was hot with fever. The boy looked round for his Mum and saw shadows, ghosts in the mist.

'M-m-mum!' he called, his throat rusty again, but it was Paul who came to his son and leaned over the box. Peter covered Nipper with his hands, calling again for his mother.

'C'mon lad, let's have a look. I'll not eat him yet,' said Paul, taking the boy's hands away. 'Joan, get us that little bit of cooking brandy you said you'd used for the cake.'

'If I've used it, you can't have it,' said Joan.

'Oh, you know what I mean. The pup needs a swallow.'

'Don't we all?' said Joan, but she rummaged in the pantry and brought the bottle. 'Poor little mite. We'll look after him, won't we Peter? He'll be all right.' Her eyes were serious when they met Peter's. 'Why did you bring him back? Shouldn't be moved, I fancy.'

'We had our reasons, didn't we lad?' said Paul. 'How do we get it down him?'

Joan fumbled through the odds and ends drawer and lifted out a

91

tiny feeding bottle. She hastily popped a little milk into a pan and added brandy, warming it gently. She sluiced out the bottle and rubbed down the teat with a pinch of rough cooking salt, then carefully tilted the mixture into the bottle.

'That takes me back a year or two,' she said and went back to the pup. Peter seized the bottle and very carefully tipped it until beads of brandy milk spilled on to the side of Nipper's mouth.

'Hold on, lad,' said Paul and he lifted the lip with his huge thumb. 'Try now.'

The boy tilted the teat into the little gap and coaxed the liquid between clenched teeth.

Claire came over. 'Me do,' she demanded, grabbing at Peter's arm. Her brother snatched his fist away and flailed with his spare arm, knocking his sister to one side. Joan caught her up, stifling her scream. Nipper shivered and swallowed.

'Yes,' said Paul grinning. 'He likes that.'

Four faces watched as bubble by careful bubble Nipper drank.

For the rest of the day Peter stayed loyally by his pup. He put newspaper beneath him and took out soiled pieces when necessary. Joan brought him a cushion to ease the hardness of the stone floor. He refused to move for his food and, ignoring Claire's anger, Joan allowed him to eat where he sat.

With the midday meal out of the way and the washing completed, hanging high on the drier, Joan decided to attack the bedrooms and work her way down through the house, but she mentioned the pine table to Paul, asking after sandpaper and varnish for later. Paul ran his fingers over the table, rubbing at grease marks in the dark wood as if he were a master craftsman.

'Might polish up all right, I suppose. I'll have a look at it myself – no job for a woman.'

'Mr Eldon said it was a very nice table and would polish up well.'

'Mr Eldon!' Paul aped his wife's tone. 'He wouldn't know his arse from his elbow.'

'You seemed to like that bit of pie you had yesterday. He cooked that, you know,' Joan smiled derisively. 'Not all men are cocky layabouts.'

'There are fairies at the bottom of my garden,' laughed Paul, refusing to be drawn into anger.

'They say the best cooks are men!' Joan concluded as if she were clinching an argument for herself and then, as she took Claire out of the room, she wondered.

Paul pottered out to the shed where he kept his decorating stuff – the ends of paint, stiffened black brushes, turps, scrapers, papers and varnish. He brought in three different grains of sandpaper, a block of wood, his old plane, the pot of clear varnish and then, vaguely remembering another comment of Joan's, dug out a half-used tin of cardinal red for the bricks round the range.

Early afternoon quickly turned into dusk. Cloud increased outside and snow, like swirling goose feathers, flew crazily round the house. Peter, sitting by his pup, stared unseeingly through the window; he became caught up in the dance of creamy white, his eyes trying to dodge the flakes, seeking the black between; the sky, bruised and sullen, shed its frozen tears and the window became an ambulance-black shield, reflecting the gas lamp that Paul lit as soon as Joan had left the room.

Paul leaned into the tabletop with the plane, slicing off lines of black gum, the old ingrained varnish. He caught against knots and violently crashed through them until the surface was a deeply scored, uneven grey and yellow, with splinters splitting off and black threads still winding through. With the tip of Joan's best sharp knife, he picked out old food particles, scrapes of ancient gunge, from between the tongue-and-grooved slats. Curls of black and yellow littered the floor like hair from a barber's shop. He folded a sheet of thick-grained sandpaper round the wood block and started a circular scraping. Flecks of sawdust sprayed over the sides of the table, highlighted by lamplight, and drifted down to the floor, a snowstorm inside the house. Peter became coated with the flecks, and whenever his father blew noisily at the surface sawdust flew everywhere, even over Nipper.

In an hour Paul's face was caked, his eyebrows sandy, his stubble like a sand dune flecked with reed and his hair sprinkled with dandruff. His arm ached and the table looked as if a giant had stubbed his thumb again and again on the wood. Wearily he folded over another piece of sandpaper, the next grade finer, and began rather half-heartedly to smooth the wood, knowing that he had a very long task ahead. He pushed the block to one side when he discovered that it was making very little difference to the scarred pine.

'Well, I've made a good start,' he announced to the world in general. 'Give us a hand clearing up, will you Peter?'

Peter didn't hear. His father took him by the arm. 'It's you I'm talking too. Give us a hand.' Peter came back into the world of the living, shaking his head.

'L-l-look after N-n-nipper. L-l-look a-after Nipper.'

Paul shrugged, raising his eyes to the ceiling.

'He'll be all right for a few minutes. He's not going to run away, is he?'

But Peter sat tight on his cushion, shaking his head. Paul could not tug him out without endangering the pup.

Joan and Claire came into the room at that moment, having finished their tornado of bed-making, sweeping, polishing and scouring upstairs. Mother's and daughter's mouths dropped open in identical fashion as they came in through the door. Condensation from the morning's washing and the clothes hanging above had provided a beautifully tacky surface. All surfaces were gritted with what appeared to be a virulent sandstorm. Jaundice, heightened by yellow-fever lamplight, had swept through the kitchen, invaded even the cupboards where doors hung habitually open. Half expecting Mr Eldon to drop in later in the afternoon, Joan was ready to clear away the washing, sweep up and clear the odd crocks, put her mum's old lace tablecloth on the table and make the room tidy for a bite of tea. She'd even made time to bake a cake in the morning just in case the minister came with news about Paul. Now her kitchen was transformed into a beach after a high tide.

All of Joan's high purpose, her resilience and determination ran out of her. She had no fuel on which to stoke her anger; no blaze could flare from the embers of pain after pain, disillusion after disillusion. It was especially cruel because it seemed such a minor matter. What did a dirtied kitchen matter when compared with a court case, a son without a rabbit or a voice? Yet even Peter's new-found words could not comfort Joan. She slumped at the table on which were scored lines that hurt her and wept.

'It'll clear up quickly enough.' Paul wiped a dishcloth across the tabletop. 'You wanted the job done, but it'll take a bit of time. You don't make omelettes without breaking eggs.'

Joan looked disbelievingly at her husband and then buried her face in her hands. She rocked as if trying to soothe herself with the rhythm of a lullaby. There was nothing she could say to this lump of a man, this unfeeling blustering cocky sod who always had an answer, made her feel guilty when he had done wrong and now patted her on the shoulder as if she were a vaguely embarrassing nuisance.

'Well it's not that bad, Joan,' said Paul, a trace of anger in his voice.

Claire came to her mother, put her hand awkwardly on to her lap, leaned her face into her side.

'Now you're upsetting the children!' Paul continued. 'There's just a bit of sawdust about, that's all. Now pull yourself together.' He stared at his wife's broken back and then, with a gesture of annoyance, walked out, taking his plane and sandpaper with him.

Joan shuddered, hands falling to her sides, and looked blankly ahead of her. She had to stay calm, she thought. She must not allow this man to trample over her, not allow herself to become a weakened vassal. Her tears merely confirmed Paul's attitude. She wouldn't be a hysterical, emotional woman, pretending to rely on her man, accepting his terms for her life. She took Claire's hand in her own in a numbly self-conscious way.

In an empty voice, no challenge within it, she said, 'Don't worry, Claire. Daddy doesn't understand or doesn't try to understand when he hurts us, but he can't really hurt us any more. You have to be intelligent, know what you're doing, to hurt people on purpose. Daddy sometimes seems to try to hurt us deliberately, but he doesn't really. He hasn't got the brains, but he also hasn't got the heart to apologize when his stupidity might hurt us. All this washing,' Joan sketched the airer with her spare hand, holding her daughter firmly now in the other, 'doesn't mean anything to him. It might just as well be rags because he only thinks of himself all the time, not of how much time and effort we might have put in to keep him in clean clothes . . . but polishing up a pine table is a man's job . . . more important than a woman's job, so it doesn't matter if he spoils everything.'

She stopped and the silence behind her made her look round apprehensively, wondering why Paul had not interrupted her, even hit her. She hadn't noticed his leaving. Now she patted Claire's hand and stood up. 'Life goes on regardless' echoed through her brain. Even as she stood, she resented her everlasting ritual of despair and slow recovery until the next debilitating blow.

'If this keeps going on much longer,' she said to the kitchen, 'I'll go under. I know I will.' Once again she shook her head, this time as if to clear from it the clichés which welled up so readily and tumbled out like little bits of ineffectual sticking plaster. What does 'going under' mean, she thought. She was already underwater and beginning to gasp for breath as the reeds confined her. And her children relied on her to keep them afloat. Claire, at least, did so, and Peter – well, how could she leave Peter? She had read somewhere that humans used to live like amphibians once, babies clutching on to females' long tresses for security. Thus the legends of mermaids arose.

'I,' she smiled round at Claire and then at the oblivious Peter, 'I,' she repeated with a slight giggle, 'am a mermaid!' Claire's eyes grew round and very intent.

'You haven't got a tail,' she said accusingly.

Paul burst back through the door.

'It's that Eldon. Surprised he's risked his precious suspension but then the snow would be more than he could manage on two feet. Could get lost in a snowdrift, couldn't he?'

Joan smiled serenely at her husband, who stopped abruptly.

'Of course it's *Mister* Eldon. He said he'd come this evening. That's why I wanted the place to look nice.' Joan twirled round as if showing off a new dress. She ran to the window, peered out girlishly, and then whisked round, winking at Paul.

'And where's he got to then? Front door or back door? Upstairs or downstairs?'

'Don't be so bloody stupid,' Paul muttered.

Joan clasped her chapped hands beneath her chin and tucked her head to one side.

'Ah,' she sighed, 'if only you knew all that is to be known about Mr Eldon, or should I say Arnold? You would not doubt his loyalty nor his wish to help a little girl lost.'

'I don't want him sticking his nose in where it's not wanted.'

'Oh but it is,' smiled Joan, rapidly skirting Paul beyond the reach of his arm and making for the front door. 'He has the dearest little nose and he can stick it anywhere he likes.' She flung open the door.

'Mr Eldon,' she called and a snow-shrouded figure slipped into the house like the white rabbit into his burrow. A flurry whirled around the draughty hallway for a moment and then the storm was excluded. Mr Eldon brushed down his coat with small, deft, leather-clad hands, popping his trilby over the banister head and chirruping excitedly.

'Such a journey! Short indeed Joan, but treacherous – a veritable swirligig of snow unlooked-for and suddenly upon us. I thought to turn back, but then I was in snow so deep I might just as well go o'er, to paraphrase murderous Macbeth for totally innocent intentions! And then your drive, my dear, is cloaked and nasty ruts are lurking for the unwary. My little car has bobbled and bounced its way to see you kind people, but I did promise I would come and here I am. Like Good King Wenceslas I have dinted the snow with tyre tracks and hope to return upon the very same.' Arnold Eldon finished shaking his coat and Joan put it under the hat on the same banister. 'And Mr Townsend,' the minister turned the full beam of his adventurous journey and happy arrival upon Paul, 'I trust I find you as well as can be expected in these difficult days.'

'Paul,' interrupted Joan, matching the minister's high-pitched squeak, 'has been making a start on the kitchen table, haven't you?' Paul did not reply. With a flourish Joan opened the kitchen door to usher in her guest. Mr Eldon walked through and Joan grinned at Paul.

'Oh my goodness!' exclaimed Mr Eldon. 'Yes, indeed you have made a start, Mr Townsend, but your finish remains a little ahead of you.'

Paul grunted, seemed about to speak, but thought better of it as the minister turned his attention upon Claire, asking how she'd enjoyed the flan and whether he could give her races in her pushchair when the snow had disappeared. Claire huddled into Joan's skirt and giggled. Then he turned to Peter, suggesting a snowball fight once the storm had abated, but Peter just gazed back at him.

'A lot has happened since you were last here, Mr Eldon,' said Joan brightly, brushing off a chair.

'I'm happy standing for the moment, my dear. I've been sitting all the way here.'

Paul snorted and sat himself down on the sawdust. Joan threw a couple more daggers at her husband and then realized, with a pang, that the main news, the best and only news, was really Peter's ability to speak and she had forgotten it in all the hullabaloo. With a gradual return to sobriety she explained how Peter had come to speak about the pup and was now able to talk about anything he wanted. She told how the pup was accidentally injured. She omitted reference to the school and the involvement of the Westby family, but then she knew nothing of her husband's exploits at the gamekeeper's cottage earlier that day.

'Talking, eh?' Mr Eldon twinkled at Peter. 'Stringing together those little pearls of communication, eh? How wonderful and how cheering! May God be praised, my dears.'

'He's very upset about poor Nipper at the moment, but I'm sure he'll say something for you before too long,' said Joan, smiling towards Peter's crouched figure.

'Left it a bit late, didn't he?' interposed Paul truculently. 'Thought God could do what he wanted – flicked his fingers and hey presto! As the Italian magician said when he forked out the rabbit by a paw.'

'Oh the best treats are sometimes the ones we have to wait for, Mr Townsend.'

'And we've been waiting a very long time, haven't we?' chirped Joan, smiling confidentially at the minister. 'Would you care for a cup of tea and some cake?'

Hardly waiting for the minister's effusive thanks, Joan set out her best cups and saucers, blowing each one individually to remove the dust, and took the cake from the top of the range, flicking it over with a teacloth. Meanwhile Mr Eldon turned his attention to Peter but the boy remained silent. Claire prattled round the minister, holding on to his arm and trying to pull him away from her brother.

'Now do sit down, Arnold, and have some tea.' Joan seized another chair and vigorously rubbed it clean with her apron. 'If we don't breathe too heavily, the dust won't choke us!'

Arnold was prevailed upon and he sat gingerly on the edge of the chair, sipped tentatively and then nursed his plate of cake.

'We would be in the front room,' announced Joan, 'but there is no fire in there at present.'

'You said you wanted to use the kitchen,' stated Paul baldly.

'Oh no, this is fine for me, dear. It could be a most pleasant room when you've finished.' A vision of his own little kitchen flickered in Mr Eldon's mind. He much preferred cosy little nooks, but at least the old range was warm after the snow and the yellow light was comfortable on the eyes. At one stage in his skidding progress from the village he had wondered whether he would reach any sort of haven. Still, duty was his watchword, if only that duty were not so unpleasant. He hated unpleasantness, avoided it whenever he could.

The information was bleak. Joe had insisted on showing him his old bandage with the rusty bloodstain on it to prove his injury and the Luffmans in the village store confirmed that he had become a doddery old man overnight. PC Bates had sounded ponderously damning as he attempted to present a cautious picture of a case in process. George, the landlord, had been implacably intent on sending Townsend to jail for attempted murder and Johnny glibly confirmed the landlord's story. He had also visited Mrs Gribbons, and learned of the accident to Nipper. He knew more than Joan had told him.

Such a messy tangle, thought the minister distastefully. You start unravelling one thread and are caught on horrible knots that can't be tugged loose.

'I really need to talk privately with the two of you,' he stated, more suddenly and pointedly than he had intended.

'Claire!' Joan called her daughter to her side. 'Go over by Nipper and play with your doll. Don't disturb Peter, there's a good girl.' Claire's face puckered.

'Oh no, my dear. Let Claire stay here. She's not old enough to understand.'

Joan didn't know so much. She had respect for the quickness of children in picking up what adults didn't want them to follow, but she didn't say so and Claire was reinstated, ostensibly playing with Annie, her old rag doll.

'I must suggest as strongly as I may that you consult a solicitor if you have not already done so, Mr Townsend.'

'That's what I told him,' said Joan, 'but will he listen to me?'

Paul remained silent.

'It's just that he'll know the ins and outs of the law, you see, and may be able to suggest a way forward for you.' The minister's voice was warm, persuasive. To Paul it sounded insufferably condescending.

'I don't need a lawyer,' he stated. 'I just need a bit of justice. George as good as admitted I didn't mean to hurt Joe.'

The minister looked apologetically towards the couple.

'George says he only appeared to agree with you to try to get you to leave his public house; he says he was frightened you might shoot somebody and wanted to get you out.'

Paul brought his knuckles up to his mouth and scraped them along his teeth. He rubbed his fingers together where they irritated and then brought his two balled fists down on the table. He had run through the unfairness of his treatment so often that any suggestion that he might have been to blame merely fuelled his resentment. Eventually he managed to speak, his tongue thick in his mouth.

'Well, you've been a great help, I must say – stirring it all up again. Don't think I can't see what you're after, jumping round here on your pretty little tootsies as soon as Joan flutters her eyelashes. I'm not having my marriage messed up by a conceited little . . .' Paul stopped, dragged in breath to steady himself then suddenly lurched across the room to the dresser where he found an old pack of cigarettes with one left inside. Drawing smoke inside himself, he pointed at the minister and Joan, setting them together by the gesture.

'You two want me inside. I'm not daft. Now get out of here, Eldon, before I throw you out!'

Joan rose. 'You're talking to the minister, Paul.'

'I don't care who I'm talking to! If he was twenty years younger, he'd end up in a bleeding hedge with a broken nose. Out!'

Mr Eldon stood up and placed his plate, cake untouched, on the table. His hand shook slightly, but he asked Joan for his coat in a steady voice. As she hurried out, Claire rushed at the minister, kicking at his shins furiously. Mr Eldon tried to push her away gently, but she screamed.

'Don't you hurt my Daddy! Don't you hurt my Daddy!'

Joan ran back and pulled her daughter away roughly. Mr Eldon found his voice.

'She doesn't understand, my dear – think nothing of it.' A spasm flitted across his face and he went on simply and seriously, ' "Suffer little children to come unto me," the master said, and however they come, bearing their own suffering with them, we must accept and cherish them.' He turned towards Paul, whose eyes laughed in mockery. 'I promised your wife to help you as best I could. If you would like a lift into Norwich I shall render you that service.'

'I'm not going anywhere,' Paul said emphatically.

'Goodbye, Peter,' said Mr Eldon, clutching his dignity to him. 'I hope your little puppy recovers.'

Peter stared at the little man, a grin twisting over his face.

'F . . . f-fuck off!' he blurted and Paul laughed triumphantly.

Mr Eldon pattered down the corridor and out of the front door with Joan close behind him. The snow storm was unabated and the minister's car was already capped with white, the windscreen clogged.

'Oh dear.' The minister stopped at the doorway, peering out into the gloom. Yes, there was the car and the drive, but the car was facing the wrong way and what could he use to clear the windscreen? He looked briefly at Joan, tried to smile reassuringly but his face crumpled. The kitchen door slammed. Joan flinched as if she'd been slapped.

'Please don't leave me with him,' she blurted out. 'I'll bring the children and we'll find somewhere else to live, but I can't stay any longer. We could all fit into the car just down the road.'

Joan put out her hand to touch Mr Eldon's shoulder. Beneath the overcoat, the minister was rigid.

'I shouldn't have come out on such an evening – snow like this and so suddenly down.'

Joan went on desperately, knowing that what she asked was beyond imagination. 'You don't know what he's like. I can't trust him – up and down like one of those yo-yos. Please, please let us come, just for a short time until this court case is settled.'

Mr Eldon forced himself to look into Joan's feverish eyes. Dear God, he thought, this isn't happening to me.

'I'll need something for the windscreen, my dear,' he said, trying to keep life to simple things. 'To clear off the snow. It's really remarkably thick in such a short time.'

'Shall I fetch the children?'

'Just a piece of wood would do the trick. I really don't want to wet these gloves, you see. Leather tends to dry out with continual damp. Please help me, my dear.'

Joan called back down the corridor, her voice crackling falsely.

'Claire darling, come and see me for a moment, dear.' She pulled open the cupboard under the stairs and rummaged through it.

'I've got another coat in here for her – found it at the school sale, and she'll have to manage in shoes for now.'

The minister could wait no longer. He gingerly picked his way across to the car. With a stretched sleeve he rubbed sticky snow from the black glass and then skirted a rut round to the back. By the time he'd reached the front of the car again, the windscreen was lightly coated. He rubbed once more, fighting the cloud mantling his precious machine. He climbed into the driver's seat, knees first, kicking his feet behind him and then swivelled his bottom round and in. He automatically pulled down his coat to clear the wrinkles behind him and fumblingly found the key and ignition. The headlights blazed forward, bouncing back a myriad whirling stars into his eyes. All around the car was blackness and ahead of him a moving maze of dazzle. He'd met London smog, London wet black snow, but never anything like this vast expanse of choking cold.

With painful care and inch by inch, he manoeuvred the car back, his spine locked lest he hit something, and then forward again. He was just about to pull away when the passenger door was flung open and Joan hurtled into the car, thrown by an unseen arm. She banged against the minister, her head cracking against his shoulder, and he ricocheted against the door with the impact.

'You can have her!' bellowed Paul and his face loomed menacingly through the window. Mr Eldon crashed into gear and with a squeal from the skidding tyres, the car plunged off along the track, like a horse bolting from a slap on its rump.

Maybe divine providence was caring for the minister because the track ran closely round the edge of the quarry, known as Fen Dyke Edge, and here the fence was broken – not that fencing would have held a car. But somehow the car maintained its proper path, grooved by ruts perhaps and involuntary twitches on the wheel. Miraculously the car hissed silently on to the road and Eldon instinctively directed it towards the village. Joan lolled on the front seat, only half-conscious, uncertain whether the whirling specks ahead were snow or a maelstrom in her brain.

The minister reached Barham, and stopped outside his cottage. At last his refuge was in sight! He tottered out. For a moment he was tempted to leave Joan, pretend she wasn't with him, but he stoutly resisted the temptation. The passenger door was stiff with ice and Joan almost toppled but, after steadying herself against the door frame, she managed to walk to the cottage. Arnold pulled up the side of his overcoat and scrambled in his pocket for the key and the two went inside.

As he ushered Joan to an armchair in the warmth, he felt obscurely guilty, resentful and rather scared. Guilt is often propagated in innocence, finds rich soil in righteousness. Paul's belief in his wife's infidelity and his violence were based on false assumptions, but nevertheless the minister felt guilty that such notions should have even been possible.

'The man must be mad,' he muttered, putting the kettle on to boil. He tried to add his normal appellation of sympathy to anyone he slightly criticized, but found the words 'poor chap' would not come.

Yes, he resented this invasion. He could not view the matter dispassionately. He resented the physical invasion of his car, but felt more hurt still by the assault on his mind. Of course he wished to help Joan – had assumed that by helping the husband, he would assist the wife – but now the demands of the two were distinct and harshly conflicting.

He poured boiling water on to the tea. His hand was trembling so that splashes of water fell on the work-surface and, when he poured sugar into the bowl, some grains spilled and gritted the lino by the sink. He did not notice.

There was no doubt of his fear. He had often prayed to God to give him physical courage and moral strength; it was a prayer born of his size and his deep sense of inadequacy. It was a prayer unanswered as yet, he thought, although when he had told his father about going into the Church, that had required courage. He still quivered when he remembered the occasion.

'God give me strength for I have none without your help,' he pleaded, managing to place the teapot on the tray without further mishap. He even popped the tea-cosy on, with greater resolve. He began to feel angry – righteous indignation, he thought, after his treatment.

Joan was sitting exactly where he'd left her, still in her coat, her face waxy. Her skin was very cold and the warmth of the room had not stilled her shaking. Beneath her eyes purple bruises of tiredness and strain twitched with the impulses of an uncontrolled nerve.

'The doctor, I must fetch the doctor. She may be concussed,' said Mr Eldon, but he felt uncertain about doing so. The doctor's arrival would demand explanations, explanations which he would find difficult to give and which Joan might regret later. The police were wary of coming between man and wife in domestic disputes. Ministers of religion also had to be careful.

'Perhaps if you were to sip a little sweet tea, my dear, you would feel better.' He pushed a cup and saucer into Joan's hands and she clasped them, her knuckles the colour of the pale blue china. He sat down opposite her and sipped his tea with bird-pecking dips, keeping his eyes on Joan all the time. Eventually she raised the cup to her lips and drank, but her stillness remained and her silence was unnerving. Arnold found a large plaid shawl which he sometimes used of a cold evening to keep his shoulders snug and wrapped this round Joan. He was rewarded with a small nod of recognition.

'Maybe it would be best for you to stay with the Luffmans at the village store, my dear. I'm sure . . .'

'No!' came urgently from Joan. 'The children – I can't leave the children with him.'

Mr Eldon shook his head, acknowledging ruefully that there was no simple solution.

'There is little we can do for this evening, my dear.' He took a prim poised position on the edge of his chair and spoke in a consciously avuncular and judicial way. Joan just shook her head violently as if trying to avoid the attack of a persistent wasp. The minister's voice rose. 'Just look at the snow, Joan. It is swirling down harder than ever.' It was true, unpalatably true, impossibly true for Joan to accept. Beyond the light and warmth of the minister's haven the pus of the sky's poison was congealing as it met the ground, larding it with white icy grease and muffling all the clear-cut lines of buildings and contoured fields and bushes into an amorphous pale leprosy.

'Peter and Claire will be safe at the farm. The range is warm and your husband is not quite the monster you imagine.'

Joan shuddered, but even in her distorted vision she knew that her husband never attacked the children except to administer legitimate punishment. He used his leather belt on Peter, but this was part of Joan's image of acceptable chastisement for boys. She'd given him a resounding slap herself only that morning and, by God, Peter had deserved it. No, she was terrified that she had lost them, that her mental terror was being reflected and magnified in their susceptible minds, that they would think she had deserted them, that she had no love for them. She imagined what Paul would be saying, justifying himself, accusing her of leaving the family, filling their heads with wicked stories of her betrayal.

'I must go back to them,' she blurted out. 'There's no need for you to worry about me. I'll walk; I know the road like the back of my hand.'

This time Mr Eldon shook his head slowly, sorrowfully but definitely.

But Joan was standing up. She imagined Peter shrinking into his corner, the newly minted words shrivelling inside him again with the sorrow of his pup's injury and with her own desertion. Her eyes glittered and little red patches blistered her thin cheeks.

'I shouldn't have come in the first place,' she said stoutly. 'It was good of you to allow me to come. I must go back to my children.' She had made too many wrong decisions already, gone against her instincts to take her children to safety and stayed to battle on. It was clear now. She would return and bring her children away as soon as the weather cleared.

Mr Eldon struggled up, his legs stippled with pins and needles, but he pulled himself to as full a height as possible and tried to persuade, cajole and even demand that Joan should stay. The weather had assumed monstrous proportions in his mind and images of sheep trapped in floundering drifts, the old peasant holed up waiting for release from Wenceslas – who must, he felt sure, have been a very tall man – the moon of Paul's face peering through snow and windscreen all combined to strike horror in the man. And if Joan were to go, would it not be his duty to accompany her?

'Tomorrow morning we shall be able to go together.' His words did not touch Joan, who felt lightened by her decision. Tomorrow morning would be too late. The roads would certainly be beyond the tread of human feet if the snow continued, and she did not need the light of day to travel a well-known path.

'It's all right, Mr Eldon.' The minister winced slightly, palms spread in supplication.

'Please call me Arnold, my dear.'

Joan had a sudden impulse to laugh, but she controlled the bubble of hysteria.

'You don't have to come with me, Arnold. I can manage by myself.'

How had she ever believed that this elderly minister could save her? She was speaking to him as if he were a child and he was looking at her with the gratitude of an infant awarded a sweet for good work. Mr Eldon made a token gesture of determination.

'Oh but I can't allow you to go alone, Joan. You've had quite a knock on the head. It would be wiser to rest until morning, but if you must go, I should come too.'

'No point in a double journey for you,' said Joan, with practical good sense. 'And your tea has helped me recover my senses. I couldn't possibly stay away from the farm for a night. What would the village think? Just imagine the local headlines after my husband had finished? MINISTER STEALS FARMER'S WIFE!'

Joan did laugh then but Arnold did not. His face filled out with pink and he was consumed by an immediate and ferocious anger.

'Even if your husband wished for such unpleasant publicity, you know there would be no truth in such a story and where truth lies is where I lie.'

Even as he spoke, he knew that Joan would have to go and he would have to stay. There could be no compromising his position so early in his ministry in Barham.

With another cup of tea refused, a roll of thinly sliced ham and a thermos of hastily prepared soup reluctantly accepted, Joan set off leaving an exhausted and ineffectual minister behind her. No knight in shining armour existed. Her experience with Paul, heroic from the war, should have taught her. How her imagination could have placed Mr Eldon in that role was a mystery born of despair and loneliness.

# CHAPTER
# TWELVE

It was barely seven o'clock in the evening but the village was swathed in white, nursing its single-minded nature and excluding the stranger. Joan was a solitary traveller trudging through the masked lanes. Cottage windows were her sole illumination along the way. Gradually these specks of light dwindled and the snow became a grey spectre of icy fingers always just ahead of her, mocking her progress, trying to guide her astray. But Joan knew her route and, head down, plodded along it, her boots accruing wadges of snow, weighing down her legs like those of a deep-sea diver. Her steps took her directly into the north-east wind, which swirled eddies of sticky paste into her eyes and under her hood. But she did not feel daunted now, nor yet scared of what the journey or her arrival might hold. She was sufficiently content to be travelling back to her injured children and the devil she knew.

When she left the final cottage behind, she felt a momentary pang of isolation, turned her back on the snow and crunched backwards for about twenty yards, looking at the silhouetted buildings of Barham, picking out landmarks with difficulty. Occasionally the snow lifted, showing only tiny black chunks of stone, before the storm wind whirled another flurry between walker and village. Joan returned to forward motion, clenching her jaw and spare fist as the wind buffeted her face again. In her right hand she carried one of Mr Eldon's shopping bags with her emergency rations. The hand clutching the bag was becoming increasingly stiff and numb, despite the glove. She switched the load to the other hand, but within fifty yards the left hand was as bad.

It's not worth carrying it, she thought. There's a bit of food at the farm and the trip is hardly to the North Pole and back, but she did not discard the thermos and roll, just went on swapping hands. She reached the track to the farm buildings. Here the swing to the right was accompanied by a steep slope and then the route ran along the top of Fen Dyke Quarry. Even since the car's passing the snow had drifted across so that the way was reduced to single-file walking by the edge of the dyke. If snow continued all night, it would be impassable by morning, although the approach over the back field might still be open.

As Joan's feet began to sink into the rapidly accumulating drifts her confidence ebbed from her. The world was a white sameness and secure boundary markers were now obscure invitations into an abyss made all the more treacherous by its apparent smoothness and lack of depth. The snow and night took not only colour from the earth, but also all normal sense of perspective. Joan knew that the dyke tumbled headlong at least fifty feet on to scree rocks beneath, and through hissing wind, panting breath and scrambling feet, the swollen quarry stream growled. Joan knew that if she were to stop and look down through the jinking maze of white her balance would leave her and she would fall. She had to keep moving and keep hugging into the drifting snow, so that her legs became clogged above her boots and ice packed uncomfortably against her shins, water trickling to her ankles and through her socks.

Only a mile to go, she chanted to herself. Then, her night eyes straining ahead, she thought she saw two black shapes move. They disappeared like spots before the eyes and yet Joan was certain of some presence ahead, something more tangible than the spatter of deceitful snow. Her heart missed a beat. Next moment she was flung into the drift, and the thin air became a solid force rushing past her and on down. As she fell she opened her hand to catch and save herself, terrified of the oblivion by her side. The bag was hurled one way, she the other.

For a moment she was filled with panic, scrabbled frantically and, by doing so, forced her body weight down the slope towards the very fate she was struggling to avoid. A great heaviness of spirit seemed to invade her, a feeling of futility and drained helplessness. She lay still and the cold seeped into her. It was too much bother to go on, but the image of Claire sitting in the washing came to her and the sight of Peter holding Nipper prompted her. With painful slowness she lifted her bottom into the air and winched herself to an apex before pulling her torso into an upright position. On two occasions her boots, now solid with ice, slid out from underneath her, but she recovered more by luck than judgement by forcing her heels into the surface. She stood, a rigid, tense figure, peering into the blackness and taking in nothing.

'I must go on. I can't stay here.' Tears scalded her chapped cheeks, but she hardly noticed. Inch by inch she shuffled on, leaning back away from the edge, making it all the more likely that her grip would fail. She kept her eyes fixed on the lip of the path as best she could, but the old fenceposts were her only sure guide and these were at ten-yard intervals. After some forty yards her crab-like motion was checked. Her boot struck a consistency different from snow, firm under softness. She tried to push on but could not move the obstacle. Panting with fear, she crouched down, feeling for a clear path, but her hands met solid mass. It felt a bit like the old scarecrow. She followed its shape with frozen fingers and recognized the outline of a shoulder in the drift. She tugged her hand away, but the ice on the glove met the ice on the cloth beneath her and stuck so that the shoulder shook and an unmistakeable groan welled up from the body.

Storm-wearied and frightened, Joan found this shape first and foremost a lump in her way, an obstacle to her safety. A sprawled body is a difficult size to straddle when teetering on a precipice in a blizzard. Joan wanted just to crawl over the top of the body, but she didn't. She found the head and twisted it round, peering closely into the black roundness of it. She could barely make out the features but there was no doubting the identity. It was Paul, her husband, lying across her path, threatening her life. She patted down his body with cold certainty until she found a pocket that held a small oblong box. Then she slid her fingers under the flap and drew out a box of matches. With huge sausages for fingers, she eventually managed to strike one, shielding the flame as best she could. It only flared for a second before being blasted away by the wind, but in that second Joan saw Paul's face. A great weal and a bruise darkened his left temple, but more shocking still were the open eyes, definitely conscious, definitely aware.

Joan screamed silently and tried to stand again, but her feet slid behind her, back down the path so that she fell forward, her face smacking into Paul's side. She felt a dull pressure as he pushed up from under her. In desperation she lifted her head and pulled her right hand down on to the man's shoulder. Like a released toboggan he skidded smoothly across the path and slipped feet first over the lip and into the void. One moment he was a dark immovable wall, and the next the path was clear and he might never have been there at all.

Joan crawled forward on hands and knees for a few yards and then, with no reserve of thought or feeling left to her, she pulled herself up and resumed her journey, putting one foot in front of the other fatalistically. She reached the farmhouse in half an hour. It had taken her over two hours to walk barely two miles.

The back door was unlocked. Joan stumbled in and pushed the door closed behind her with her back. The kitchen seemed strange to her, as if she'd never seen it before. She took in information dispassionately. Nipper looked better; he was questing with his nose into Peter's palm and had licked up milk from a saucer. Some of his covering blanket had fallen down and he was twisting his head round to tease at the wrapping round his rear, but he did not seriously worry it. If he twisted too far the pain caused him to whimper and then he would lie back down, puzzled and distressed by his immobility. Peter's hand had slipped from the pup's back and now lay by his side, and the boy was curled up on a makeshift bed of cushions and blankets.

Joan heaved off her sodden coat and tugged off her boots on the scraper. She padded across the kitchen and gazed down at her son with greedy eyes. Here in the ordinary warmth she could imagine that all was well, that the nightmare of the snow and Paul were part of another existence. Already the range's heat was transforming her. With a tentative finger she brushed back a little damp hair that fringed Peter's face, touched his closed eyelids. He'd had a wash before bed then. Good lad, she thought.

She stood up and glanced round the room. There was a pile of rough dry washing bundled together in a basket in the corner and the Dutch airer was back in its high storage. A cloth had been smeared round the room and the table was covered in an old sheet from the mending basket. Crocks were washed up and piled carelessly to drain. A dish perched on the edge of the draining board. Instinctively Joan picked it up and put it safely on the table next to the old enamel bowl, half full of scummy water. On tiptoes she crossed the room, eased open the door to minimize the slightest squeak of its hinge and then, feeling both at home and an intruder, moved quietly up the stairs to Claire's room. Yes, her daughter was safe, lying flat on her back, blankets up to her chin and heavy breaths blowing from her full lips. The girl moaned slightly and then twisted over on to her side, curling into the fetal position. Breathing became easier. Joan stroked her hair and kissed the top of her head with great gentleness. Satisfied, she returned to the kitchen. Exhaustion was quickly eating into her. She wobbled to a chair and collapsed.

The next moment she started up, eyes staring at the back door. The house was full of echoes. Suppose, she thought, he is not dead but comes back in the night. She could see the doors of the house swinging wide simultaneously and Paul standing huge in the entrances like two abominable snowmen transfigured into instruments of revenge. Yet when she tried to stand and walk to the doors to slip the bolts, she found she could not move.

She sat transfixed for about a quarter of an hour and then sleep conquered her and she fell forward, head on her arms, and slept, but nightmares hammered through her head, extensions of her waking terror. When she next awoke, at midnight, she managed to wrench herself up, ache stiffly to the doors and bolt them securely from the inside. She even propped one of the kitchen chairs under the back door handle because the top bolt refused to scrape across fully – damage caused the last time Paul was locked out, she supposed. She remembered how he'd burst through upon her then, when she'd eventually plucked up courage to let him in, and how his hand, his fist, had exploded into the side of her face and she'd been thrown against the table. Her side still bore the bruise. She would never let him in again.

She returned to her chair, unwilling, unable, to leave her kitchen and face the cold bedroom of shadows above. She took up her vigil again and, as she sat, the howling wind outside died away and the house was enveloped in a silent, menacing dark. At four in the morning, when next she woke, she was cold. She stoked the range, soothed Peter back to sleep for he stirred and whimpered at the noise, and made herself a cup of tea. By seven o'clock she had laid the table for breakfast and Peter was awake. Although it was still dark outside, the daily round had started. Leaving Peter to potter in the kitchen – the boy seemed quite happy to leave Nipper for a few minutes at a time now – Joan scraped open the back door. Whatever her nightmares, the cows needed milking and there was snow to clear.

The great storm had passed and the fields lay bare to a high clear sky. Dawn pinks were lifting through the darkness above like watered-down cochineal through icing sugar. It was as if the eastern horizon was spreading frozen tentacles into the sky. There was no wind, just an infinite creaking of nature under strain in the silence of the snow. It was all new, cleansed and perfect in Joan's eyes. There was no guilt, no fear and no struggle. Her mind was calmed by the rolling acres of grey leading into a dazzling promise of reflected sun.

'Peter!' She had to clear her throat to speak. 'Peter, come here a moment. Put your coat around your shoulders and come here.' Peter obeyed, stood by the door and peered round it nervously. There was nothing to fear.

'It's as if there's a clean sheet for us all, isn't it?' Joan whispered, putting her arms round Peter and pulling him in front of her. The boy stared out across the yard towards the gate. He could just make out its top bar. He looked down at his feet. There was a good hour's spade work to clear the path. Dad and he normally did that, the shovels being kept in the cupboard under the stairs. He wriggled out of his mother's grasp, hurriedly pushed his hands through the coat sleeves, hobbled off to fetch the shovels and brought them back.

The cows were setting up their morning call with greater insistence. Joan grasped the larger shovel, Dad's shovel, and started to push it into action.

'W-w-where's D-dad?' asked Peter. It was an unlikely question because Dad often woke late, but something had triggered its asking.

'I don't know. He's not upstairs.' Joan bent into her task, scoring grating black lines into the piled-up pillow, rucking it aside.

'He w-w-went with that man. He d-d-didn't want to,' said Peter.

'Oh no,' grunted Joan. 'He's always off to the pub with that man or another. Now let's get on or those cows will never be milked.'

The two of them pushed, lifted and twisted the spades in tandem, Peter keeping up with his mother by virtue of quicker, more economical movement. This pleased the boy and he made the snow fly about him, his cheeks beginning to apple up and his thin frame glowing from the work. They trampled the snow, forcing a path through, churning up chunks streaked with black and brown earth. When they'd covered half the yard, their boots had marked all around and the purity of the view had been partially destroyed.

As her spade cut into the loose flakes, Joan began to lose her early morning exaltation and became fearful that every stroke of her shovel could strike a foreign body hidden in the snow. The earth's covering could be a shroud for her husband. Suppose he had tumbled down from the quarry edge and fallen into a drift and then recovered, managing to stagger back to the farmhouse before collapsing for good. He could be lying hidden anywhere nearby and when the snow melted, then he would be found preserved with the hideous wound on his head and no explanation. Perhaps that was why she slowed her digging to match that of the boy. The snow, her enemy last night, was now her friend. She did not want to discover anything beneath it.

She was relieved when she reached the cowshed, but then panic struck again. What more natural than for Paul to shelter here in the warmth of the steaming cows?

'Go back to the house!' she ordered Peter. 'I'll do the milking. Get back inside.'

Peter trailed his shovel loudly back up the path they'd made together, his face losing its round natural relaxation. Joan, swallowing dryness, stepped into the gloom. The cows were showing their normal impatience, their eyes rolling white towards her as she passed and their feet shifting in the night's trampled manure. As

Joan sidled through, peering into the darkened corners, she saw no huddled figure in the straw. The paraffin lamp still on its hook inside the door was further proof of the cowshed's emptiness. She settled to milking.

Then she heard footsteps and a sudden voice clear and cracking through the ice-held dawn.

'Mum!' it called and all the taut nerves sprang and twanged so that the bucket almost spilled and Joan's hands jerked on the teats making them slither and the cow sway restlessly away. Peter hurried into the gloom.

'It's N-n-nipper!' the boy shouted. 'H-h-he's w-w-walking again!'

She swung round on the stool and Peter stood there gazing first with eyes alight with pleasure and then, as his mother's frightened expression took hold, he flinched automatically. Joan forced an unnatural smile.

'That's good dear. You'd better go and look after him, hadn't you?'

Peter turned away and shuffled his silhouette through the blazing barn entrance. The frozen sun had reached the house and yard, spreading its coat of gleaming ice. The whiteness glared through to Joan and she huddled back to the cow, finding the intensity of light outside too great, too all-seeing and threatening. The slow tender rhythm of the cows' spurted milk gradually exerted its influence, and she buried her head and shoulder in the beasts' flanks, taking strength and consolation from their endurance. For once, their placidity soothed her hands and mind and she worked steadily, her thoughts in abeyance, a temporary shield erected round her.

There was nothing she could do until the milk lorry came through and, from the look of the snow, that would not be for a few days. Paul would normally have loaded up the churns in his cart and forced a way down to the road, but she could not do that. More than a physical reason prevented her even thinking of the attempt. Perhaps someone would notice that the churns were not in place or maybe the milk lorry would report it, but the farm was cut off from the village fairly regularly during a severe winter and there would be no rescue bids. With a good stock of tinned foods, a fair supply of root vegetables stored in their straw clamps and enough milk to swim in, there was no fear of starvation. It was a pity Paul had not replaced all the hens. There were just the three and, in this snow, it was very unlikely that they would lay. Nevertheless, away from the world, isolated within their own little existence, they would be safe. The snow was a godsend.

Inside the kitchen, Nipper was exhausted. Claire was sitting on the blankets by the stove and Peter was kneeling by his pup, stroking it gently behind the ears.

'Where's this miracle pup then?' Joan asked cheerfully, leaning over Nipper. 'Looks much the same to me.'

'H-he's t-tired Mum, but h-he can move, c-c-can't he?' Claire nodded, thumb stuck in her mouth, eyes wide. 'H-h-he h-holds up h-his back leg and w-wobbles along.' Peter motioned with his hands to show the type of movement he meant, caught up in the dog's recovery, finding words almost without effort. Joan smiled, tears pricking behind her eyelids, and pulled the boy to her so his face nuzzled into her apron.

'I am pleased, Peter,' she said softly and rubbed his hair in an unconscious reflection of the boy's caress of Nipper.

Claire removed her thumb with a loud plop. 'Like Peter,' she stated clearly and then giggled.

'What's like Peter?' asked Joan.

'Oh shut up you!' Peter wriggled away from his mother and shook his fist at Claire, without malice.

'Nipper's like Peter.' Claire scrambled to her feet and hobbled across the room, her face alight with mischief. Peter lurched after his sister in mock chase. She screamed with excitement and dodged back round the table to the safety of Mum's legs, clinging like goose grass. Nipper, disturbed by the sound of bustle, flickered his ears and whimpered. Even in mid-flight, Peter caught the noise, stopped and went back to the dog, his face serious. The little explosion of pain died away with the boy's renewed stroke, but the bubble of laughter created by the children's teasing supported Joan as she bustled around, preparing breakfast.

'No school for you today, Peter,' said Joan. 'Nobody'll get through that snow for a bit, will they?'

Peter nodded, unworried.

'We'll have to go easy on the bread, but there's plenty of porridge and you can have a few prunes with it today.'

Peter hastily scooped the lined liquorice sweetness of juicy prunes into his mouth and sucked the flesh away from the stone. As he ate, he thought about going to school again. A few days would allow Mrs Gribbons to forget about what had happened to Nipper, allow him to forget that awful scream and how the Westby boys had stolen his dog. Then he thought of the night before and how his Dad had gone out. If nobody could force a way through the snow, where was Dad? Why had he gone out into the storm? Was he stranded in Barham? Mum didn't seem to want to talk about him, but hazy images of the kitchen the previous evening swam before the boy's eyes. He had been so caught up in Nipper's plight and the horror of how he'd carried him home from the Westbys that he'd hardly noticed anything. Only when Dad had leaned over with a wet flannel and rubbed his face or picked him up to rearrange his cushions and blankets had he become fully conscious of life beyond Nipper and himself. After Mr Eldon's departure he had tried to close up, like a winkle trying to seal itself from the pin. He didn't want to think about it now, but his head kept telling him that Nipper being able to walk again had to be paid for, that there was something wrong about the night before. He finished his porridge and gulped his milk. Suddenly tired by all his digging and the long watch over Nipper, he returned to his corner by the range, seeking a place alone again, a place where he could think and remember.

'Help wash up, Peter,' said Mum, but he looked blankly at her. She shrugged. The boy seemed so much better that she didn't try to force the issue, just let him curl up by the pup.

The kitchen had been empty – Dad no longer there but the door through to the front open and a freezing draught cutting across the stone and attacking Nipper – must keep Nipper warm – put wood in hole – but the ice had reached the range. There'd been shouting –words like bitch and bloody and bastard. Mum was outside with that Mr Eldon and where was Claire? He didn't know where Claire was but Mum had called for her. She didn't know where she was. Then there was banging and Dad stomped back into the kitchen, kicked over the stool by the dresser so that the windows rattled and the sawdust motes shivered and gusted up in the yellow lamplight.

He'd been scared then, remembered huddling up small, wanting to find his wardrobe but tied to Nipper – mustn't leave Nipper. There was dull throbbing in his ears. Dad kept on beating his fist on the table, mouthing dirty words. Mum didn't like him doing that. He only did it to annoy her, so she said, but she wasn't there to be annoyed so perhaps he was talking to him, Peter, threatening him. Dad's fist was a war drum, something to hide from even more. He pulled himself even more tightly into a ball in unconscious imitation of the night before.

There was light on his face and he'd been in the darkest corner. The beating had stopped a while ago and now the airer was up and wrinkled hanging shrouds spilled from the edge of the table. The light was no longer cut off by the sheets. That was why there was shining on his face. He'd wanted to wriggle away into blackness but he'd peeked. Dad's old coat was lying across a chair, its arms hanging down like an unconscious body. He could hear water dripping. The old tap needed a new washer – 'if I've told you once

114

I've told you a thousand times to change this washer,' but Mum wasn't there to say it, although Dad was breathing heavily as if she had and then came the trickle of water hitting enamel as a cloth was wrung out and then heavy breathing again in a rhythm of smear and scrub. Peter stole a glance, saw his father's hairy forearms, the tattoo of his tank regiment's insignia and the roughly rolled-up sleeves. 'Won't catch me doing the housework – woman's work that is.' But Dad was cleaning up, soaking the cloth, wringing it out, plastering it over cupboards, table, range and door frame.

How long this went on Peter didn't know. He became lost again in a reverie about Nipper, but his next awareness was of a frozen stillness. Dad was clutching the cloth, standing, looking down at the bowl. Suddenly one hand went up to his hair, snatched at the nape of his neck and the other flung the cloth into the bowl so that the dirty water lapped over the edge. Dad was looking wildly about him, his eyes blazing. Peter buried himself in his blankets. Dad was going to hit him. He was going to pick up the poker and smash it against his skull because he'd hurt Nipper. Then came the shout, a desperate shout.

'Claire! Where are you, Claire?' Then that silence, more dreadful than sound, more fearful than action, listened, but nobody interrupted it. Nobody said it was all right because Claire was upstairs in bed already weeping under the bedclothes, scared to come out because Daddy might hurt her. Peter didn't know she was there because Mum had called for her and she could have gone with Mum, but he didn't know where Mum was.

'She must've been locked out!' Dad's arm seized the coat, struggled into it. 'She must've been bloody well locked out when I came in. I told her to go inside. I bloody told her she wasn't going with Joan.' Dad had roared again then, making the whole house tremble with the noise and he'd charged upstairs but Claire wasn't in bed as far as he could see in the dim room. 'I bloody told her to stay inside.' Dad hurried to the front door. The coldness came again – must keep Nipper warm – put wood in hole – and then there was the banging on the back door.

He didn't want to remember any more. Dad had gone out to fetch Claire, but he didn't want to go out when he'd wrenched open the back door. Peter didn't want him to go out. Claire wasn't out there.

'What's the matter, Peter?' asked Joan, leaning over her lad. Tears were streaming and the boy was panting, 'No, no, no,' between clenched teeth, his body tight like wound elastic and nowhere to go. She put her hand on his shoulder, holding him urgently until eventually Peter returned to the morning. Joan put her fingers like

# CHAPTER THIRTEEN

December snow rarely holds its grasp on the earth for more than a few days. On the third day after the great storm a warm wet westerly brought clouds of misty sleet, turning into gobbets of steaming rain to splash into the white crust and turn it grey. The snow began to shrink into slush and the cloak began to sink towards the blackened vegetation and stone until outcrops of rock, clumps of hardy grasses and reeds, the cattle feeder by the barn and the gate stood clear and ugly like dirty scars on unhealthy flesh. Water trickled down slight inclines, forming deep puddles which in turn seeped through the earth as the frost yielded, cascading from the quarry edge until the stream below swelled and roared like a beast bellowing in pain.

The rain stopped by midday but the thaw continued. It was then that Peter said he was taking Nipper for a walk.

'Oh no you're not, my lad,' said Joan.

'B-b-but it's stopped r-raining.'

'It's still very slippery out there. I've told you you can stay in the house and yard, but you're not to go further. Some of the drifts take a long time to clear. That pup's still too poorly to go gadding about.'

Yet Nipper was making remarkable progress, and trundled round on his dot and carry quickly and confidently.

'I can c-carry him – I won't g-g-go far,' said Peter, his face pinching up into obstinacy. 'I c-can go and m-m-meet Dad.'

'Will you just do as you're told!' Joan screamed, launching her fist at the boy's ear. Peter slunk out of the kitchen, Nipper following. Claire went to run after her brother, but Joan caught her by the back of her skirt and dragged her in.

Joan looked out of the window where the clouds were tumbling away towards the coast and the sky was lightening into a hazy blue. Sunshine gleamed fitfully, wet and warm, into the room through glistening raindrops. Why did the thaw have to come? She hadn't wanted any interruption, and now the earth would reveal its secrets. She was being forced out of her limbo of forgetfulness. She flung the window open and called out to Peter.

117

'You heard what I said – no further than the gate.'

Peter dabbled a stick in the sea of mud by the cow barn and then flicked it so that black chips of melting ice flew across to the little mound where Nipper stood. The pup mock-rushed the spattering flecks and then inspected the marks as if investigating a great mystery. The pup set off away from the mound round the back of the hen run where snow still clung to shrivelled brambles and on towards the front of the house, out of sight of the kitchen window. Peter followed, scuffing his boots through slush and making monster slug trails. When he looked back at the house it was in shade, dark and dead-looking. He looked out along the path. It was running with muddy water under a slimy translucent slush. Nipper stopped by its side, put his tongue like a pink rosebud into the water and then jumped along the track's ruts as if the running water was alive and he its shadow. Peter picked up the pup and put him into shallow water. Nipper held his injured leg high above its rippling surface and sniffed excitedly at this strange odourless material that talked. He followed the tiny river and Peter placed his boots into the rut behind his pup. By almost imperceptible degrees, the couple worked their way down the path towards Fen Dyke Quarry.

When Peter realized he'd come a good three hundred yards, he was too far away to worry much about what Mum would say. Besides, Nipper seemed happy enough and the fresh warm air was blowing away the cobwebs of being stuck in the house all morning. Still, he didn't want to be seen and the track along the top was visible from the front of the house. He took the narrow zigzagging path down towards the quarry floor. He carried Nipper here because the surface was uneven and certainly slippery. He fell on his bottom and scooted down, smearing his old coat with slush. As he fell he released Nipper, the memory of his accident at school flashing through his brain, and the pup scampered on ahead, his tiny tail upright, quivering with the excitement of this long walk. At the bottom of the track, Peter called his pup.

'Nipper!'

But there was no sign of the creature. The boy lurched on round an old heap of boulders to where the stream crashed by. Ah, there was the puppy, he thought with relief, by an old broken lump of tree that must have been swept downstream.

'Come on, Nipper.'

The pup didn't move, though, didn't hop, step and jump it back to his master, but went belly down, his tail tucked between his legs as if he'd done some terrible wrong. Peter walked towards him. Perhaps Nipper had been frightened by being dropped. The outspread branches of the broken tree were like sprawled arms and legs and their colour was the deep shining black of drowned and rotting leaves. Nipper bellied towards Peter, whining a little, but the boy's eyes were riveted on the broken tree where a pale roundness like a great wadge of Mum's pastry dough grew out of the trunk. It could have been a massive fungus, a muddy snowball, part of the sodden sponge Mum used in the peggy tub or the disfiguring bole left to swell on the wood after the lopping. But Peter knew it wasn't any of these things.

The boy stopped and a shaft of bright sunlight shone its silver into the valley bottom, making the water sing and the shale flash. The shape stirred as water caught it and Peter thought the dead was coming to life, was not in fact dead at all. He snatched up Nipper and ran back along the path. Half-way up he stopped, panting, and looking back – he couldn't stop himself. The felled tree lay there still and any resemblance to a human shape seemed unlikely. He looked up to the crest where a black silhouette walked, strode as his father would stride, towards the house. It was Dad. It had to be Dad. Peter launched himself on up the hill and burst over the edge just as the figure reached the path.

'D-d-d-da!' bleated Peter and the figure stopped, looked towards him. It wasn't Dad. It couldn't ever have been Dad. It was the postman in his dark blue uniform.

The postman smiled at the soaked pale figure clinging to his pup. Peter turned away and looked down into the valley. The tree was hidden by a knot of hawthorn.

'D-d-dad!' Peter mouthed and pointed a trembling finger down the quarry face.

# CHAPTER
# FOURTEEN

At the inquest the details of an accidental death were elaborated: the treachery of the track, the significance of snow-blindness and the desperate weather. Mr Eldon explained with gentle grief how he had given Joan food and a thermos flask for her walk even though he was unhappy about her returning to the farm on such a violent evening. Joan, pale and apparently calm, described how she had slipped, almost lost her footing and had let go of the bag to save herself. She presumed her husband had been trying to meet her, to escort her home, but had fallen from the track instead. A doctor described the state of the body, attributing death to the violent bruising on the head and then exposure. When asked by the coroner how the injuries seemed to have been incurred, the doctor assumed that the fall had been responsible. There was no other damage to the body because snow had cushioned the impact. PC Bates agreed that a few strewn boulders at the base of the cliff could have inflicted the damage. The coroner took little time to confirm death by mis-adventure.

Joan cried then. She had remained coldly in charge of herself throughout the discovery of the body, the questioning and the wait before her husband had been taken away in a silent ambulance. Now she wept unexpected tears. She sat on the wooden bench of the Thurriton court room and bent her face to her hands. She wanted to stop, told herself to do so, but the tears kept coming until she felt a hand on her arm. A woman police constable was patting her, and Mr Eldon hovered behind, looking embarrassed and helpless. For a moment Joan thought she was being arrested after all and she stood up, brushing her eyes with her handkerchief.

'Delayed shock – perfectly understandable,' murmured the minister.

'She's been very brave.'

'I haven't been to the dentist,' Joan tried to smile, but her bottom lip quivered again.

'Would you like a nice hot cup of tea, dear?' asked the WPC, but

Joan did not. She wanted to be away from the court now that she had heard Paul was legally and irrevocably dead. She wanted that feeling of blessed relief that had buoyed her through those precious two days of snow and ignorance.

She waited for release throughout the car journey home, but it did not come. The tears gave way to an emptiness, a barrenness she had not expected. The verdict should have given her freedom from guilt. She sat in the car with Peter and Claire on either side of her and watched the charcoal-lined hedges bound past and the wide fields dawdle on the horizon. She saw nothing except an expanse of greyness and Paul's face reflected in the glass, his face as she had last seen it, lit by the pallor of death and the recognition of her presence. Perhaps it wouldn't have been so bad if he had tumbled over like a sack of potatoes, but his eyes had known that she was there with the power of life and death over him, and what had he seen in her face? Had she intended that sudden pull on his shoulder, or was it a jerk of panic and self-preservation? She'd hated him, wanted him dead, but she'd also lived with him, borne his children and suffered with him. His death left a grave inside her.

Claire nestled into her side, but she felt no warmth towards her. She turned incurious eyes to her son. He had not spoken again since the discovery of the body and his every glance seemed full of accusation, as if he knew how she had pushed his father away. He no longer fondled Nipper, as though the pup had been tainted by Paul's body. The children seemed to be building walls of ice around themselves. They could not speak of the dead man, as if his death was part of the natural order of an adult world, to be endured but not questioned, something that denied curiosity and created an uneasy silence of hidden responsibility in their hearts. Paul remained the unspoken subject of the family's mutual insecurity.

Mr Eldon turned the car into the lane leading past the entrance to the Townsend track. He accelerated a little as if to leave the farm behind for as long as possible. The three passengers sat, still and heavy, staring towards nowhere. Their arrival at the manse cottage for tea was subdued and serious.

'I hope that puppy of yours has behaved himself, young Peter.' The minister twisted his key in the lock and pushed on into the small hallway. Nipper scuttled forward, his black nose bright. The light discovered a pair of slippers chewed into dark soggy maroon shreds.

'You'd better take him out, Peter, just over the green.' Mr Eldon forced a smile and Peter glumly led Nipper outside.

The green shelved gently towards a cluster of creaking elms and a shallow pool created more by rain than a natural spring. The melted snow had added to its volume, but it remained only an inch or so deep. In the early evening, however, it appeared larger, and the shadows from the tall trees threw strange shapes upon the rippled surface. Taking the line of least resistance, Peter faltered down the slight slope ignoring his cavorting pup as he caught his lead between his front legs and extricated himself more by fortune than design.

Beneath the trees, Peter felt alone and safe, sheltered by the gathering dusk and the surrounding tree trunks. The branches grew like umbrella spokes with ragged shreds of old black cloth clinging to them, like bats struggling to fly but limed there. Evening clouds rapidly drew a veil and when he turned to wander back, the yellow squares of light in the cottages along Pond Street emphasized his sense of isolation. He moved between two trees and passed along the staked chain fence by the road. There was a bench here and on it a slumped figure with a glowing red stub stuck on its face like a clown's nose. Nipper jerked away from his slack fingers.

There was a yapping and snarling.

'Gi'o'er, will yer!' grunted Joe and the old man wrenched his two curs under the bench. 'Take your pup away, lad,' he continued. 'My terriers are too old to put up with his scatting.'

Peter found his pup and caught the lead again. He went to walk off without speaking, but Joe mumbled on.

'Not that these two could do much nowadays – all mouth and no teeth. What's your pup called?'

Peter stared at him. The dusk light caught Joe's face and a faint stubble greyed his pallid cheeks. His eyes were dark sockets.

'What's the matter then? Cat caught your tongue?' Joe wheezed and the cigarette glowed fiercely.

'Nipper,' said Peter, aware of the dark closing around him, his anonymity secure. Joe sniffed as if testing the name.

'Haven't seen you walking him before,' he muttered. 'Visiting is it?'

'Not really,' answered Peter. He felt no hesitation about talking to the old man.

'What sort of an answer's that then?'

'My Mum's at Mr Eldon's, across the green.'

Joe stiffened on the bench. This was Paul Townsend's lad, of course. He'd seen him often enough before but always at the farm or on the road there. When Joe had heard about Paul's death he too had felt guilty, wondering if there was some truth in the village rumour that the man had killed himself from desperation about the court case. There was also that story about trouble out at Westby's that had percolated through from the doctor who had visited Mrs

Westby for her nerves again. Now he looked over to the lad and felt sorry for him. He was such a thin and shambling figure. A boy should be running round with his pup, not kicking along through the mud with his head lower than his shoulders.

'You're Paul Townsend's boy, aren't you?' asked Joe.

Peter darted frightened eyes towards him. He pulled at Nipper's lead. Joe called after him:

'It's all right, lad. I won't bite, you know.' But Peter did not return.

'Poor bugger,' muttered Joe. The bench was beginning to chill his backside. It was all very well for his friends to say 'Good riddance to bad rubbish' when they heard of Paul's death, but even bad rubbish left a nasty smell. 'I was your Dad's friend!' he shouted after the solitary figure, then yanked his dogs beneath the chain after stepping over it himself. He began to walk stiffly back home. Too hasty by far, that was Paul Townsend's fault. Too much jumping in when standing back and watching would have paid, and now there was the boy mooching round with the world on his back.

'It's the war I blame,' Joe muttered. 'Like that young Frobisher running off the rails. Nerves takes people like that. Poor little sod. A boy needs a father, he does.'

By the time Peter and Nipper returned, his family and the minister were ready to eat. Only Claire tucked in. Joan picked at her food and Peter bit into a sandwich automatically and chewed it to a liquid paste before swallowing. Mr Eldon, who had been unusually silent, began to find his voice.

'I know it is early days, my dear, but have you thought about what you will do now your husband will be unable to run the farm?'

Joan smiled slightly as if he'd asked about the weather or some unimportant matter, tapped her spoon against the cut-glass fruit dish and shrugged. There were all those old papers still to sort out in the kitchen drawer, but they could wait for ever as far as she was concerned. She didn't want to worry about the business of the farm, just wanted to be there with her children, away from the meddlers.

'Perhaps you would like to return to London?' Arnold persisted, but Joan shook her head vacantly. There was nobody there she could turn to; there was no community there now. Bomb Alley, that's what it had been called, where she'd lived. The German bombers had growled in towards London, aiming at the centre, but had dropped their loads too early, eager to be away and free from the tracer bullets around them. The bombs had cut a swathe through Clapham and most of Joan's friends and distant relations had been killed, or made homeless and rehoused in new developments, or had moved of their own accord. No, there was no future in London.

'You are hardly in a position to keep up the farm, are you?'

Joan felt increasingly like a child under inquisition for a misdemeanour. Arnold Eldon obviously hated untidiness of any kind.

'Paul wanted it for Peter,' she said, remembering a time when Paul had moaned about the farm's uselessness and said that it would suit Peter when he had grown up, both as bad as one another.

'But Paul, I'm sure, had not considered this sad occasion. Peter is far too young for such a responsibility yet.' Mr Eldon sipped a little tea and continued. 'Perhaps if I were to make a few small suggestions for you to consider. Of course, my dear, I do not expect instant decisions. Instant decision so often leads to extended disappointment, but you must have some focus, some intention in your life, if only for your children's sake.' He put down his cup and saucer and brought his fingers into a spire under his chin. 'I, of course, would say that Christ gives that purpose and changes it into a divine pleasure, leading to unselfish fulfilment in others' lives and in the personal hope of spiritual blessing, but you might think, at the moment, that you need some more concrete and immediate solution to your problem of loss. That is not to say that Christ is not concrete nor immediate, but that our perceptions of him tend to suggest that he doesn't put butter on the bread here and now. I know this is theologically unsound, my dear, because there can be no bread without Christ, but that is how so many people view religion – a way of life for people once they have achieved material security. In fact, to cut a long story short, you have that finest of man's purposes to consider, have you not?' He smiled confidingly round the table at Claire and Peter and continued, 'You have motherhood – the sacred trust of care and security of the generations. What would be best for the children? That must be your first and last consideration at the moment. Is it best for them to live on in the seclusion of a somewhat run-down farmstead, or would they do better caught up in the life of a community? Would you find motherhood without your husband more easy trying to maintain a farm or with the support of villagers about you? These are not stark alternatives I know. Life is so often grey around the edges. Perhaps you could start, when you are able, from this point. Do you wish to stay at the farm for the well-being of your children or not?'

He is a monster, thought Joan. His words made her want to return to the farm even more, to brave the memories and insulate herself from this prying concern. Another thing jarred on her in the minister's words, something that made her feel guilty even as she felt annoyed. Was all her own life completed in the rearing of her children? Was she so old, so used up, that no independent action of her own could be countenanced? Yet so much of her did regard Claire and Peter as predominant.

'I don't really know what I'll do yet,' she said hesitantly.

'Of course you don't,' agreed Arnold, nodding enthusiastically. 'I only try to put forward the possibilities as I, an interested but unprejudiced outsider, may do perhaps better than somebody closer to you.'

There is nobody close to me, thought Joan. She had thought the minister might have been a friend, but now he had assumed the seat of judgement.

'Wipe your hands on the napkin, not the tablecloth, Claire,' she said automatically.

'Of course, now you've lost your husband, money may be a difficulty for you. Or perhaps insurance will provide a little security?' Arnold leaned over, took Claire's hand away from the cloth and wiped it thoroughly with his own napkin.

How careless of me to lose my husband! Joan's thoughts continued. A picture of two black tubes and a flapping arm skidded across her vision into a swirl of white, a possession being lost, the one possession to afford her security. Without that black sliding torso, she was alone and incapable. With it she had been haunted.

'There's the farm. Paul left it for Peter, as I said, and there's a small pension and the insurance I took out when we first married.'

Arnold wiped his own neat mouth and folded his napkin precisely. He nodded as if Joan had confirmed his already unassailable logic.

'I would suggest, my dear, that you sell the farm and find a smaller place here in the village. Then we could see about a little housekeeper job for you to keep you ticking along. I, as an old friend, would worry about you and the children tucked away up at the farm, particularly in hard weather. Naturally, young Peter here should still apply to Greelham's, and in his present circumstances I would hope for a successful scholarship. With only Claire to worry about, you would be able to lead a very pleasant life in Barham.'

'I can't sell the farm,' Joan said obstinately, fighting against the trim solution. And why was it 'only Claire to worry about'? Was Joan only safe to look after her little girl? Did her boy need more than she could offer? Joan remembered how Claire had kicked the minister's shins in protective rage for her father but now, after the first floodings of tears and refusals, she had shown little grief and had accepted Mr Eldon's authority. Were both of her children to be weaned from her? Perhaps that would be justice.

Arnold smiled round the table at the little flock, but the lambs did not smile back.

Joan pulled herself up abruptly. Her husband had beaten her, raped her and treated her like dirt, but now he was being talked about as somebody to mourn, and she did feel the need to mourn his death, but, more than this, she needed to feel the relief that he had gone, that wonderful sense of freedom and joy. Every word that the minister said seemed to drag her into the leaden rites of duty. She bundled Peter and Claire into their coats, pushed Nipper's lead into Peter's limp fingers and set off across the green with a temporary sense of that great relief she yearned for. She did not, however, take the obvious route along the quarry-top pathway, but led her children over the back field. Nipper caricatured Peter's hobble until he picked up the pup and lugged it along.

On Christmas Eve the church was crowded with parents, aunts and uncles, grandmas and grandfathers. The lights on the rostrum were shining and the congregation was in bulky shadow. Large heads peered round stocky shoulders to glimpse their haloed children. In the vestry Joan hurried Peter into his long white robe and headdress fixed with old pyjama cord. Excitement squealed under the door, but the adults chattered busily like magpies and didn't notice. Despite Mrs Gribbons's strict instruction, the angels in the choir waved to their mums and dads. Mr Eldon walked to the front, raised his hand and coughed wheezily once or twice for silence. The cold often brought a touch of bronchitis.

'Ladies, gentlemen and children – how lovely to see so many of you.' His chest swelled like a plump budgerigar's. 'Welcome to our special Nativity. I'm sure you are going to enjoy the music led by our capable organist and schoolteacher Mrs Gribbons, and our mime created by Mrs Luffman, our Sunday School teacher.' He paused as if waiting for applause, but all hands stayed plunged inside pockets. 'May I remind you that there will be a collection at the end, the proceeds to be divided equally between the church heating appeal and the National Children's Homes. Perhaps now we could start with the prayer our Saviour taught us ... "Our Father ..." '

The congregation rumbled along behind Mr Eldon's lead. Peter, waiting in the area at the back, shivered. The other shepherds and the wise men around him brought their hands together and mouthed the words. Peter stared down the aisle towards a leaded window at the left of the rostrum. 'Our father witch – art in heav'n . . .' The window was spilling darkness into the church; the darkness was of his father witch art in heav'n wanting his will done as long as he was forgiven for trespassing. Get off my land and a shotgun to the head of old Westby and he was going to trespass if he could. But mine is the kingdom, the power and the glory ferever and ever armin. He wondered what his father was wanting him to do in the dark window leading out to the heaven of a dirty grey dishcloth sky, but Mr Eldon was talking again, calling to Mrs Gribbons and the carol of the Angel Gabriel started so Claire was running from the vestry door into the light and Mary, Mrs Luffman's daughter was waiting to hear about being pregnant as if she was getting the tricycle she'd asked for for Christmas. It was hidden at Mr Eldon's house. Peter knew because he'd seen the grey cardboard tubes round the handlebars in the kitchen and had heard Mr Eldon telling Mrs Luffman he'd look after it because there wasn't anywhere in the shop they could put it without little Miss Pry finding it, but Peter hadn't told Mary because he didn't talk.

Peter wanted to stay at home for Christmas. He didn't want to spend his day in church and Mr Eldon's house, but that was where they'd been invited and his mother had not refused. She no longer tried to fight.

The window was a black hole of yellow light and occasional shimmering figures gleamed through it. They were the dark angels of the night bringing messages from heaven from his father but they couldn't come through the patchwork squares of the leaded glass. Nipper though was tied to the boot-scraper outside, waiting for Peter to collect him and wrap his sheepskin round him, a puppy in sheep's clothing. Young rats grow into old rats, puppies into wolves, wolves in sheep's clothing and Mr Eldon was there whispering about being all ready and remembering when to fetch the pup, but the dark angels outside the church were waiting for him and Nipper was like him – more trouble than he was worth, like teeth Mum would say – trouble coming, trouble going. That's what he was.

He felt a little push in the back and found himself hobbling out of the door. He could not see. It was black night now. The wind blasted through his thin robes and blew him sideways towards a high-pitched whimpering plea. He was a ghost gusting through the churchyard and crumpling down like a falling sheet before billowing up again and disappearing back into the infinite blackness.

Gasping, Peter returned to the yellow haven of the church. Nipper scrabbled in his arms. He could feel his scratchy paws through the robe and the eager wriggle of his pleasure, but he held the pup stiffly

# Part Two

# CHAPTER FIFTEEN

When Peter arrived at Greelham School for the interview he was eleven years old. His mother and the minister flanked him, but his memory of the occasion excluded them. He was alone and isolated, so that when he stood at the bottom of the white chipped steps looking up to the red-brick Victorian facade of the school, he was looking from a perspective that denied external influence, and denied even his own part in the arrival. There were no tears in him and no conscious feeling, just an aching inevitability. He scarcely saw and scarcely registered place, people or reason, yet this moment of arrival remained with him as a complete and vivid memory – the white steps, third flight badly scarred on one side, the black double door complete with huge brass handles polished to reflect the vast acreage of green and tall trees to the left. Fire escape, black iron grid to the right, up past dark ruddy patches of worn brick in the wall and the bottle-green doors floating at each storey. Back at the top of the steps by the black door was an elongated man casting a shadow across the grass, looking down on him as if from the summit of his dreams. There was no smile but a distant welcome in a clear voice, such as the angel Michael might deliver to a sinner.

'Townsend, isn't it? This way please.'

To a lost soul, a definite path appears as wisdom. Peter pulled back his shoulders, did not feel the encouraging pat his mother gave him on the small of his back, and walked steadily up the steps. He kept his eyes firmly on this important person's back. The trousers were shiny and the creases were razor edges. A tag-end of white thread clung to the bottom of the right buttock, just below the jacket.

'This way please.'

The important person swung open a polished door and Peter edged in, ahead of his leader. Somewhere voices said thank you and he sat gazing at a dark brown desk in front of a high window and more trees beyond. Pigeons in those trees, he thought. At the apex of the windows – like church windows – were stained-glass sections in which pears, apples and plums shone with early June sun, but the room seemed dark.

Old Salmon came in, a large sandy figure. Peter stood up, the tops of his thighs squeaking off the cold leather. He did not know it was the headmaster but he found himself on his feet.

'Mr Salmon? So very pleased to meet you. I am Mr Eldon. This is Mrs Townsend and here is Peter, her son.'

A red face, full of feature, pale blue eyes and eyelashes pricked out like thin stiff bristles from a scrubbing brush, acknowledged the introduction and a wide hand opened, proffered chairs.

'Give Mr Salmon the little report your teacher gave you, Peter.'

A report? In slow motion his brain recalled the envelope in his jacket pocket.

'Oh yes, I see . . .' Mr Salmon skimmed the contents quickly. 'Most useful . . . wish more would do it . . . most handy.' But, even as he spoke, Peter knew that the report was valueless, insignificant, belonging to a life where Greelham's held no sway.

'Now Peter – take this.' Peter found he was holding a large book bound in leather. 'Find a page . . . any page . . . and read a little for me . . . any piece will do.'

Rules for turning pages in a book: lift them delicately from one corner. Do not scuff them across the surface. Rules for recitation of an unseen piece: stand firm and tall; address the furthest wall; speak slowly but do not stall – no problem for a steady boy at all. He performed obediently. It was about a wolf dwelling with a lamb and a leopard lying down with a kid.

'A very appropriate piece indeed,' interposed Mr Eldon, but Peter knew that everybody knew that wolves ate lambs.

'Jolly good, young man – your reading will do nicely. Quarter of a hundred?'

Peter looked back at the silky pages of the book, caught out, worried. Quarter of a hundred what? Where in the passage did it mention this figure? Was he supposed to know how many words in each sentence?

'No?' continued Mr Salmon. 'How about two thirds of nine?'

Peter looked hastily at Mr Eldon, who mouthed incomprehensibly at him. This was the only time he was physically aware of the minister but Peter was settled. He spoke firmly. 'The answer is six, sir.'

Mr Salmon appeared not to have heard him. 'He seems to read well, but is less confident with number.'

Joan nodded to the man's superior wisdom. Peter listened and believed this sudden analysis. Mrs Gribbons's report lay on the desk.

'Don't worry, my boy,' Mr Salmon continued, even managing to prevent Mr Eldon's intervention. 'Lots to learn, lots to learn but lots of time to learn it.' The man leaned back in his high leather chair, drummed his fingers momentarily on the beaded edge of the desk and smiled as if he'd reached a momentous decision.

'Well, Peter Townsend, you'd like to come and work with us here, would you?'

'Yes please sir.'

'Good. Keenness is always to be applauded. We like boys here to work hard and play hard, to try hard and to obey the rules. I'm sure you will be a credit to us.' His smile broadened; his teeth were wearing away into a mottled yellow. 'I'm also sure you would like to have a look around the rest of the school, see where the dormitories are. You might even meet a few of the boys. I, meanwhile, would like a short conversation with your mother and Mr Eldon here. If all seems in order you would be able to start with us in September.'

He was so sure, so certain and on such flimsy evidence, but Peter knew he was all right; he'd been accepted. His mother might reject him; his father might leave him; Floater could be killed and Nipper limp in parody of him, but by learning some of the minister's tricks he could become wanted and accepted.

'Foster!' The Headmaster called through his door and the tall man in the dark suit returned. 'Please escort this young gentleman on a tour of inspection. Bring him back in about quarter of an hour.'

The tall man leaned slightly from the waist. 'Of course, sir.'

Peter followed Mr Foster again, looking neither to right nor left, amazed that this man, whom he had considered so important, was spoken to as a servant. His black shoes squeaked along wooden shining floors.

'The young gentlemen are not normally allowed in this area of the school. It is reserved for staff and visitors.' Sober portraits watched him walk along.

They reached a small door with a large instruction painted on it that it should be kept closed at all times. The tall man pushed it open with a long broom handle of an arm and Peter passed through. It sighed and closed behind him. The floor was scuffed linoleum and the walls bore the black marks of kicked heels along the grey skirting-board. Foster strode on along the dingy way, pausing

131

momentarily at windowed doors which led into brown and sullen classrooms. Peter only gained glimpses of rows of desks, a slight noise of a teacher speaking, and then the wall intervened. Peter found himself losing his newfound walk, his limp becoming more pronounced as he tried to keep up.

His guide reached the far end of the corridor and waited for the boy, pointing along to the left. His figure was set against a small window and, for a desperate moment, Peter thought it was his father leading him again, as he did so often on the farm. He scuttled forward and, as he passed the tall figure, he twitched involuntarily, as if expecting punishment for delaying the tour. He imagined he saw Foster's eyebrows rise in disdain.

'That leads to the quadrangle and the playing fields. Up these stairs and you reach a similar corridor to this with more classrooms, including the science rooms. This corridor here is reserved for boys arriving from preparatory education in the nursery block. You will start here and work your way up, I presume.'

They passed through another door and Peter felt as though he would never be able to find his way out. His sense of direction had left him. He kept thinking of the rabbit hutches at the farm and the way Floater used to slip along his wire netting, leaving wisps of his black fur to mark his route.

'This room is the junior prep and common room.' Once again Mr Foster pushed open a door and Peter peered in round his ungainly long legs. 'These young gentlemen will be in the second year when you arrive in September. First and second years share this room.'

There were six boys there sitting at desks near the door. Beyond the desks there was an old table-tennis table and a high wall of wooden lockers beyond that. In the corner a tall cupboard reached almost to the ceiling, its door half open. There was a musty smell of old books and lack of air. The boys looked round incuriously like the cows in the barn when Mum went in to milk them, and then bowed down over their books.

'I'm afraid these young gentlemen have broken school rules and have to work in silence here for a while. The room is a silent work room during lessons, but it fairly hums at other times. Isn't that right, Atkinson?'

The boy nearest the door looked up. 'Yes Foster,' he said dispiritedly.

The door creaked closed again. Foster bent low down until his face reached the level of Peter's. The boy half expected to hear the joints creak as they fought against the creased clothes.

132

'One of the teachers keeps an eye on them. A single word and they have to face the founder.'

The tall back presented itself again, leaving Peter to ponder the meaning of those awful words, and then they were both out in the open air.

'No time for a full inspection, young man. We will return round the front of the school – out of bounds normally, but a little laxity is warranted on this first occasion.'

The walls were clad in ivy and finely trimmed lawns lay on either side of the path. Far away to the right a line of boys in white vests and shorts ran into a tall building. A door banged, echoing against the quadrangle and walls. Foster did not speak and they reached the white steps. The sun burst through and swept across the grounds in a cascade of brilliant greens, and the tall trees leaned like a row of Fosters, their leaves glinting like half-crowns. There was Mr Eldon's car, tiny in the sweep of the drive. There was Mum shaking the headmaster's hand and then trotting down the steps. He joined her and climbed into the car. A moment later and Mr Eldon wriggled into his place and back through the grounds they went, out into the narrow road into the village of Greelham itself and then away.

The two and a half months that followed whirled by in a kaleidoscope dream of congratulation and fearful expectation. Joan was reassured by the presence of a matron in the school, but her worries about school uniform were fully realized as she tried to buy appropriate sports clothing from main-line stores in Norwich, rather than the school's own expensive outfitters.

'I'm sure it will do perfectly well,' she'd say as Peter stood uncomfortably in black cotton shorts, his legs shining like milk bottles below them.

'It says dark blue,' Peter would mutter, resenting the public display, his mother's desperately cheerful attempts to fob him off with less than the required clothing.

'Nobody would see the difference.'

Peter, though, was not convinced. He knew that his appearance was different enough without the addition of clothing not quite in line. He refused to accept anything not exactly according to list, which meant that the shopping expedition resulted in one pair of white plimsolls. Joan couldn't find a pair of rugby boots to fit. One of Peter's feet was markedly larger than the other so that he required a size three left boot and a size four right. Shops were not prepared to split pairs. By the time they reached Barham again, Joan had a headache and was in a foul mood.

'They give you a scholarship and then you can't buy the school uniform. It's too expensive. How are people meant to manage?'

Peter couldn't answer.

'I've a good mind to write to that Mr Salmon – tell him what I think – traipsing round Norwich all day with you whining and moaning. It was enough to find the train fares without all the extras thrown in.'

'I won't go then,' Peter blurted out angrily. 'Whose fault is it? It's not mine.' It was his mother's fault that there was no money for proper clothes. She'd have to go to Mr Eldon for help, and Peter resented that. If he were old enough, he'd make sure there was money in the house. It wasn't right to be scrounging off the minister. It made you feel as if you didn't belong to yourself any more. Peter hated thinking that. It made the back of his neck crawl.

On the Sunday before Peter's departure for Greelham's, the minister preached a beatific sermon on the lost sheep who is found, pointing forcefully to the rejoicings in Heaven. His voice was still husky from the bronchitis that had lingered through his training of Peter and caught at his chest despite the hot dry summer. Joan sat with her two children in a pew towards the back. It was as if Mr Eldon were addressing her. She gazed at the light blue wall behind the lectern, trying to cut out the words and find quietness.

She travelled back to a chilly day in early spring, with evening darkness closing in outside the village school. Peter's pinched white face had mooned up beside her and Claire had stood by a low wall kicking at it with the heels of her boots. The minister had left them to spread good news to Mrs Gribbons and the restraint between Peter and her had thickened like the clouds above them. She had been holding a blue envelope and she recalled Peter's eyes fixed on it as if it were a sword.

'Is it Dad?' Peter had asked. The dead were always with him, but he must have known that his father would not have written even when alive. She had tried to smile, but her heart would not lift to the occasion. She had been performing a ritual in obedience to plans beyond her control.

'It's from Greelham School. I agreed for Mr Eldon to write. They want you to go for interview.'

She held her breath because she had not known how the boy would react and he had kept on staring at her. His face, although thin and small, had seemed to fill her world, and she had peered worriedly into his eyes, trying to gauge his feelings.

He had shuddered and taken the letter from her. He had seemed

134

to accept, as she had, the role he had been assigned. She had touched his arm. It had felt like frozen meat, but she had moved gently and brought him reluctantly to the minister's teaching. There had been no alternative.

She looked sideways along the pew. Peter was pulling at the edge of his jacket, teasing out a loose thread with nervous fingers. How can a boy so young have such power over me, she wondered? She, a grown woman, waited with bated breath for her son's responses and could not stop the pain of anxiety filling her. Had he assumed she was rejecting him, throwing him out into a hostile world because she did not love him? Had he realized that Nipper would have no place at Greelham's? Even now she winced when she recalled how he had behaved when Nipper was taken from him at the village school. He seemed to resent her even more now, claiming his role as head of the house. He had taken to trying to lug the milk churns into place for the lorry every day and screamed at her when she offered assistance.

Perhaps I am the sinner, she thought, and my son is leaving me to rejoice in an opportunity that I never had because I cannot be saved. I have killed my husband and can neither admit it nor regret it. I shall lose my son to a better world and my daughter is off to the Luffmans at every chance. The blue wall of the church seemed to open into a great clear sky and she was lost in it. I must devote myself to God and pray for healing, she thought, chiming in with the minister's words, but, when she tried to pray, she couldn't help observing the ridiculous manner in which Mr Eldon held his little white hands over his belly-button and how his suddenly thin voice would try to deepen a little at the ends of sentences. I should be able to ignore things like that, she said to herself violently, but the little things continued to obtrude. The wall became a wall again and she began to feel as guilty about the petty as she did about the major sin in her life. She could see that the black shape of her husband's body sliding away from her was no accident but the deliberate act of another woman, a woman elsewhere, not sat in church, and she need feel no compunction about it. It was other things that made her suddenly quake with terror. She was frightened whenever Claire woke up at night, scarcely able to control her trembling as she rushed along to the girl's room. She hated going beyond the immediate area of the house, although the inside of Mr Eldon's car seemed a safe haven. Standing in the queue at the village shop was a torture to her. She wanted to swing out her arm and sweep all those ahead of her into oblivion, and when people talked with commiseration in their voices her pupils dilated and she often cried, outwardly confirming her love for the dead man and inwardly horrified at his continuing power to evoke terror within her. Then there was the minister standing above her, preaching his word of salvation. He too appeared frightening as if he were demanding payment for services rendered, as if he knew her crime, and had put his own soul in jeopardy by supporting her, a murderess.

Her thoughts returned to her son. When he has gone, she began to think, I shall have suffered my punishment and found my release. I will be able to repay the minister's kindness then and become myself again.

Peter was growing daily more aloof, more arrogant and more like Paul. Rather than the timid, silent child of the past, he was becoming clear in his speech and his words wounded her. He treated his mother and sister with scarcely veiled contempt. Joan could do nothing to change him. She could just about accept his enforced leaving to go to Greelham School, but she could not cope with the way he had already divorced himself from her. Mr Eldon talked of having a proper respect for yourself, holding your head up and facing the world with confidence. By doing so he had achieved a place at Greelham's and everybody seemed to congratulate him. She had lost her right to preach, had been shown to be fallible, and now Peter would follow his father's example as it was transfigured by the minister's words into a noble creed.

The sermon reached its end and the hymn thundered out.

'And though they take my life,
Goods, honour, children, wife . . .'

Wife comes last, she thought, life first and why should God want to deprive man of all things just so that He can have everything? She could not believe it, but Mr Eldon was looking at her again and she felt deeply sorry for him suddenly. Perhaps God required an act of renunciation and sacrifice from her. Perhaps she should marry the minister and heal the wound of her first marriage with the salve of service to this old friend. She desperately wanted to act for herself, but she could not do it. She could only think of herself in relation to other people and the demands they made upon her. She was confused by the contradictions – mother, widow, churchgoer, receiver of charity, farmer, murderess. At the end of the service she left the church with no peace in her mind and she confirmed her own analysis of Peter's state by chivvying him along the road home with a thick ear.

Later Joan rummaged through the old cupboards in her bedroom until she found a large green trunk ribbed in wood. It had been Paul's. He'd used it during the war and it was patched with various exotic stickers. She lifted it on to the bed and pushed open the catches, which were stiff and slightly rusty. The lid eased up and balanced, revealing a bundle wrapped in black oilcloth and a tin box. She lifted the bundle. It was surprisingly heavy for its size and, although she was anxious to get on with Peter's packing, she could not resist unfolding the stiff material. She knew what she would find inside, but nevertheless started when she saw it. The barrel gleamed through a sheen of oily grey and when she put her palm round the grip the coldness froze her fingers. She could not reach the trigger easily, but winced away from touching it. She hastily put the pistol back in its wadding and rolled it up. Paul had shown it to her shortly after their marriage and the circumstances came back to her vividly. He'd been standing by the window, chest naked, belt undone and trousers hitched casually on his hard slim hips. She'd said he looked like a cowboy in the films and he'd laughed, fetched out his trunk and shown her the gun, prodding it towards her suggestively so that she felt both alarmed and excited by him.

'Officer material this, you see – not for the likes of ordinary men like me, but who's to know? Certainly not Lieutenant Philpotts. Don't laugh, that was his name and that's what he did every time the guns sounded – filled pots! A shell had his name on it and I inherited his gun.'

Joan stared at the bundle, remembering her fascinated horror. It had belonged to a dead man and had been stolen by her dead husband. She ought to take it to Bates, but she might get into trouble for having had it in the first place. She picked it up with the tin and stuffed both items deep into the back of the blankets drawer.

She turned back to the bed where she'd piled the new clothes, the new identity of her son.

'Peter!' she called through the house. 'Have you chosen those things to take with you? Bring them down here, will you?'

She heard thumping on the stairs down from the attic bedroom and returned to the trunk, wiping it over with a cloth. Her son came in carrying nothing.

'Haven't you found anything?' Joan asked. 'The headmaster said you could take a few personal items – what about your old ted?'

Peter sneered visibly. 'I don't need anything.'

'Your woodwork book?' Joan persevered. 'You like that one.'

Peter walked out, leaving Joan to the packing. She picked up the clothes carefully. They smelt fresh and they reminded her of her schooldays, the gingham checks and heavy felt hats, the gaberdine mackintosh and ribbed long hose.

At teatime Joan tried to talk with her son again, explain some of the feelings that she harboured for him, wonder how he would feel about leaving Nipper behind, assure him of her love, but the words would not string together. I shouldn't have to say these things, she thought. He should know already how I feel.

'I'll look after Nipper for you, Peter,' she said. 'You needn't worry about him.' Peter shrugged, but he had to care, Joan thought. He'd spent hours nursing the pup and fought for it at school. Why did he just shrug as if the pup meant nothing to him? After a pause, Peter muttered,

'H-h-he'll always be a c-cripple, w-w-won't he?'

'Well yes, I suppose he will, but he is a fine young dog now, able to manage.'

'H-he'll never w-w-work. I'd w-w-want a working dog r-really.'

The next morning Peter woke very early. Mist was huddling over the earth and only a little bleary light was spilling from the east. He shoved aside his blankets and dressed quickly in his old farm clothes. He could hear his mother stirring down below and he wanted to be up and out on his final rounds without her knowledge. He slid downstairs, put his boots on and took an excitable and whimpering Nipper with him out of the back door and over the yard. Once in the shivering air, the urgency of his movements was lost and he began to poke about in the old outhouse, peering into the gloom until he found the canvas bag he was looking for. Slinging this over his arm, he set off with Nipper tumbling and lurching at his heels.

Peter trotted quickly along the quarry path and then down into the bottom where the stream trickled after its summer drought. False dawn light gave him his direction. Although he had seen his father's body, he now did not know the precise place and had chosen another spot which marked for him the symbolic presence of his father. There was an actual grave in the village, but here was Peter's memorial, beside a large fissure in the quarry wall and next to a lump of clay that formed a natural seat. The stream was held up here by fallen quarry stones and the water made a pond which Peter had increased by daubing clay and stones together to make a partial dam. He sat down and gazed up at the high quarry wall. The mist shrouded its ridge and he could hardly make out where sky turned into the dark stone face. A little wind sighed and wisps of dank air fluttered.

Quickly Peter unbuckled the bag, his fingers tugging impatiently at the stiff straps. He turned his eyes again to the cliff. The black and huge silhouette of his father was there now, striding along its edge. Although the story had it that Paul was looking for his wife when he fell, Peter knew that this was not so. He had been protecting his children, guarding them. His voice rang in the cold air.

'Peter! Peter! You shall be a fit son for me. The halt shall walk and the dumb find words.'

They were Mr Eldon's words but it was his father calling for him.

'And Abraham took and bound his first-born son to be a sacrifice unto the Lord.' The voice took on a warm and rhythmical tone and the figure seemed to stretch his arms over the whole valley floor in a gesture that lifted Peter and took him to the edge of the water where he paused and raised his hands as if to dive, but then the voice came again.

'And the father saw that his son loved him and would obey him.' Peter turned from the water and his eyes were full of tears. There was no future time. Nipper was burying his nose in the canvas bag as if he could smell rats in it. Peter collected a number of stones and loaded the bag with them, then pushed the little terrier into the opening and started to do up the straps. Nipper, enjoying the game, wriggled his head round and began to nip playfully at Peter's hands, squirming and pushing through the gap so that the boy could not contain him long enough to fasten him in. Peter began to shove the pup harder, staring up at the figure on the cliff and trying to buckle at the same time. With a lurch and a final wriggle, Nipper scrambled out and, as he did so, the black figure fell, arms and legs like a falling cross, blotting out the sky, the cliff, the whole world in a black cloak enveloping, suffocating and choking the boy so that he stumbled and crouched as if crushed by a formless and invisible weight.

When next Peter dared to peer out from between his fingers, there was Nipper scrabbling and teasing at his feet. The mist had lifted with the pale insistence of the sun and the pond in front of him reflected a bare horizon on a pale blue sky. He rose clumsily, the invisible cloak of failure wound around him, and he walked stiffly back to the farm, his limp exaggerated by an acute sense of kinship with the lame and unsuccessful. He had tried and failed. He had been tried and failed by his father. He should have followed his father out into the storm, not stayed clutching his puppy to himself like a toy.

Now he would move on without the consolation of his father's blessing. He had steeled himself to end Nipper's life but was leading the pup back home to a life without him, a continual reminder to his mother and sister of his own imperfection. They would look at Nipper and think of him, the crippled child. He wanted to be redeemed from his childhood and made whole by Greelham School. No longer should death and sorrow haunt him. He would become known for his confidence and cleverness, not his hare-lip and limp.

'You would have killed him if you'd really wanted to,' murmured an inner voice, quite different from the voice at the cliff. 'You only wanted to deceive your father into loving you. Cheats never prosper!' It was true. He could not stuff Nipper into a bag and thrust him underwater, holding him there until the breath was replaced by gurgling water and the spry bright eyes clouded with darkness. There was such life in the little dog now, cocking his leg and sniffing at early morning scents all at once, almost falling over himself in obedience to need and curiosity.

Suddenly Peter picked up a stone and flicked it at Nipper. It span past the pup's ear and cracked against a rock. Nipper started, tumbled and then skedaddled towards Peter, his head rocking up and down, teeth bare in a mock grin. Peter bent down, plucked the pup up under his belly and, cradling him, carried him back to the yard. But before going into the house he put the dog down and kicked him into the kitchen in front of him, not wishing to show his feelings on this special day of emancipation.

# CHAPTER
# SIXTEEN

The new boys gathered at the buttery, a building set alongside the gym and used by Upper School boys for their refreshments. On this occasion it was entrusted to the test for new boys. There were about forty-five pupils – three classes in all, A, B and C – but Peter did not know this. He filed into the echoing old room with the others and sat at one of the long refectory tables on a scratchy-sided but silver-smooth-topped bench. Most of the boys seemed to know each other and their light grey flannel suits were old, worn carelessly with ink-blotched patches and shirt collars flipped up at the ends, ties scrawnily thin and legs long in very short shorts.

Opposite him sat another new boy and Peter felt rather reassured to see him. He knew that he was a potential victim for bullies and saw in the fat, pale-faced and uneasy-looking boy an alternative butt. A white sheet of paper was slid in front of him and a chill silence augmented the hush that already existed. Peter took out his new fountain pen, given to him by Mr Eldon in a little ceremony at church, and a pencil. He looked around surreptitiously.

There were four men, all clad in black gowns. Three were giving out paper and the fourth stood by the buttery hatch, his arms spread out across the bar, leaning backwards casually. His hair was white, and shone in the early autumn light. He tapped his fingers gently on the counter as if playing the piano, waiting for the other teachers to complete their task.

'My name is Mr Grant,' he said in a harsh voice. 'I am head of first and second years and in charge of music in the school.' The word 'music' rang out like a clarion call to the charge. Music was obviously the more important of his tasks. 'You have in front of you a short test in number and words. There is also a section devoted to Latin. The test will last one hour and will help us put you into appropriate classes. You may begin.'

Peter had no Latin but Mr Salmon had said that he would be able to learn enough as he went along. He wondered whether he ought to tell one of the teachers, but a single frightened glance convinced him that he would have to make the best of a bad job. He sailed through the numbers section, managed the words quite happily and then boggled at the few short Latin sentences in need of translation. He looked up again. The fat boy opposite was breathing heavily, his bottom lip stained blue by pen-sucking. One of the teachers, a tall, heavily-built young man, was leaning against the wall inspecting his nails and then gazing out of the window. He looked incuriously back round the tables and Peter hastily lowered his head to the page. Perhaps Mr Eldon had been wrong. Perhaps he had been expected to go away and learn Latin during the summer. He would be discovered as an imposter and thrown out. He looked at the first sentence. He vaguely recognized 'urbs' as a funny part of 'urban'. He wrote that down and then went through all the sentences looking for bits that looked like English words. By the end he'd found about ten and the hour was up.

Peter was allocated to 1B. Nobody mentioned his Latin or lack of it. His final mark had sufficed to put him in the middle group and his form teacher was Mr Feeling, in classroom 2 along the bottom corridor, a grey, chalk-dust-filled repository for mathematical textbooks and Latin primers. There were only fifteen boys in the group and they sat in rigid rows of five with the teacher on a dais beside a blackboard on stilts, which occasionally slid off the uncertainly fixed pegs. On this board Mr Feeling performed hieroglyphics while the boys communed with marble runs, scribbles on desks, whispers, daydreams, fumbling under desks to grab other boys' privates, kicking books over the floor and waiting for that delicious moment when the marble secretly inserted through the inkwell hole plopped into the hand through the hole bored in the base of the desk.

Teacher and pupils reached a reasonable truce. As long as the boys remained comparatively quiet Mr Feeling did not disturb them, maintaining his monotonous explanations of mathematical formula and setting prep work. Peter managed the work easily. Even the Latin followed simple lines of rote learning and he found himself completing Alan Wright's work for him and charging a penny a sum for prep. He had not thought to charge, but Alan, his desk partner, automatically handed over the money.

Early on the first day Slater made it clear that he was to be class leader, the boss. He came from the Nursery School with that reputation and wanted to impress himself on Peter Townsend. He took the prime back seat next to the window, flashed pounds round the side of the buttery, persuading older boys to buy him things and sharing them with his favourite cronies. You knew you were all right if Slater gave you a bun. You knew you were in for trouble if he stuffed one down your neck. He was tall for his age and a good athlete, manoeuvring himself into all the best positions on the rugby field where he could shine without becoming too involved in close scrummaging. Peter's silence – he still spoke rarely – and his physical insignificance quickly made Slater ignore him, unless he wanted some work done. There was never any question of Slater paying a penny a sum, and when he found out that Wright was occasionally forking out he took a halfpenny cut on each deal. These halfpennies he kept in a tin in his bedside locker, and claimed he would buy end-of-term cakes for the whole class with the proceeds.

One day during break Peter was stopped in the yard by three older boys and interrogated. They had kept returning to one particular question of intense importance.

'Are you fee or free? Are you fee or free?'

Peter did not know what they meant, nor the distinction that the additional 'r' gave him. To be fee was acceptable because the majority paid fees; to be free meant a victim. But the Westby boys had taught Peter well, and when he turned impassive eyes on the bullies and refused to show any fear or interest, he was left alone, branded a strange fish.

It quickly became clear that there was already a butt for teasing and torment, a boy sufficiently fat and ineffectual to protect others, like Peter, from being branded. Keeping, the son of a Norwich shop owner, was wheezy and dense. It was a mystery how he came to be in the B stream.

'Bribery and corruption, Keeping – offered old Grant his Billy Bunter bag of toffees to keep out of the Cs,' jeered Slater.

'Cheated off Townsend more like,' grinned Smith. Keeping also wore glasses. But his size, lack of intelligence and poor eyesight would not have created his private hell had it not been for his high and squeakily petulant voice. There wasn't a boy in the group and not many in the house who couldn't do a passable imitation of Keeping within a fortnight. It whiled away the hours spent poring over dry and dusty volumes of fact to squeak out complaints and hope that Keeping would get into trouble. He often did.

'Was that the cry of the stranded walrus?' Mr Feeling looked round from the blackboard, wiping his brow in mock despair.

'Yes sir,' Slater said. 'He doesn't know he does it sir.'

'It wasn't me sir,' Keeping bleated as all eyes turned towards him. The boys laughed.

'It never is, is it Keeping?' Mr Feeling looked sternly at the round and unhappy moon in front of him.

'No sir. It's the others sir. They do it to get me in trouble sir.'

A low moan of angry horror grumbled round.

'I don't think it's particularly praiseworthy to try to blame others for one's own faults, Keeping.' Mr Feeling carefully placed the pale brown sweep of hair that fell over his eyes back in place over his bald patch.

'But it's not fair sir.' The boys howled with laughter. This was the magic phrase, the one they angled to hear and then imitated, squeaking higher and higher until Keeping squealed above them, appealing to the teacher for justice.

'The only thing that is not fair, sir, is you sir,' said Mr Feeling and another gale of laughter swept the class. 'Now we must proceed without interruption.'

The boys returned to work, copying from the blackboard and the old text books, waiting for the clanging of the brass bell which Foster sounded every hour to mark the end of breaks. He came through from the holy sanctuary of the main entrance area like a blackened stick, his thin twig-like fingers clenched round the bell's clapper lest a whisper of his arrival should escape before the allotted moment. He checked the time on his fob watch and then heaved the handbell up and down until the peals clattered their way to the top of the building where senior pupils studied. Slater said he was going to steal Foster's watch one night, but it would be difficult because he never took his clothes off.

Every morning straight after breakfast came a change from the cream walls of the classroom. Mr Grant took the whole lower school for singing. Nines to twelves were paraded into the school hall and set in rows, no chairs, no bags, just rows of boys looking at the dais in absolute silence. Mr Grant strode to the lectern, his feet cracking into the polished floorboards, his white hair flowing and his gown billowing. A brief prayer boomed out and then he turned to important matters.

'I want to see your mouths in your foreheads and I want to see every word framed. Work your faces until they ache.'

Slowly heads began to look up from the planked floor and eyes focused on Greelham's eccentric music master. Grant swept a long purple-silk-sleeved arm and brushed away a lock of hair from his eyes. Small, bright blue eyes glimmered into the head of every boy in the hall. Peter stood with the older boys at the back, behind Slater if he could manage it, but he knew that one day those gimlet eyes would fall on him and he would be castigated for not opening his mouth wide. He couldn't unfreeze his jaw and work his lips as Mr Grant insisted he should.

'Each word is known by heart – we chant them now – "Res Superbae Negavunt". Let me hear the "re" and "unt"!'

Now the voices raised a shade; the early morning mumble became a mutter. Another long emphatic gesture brushed the hair aside.

'Any boy who fails to chant will lose all free time for a week.' Another stare round the hall. Every word from this apocalyptic figure was pointed, precise and poised.

'Again, again, again and again, sing this bloody awful refrain.'

Gradually the boys began to repeat with higher volume and the purple arm rose and fell with increasing emphasis.

'But now to sing the holy song, Lully lullay my little one . . . volume high and clearest words – "Lully"!' This time Mr Grant sang the opening lines and his voice, although strident, even unmusical, had a magnetism that held and drew the sound from the boys. Suddenly the whole congregation, perhaps one hundred and fifty boys, was away, in full voice, and on they sang with little interruption for twenty minutes. Then was the dangerous time for Peter because Mr Grant went his rounds, crouching down along the rows listening to the voices as they breathed their treble notes. In this way Mr Grant made his selection for the school choir and, fortunately for Peter, he tended to listen to the younger boys because the older ones were already heard. Alan Wright was in the choir, one of the foremost members, and Peter also tried to be away from him because Mr Grant often came along to check that his angel's voice was still pure and unclouded by incipient manhood. Throughout the patrol Peter stood with his face as close as possible to Slater's back and his mouth twitching through the words. He felt like a hunted animal and could see no way of avoiding the trap.

Eventually Mr Grant raised his hands and brought the singing to an end.

'To classes, rabble! Waste your time until tomorrow morning. Music is the complete teacher of time, place, relationship and movement. There is no other subject.'

Mr Grant turned and left as quickly as he had come.

A month or so into the term and Peter had begun to adjust to the school routine, to know what to expect, where to go and how to survive. He'd suffered the ritual bowl of cold water thrown over his head in the dormitory and cleared up the puddle the best he could before sleeping on top of the blankets. Alan had told him to turn the mattress over so matron didn't think he'd wet the bed, but nobody warned Keeping and he had to go to matron every evening for a week. Food in Barham had been basic and food at school was similar. Slowly he began to feel part of the place, not to notice the squalor, to take as inevitable the continual jockeying for power that marked the school.

Greelham's glorified respect and created minuscule steps of hierarchy. There was a Head – always out of sight except on severely formal occasions – a Deputy, housemasters, subject staff, in a ladder of influence. There were school prefects with the power to cane you, house prefects with the power to remove your liberty, dormitory monitors with the power to throw your belongings out of your locker and class leaders like Slater, the school prefects of the future. There were also mavericks and Peter felt akin to them because they won attention and respect through different means. He even had an inkling of Keeping's need to be always the centre of ridicule, for even that attention was better than none. Among the teachers, Mr Grant wielded influence from the unlikely position of music teacher and Mr Graham, the PT teacher, was bossy with the boys and deferential to other teachers, even to Mr Feeling.

One morning after singing and another escape from Mr Grant's scrutiny Peter settled to tracing a map of Great Britain and filling in the main industrial centres. It was quiet in the room. Only the old stove in the corner made a noise, creaking its heat through the pipes and sending gurgles of hot water along the wall. Mr Feeling lifted his gown and propped his backside against the cast-iron cover. Winter was flexing its muscles outside. The long line of trees had been stripped bare of leaves by a week's harsh wind from the east and the heating had been put on before the end of October, a most unusual departure from custom. Peter knew that because he'd overheard Mr Feeling saying he couldn't remember the heating going on so early before. Because he was habitually so silent, Peter tended not to be noticed and often picked up titbits of information that he relayed to the other boys in tiny gobbets.

Mr Feeling eased himself away from the stove and moved gingerly towards his desk, his trousers just on the safe side of scorching. As he reached the dais there was a rap on the classroom door and the brass handle flicked down.

'Class stand!' Mr Feeling called out, rubbed his backside vigorously as if to remove signs of his gentle roasting. The boys scraped back their chairs and stood gazing at the visitor.

'I am looking for new boys,' Mr Grant announced as if he were in a department store and addressing a shop assistant. Mr Feeling smiled and nodded.

'Boys who are new to the school this year stay standing. The rest sit down quietly.'

Peter would have liked to sit down with the others but when he slowly shifted towards his chair seat, Alan Wright leaned towards him and whispered, 'Not you, Townsend,' and he had to stay upright.

'Just the two of you?' Mr Grant stared briefly at his catch. '1A came up with six possibles for the choir and three new instrumentalists.' He seemed dissatisfied, looked round at the rest of the class. 'Hands up other choir members,' he ordered, and four hands rose. Mr Grant fixed his eyes on Alan Wright, next to Peter.

'You come as well,' he said. 'Beauty and the beasts!'

Mr Grant flung open the door and pointed through it. 'Come along. We have wasted enough of Mr Feeling's valuable time.'

Peter always seemed to be following adult backs through long corridors. Mr Feeling often put him in the front of the crocodile. He was likely to fall behind otherwise, not because he couldn't stumble along fast enough but because he just found himself lagging when going somewhere new. It was as if he didn't want to arrive. The black back in front of him seemed threatening. It reminded him of his father.

Now, because it was a gloomy morning, the corridors were dim. Putting lights on during daytime was strictly forbidden. Mr Grant hustled through the corridors like a giant bat flapping through a maze.

'Where we going?' panted Keeping, the tops of his thighs rubbing together as he wobbled along.

'Music room of course,' answered Wright.

'What for?' Keeping squeaked.

'Woodwork,' replied Wright.

Grant turned a sharp left, trotted down a flight of stone steps and clattered through a small door. The boys followed. The music room stank of stale pipe tobacco and old manuscript paper. An upright piano littered with pieces of music and manila folders stood by the door. Music stands in various states of dilapidation and erection were piled along one wall by the windows. Only a grey wall with black iron railings on top could be seen through the grimy glass, for the room was on basement level at the back of the hall. There was another door leading out to the yard and this had a bar across it and the faded letters, Emergency Use Only.

'Names first,' ordered the teacher fishing an old exercise-book from a shelf and flicking it open.

'Wright sir,' answered Alan pertly.

'Not you, idiot.' Grant ruffled through Alan's fair curls with a large hand. 'You,' he pointed at Keeping. 'What's your name?'

Keeping had scarcely recovered breath from the chase through the corridors. He gulped. 'Keeping, sir.' Mr Grant's eyes seemed to shrink into pinheads of light as he stared at the fat boy.

'Ouch!' he whispered. Then he wheeled round to Peter as if for relief. 'And yours?'

Peter had been dreading this moment. He could manage to speak a little in class but was rarely asked to do so. His great fear was the singing at morning assembly, and now there was no escape. He swallowed and tried to remember Mr Eldon's instructions, but no help came.

'Come along lad – haven't got all day.'

'T-t-t-owns-send s-s-sir.'

The teacher looked at Peter and then again at Keeping. The man's eyes were hard and glittery blue but his mouth could almost have been smiling. The eyes turned to Peter.

'Is that stutter just nerves or because of your mouth?' he asked abruptly. Peter could not answer. Mr Grant looked at Alan.

'Does he always stutter?'

'No sir,' Alan answered. 'He doesn't say much but he speaks all right.'

Mr Grant nodded and turned to the piano. He looked at Keeping and forced a smile.

'Listen to this note and see if you can copy it.'

A strangled bleat rose and failed. Mr Grant tried again with the same success.

'You are a rare animal, Keeping,' he said finally, 'but I'm afraid you will be unable to sing in the school choir. I have been wondering where your noise came from every morning, am pleased to have isolated it, but should be grateful if you would mouth the words in future rather than sound them. I'm sure you have many fine qualities, but music is not one of them. You may return to class.'

'Yes sir,' said Keeping, and Alan, who seemed relaxed and confident in a way Peter had never seen before, giggled. It was another weapon delivered into the boys' hands against fat Keeping. Peter looked at Alan and found himself grinning back.

'Now what are we going to do with you, young Townsend? Many people with a stutter are greatly helped by singing. See whether you can join in with Alan here.'

Mr Grant ran through a scale and Alan met the notes, rising in a liquid purity that shivered in the shabby music room and caught at Peter's heart. He could never join in with that sound. His throat closed on the possibility.

'No?' questioned the teacher. 'Well, let's try something else. I'll sing a note and you try to find it on the piano. I doubt if even Alan could do that very easily.'

Peter shuffled over to the keys. He knew that bottom notes were to his left, top to the right. Mr Grant sang and Peter tried and found the note. It was easy. Another note came and Peter matched it. Then Alan sang a note and this was found as well. Eventually the sound stopped and Peter looked back at Mr Grant. The teacher was resting his hand on Alan's shoulder and he was smiling. Peter could see the yellow worn edges of his teeth where the pipe normally fitted.

'Hidden depths, eh, Townsend?' Grant walked over to a dark wooden cupboard that almost filled the wall behind the piano. He shuffled through a heavy bunch of keys and fitted one into the lock. Violin cases of various sizes were revealed like huge black beetles, or the sarcophagi of Egyptian burial. Grant's fingers strummed against one of the shelf edges and he shot another glance at Peter, measuring the boy.

'Half-size for a half-pint pot, I think.' He hoisted down a case. 'It has taken me years to build up this collection of violins. It is irreplaceable. This violin,' he plucked the instrument from its faded velvet bed, 'is German. The last boy to use it is now playing with the London Philharmonic. You may emulate him. I normally start boys on string instruments at a very early age. Inculcating good habits when very young prevents all sorts of problems later. You seem an unusual case, may even have that magical possession of perfect pitch. We shall see.'

He handed the violin to Peter, who took it gingerly. 'Alan has been learning the piano for a year. From now on you two will practise together and play together. At Christmas next year there will be a concert in the school hall. You will play your first public piece then. That gives you just over one year to master basics.'

When Peter had managed to tune the strings, Mr Grant smiled. 'That will be all for today. You will come every evening at four thirty for half an hour. You may return to class.'

Mr Grant's hand gently touched Alan Wright's neck and then rubbed his right shoulder. 'Off you go, then, and remember, Peter Townsend, I do not approve of lazy boys. That fiddle could be used by another boy to good advantage, so work hard.'

The two boys left the room but instead of returning directly to class, Alan pulled Peter into an alcove beside the exit doors to the yard.

'He thought you were good,' said Alan.

Peter did not respond.

'You normally have to be in the choir before you can learn an instrument. He's breaking his rule for you.'

Peter nodded. He still didn't know what to say but Alan seemed to be expecting him to reply, his blue eyes gazing earnestly into Peter's face.

'We ought to get back,' he eventually said, moving out of the alcove. Alan followed Peter and caught at his elbow.

'If I help you with music, we'll be quits. I won't have to pay for the sums,' he said, grinning.

'I'll soon catch you up,' Peter said.

'I didn't mean just that. I'm a favourite.' Alan's eyes turned suddenly serious. 'Mr Grant listens to me.'

Peter didn't understand what Wright was driving at and they returned to class.

# CHAPTER
# SEVENTEEN

Peter found it hard to believe he had a friend, that Alan Wright was prepared to talk with him, joke with him and help him. At first he tended to take any joke as a possible insult, any tiny enquiry about his home background as an intolerable intrusion, and a little difference of opinion as the potential end of the relationship. Other friends had been taken from him but maybe, he thought, Greelham's exerted a new law which could hold Alan to him. Even the black shadows of the corridors began to lose their power of fear and the iron band that occasionally clamped itself around his temples, squeezing anger and frustration into his brain, began to loosen. He became jealous of Alan and intensely protective of him. It was threatening to have Keeping in the next-door desk, trying to push in on their friendship, trying to be accepted. In breaks between lessons Alan and Peter stuck barbs into Keeping's blubber to consolidate their own position, but Keeping never seemed to give up lest the last little hope be dashed.

'I'll buy you some toffees if you let me come.'

'No, Keeping, you need them for yourself. Can't have you dying of starvation.'

'Please Wright, let me come. You're only allowed in the village with another boy and nobody will go with me.'

'Feeling will think two of you have gone if you go by yourself,' giggled Alan, nudging Peter in the ribs.

'Please Alan . . .'

Alan raised his eyebrows at Peter in mock desperation and Peter turned to Keeping, staring at the fat boy so that even he stopped talking for a moment. There was a natural seriousness in Peter's eyes, a natural sneer to an already twisted lip and a stillness in his face. As the year wore on Peter found he could use this power to good effect. He also maintained a slight stutter; it made people wait to hear him.

'K-k-keeping,' he said, 'you heard w-w-what Alan s-said. F-find someone else.'

There was nobody else for Keeping to find. Peter knew it. Alan knew it, but Keeping could not accept it.

'Just because you want Alan all for yourself,' bleated Keeping.

'Two's company; three's a crowd,' answered Alan cheerfully and Peter felt moved by his friendship. Very occasionally, because Alan was warm-hearted and Keeping insistent, Keeping would be allowed to trail along with them, his face wide and beaming while Peter's became closed and resentful.

At Christmas, when Peter returned home to the farm, he found the yard empty of livestock. The cows had been sold, the hen run and rabbit house dismantled, and his mother and sister were hardly ever there except for sleeping. Although his mother had written to him about Mr Eldon's continued poor health and her decision to act as his housekeeper, the holiday came as a surprise, an unwelcome return to a world he had tried to blot from his mind. Claire was virtually one of the Luffman children and Joan spent her days arranging the cleaning rota for the church, nursing Mr Eldon, even preparing his meals and cleaning the cottage. Mr Eldon had little voice. The throat infection had settled on his narrow chest and the minister could not shake it off. Peter spent the holiday walking round the old farm and the Frobisher Estate with Nipper, and returned to his sullen nature when asked about school. He did, however, avoid the quarry, and if he felt that premonition of fear scudding towards him from the far horizon, he thought of Alan, his smiling face with an ink blot on his chin, his curls after showering, his fingers hesitating then finding the right note and the way the tip of his tongue poked from the corner of his mouth when he was pretending to concentrate but was really copying Peter's maths prep. Peter's fears would disappear and the black-winged shadow would shrink and shrivel into the wide sky.

Peter returned to school with joy and there was Alan, almost as he had remembered him. The term continued on its solid course and Peter found security within the routine, but little irritations worried him. Alan would sometimes fling himself away from him, even go off with Keeping, and Slater took to walking up behind him and coughing in his ear. It became the craze of the term, but the stock response of the boy assaulted was to turn around and squeak, 'You're a bender coming up behind me.' Then the boys would both collapse in giggles, grunting 'bender' as if the word held great and dirty significance. Peter did not join in this prank, and Slater continually coughed in his ear and whispered 'You're a bender,' trying to force Peter to respond. Even the teachers were greeted by a cough and a disguised 'bender' noise when they walked into classrooms. Slater even did it once in Mr Grant's assembly, but none of the boys would reveal the culprit and they all had to stand in silence throughout the lunch break. After that the game waned in popularity and Slater stopped worrying Peter with it.

One day Peter had the prep room to himself. There were three old leather chairs by the lockers and if he curled up small inside the end one nearest the window, nobody could see he was there. It was his favourite listening and daydreaming post. There was a musty but reassuring smell of generations around him; the leather was worn smooth as glass and yet it gave beneath his weight and held him like another skin. He could see the fringe of trees at the far side of the school grounds. Above the trees a shimmering blue sky stretched and the sun shone like a furnace. All the other boys were outside. Alan was in choir practice because it was Thursday and Peter preferred to be alone, waiting and dreaming in a quiet cool corner. There was a bluebottle beating its wings against the grubby windowpane, settling for a second and then continuing to buzz angrily. Everything wants to get outside, thought Peter, but I'm happy here.

He did not hear the door open, nor at first did he notice the voices behind him, but one was so discordant and shrill that he knew automatically that Keeping was there.

'I don't know how you put up with him,' came the voice and the bluebottle flew away from the window, dive-bombed the chair next to him and then launched itself again at the pane. Should he let it out or squash it? To release it would mean fetching the long pole from the corner and boys were not supposed to use it unsupervised because, the story had it, a boy had once lost an eye in a jousting match with it. It would be cooler in the room if the window were wide open, but he had energy neither to release nor assault the fly. He tried to blot out Keeping's bleating and hoped that he would not advance to the lockers and see Peter in the chair. The voice came again, insistently breaking into his reverie.

'At least not having choir gives you a break – why aren't you there? Was Grant ill or something?'

'He just needed the altos.'

It was Alan's voice. He would recognize it in the middle of a storm. Peter almost uncurled and launched out of hiding to greet him, but he held back for a few more precious moments, enjoying the knowledge that he could hear Alan and his friend did not know he was there.

'The others are talking about you two, you know.' Keeping's voice sounded very old, his words creaking with responsibility.

'Oh yes.'

'You do get people who like boys not girls. My father says it's because their mothers hated them.' There was a pause and the bluebottle stayed still and exhausted on the window. 'It's just the way they are.'

'You're the expert, are you then, Keeping – first-hand experience?'

'They like sticking their thing into boys' bottoms,' came that harsh affronted voice, daring Alan to deny it. There was a snort of disgusted laughter from Alan.

'Shut up, Keeping. You don't know what you're talking about. That's mucky talk, that is.'

'That's what Slater said,' jeered Keeping as if he were quoting from the Bible. 'He said Townsend might be like it.'

Peter went rigid in his chair. His mother's face flashed in his mind and her warning that 'You never hear anything good of yourself if you listen to private conversations' echoed. He shoved his face deep into the corner of the chair, but he found himself straining to hear the next words as if he were being force-fed with poison.

'You don't want to believe everything Slater says.'

'He's always going round with you. You should see the way he looks at you sometimes. Gives me the shivers.'

'You give me the shivers, Keeping,' laughed Alan, but there was tension in his laugh. Peter could see through the chair back, knew how his friend's mouth would have opened and the way his tongue would have quivered with the sound, but he could see his eyes as well and they were not dancing with the light of the sun on a blue sky.

'I know I'm fat but I'm not bent,' said Keeping stoutly, crashing through Alan's laughter. There was silence again and then a swirl of movement. The door slammed and Peter could hear Keeping breathing heavily, like after running the hundred yards. He wanted to get up and tear into the fat boy, kick him into lumps of quivering jelly and tread him into the splintered floorboards so he was just a stain. Slowly he inched his head away from the leather and looked towards the lockers. The room seemed dark and each locker door that hung ajar seemed to be moving, waving in a muggy brown sea of hatred. There was a creature inside each of those cupboards and each creature was the creature inside his head. Peter brought his hands to his skull and pressed as if holding it in.

'He's just jealous because he hasn't got a friend,' he said to himself. 'Alan is just my friend.' Slowly these words acted as a comfort, a way of staving off the nightmare. He stared at the locker opposite and said those words until the black anger subsided and the locker door stilled. He heard Keeping leave and then he unravelled himself from the chair and fled from the room like a wraith. He found himself patrolling the corridors, peering through windows, hoping to see Alan again, to be reassured that Keeping's words had had no effect on his friend.

He arrived by the stone steps near the music room. Voices from the hall told him that the altos were still practising and so he went inside and across to the emergency door. He peered up through the window to the yard above and the railings there. There was a line of boys' legs. They were twined into the railings and then suddenly they bolted away, flashing like stars. Alan was there. Peter was sure of it. He pushed on the bar of the door and it gave. Next moment he was standing in the well. Stairs led up on either side. It was a favourite place for chasing and dodging games.

'You're on, Wright,' came a shout and then feet pattered away. Peter heard Alan's voice rising clear in the darkness, counting to forty. Next moment there were footsteps on the stairs to his left as Alan charged down to catch the grey shape of a boy who was trying to hide by the music-room window. Peter did not run, did not try to join in and reach home before Alan. His friend clattered down and stretched an arm out to touch him, expecting his prey to dodge and run away, but Peter stayed still and Alan's hand flapped against his chest. Peter looked at Alan, who had only just realized whom he had caught. Peter saw how Alan's face changed from life to death, from joy to a sort of fear.

'Oh,' said Alan. 'I'm sorry. I thought it was Peach.' Alan was away back up the stairs to guard his railings. Peter turned back into the music room. It was Keeping's fault that Alan had looked at him like that. He was used to others reacting with that flicker of fear when they saw his face, but Alan had never done so before, never winced away from him as if he were diseased. Peter went to the cloakroom and leaned his forehead against a cold metal bar. He hated Keeping and the blackness shrouded him in that fierce and certain power. It was his father come again. His mother would reject him; his joys would turn to sorrows and the great gaunt shadow would haunt him.

Alan changed towards Peter, not greatly, but enough to tilt the scales. He was about with the rest of the class more, and joined in groups of lads. He would always ask Peter if he were coming too, but when Peter refused he would charge off regardless. Peter's hurt grew raw again.

Outwardly the veneer of Greelham life continued to shine. The routine remained secure around Peter until the end of June and the inter-house athletics competition. Peter did not worry because, although he could not enter the sprints and field events, he was able to drift round and round the track for long distances. In the cross- country earlier in the year he had surprised Mr Graham by coming third. His early training of trailing behind his father over miles of Norfolk countryside now helped him and he enjoyed that sort of running. His mind could wander and listen to the voices he found within him.

For Keeping, though, all to do with PT was excruciating. As soon as the boy entered the grey changing rooms with their smell of old sweat and lines of benches held in place by a scaffold of metal bars, his body seemed to swell even larger, beyond his control. He was inordinately shy of his shape, and the whole process of changing and showering filled him with apprehension. He tried not to look at the other boys as they slipped happily into shorts and singlets and later rushed their lithe bodies into steaming showers. He made loud self-conscious jokes when he had to follow under the spiked bulbs that shot their needles into his plump flesh.

'Flobber! Flobber! Flobber!' he would chant as he arrived and, although the other boys jeered, time had bred a modicum of contemptuous disregard, and generally a space was found in the corridor of steam where he could dab away the sweat of great energy expended to little effect.

Mr Graham, unlike some teachers with more status who had tired of calling Keeping names and ridiculing his voice, had not lost his relish for insulting the boy. Two weeks before the athletics tournament, Mr Graham stood in the gym bouncing on the soles of his large white plimsolls and swivelling his shoulders to loosen them. He bellowed through to the changing room, 'Last one in here changed knows what to expect!'

Squeals of mock horror rose and the boys scampered into the gym, tugging on their plimsolls as they hopped along. They lined up and stood waiting, eyes bright. The last boy was nearly always Keeping. Occasionally Smith lost the race because he forgot to dress himself as well as carry on his interminable chatter, but today it was Keeping who lumbered through the doors last, his face already red and oozing unhappy tears of perspiration. He knew what was coming and it was the work of a moment for Mr Graham to confirm it.

'Bend over, Keeping. Shove your gut out of the way and bend.'

Keeping tilted forward and the teacher brought an old plimsoll down on the tightly-stretched shorts. It sounded like the starting pistol firing. Keeping was so used to this that he just returned to his place and waited.

'You must have the hardest hide in the school, Keeping,' said the teacher, flicking the punishment slipper into the corner where it landed with another slap. 'A rhinoceros would have understood by now. When are you going to pull your socks up and trim yourself down?'

Keeping eyed his socks suspiciously. Mr Graham had a way of suddenly taking that turn of phrase literally and drooping socks at the start of a lesson could mean another whack. At least his white socks were pulled up, although one was inside out. The ribbing stood out clearly. He hoped the teacher would not notice.

'Right, lads, arrangements for athletics. Two competitors in each event, maximum of four events plus relay for each boy. Every boy to take part in at least one event.'

Mr Graham tugged the zipped pocket of his tracksuit and pulled out a tightly folded piece of paper that he began to unfold carefully. As he did so he looked towards Keeping again, smiling.

'Well, Keeping, how are you keeping?' A time-honoured ripple of amusement, giggles then silence waiting for the next barb, met the teacher's words as he bounced from toe to toe on the shining floor, the paper flapping. 'I asked you how you were keeping, Keeping. Is it to be four events or will you go for the relay as well?'

Keeping drew in his breath. He knew that whatever he said would be turned against him, but he also knew he had to speak.

'Well sir . . .' His voice sounded excuse-full. Graham interrupted.

'Well sir, what sir? Well sir, bottom of the ding dong pussy's in the . . . or in excellent trim sir, ready for all comers?'

The boy rubbed his hand over his forehead and flicked a nervous glance round the class. The others all seemed to be grinning at him except Townsend, who stood in front of him and hadn't looked round. He tried to grin back.

'While you're deciding what to say, Keeping, I shall read out the team.'

Mr Graham read in a staccato fashion, starting with the sixty-yard dash and working up in distance. Slater and Wright were in most events but all the boys' names were soon mentioned except for Townsend and Keeping.

'Eight-eighty,' he called out, 'Townsend and Peach.'

'Yes sir.'

'Finally, because our fat friend will have been saving up all his energy all afternoon, the mile – the summit of an Englishman's athletic dream, the Roger Bannister of success and glory. Townsend and Keeping will be our pair.'

'Yes sir,' said Peter, but there was a tiny moan from behind him.

'Were you about to say something, Keeping?' Mr Graham smiled blandly.

'But sir,' Slater put up his hand, 'we want to do well sir. Rowe House could win it this year. Do we have to have Keeping? He could help with the scoring.'

'We all have our crosses to bear, Slater, and Keeping is ours. Besides, Keeping won't let us down. He will gain one point for completing the course without stopping.'

'What if he reports to matron sir?' chimed in Smith.

'Then we'll kick him out on the field. He is going to run, and if he looks like stopping he'll receive a gentle boot to encourage him on.'

'He could throw the cricket ball sir,' said Wright.

Keeping shot a grateful glance at Alan. Above all things he hated running. The tops of his thighs rubbed together and flamed red. He could never catch his breath and needed to stop after every few yards. His mother worried that he was asthmatic, but his father just said he needed more exercise and less mollycoddling.

'He'd probably throw it in the wrong direction, Wright, but it's a thought.' He marched over to Keeping and bawled at him as if the boy were deaf.

'You want to run a mile, don't you, Keeping?'

'Yes sir,' Keeping answered miserably.

'That's the spirit, lad. What do you think, Townsend? You're to be his partner.'

Peter turned round to look at Keeping.

'H-h-he wouldn't f-finish, sir,' he said, as his face grew a little paler and his eyes sparked with contempt.

'Perhaps you have a point, Townsend. Since Keeping is a trifle overweight for long-distance running, round and podgy like a bloated parrot, like a distended porker, like, in fact, dear matron's flea-ridden great lard of a tabby cat, we could give him a chance to throw the cricket ball instead.' The boys laughed again, nervously. Keeping remained silent.

'Now, Keeping,' continued the teacher, 'we will attempt a ten-yard dash for walruses.' He plucked two chairs from the side of the gym and placed them ten yards apart. 'Now, huge and galumphing hippo, let us test your running ability. If you manage to complete the ten yards, you will not have to run in the mile but may throw the cricket ball instead. Stand at that chair and be ready to run.'

Keeping trundled to the chair, puzzled, frightened, confused but with a glimmering of hope. He had no cause for hope; time and again his hope had been dashed, but still that faint gleam brought him to the mark. Even he could reach the other chair, yet Mr

Graham was rarely so kind and accommodating. The other boys stood round, puzzled, but sensing a trick, a bit of fun.

'Now, lad, are you ready?'

Keeping nodded dumbly.

'Reach the chair, running all the way, mind, only ten yards, and it's throwing the cricket ball for you instead of the mile.'

Keeping nodded again, eyes fixed on the chair as if he expected it to be carried away from him by an invisible string, but it stayed where it was.

'On your mark! Set! Go!' Keeping, mouth open, shambled at a lolloping pace towards the chair. Slater started the 'Flobber, flobber, flobber' chant but Keeping kept going. Two yards from the goal Mr Graham interposed his body. Keeping was brought up short.

'Don't stop, Keeping! Run round me lad. Run round me.'

The boy started to do so and the teacher side-stepped neatly to prevent him reaching the chair.

'Dodge, lad. Dodge!' Dodging, however, was beyond the stranded whale; he began to puff and sweat and suddenly stood still, gasping. Heaving his voice into his mouth, he began to speak. 'It's not fair sir. 'Snot fair.'

A collective sigh went round the gym. Here was the rallying cry, the refrain that followed Keeping everywhere he went.

'You're right, of course, Keeping,' chipped in Mr Graham. 'It is not fair to waste the class's valuable time on you. You will have to run the mile.' The teacher tired of his game. 'Come on, you lads. Show Keeping how to do it. A thick ear if you're caught.'

The others lined up at the far chair, suddenly excited, while the floundering Keeping collapsed at the wall. Peter looked at him and then joined the others, standing quietly behind Alan.

One after the other the boys ran, dodged and often succeeded in touching the chair. Occasionally Mr Graham's flat palm would clip a passing lad, but his blows were light and served to encourage them. Peter stayed well beyond reach and waited until Alan whisked towards the chair, using him as his silver-fast shield. Eventually Mr Graham shouted 'Enough!' and stood panting slightly.

'Well, Keeping, are you up to another go or is it slug of the month award for you?'

Slater, Smith, Peach and the others all clustered round him, their faces red and their eyes shining feverishly. Slater began to jog on the spot and lifted his knees virtually to his chin in a frantic whirl.

'Knees up! Knees up! Get your filthy knees up.' Smith began to imitate Slater and the others laughed, but Peter slid his back down the wall until he was sitting by Keeping. The fat boy blinked at him. Peter leaned over and poked a finger into Keeping's side.

'It's b-b-best to t-try, to have another g-go. The others w-w-would respect you f-for it.' Peter smiled reassuringly. Part of him believed what he said; his mother used to say it, and mother's sayings have meaning long after they have slipped from the conscious mind. Another part of him knew that Keeping would fail, that another little revenge for what Keeping had said to Alan would be exacted and Peter would be the clever persuader, the smooth operator who could fool Keeping every time. Peter stared at Slater, who was still prancing and jeering.

'He's g-going to try again, aren't you Keeping?' Peter said, and his voice, normally quiet and stammering, cut through the raucous chant and sound of pounding feet.

'Oh, give him a chance,' Alan said and flushed. It wasn't Keeping's fault he was so fat. Alan's comment could have been made for any creature in trouble, but to Peter it suggested further betrayal, a further weakening between them. Slater began to sneer but the teacher intervened, suddenly positive and purposeful, feeling that at last his hard treatment might lead to improvement.

'Now, lad, we'll give you a chance. Who would like to protect the chair from Keeping? I won't do it myself.'

A great shout of volunteers rose. Peter and Alan remained silent.

'Townsend! You do it. You know the rules and Keeping knows you're not as fast as Wright and the others.' The skin on Peter's cheekbones pinked slightly but the teacher was busy tracing an imaginary line round the chair with the toe of his foot. 'Once Keeping has passed that line, you can try to catch him. Ready, Keeping?'

Peter took up his position by the chair. Keeping seemed far away at the end of a long tunnel, and he was shaking his head slowly not so much to indicate his lack of readiness but to show his dismay.

Mr Graham turned to Peter. 'I thought you said he wanted to try again.' The teacher's voice came to Peter from far away as well, hardly piercing the tunnel walls between himself and Keeping. Mr Graham swung away impatiently.

'You, Slater, stand behind Keeping. I shall shout for him to run. He has a good chance of touching the chair with Townsend there, but here's another line.' Once again he traced a line with his plimsoll. 'If he hasn't crossed that line in two seconds, you can try to catch him, Slater – one boot up the backside only, if you please.'

Slater smirked, looking round at Smith, his main supporter, and winking. He was a good runner – long legs, long body for his age.

His normally pale face turned a little whiter in anticipation and he grinned at Keeping as he strolled past to take up his position in the rear. He stood idly swinging his right foot as if on a widening pendulum ever closer to Keeping's rear.

'It'll be best for you to make a run for it, Keeping,' said the teacher, his voice suddenly much more gentle. 'Townsend I'm sure will help you out. He is by way of being a friend of yours – birds of a feather, in a way.'

Mr Graham looked at Peter, smiling at him, hinting that Keeping should be given an easy ride and Peter, far away in the tunnel of the chase, nodded. He would let Keeping through, he thought, and treat it as a joke; pretend to slip and flip Keeping so it looked all right to the boys. He looked back down the ten yards and he could see his victim as clearly as if a spotlight had been turned on him. There was a darker presence behind him, Peter was filled with a sense of purpose.

'On your marks. Set. Go!' shouted Mr Graham and Keeping shuffled a couple of steps down the tunnel. Peter saw the dark shape leap into action from behind. There was a fearsome roaring in his ears and a great inexplicable fear as if a black door had swung open and a storm was trying to pluck him out into the void. Slater kicked Keeping and he howled, clutched himself and was forced onward down the track towards Peter, whose hand was raised either to hit or ward off a blow. Keeping slipped on the polished floor and Slater, forgetting instructions, kicked again. Keeping yelped, turned his head as if to complain and Peter's hand met his jaw as he swivelled. Keeping, off balance, spun and crashed to the floor as Slater kicked again.

An accident? It all happened so quickly that it was impossible to tell, but Peter seemed to see the frightening speed of the event in slow motion even as it happened. When his blow landed, or rather when Keeping ran into his hand, he saw the whole terrible fulcrum of accident and purpose.

Keeping lay huddled on the hard floor, still and silent. One moment he was looming like a threatening shroud towards Peter, the next he was melting into the floor, small, featureless and defeated. Mr Graham leaned over him and the boys stood dumb and apart, no longer united. The teacher peered round. 'Johnson, Peach! Fetch Matron, quickly! Smith – some water. The rest of you changed, for lunch. Hurry!'

The boys left the gym, all except Peter, who remained, his heart gradually returning to its normal beat and the blackness receding from the shape of the boy on the ground. He had done as his father would have, and the tormentor would no longer torment him. He waited for the tightness in his brain to loosen as it always had before, but it didn't. It seemed to creep over his eyes, his nose and mouth as if his senses had to be stifled, but everything shone in startling clarity before him.

'And you, Townsend. Hurry up!'

'Is he dead sir?' Peter asked.

'Of course not. Winded, that's all. A small accident.'

Peter walked out. The man was lying. He *was* dead. Keeping was dead. Peter felt tremendous power running through him and tremendous revulsion. Keeping was dead – he had to keep repeating it – and he had killed him. The narrow changing room was silent, the boys shifting into their uniforms as if guilt had robbed them of speech. Peter sat on a side bench, alone, and nobody looked at him. He inspected the palm of his right hand, holding it like a separate part, a tool beyond his power to control, but for a moment just a hand. The last thing that he had touched had been a dead boy and Peter had known what was to happen. Death came with the blackness and the storm. He had seen his power in the averted eyes and in the pain of creatures and in the suspicion of his friend. Keeping hadn't had that power so he was dead. Alan would be his friend again because friendship stems from power. He had inherited it from his father and his father would respect him for it.

# CHAPTER
# EIGHTEEN

In bed that night the moon was Keeping's face and it gazed accusingly through the windows. The sheets were cold and unforgiving despite hot weather outside and, for once, there was silence with the dousing of the lights. Peter knew he had been lying in this metal-rimmed bed with these thoughts and this same knowledge inside him throughout his life. When the school clock cracked its long midnight chimes, it was the tolling of years. Slowly and desperately Peter tried to push away Keeping's death into another existence beyond himself in which there was no responsibility, no duty. It was an accident. That word passed like a sibilant reassurance through the boy's lips as if by saying so, it might be so. Why then had Alan flinched away from him at break and run by himself towards the music room, his golden hair like a halo round him? Why had the other boys stayed silent, even ignoring Slater's attempts to bluster about 'one of those things'? Everyone was saying 'accident' but Alan's blue eyes were clouded and troubled. He had slipped into his bed with his back to Peter and his mumbled 'good night' seemed perfunctory, words of duty not of love.

The deep breathing all round Peter measured further long time and still his eyes would not close. Time after time, minute after minute, the sequence of kick, slip and hit ran through his head and his brain said it was another boy, another place and another time, but Keeping's moon-face repeated that it was Peter and Peter knew it, could not regret it and sent up a prayer to his father that he would now be recognized. No recognition came, but his mother's face loomed over his other shoulder when he twisted away from the moon and it was bruised with the shadows on his pillow and damp with grief.

Now his bed was hot, crumpled, uncomfortable, and he moved restlessly to escape, but the tightly turned sheets held him and he found himself looking more and more at Alan's back, holding out against him.

Peter crawled out of bed and tiptoed round to Alan, to where the

163

moon shone upon the precious friend. Peter crouched and his shadow fell across Alan's face, but his friend's eyes were already open. Peter stared solemnly and ached to touch him, ached to be held by someone who understood his unhappiness.

'It was an accident,' he whispered. 'I didn't mean to hurt him.' Alan tried a shaky smile.

'I know,' he said as if he didn't know anything at all. 'You seemed to hit him though.'

'He ran into my hand,' Peter pleaded and put his hand towards Alan as if to show how gentle he could be and the hand's shadow crossed Alan's face so he brought it down just beside his face and touched a cheek as if by accident, but Alan moved a bare inch away. Peter withdrew. He brought his face closer to Alan's so that his voice would carry.

'I'd never hurt you, Alan. You are my friend,' he said, and tears began to well but because the moon was behind Peter and Alan was afraid, they were unnoticed. Alan lay still while Peter put his hand upon his curls and rubbed his palm across his head.

'Go back to bed,' Alan managed to say. 'It'll be all right in the morning.'

Peter rocked slowly back on his heels, pulled himself up and padded silently away.

Next day Old Salmon called a whole school assembly. In whispering funereal gowns the teachers processed to their seats and the boys stood, their eyes shivering along the serious line of adults. Mr Graham, normally relegated to the back row, sat on one side of the Head's chair and matron occupied the other. Mr Grant waited until the Head had taken his seat and then whisked away from his position by the founder's portrait and took his seat. Old Salmon stood up and the silent boys became as still as Medusa stone.

'Boys, boys,' Old Salmon shook his pepper-pot head in time with the words, spicing them with sorrow and deep disappointment. 'As you may know, a terrible accident happened in class yesterday, a total accident and a total misfortune. A young boy in the first year, Keeping, slipped as he attempted an exercise in gym and was caught by another boy's swinging hand.' There was a space where Keeping normally stood and Peter wondered whether he would now be arraigned and dismissed from the school, as he was only free and not fee. 'I have to tell you,' continued Old Salmon in his measured delivery, 'that the poor boy must have broken his neck – perhaps there was a weakness of which we were not aware.'

A short silence suggested that Keeping should have told the school that his neck was weak and that any other boys with similarly weak necks would do well to notify matron of the fact or else for ever hold their peace, as Keeping was now holding his.

'But what is clear,' the Head resumed with more confidence, 'is that this was a terrible once and once only accident born of a boy's lack of athleticism, another's high spirits and the teacher's genuine desire to help. We have, of course, notified the authorities and you may have to answer a few questions. We have told the poor parents of the boy and we shall write to all parents about this horrifying affair so that they may be reassured of our high standards of care and compassion. Poor Jolian' – Keeping's first name only used with his decease – 'poor Jolian was, unfortunately, not the most lithe or active of our pupils, and efforts to help him master some skills were only slowly reaching fruition. We must all try to help each other and avoid accidents through careless or thoughtless behaviour. I must ask all of you to say nothing of this episode except to the police. It is at times like these that Greelham's must show that proper sense of loyalty and common decency of which we are rightly proud.'

During the last few weeks of term, headlines appeared in local newspapers and two boys, including Slater, left the school because, as Slater explained, his parents weren't happy about him and the accident was the last straw. When his trunk was carried downstairs on the last day of term he followed behind it, face paler than ever, set and arrogant, but because all of the boys were excitedly gathering their belongings his departure went unremarked except by his own particular gang. The other boy was transferred to a crammer in King's Lynn with cheaper fees and, although a few staff wondered whether his departure would herald further defections, the long-standing reputation of Greelham School remained untarnished.

The boys themselves did most to keep the school's good name abroad. A sort of collective guilt swept them. There were few who had not tormented Keeping from time to time, and a whip-round among them provided a magnificent wreath for the funeral in Greelham Chapel. Mr Grant gathered the choir and trained them for a special commemorative service of re-dedication. Alan sang a solo part and Mrs Keeping cried. He was so beautiful and his voice was so pure.

Mr Keeping, a large florid-faced man, was at first bemused by the many letters arriving penned in schoolboy handwriting, but eventually he was convinced that there must have been more to his son than he had ever observed and he too began to cherish the memory of a son about to discard his slough of sluggard fatness and become a popular, witty and sociable member of an elite society. He arranged an interview with the Head and endowed the school with the Keeping Room, an area off the main hall for weight-lifting, table tennis and set-apparatus gymnastics. His chain of stores was flourishing and, with tax adjustments, the room cost him nothing financially and rewarded him greatly in the boardroom.

Peter left for his summer holiday with no such consolation of memory. He knew now as he had known before that the dead have more power than the living. When he and Alan went to the music room for their daily practice, Keeping went too. He never used to be there, but now he was, deflecting Alan's smile and twisting the violin in Peter's hands so that Mr Grant would stop them and check that the bow was properly resined. From the beginning Peter had found that he could play with Alan, fit his time to the piano, almost sense when Alan's fingers would stutter slightly over a difficult chord and he would need to adjust accordingly, but now Keeping kept their timing out and their duets became competitive solos. Peter wanted to play in time, lose himself in the music of friendship, but it was Alan's playing that became unpredictable. Mr Grant did not see this and would upbraid Peter for not listening to his partner, for losing the beat, for not counting the bars and coming in too late or too soon. Keeping jeered at him as others had jeered at Keeping whenever he tried to talk with Alan or suggested they go into the village.

For the first time he was pleased to be leaving Greelham School for Barham. What had appeared to be an escape was another trap.

# CHAPTER
# NINETEEN

The train into Norwich from Thurriton had been slow and they had to wait an hour for the bus to chug along the lanes to Greelham. Joan had had time to dwell on the past few months and her move to Pond Street to be close enough to the manse to nurse the ailing minister. She knew that people looked suspiciously at her. Now that Arnold's chest seemed so bad and his throat so painful, she, as housekeeper, wanted to do the best she could for him and she tried to ignore the backbites of a small village.

She glanced at her coat. At least Peter would not feel diminished by her appearance as she collected him for the summer. Arnold had insisted that she buy a new light coat and summer outfit, right down to the trim fawn leather bag and matching shoes. Claire, perched next to her on the bus, was also clad in finery, a pretty little thing with a strawberry pink dress and ribboned bunches. Arnold took as much pleasure in dressing her as a little girl with a favourite doll. In fact, Joan thought with a stab of discomfort as the bus lurched round a corner, all three of us are now his little playthings. He had so much wanted to drive over to Greelham School to fetch Peter, but he was confined to a chair by the front bedroom window.

Joan fumbled in her handbag and brought out Peter's last letter to her. He never wrote a lot and had not acknowledged her change of address. But his writing was legible and less like the meanderings of an alcoholic spider than before, and it said he looked forward to seeing her at the end of term. Perhaps Mr Eldon would again be proved right. Time away can show the virtues of home more clearly than preaching about them.

The bus jolted over Dinsbury level crossing. It was very stuffy in the bus. The narrow window along the side was open but it let in thick heavy air so that Joan opened the buttons on her coat and shifted a little on the seat, hoping the stickiness would not crease her dress. Her appointment with Mr Grant was for three o'clock. They should be away from the school by three thirty but would certainly take a taxi back to Norwich and another from Thurriton to home.

Arnold had wanted her to hire a car, but she would not countenance such expense.

Claire sat back in the seat folding and refolding the bus tickets until they became pellets of softened card which she then chewed at with tiny sharp teeth.

'Whatever will the inspector say if he wants to see the tickets?'

Claire ignored her mother. She had wanted to play with her friend Ann Luffman. She liked it there at the village shop because it was busy and she could help count out sweets for customers or carry in the boxes. She didn't like being at the manse because Mr Eldon was wheezing and there were hushed voices from old people and tiptoes on the stairs.

'It will make a nice change for you, dear,' Mum had said, wheedling.

Claire looked out of the window at flat fields and blue sky. She didn't like being dressed in her pretties, as Mr Eldon called them, and wanted to be off in her grubby pinafore and apron, able to tumble or play hopscotch in the village store backyard. She yawned, her eyes watering with the stretch.

'And don't you go doing that at Peter's school! Whatever would they think of you!'

Peter was on the lookout for them. He had forgotten that Mr Eldon was not coming and so at first he did not realize that the two figures approaching up the drive were his mother and sister. Alan was sitting on his trunk with him because his parents were due immediately after Peter's, his surname being next in the alphabet.

Peter jumped to his feet.

'Is that them?' asked Alan, trying to find warmth for this last day of term.

Peter opened up the wide swing door, beating Foster to his post. That was the game they all played on summer break-up and Foster pretended to be displeased. In they came and Peter suddenly froze. He'd seen how Smithy had thrown his arms around his mother, almost knocking off her feathery hat. He'd heard from Alan how his father always put his hand on his shoulder and patted him, saying, 'How are you, old chap?' a couple of times. He did not know how he would greet his mother. She was so smart. For that he was pleased. But she had sent him away and blamed his father for his unhappiness. His head went down and he waited silently.

'Mr Eldon said he is sorry he couldn't come. That drive is longer than you think when you're walking, isn't it?'

Peter looked over at Alan, who was still sitting on his trunk, pretending not to notice how loud his mother was.

'I hope they've been looking after you. You still need fattening up, I'd say.'

He felt his shoulders being held and then a perfumed finger brought up his chin. He'd expected the smell of carbolic or cows and wasn't sure he liked the heady scent. Her voice was the same, but all else about her seemed totally different.

'Hello,' he said and turned towards Alan. He had to introduce him even though he'd think his mother was coarse. He needed to show her that he had a friend. 'This is Alan, Mum. I mentioned him in my letters.'

Then Alan stood and smiled, running his hand through his hair and shaking hands in such a proper way that Joan was impressed and Claire, who had been hiding, came out and said,

'My name is Claire. I'm his sister.'

Then Alan shook her hand too and she blushed as pink as her dress.

'You have to go and see Mr Grant,' said Peter. 'He'll give you my report.'

'Do you come too?'

'No. It's all top secret,' explained Alan. 'And it will give Peter a chance to run away.'

How Peter envied Alan's relaxed and confident words. It was as if there had been no tragedy during the term, no suggestion of the fear that had riddled their relationship, but Peter could hear that Alan's voice was fragile in its smiling friendliness. Mum was escorted away by Foster. Claire sat next to Alan on his trunk, chattered to him about the village shop and asked him all about himself while Peter watched for the Norwich taxi.

'Alan seems a very nice boy, and your teachers are pleased with your progress on the whole. You've done very well for yourself, young man.'

The taxi rolled quickly along the lanes that the bus had crawled through and spurts of a fresh breeze slipped through the windows, brushing Claire's hair and flicking Mum's straw hat so that a cherry bobbled.

'Is that the report?' asked Peter, pointing to the long envelope in Mum's hand. 'Can I see?'

'Well, it has been stuck down and I think perhaps it would be nice to open it at the manse. If it hadn't been for Mr Eldon you wouldn't be at the school, would you?'

'But it's my report,' said Peter, his fingers clutching at the leather edge of his seat.

'Of course it is, but you can't read it while we're driving along and I thought you could open it with Mr Eldon there to see. It would be a treat for both of you.'

Slowly Peter controlled his anger. She had forgotten that it was he who made decisions now. The boys in the class were controlled by him since Slater had departed; they were scared of him. His mother had to realize that he had grown up. Mr Eldon did not own his mind or his future. He looked down at his knees. Next summer he would be old enough to wear long trousers. Next term he would be in the second year of Greelham School. He should be allowed to see his report when he wished and not at the whim of this strange smart woman with a voice that echoed with his own unhappiness.

'I w-w-want to s-see it n-now,' he said, turning his eyes towards his mother's ear and leaning across towards the envelope. 'It's nothing to d-do with him.'

Joan turned to look at her son, surprised and sorry that his voice had caught his stammer again. His fierce eyes burned and his lip was livid. On the journey to Greelham she had decided to treat him firmly but kindly, not allow him to play games with her, or use his speech as a weapon, but now she found herself relinquishing the envelope. Peter slid it carefully into his inside jacket pocket.

'Aren't you going to open it, then? That's what you wanted, wasn't it?'

'It can wait now,' Peter replied.

He was prepared to do his little duty then, present the envelope to the shrunken white-haired man propped in his chair and listen to the eulogy that flowed from the minister's strained body, watching the flickers of smiles and the poise of fingers sketching their patterns. Mr Eldon could not speak long and teetered along the threat of a coughing spasm, so Peter felt no challenge and could nod and leave him when he wished. He tried to understand why this was so, why his mother no longer hurt him with her demands, why his sister seemed so insignificant to him and why the minister was to be ignored. He decided it was because Keeping had made him invulnerable to their angers and persuasions.

He spent the holiday wandering the fields and visiting the dyke and quarry. These too seemed tame and Nipper, his terrier, was fat and irritable. It was just spoiling and lack of exercise, though, and as the summer passed the terrier regained his trim and ran boisterous circles round Peter's feet. He received a postcard from Alan in the South of France which said he wished Peter were there and, for a moment, Peter's heart twisted with joy before he realized that Alan was only observing the rites. He would have sent cards to all the boys. The feeling of fear and power flashed through him then, but he pushed it away easily by taking Nipper on a long walk, leading him through brambles that caught in his undercoat and held him there until he mewed for escape. It made Peter happy to release the pup and feel his gratitude bubble through his sides and his tail flap with pleasure. Nipper held no grudges, didn't know that it was Peter's whim that made the brambles catch his fur.

He didn't like living at Pond Street and the manse, sleeping at the one and eating at the other. Often he would take the path up to his farm, for his mother told him he could have it when he was old enough and silly enough to want it. The buildings were all dead, faces closed against the world and the little signs of a previous living were fading. He found the rusted spokes of a pushchair wheel behind the old sink which used to be planted with herbs and had now run wild. The scratch marks he had made with a chisel down the back planking of the outhouse when he had pretended to be Floater were scarcely visible, just little darker lines of greeny brown. When he peered through the windows on the ground floor, all he could see was dusty floors and creamy sheeting. It all appeared smaller than he'd remembered it. It did not rule his mind, nor did it conjure up the giant shadow that had haunted him to Greelham. It was waiting and was patient in its waiting, but Peter could leave it behind and walk the high path by the quarry without a qualm.

When his mother told him that the minister would have to stay in bed and would Peter mind helping a little more about the house, he could just ignore her, nodding gently and walking off as he wished. Why did she think that it was part of his duty to be a nurse?

'He's becoming an insufferable little monster,' she said to Arnold, popping extra pillows behind his wasted frame. 'He turns his nose up at whatever I give him for food and the way he treats Claire makes my blood boil. It's as if he doesn't care about us.'

The little man no longer interrupted with tendentious advice. Now he managed just to think that the boy felt great pressures on him from the school and the only time these could be shown was at home. It was understandable, but regrettable. He would grow out of it. Arnold remembered going through a similar stage with his father and mother. Rebellion was a natural state for the adolescent. But he did not express these thoughts. He was becoming almost used to a silent dialogue in his head, holding his body in a corset of stillness lest the coughing catch at him again.

In September, when Peter returned to Greelham, Mr Graham did not and a new teacher, a Mr Firmani, replaced him. He was a Brylcreemed, dark-haired, India-rubber ball of a man, once a schoolboy wing three-quarter for the Southern Public Schools and a weight-lifter of some repute. His Italian background had prevented any further achievements. The Second World War placed him in internment, although his mother was English and his father had lived most of his life in England. Now he was still fit, still outwardly deferential to authority, but he found it hard to forgive a British establishment that had robbed him of his position. This anger occasionally showed in outbursts of eloquent support for international socialism.

If Old Salmon had known this, Mr Firmani would not have been appointed to the school, but the gap left by Mr Graham's departure had not been easy to fill. Fit young men with a public school background were fairly rare and Mr Firmani had impressed at his interview. He had good qualifications in sport, although he omitted to mention that he had transferred his allegiance from rugby union to soccer. He had no trace of an accent.

The boys liked Mr Firmani, but they knew he would not stay for long. He was a creature of the moment, but moments can be long in an education and Peter responded to his idiosyncratic methods. It became the craze to mimic a mock Italian accent and bounce around the corridors like a basketball.

'You watcha me then and you learna it good,' called Alan, bounding like a golden child god from side to side of the first-floor corridor, his hair bleached by Mediterranean sun and his eyes the blue of the sea. Alan and Peter sat together still. They would never not be friends, thought Peter, hopping ridiculously after Alan and shouting, 'You joina the firma and you joina Firmani.' They were second-year boys. They could pick on first years and call them free or fee; they could tell them to hand over their milk; they could use the buttery after the third years. They had a table-tennis table and a darts board. They could burst into their classroom and Mr Firmani would not sigh and raise his eyebrows as if they hurt his eyeballs, but he would point with his finger at their desks and chant:

'You're late! You're late! You're late for an important date! But now you're here, let's raise a cheer with a bottle of beer – you're late!'

Yes, Mr Firmani was mad. He would never last in Greelham School. His classes were noisy, his attitude casual and he exuded electricity.

'Zip! Zap! Zither, children – listen to the teacher – he tella you alla you needa to knowa. You!' A dramatic pause and an outflung hand, 'ze boy wiz ze mouldy hair, what zings frightens peoples?' Suddenly he changed his patter. 'A serious question – what frightens people? A list please.' Then just as suddenly back into fraudulent Italian. 'Eeez eet ze leetle creepy crawlies in ze corners – ze trap-door spiders, ze tarantulas? Come on, haystack-head – you with the pale blue eyes and sneer – don't look at handsome there – it is words I want, words, words, words and more of these strange magical words.'

Peter, caught up in the whirl, stared transfixed at the jerky bouncing of the man, the quick deft flick of the fingers at each emphasis. The list proceeded in a hackneyed way.

'Dark alleys.'

'Old Sampson.' Giggles.

'Matron hearing you cough.'

More giggles, until slowly more thoughtful offerings occurred until Peter's turn returned and he said without thinking, 'Death.'

Then he swallowed, blushed, doodled in the margin of his exercise-book because Mr Firmani didn't care if you drew pictures over the cover. Then he became aware of the teacher's gaze.

'This death, Townsend, whose death? Which death? Your death?'

Peter dumbly shook his head and the other boys told the story of Keeping to the new teacher, but he cut it short with a story of his own, a story of heroism and also of betrayal.

'The flying man's name was Giuseppe Algontino, a friend of mine at school and now at war.'

'But you said you didn't fight in the war,' said Johnson. He liked everything to be absolutely clear and factual.

'This is a true story. All the best stories are true and all are lies that smell of truth,' replied the teacher. 'I now continue. Friends at school and war. The two are similar, we understand. All is simplified in both cases, clear enemies, clear propaganda, clear hatred, clear loves.' A few boys began to cough or fidget. Mr Firmani suddenly shouted, 'That the words I use are beyond your present understanding does not matter. You must listen to this story I tell.'

Silence fell.

'Giuseppe, then – he was one of eleven children, living in Naples, poor, poorer than you know of poverty – slum poor – shoes no, socks no, clothes no . . .'

'Balls no,' whispered Osman, always ready to smirk at furtive possibilities.

'But when the war came, he, Giuseppe, was suddenly no longer naked. He had a focus in his life, an aim. He was no longer one of millions of starving slaves. Mussolini gave him that focus, that aim. "Here you are, Giuseppe," said Mussolini, "have a gun turret in this aeroplane and look through these two sight-finders. Here is your aim." It was all simple. The dusty streets of Naples, the flies and rats, the stench to which he had belonged, disappeared and a target appeared. For three years Giuseppe sat in the bottom of a plane and viewed a toy world from which fireworks blossomed as he pressed a black grip and he was happier than he'd ever been before, serving Mussolini, his country, himself, with cause and effect, aim and fire. He spoke of justice, law, order, obedience and patriotism and prayed to the Virgin Mary for fortitude in danger and service to his fellow man because he was a good Catholic and an Italian.

'One night,' and here Mr Firmani looked at his class as if to gather all the threads of life into a tangible knot, 'one night, Giuseppe went on a reconnaissance flight – a doddle, a piece of cake, or so he was told. He snoozed at his post as the giant plane rumbled along the runway, still thinking of the drinks he had given and taken the previous night when Alonzo had not come back. And, as the black giant shook off its weight and flew juddering on, he gently hummed and slept a little, just as some of you poor sewer rats are doing now. Suddenly, as Giuseppe was thinking of Teresa, a girl he had met in Verona ten months before, an icy wind blasted him against his straps and seat and a howl savaged his eardrums. Wildly he looked out and saw the familiar pincushions of light and then the great exploding party balloons around him. He did not know it but he screamed into the intercom, but there was no one to hear him, no one above him, except perhaps God. The first black hand had hit the pilot and co-pilot and they had died. Giuseppe wriggled through the tunnel leading to his parachute pack and prepared to jump, when he heard a noise so slight that given the wind and the rushing of bombs and tracers, it was perhaps a miracle he heard it. The intercom was breathing the one word "Help!" and it maintained a low breathing. What would you have done? I? I would have leaped from the burning plane, leaving the help behind me, but no, Giuseppe pushed his way to the central hold and there, amazingly, huddled in a corner, against a fuselage strut, was a figure, lolling and hugging himself as if suffocating a wound with love and pain. Giuseppe lurched forward as the plane tilted and screamed. He took his parachute, strapped it to the injured man's back, clasped him firmly round the waist and fell into the black void. A sudden jerk almost dragged the man from his wrists, but his grip held. It seemed only a moment later that he was tumbling shaken to the earth. He stood up, unhurt, and turned to his companion, but there was nobody there – no body, no sign – nothing except the parachute lying extended but unconnected to any human. Giuseppe was bewildered, but there were pressing needs for him to look after himself, for he was now in enemy territory.'

The boys stared blankly, but Peter Townsend sat fascinated by this catalogue. He knew about the black void and the disappearance, the storm and the nightmare, but how had Mr Firmani seen into his mind? The teacher refused to explain further or to answer how he'd known about the intercom if he hadn't been there, turning the story into a sum instead.

'The question is, therefore, if two bodies fall at the rate of 50 feet per second from a plane travelling at 150 miles per hour into a field swept by fifteen accurate arc lights, how often will one of the bodies disappear and how much guilt does the survivor feel? Giuseppe could not answer the question. He is now a monk. He neglected Mussolini and needed a more sanctified dictator.'

Where were the bodies? Two people were dead and now their bodies had disappeared – he could hardly recreate them in his mind – and he remained. Perhaps the creatures had never existed; he had never had a father nor seen a Keeping. They had been strange ghosts of life that reached their end and now called on Peter to join them in acknowledging the futility of this world. Where was the rational explanation of his father crying for a sacrifice to release him? Where was the rational explanation of the thunder in his ears before Keeping's death? Why did both make him tremble and feel full of power? His father had been a soldier. Had he disappeared like the man in the plane? No, whenever he thought of his father's death that black void opened up inside his head and his mind shrank away into a closed vise, squeezing oblivion into his brain so that he even found it hard to think of Alan and tell himself that it was all a story, as Mr Firmani had said.

# CHAPTER TWENTY

The days merged into a hazy autumn mist in which Alan darted, jumped and played with unselfconscious freedom. He did not seem to mind Peter's company and a sort of feverish joy transfigured the lame boy so that he kept up as best he could, joining in when Alan took part in the chasing games in the yard, helping to make a guy from old sacking stolen from the back of the pavilion and trying to accept the company of other boys. Peter revelled in the influence he achieved in the class. No longer did Peach look askance at his lip and no longer did Smith try to jeer. Peter played the part of joy and almost convinced himself that he was healed.

Only on Sundays did the old loneliness return. Mr Grant took the choir to St Wilfred's in the village where he acted as organist. A crocodile of about fifteen would follow the white head out of the gates. The other boys called the acolytes 'the Saints' and pretended they didn't mind being left behind, but Peter used to watch Alan leave at the head of the line, his fair hair bobbing in early morning sunshine, his face wheeling round and a grin splitting his features like light reflected in glass, and his legs growing even longer and more gangling. Peter felt proud of Alan, almost as if he had helped him become one of Mr Grant's cream performers, but he wished he could be there beyond the school grounds, watching him sing.

The Thursday evening choir practice continued but Peter discovered a way of attending that occasion in the hall. There was a small niche beside the organ in the loft where he could hide. Alan didn't know he was there. He somehow sensed now that he should not appear too possessive of his friend and tried to hide his love for him, but the pleasure of listening unnoticed heightened Peter's joy.

One evening in November Peter slipped into the organ loft before choir and peered cautiously through the railings into the darkness of the hall. It was a large room with an imposingly high ceiling, stained wood panelling, a rostrum of wood and a mock Tudor gallery into which the Victorian organ had been built. Very little light gleamed through the high windows and the shadows smelled of polish. Just a few yards away the school was teeming with life, the dark corridors banging and rattling, the classrooms echoing with high shrieking excitement, but inside the hall there was a hallowed stillness, the secretive aura of a special place. Peter could hear the choirboys gathering outside, waiting for Mr Grant to arrive and flick on the lights, to bustle life into the darkness. Peter imagined him striding along the narrow passage from the music room, mounting the stone steps three at a time, a bundle of brown envelopes under his arm. The door creaked open and Peter shrank into cover as the choir tumbled into the hall.

'You are not a herd of stampeding buffalo. Stand still and wait until a little light is thrown on our proceedings.'

Peter pushed his back into the gap between organ and wall and the lights clicked on. Slowly he inched his head round the side. The lamps hung down from the ceiling below the level of the gallery. Only a small glow rose to touch the ceiling with a faint mist. Peter was above the light, safe in the gloom.

There was Alan folding himself down on the rostrum, his knees like silver darts and his socks rolled down. The boys looked up from their squatting position towards Mr Grant, who balanced on the edge of the rostrum. Peter could almost imagine that they were looking up at him.

'This is for the benefit of new choir members and a reminder to old ones. As you know, we practise in the hall because singing needs space and because performances are rarely carried out inside cupboards. We practise here with just your voices so that you become confident that the audience have come to hear you sing and not the accompaniment. There comes a time, however, when you need to feel the performance as it will be.'

Mr Grant paused and looked along the lines of serious faces. Peter knew that look. It seemed to rivet you to the floor with chips of blue ice, but Alan said that Mr Grant was soft when you knew him better.

'Now, today, we will perform the twenty-third psalm arrangement that we have been practising. You will be standing in your precise positions. You will concentrate with every inch of your beings and you will sing like angels.'

There was a scurrying, a squeaking of shoes on the floor and a muttering about boys who had grown and had to stand at the back. Mr Grant was striding down the hall, and only had to look up to see Peter's white face by the railings. The boy slipped back behind the organ but the footsteps didn't pause underneath the gallery. The door was opened and then feet clipped up the stairs and entered the loft. There was a click and Peter pushed himself urgently into the small triangle of shadow left now that the light was on. He could not escape being seen, he thought, but a large bulk settled on the organ seat and then there was a flapping of papers and more clickings. The organ seemed to sigh and move behind his shoulders like a sleeping giant that it would be unwise to wake.

'Wilkins!' came a booming voice above him and Peter shuddered. He could stretch out a hand and he would be able to touch Mr Grant's left foot as it danced over the pedals. 'I can see you, boy!' There was a dark thread hanging down from the teacher's turn-up and his socks were green. 'Picking your own nose is reprehensible enough, but attempting to transfer the proceeds to Collins's sleeve is repellent! Don't look round and giggle, little flowers. I do not jest. Wilkins! Turn and face the founder. Yes, now the silence falls and the listening comes. If you can count, if you can speak, if you can laugh and if you can cry, you can sing, and now is the time, my little flowers.'

Peter shivered with the illicit pleasure of listening to that great harsh voice rolling round the hall, part of the giant's clearing of pipes, the preparation. He felt no temptation to look now, his fear of being seen diminished and he leaned his forehead to the cold wood and listened. He could count; he could cry, though rarely, but speech and laughter were imperfect. He could never sing.

The piece was a beautifully clear expression of Mr Grant's gifts as a composer for young voices – precise articulation, a flowing and powerful pattern of sound and supremely pure high notes given in simple silence. He was a master of contrast, and the organ which created it was only occasionally used: in introduction, to deepen the 'valley of the shadow of death', to warm 'goodness and mercy' and to give body to the 'Glory be to the father'. Otherwise the choir maintained almost unaccompanied singing. Mr Grant's ambition was to win the crown of best choir and best composition for unbroken voices.

Above the creaking of the pedals the slow, mellow, poised notes hummed from the organ, moulding the first phrase of the psalm and leaving it to the boys. Their ethereal voices pierced Peter's brain, sent light into his heart and by degrees turned his eyes to water. He knew each phrase, each harmony and each line, having sat patiently through each painstaking rehearsal, and now he felt part of both the music and the process of performance.

Slowly silence stole into the hall with a peace distilled from music. Mr Grant enjoyed the moment. There was something infinitely satisfying in the ordered framework and security of making music. It was far better, far more rewarding than everyday life, but he had to return to his choir, to the mere boys who could transmute dross words and scrabbling tadpoles of notes into glorious leaping frogs. The boys were already beginning to rustle with an impatient desire for praise.

'Splendid! Splendid!' the teacher intoned. 'A little more volume from the altos at the repeat of "fear no evil". Make it strong and assured. Just that phrase then. One, two, three . . .'

The altos sang dutifully.

'Now, top trebles, let's see what you can do with that "Shall follow me all the days of my life." Follow me . . .' The descant line followed and Mr Grant expressed satisfaction.

'Final performance for today then. Wilkins, rejoin the altos. They need your voice if not your manners.'

Once again Psalm 23 was performed and Peter traced his friend Alan's voice through the treble line. This time the teacher allowed no pause at the end, and Peter desperately wanted the music to continue flowing through his brain.

'Enough for today. Wait there.'

The organ settled into slumber; the gallery was empty. Peter heard Mr Grant remind the choir of rehearsal times and then the roar of departure dinned round the hall. Lingering pipe smoke alone told Peter that Mr Grant had been just a yard away from him.

Peter squeezed stiffly out of his corner. His head was still buzzing with the music and he did not notice Mr Grant and Wilkins in the hall until he reached the gallery rail. Then he froze, unable to duck or retreat to the door.

'Well, Wilkins, what have you to say, if anything, for your disgusting behaviour?'

Wilkins, a dark-haired and normally confident boy, shook his head, looking at the floor.

'Have you ever had to face the founder before, Wilkins?'

Another shake of the head. Wilkins may have stolen his grand-mother's false teeth or threatened to murder his younger brother in the past, but to his mind there was nothing so serious as this breach of discipline and then his rude gesture among the Saints. It would mean automatic exclusion from the choir and other school and house activities; he would have to sit with the youngest boys in the school, act as their monitor and make their beds for a week. During that time he would be ridiculed by pupils and teachers alike. Few children would be able to cope with such humiliation and, to do Mr Grant justice, he rarely resorted to this punishment. But Wilkins had been trying insubordination recently, muttering behind his hand about teachers who had favourite boys. Mr Grant felt that his behaviour was more than innocent fun.

Peter listened, horrified. If Wilkins were in such trouble for picking his nose, how much worse would be the punishment for a boy spying on the choir from out of bounds? Mr Grant moved away from Wilkins, circling him like a vulture. He looked towards Heaven to declaim and denounce further just as Peter tried to skip back out of sight.

'Who is there? You boy! Come here this instant!'

Wilkins started forward and then realized the teacher was talking to another boy. He looked up from beneath his black thatch. Townsend?

Peter limped rapidly down the squeaking stairs and into the hall. Even with his raised shoe, stairs were clumsy walking and now his feet seemed too large for the treads, fear making him stumble and scuff the floor. He stopped again just inside the door and had to be summoned on by Mr Grant.

'What were you doing up there, Townsend? You know that the gallery is out of bounds.'

Peter looked at the floor, his mouth working but without speech to explain that he had come to watch over Alan and to hear the music.

'How long have you been there?' Mr Grant peered fiercely at the strange boy in front of him.

'All the t-t-time sir,' muttered Townsend.

'All what time?'

'P-p-practice t-t-time . . . I w-was l-listening, sir.'

'Did you have teacher permission? Did Mr Firmani give you that permission?'

'N-n-no sir,' replied Peter, misery invading his body. He would be thrown out of school for this; he would lose his friendship with Alan and his security. The trap was closing again.

The teacher looked at the small boy quivering in front of him. He had never seen such abject submission. Wilkins, in comparison, appeared jaunty. The boy was unusual, had an unusual talent, but Mr Grant could not bring himself to like the lad. It was not just his ugliness, his misshapen features. There was a brooding sullenness about him that made the other boys uneasy. That darkness was, however, entirely subsumed at that moment in a squirming fear, which did nothing to win the teacher's sympathy.

'Wait by the founder while I finish with this boy,' said Mr Grant, gaining time to consider what to do.

'Well Wilkins,' Mr Grant turned abruptly to the other boy. 'That's good to hear, isn't it? You can't be bothered to listen and break the rules and Townsend there breaks rules in order to listen. I

180

somewhat prefer the latter to the former. You, Wilkins, will report to me tomorrow morning after breakfast. I shall give you my decision about your punishment, and whether you will be facing the founder, then. Meanwhile you will write out the full text of the twenty-third psalm and be ready to recite it to me. Now go!'

Peter heard feet scamper across to the side door, felt the air move beside him as the swing door opened and closed, but he did not take his eyes from the portrait above him. How many boys had looked into the eyes of John Greelham and read messages of doom within them? They were distant and yet angry, as if he'd been brought to make this foundation for boys of poor families by some trick of financial need and resented the intrusion. His pale face gleamed above an equally pale ruff, the sort of ruff Alan wore in the choir at the church on Sundays. It was difficult to believe that John Greelham had ever been a boy. There was a censorious bitterness in his mouth that refused the idea of innocence.

Mr Grant looked across at the waiting boy and then glanced at the portrait. He too did not like the picture. Beneath its finery and dark velvet colour lay disappointment and self-hatred turned against the world. Greelham had stood on the edge of court patronage all his life and been disregarded so often that he was reduced to playing large fish in the small pool of Norfolk. All his work in the wool trade did not win him favour and he died a disappointed man. It was fine brushwork, thought Mr Grant, but the artist was too honest to disguise the character of the man. The same pinched narrowness and sense of thwarted power crossed Townsend's face from time to time.

Peter winced as a large hand landed on his thin shoulder and he was turned round to face the pale eyes of Mr Grant. He tried to think about Alan and the way his friend talked to the teacher at music practice, but he could not. He could not believe Alan's confidence in the teacher's essential kindliness.

'You must have been only a yard away from me when I was playing the organ.'

Peter nodded and his hare-lip shone white and then red with embarrassment. He could see the teacher's hitched trouser leg, the flexed ball of white and grey calf above the green sock and the deft, dancing feet. He felt as the man in the story of Godiva felt, who peeped at nakedness and was discovered. Alan, of course, could speak to Mr Grant as he did because Alan was special. That was Alan's power, not his.

'What induced you to hide away up there? If you wished to listen at practices, you only needed to ask.'

Peter could not explain that he did not want Alan to know he was watching, that he feared his desertion if he pestered him. The memory of Keeping's words to Alan was too raw and hurtful to be forgotten, but now for the second time he had hidden and been made unhappy by doing so.

A large dry finger touched his chin and brought his face up so that he had to look at the teacher.

'There is a mystery here,' murmured Mr Grant. 'I shall have to talk to Alan Wright about it. He is a straightforward honest boy.'

Blood flushed up through Peter's face and his cheeks burned so hotly that they scalded his eyes. The teacher nodded slowly, as if he had seen what he wanted to see. 'He is a very beautiful boy,' he whispered. 'We are lucky to have him with us.'

Peter nodded dumbly and the large cool hand patted him gently on his cheek. The teacher's thumb touched his mouth as if to seal it and still the blue eyes held his gaze, trying to dominate him.

'If you wish to act as choir monitor, you may do so, Peter Townsend. You may not be able to sing, but you have musical talent and that should be recognized. You would be responsible for the correct copies of music appearing in the correct places at the correct time. Would that please you?'

Again Peter nodded. The white eyebrows bristled down towards his face and Peter felt the teacher's warm breath.

'Good boy.' The man stood to one side to let Peter walk past and out of the hall. Just before he left the white hand touched his shoulder and then rubbed down the blade. 'Off you go then,' came the teacher's harsh voice and the same hand patted his bottom.

The term seemed to fly by from one music lesson to the next, and the end-of-term concert began to loom and concentrate Peter's mind on perfection. He was now able to play the violin in the first two positions and his initially stilted bowing had suddenly given way to relaxed and sensitive movement that showed the music within him. It was Alan who tended to skip practices, had to run through scales and sequences a few times in the music room afterwards. Peter found himself hanging around waiting for his friend outside the room because Mr Grant said Alan needed to concentrate alone. Peter felt dirty and jealous at the same time as he stood leaning against the stone wall, tapping his heels against the runner.

Then Alan would appear, eyes shining, excited and apparently pleased to be out of the room, charging off down the corridor so that Peter had to run at full speed to keep up with him and Mr Grant's roar behind them, 'Don't run in the corridors!' seemed to hold the same sort of reckless laughter.

182

In the music room itself Mr Grant would stand beside Alan, his hand occasionally reaching over and guiding his pupil's tentative fingers to the right note while his other hand rested on the boy's shoulder. Peter played apart from them, his face transformed with active concentration. If he made an error, Mr Grant would slam the palm of his hand on top of the piano.

'Beautiful people may wander through the Elysian fields without purpose and Alan here will succeed quite naturally, but people like us, ugly by birth or age, must struggle merely to be accepted on this strange earth.' And the teacher would punctuate his remarks with little pats across Peter's cheek and his blue-chip eyes would congeal, but Peter knew that Mr Grant did not mean to hurt him, that he was as soft as Alan had told him. 'Now try to find that B-flat immediately, precisely and with a dying sound.'

On the Sunday morning excursion, Peter accompanied the others as monitor. All he had to do was carry the envelopes of music and hand them out before the boys processed into the choir stalls of the old, huge and beautiful church which had once marked the centre of the country's religious and economic wealth, but which now seemed far more precious to Peter because Alan's voice soared through the high pillars and left its pure notes to hover among the angels. The white gravestones in the yard, the dark inscriptions in the church walls and the nails in the tortured Christ could have no power while Alan sang, leading the choir and congregation into glorious communion with an unseen majesty that banished the dark powers. When he left the church it was as if he had been cleansed of deep sin. His heart leaped with the scampering through the wintry roads and the relief of being free from the discipline that they had to resume before they re-entered the school grounds. Mr Salmon thought that running about was unseemly on Sundays.

In his lessons, Mr Firmani joked and jumped, read *Hamlet* and asked impossible questions that seemed to lead to inevitable answers in Peter's impressionable mind. The stepfather was to blame. It was like any fairy story. How could he hurt Mr Eldon without hurting his mother? Not that Mr Eldon could marry his mother. He was too ill, but he had taken her over and used her for his own ends. The ghost of Hamlet's father spoke with his own father's voice and it was the fear of him that launched him to suspect Mr Eldon of foul practice. Hamlet was sent to England and he to Greelham's. The farm was his Denmark. There were parallels enough for Peter, but the magic of Alan and music, the routine and encouragements of Mr Grant held him in a spell he did not wish to break.

# CHAPTER
# TWENTY-ONE

A week before the Christmas concert, Peter woke up in his pallet bed and pulled himself from the covers. It was very cold in the dormitory and it took a foolhardy courage to face the icy floorboards in the darkness of an early December morning. Peter's system was heroic. He counted to ten slowly and audibly, gradually pushing his head out from under the covers and watching his breath turn to white mist. On the count of ten he wrenched back the blankets and hurtled out, shoving his feet into his slippers and his arms into his dressing gown which he kept, contrary to regulations, under the blankets. Then his task was to wake up Alan and help him to face the chill of the new day. It was a self-imposed sacrifice to get up first in order to help Alan, for his friend was never at his best first thing, taking a few minutes to wake and a few more to realize where he was.

On this morning it was clear that Alan would not be greeting the new day with a bright smile. He had gone to bed the evening before complaining of a headache, and now his flushed face and croaking voice showed that he had fallen victim to flu, which was scouring the school and filling the hospital dormitory.

'You look terrible,' said Peter, inspecting Alan's face in the dim light and seeing with a pang of concern how his glands were puffy in the neck and his eyes were rimmed.

'Like you then,' gasped Alan. 'Makes two of us.'

'Ha! Ha! Very funny I don't say. I'll tell matron.'

Alan made a half-hearted protest, his clammy hands trying to push back the top sheet.

'I'll be all right,' he said feebly. 'There's concert practice.'

Peter hunched himself into his dark blue dressing gown, pulled the cord tight around his waist and scuttled out of the dormitory along the corridor and up the stairs. He met matron bustling down them.

'Mrs Byers,' he said, clutching at her skirt as she went to sail past. 'It's Alan Wright in 2 Rowe. He's ill.'

'Another one,' the matron grunted as if it were a deliberate attempt to undermine her position in the school by introducing unwanted germs. 'What's the matter with him?'

Peter didn't know how to answer that except to say that he was all hot and red. Mrs Byers walked on down the corridor towards 2 Rowe dormitory, her black heels cracking on the floor and her wide rear waving in front of Peter. It was the work of a moment to pronounce the diagnosis in loud and assured tones.

'Can you manage to walk to the hospital dorm?' she asked. 'I need to isolate my flu customers from the other boys as much as possible.'

She put her strong arm underneath Alan's back and heaved him out of his covers, wrapped his dressing gown around him and half-carried him out of the door.

'Bring his toothbrush, towel and soap, will you?' she called back to Peter, who hastily gathered the materials and ran after his friend.

Later that morning, when Peter arrived at the music room with his violin, he was unaccompanied.

'In b-bed with f-f-flu sir,' he explained, taking his bow and checking its tension.

'Poor lad,' said Mr Grant.

'P-p-p-please sir,' Peter leaned forward, plucking the violin from its case. 'I think I can do that vibrato.'

'Oh yes . . . good for you.' But the teacher was not listening. 'High temperature has he?'

'Yes sir.'

'Well, better get on. You can play this Hebridean lullaby, smooth and slow, smooth and slow and no vibrato, just the clear notes of the Scottish highlands. How is he – in himself I mean?'

Peter, bow in hand, paused. 'Well, he's all right sir – j-j-just flu, matron says.'

'Quite – lots of it about – too much for comfort just before the concert. Up to playing your pieces solo, Townsend?'

'N-no sir,' said Peter. He couldn't play alone. 'H-h-he'll be better by then sir.'

'Of course he will,' murmured Mr Grant.

Mr Grant turned to the grimy window and listened to Peter's clear grasp of the second position.

'Good. Good,' he said. He tapped his finger idly on the windowsill, but his rhythm was not that of the lullaby. Peter faltered and stopped, but Mr Grant remained against the window. A jagged line of frost slowly slipped down the pane in a gritty sliver as the warmth from inside the room touched it. Mr Grant did not seem to notice Peter's silence for a moment, and he suddenly pushed himself away from the wall and went to the outside door.

'Keep going, Townsend. Keep going. Try it with a little vibrato now and see which you prefer.'

He shoved his heavy palm down on the emergency exit bar and the door swung open, letting in the cold gloom. He left. Five minutes passed and Peter completed the piece twice, conscientiously, then stopped. Silence pressed in on him and he became vividly aware of his surroundings. He was so used to being with Alan that he had never really noticed the musty clutter of the place, the rack of pipes by the door, the manuscript paper covered with the teacher's notation pushed into a cavity beside the cupboard, the yellowing posters of instruments in an orchestra lining the old picture rail and the chipped corner of the great globe light that hung on a rusty chain over the piano, flooding the area with a jaundiced fug.

Furtively, he slipped his violin back into its case and tiptoed over to the window. If the teacher were to be coming down the steps he would be able to pick up the violin again as if he had never stopped, but there was no sign. He leaned on the door bar and it yielded. Slowly and quietly he eased himself through and then scuttled up the steps outside until he could see across the yard through the black railings. Along to the left the area known as the arches lay. Here the daily milk crates were stacked and iced in the mornings. Here pupils congregated on bad weather days when the regulations enforced their exit from the buildings during breaks and the covered area afforded the only protection. The hospital dorm was above the arches. Peter could see Mr Grant leaning against one of the pillars, apparently conducting music gently with his left hand. He almost ducked back out of sight, but the teacher was gazing up towards the school building and then, with an abrupt clenching of his fist, he stalked under the arches, presumably to the door into the school that only sixth-formers and teachers could use.

Peter shrugged his shoulders as if it didn't matter that he had been left behind, and returned to the music room where he packed away his bow with the violin and chin rest. Normally he was very careful to wipe off all traces of resin from strings and bridge, but today he did not bother. Then he went out through the emergency door again.

At the top of the steps he paused. He found himself looking towards the arches again, and the area beneath them seemed to darken into impenetrable black and then swell out from under the building like a cloud of smoke. At the same time the roaring sound began to buzz towards him from the shadow. Peter could see it coming. It was going to envelop his head and hold it. His mind brought the talisman of his real security into focus, the image he used to beat away the darkness. Alan's face stared into his from within the cloud, but it did not dispel the force with its light because Alan's face too was darkened by illness and unhappiness. Alan was in danger. He had to see Alan. The cloud reached him, swept round his head and seemed to drag him on through the forbidden doorway and up the stairs to the dormitory.

Matron was not pleased to see him standing shivering at her door. She had quite enough flu patients already.

The clamp on Peter's brain was now tight. Mrs Byers shoved a thermometer into his mouth and clasped his wrist before he could summon words from the distant nightmare that had pressed itself upon him so suddenly and so disturbingly. Part of Peter's mind struggled still to be free of it, kept saying that there was nothing to worry about, that Alan just had flu and Mr Grant was just concerned for him, but the vice would not grant the rational world its place, slowly crushing its voice into fragments of futility. Mrs Byers took his arm and sat him on a hard chair, checking the thermometer was tucked under his tongue. Sounds and smells of vomiting exuded from a nearby bed and pressing business called her away.

Peter stayed glued to his chair, staring along the rows of starched white beds, expecting at any moment to see a gaunt figure emerge with his arms wide as if to invite him to join in. There was a picture in his history book of a medieval vision of the devil in the black cloak of a priest. The inscription spoke of the evils of translating the Bible into English. It was that creature and another vision from an earlier memory of his father that Peter could see between the beds, searching for Alan. It crouched down beside a bed at the end of the dormitory and then blossomed up like an evil tree before it strode closer and closer to Peter as if it intended to march inside his brain and take up residence there. He felt the great palm on his head as part of the clamp that held him rigid.

'Another patient, Mrs Byers?'

'Looks like it.' Matron was back, rubbing her pink hands on a white towel. 'Anderson can't keep a thing down. Fancy trying to chomp chocolate in his state!'

She pulled out the thermometer. Peter winced, ready to be discovered as a fraud. She frowned at the measure, then shook it quickly.

'A few over the top. More to come from the look of you. Pyjamas, bed – second from the end, next to Wright. Move yourself, young man.'

Lying in the crisp sheets he felt confused, but much happier. Being put to bed is one of the most consoling actions for a boy, and Peter was close to Alan. The buzzing cloud had receded and he felt startlingly well, his head wonderfully clear and somehow apart from himself. It was such a pleasure to be tucked up as an invalid. He looked to his left and saw just a thatch of golden hair above the top sheet. It was Alan, asleep, he thought, and an immense deep happiness brought peace into his heart. By the bed there was a locker, on which stood a bowl of black grapes. Peter smiled and slept.

When he awoke, the light had switched from morning white to evening grey. He thought at first that he was in bed in 2 Rowe's dorm because Alan was in the next bed, but then he realized that he was on the wrong side of Alan and that he was supposed to be ill, but he wasn't. He was there to protect Alan from the danger.

'You too?' Alan, still red in the face and peering from a damp pillow, smiled weakly.

'Me too.' Peter told of matron's misunderstanding, of how he came to visit Alan and found himself in bed.

'Do you feel all right then?' asked Alan.

'Yes. What about you?'

Alan put his head back on the pillow and closed his eyes.

'Have a grape,' Peter whispered. 'Where'd they come from?'

'Don't know. Here when I woke up,' Alan sighed through puffy lips. Peter shrugged. He was used to people receiving more than he did. He never received treat boxes from home.

'Can I have one?'

Alan just rolled over on to his side and began to breathe heavily through his mouth. Peter took the gesture for agreement.

He reached across and took a cluster of grapes from the bowl. They were smooth, cold and filmed with silver. He picked one and held it, rolling it in his fingers, a beautiful marble of sweetness. He put it to his lips and with the tip of his tongue explored the tang of the skin. He drew in a breath and the whole grape popped into his mouth. He pushed it out again with his tongue. All the silver had vanished and a glossy purple-black shone in front of his eyes. With great care he placed his two front teeth into the skin like a mosquito inserting its needle and dragged them across the bloom, scarring orange and green gashes. Beads of taste clung to his dented lip. Slowly Peter ate the grape. He was left with a rancid pip that he chomped by mistake and a desire for another grape. He took it stealthily and returned the rest of the cluster to the bowl, but his head felt drowsy and rather bleary again. Perhaps he was becoming ill and his temperature was rising as matron had said. He tucked the second grape under his pillow and slept.

His next awakening came as a shock. Matron stood at his bedside with a basin on a trolley and a bottle in her hand.

'Bottle or toilet?'

Peter indeed felt ill now. His head ached, his throat was on fire and his eyes were sore. Mrs Byers touched his forehead and nodded sagely.

'Thought as much. More fun, more flu, bottle for you.' She pulled away the top sheet and gave him a china bottle. 'Do what you have to do in that, dear.'

Peter blushed and fumbled in his sticky pyjamas. The bottle was cold against his skin and he felt dry until suddenly weakness eased his bladder for him and a great flushing flood poured into the empty container. He blushed again but matron was busy at Alan's bed and took no notice of him. Next moment, however, she was back, took the bottle and gave her patient a cursory mop from flannel and bowl. Quickly she adjusted his pillow, discovered a squashed grape, tutted over it briefly and left him caught once more in a white cocoon.

This time sleep did not return so soon. His eyes flickered over the cracked ceiling and the sheets about his thin body trapped him. Wild imaginings replaced his normal existence and the cracks in the ceiling were the interlaced and confining branches of a forest. Above the trees in the snow-filled sky Mr Firmani flew like a giant crow and he croaked and croaked and croaked but Peter could not hear his message because Mr Grant thundered through the great trunks of the pillars of Greelham Church, a giant on a white stallion, white-bearded and his eyes like twin torches. He wielded his baton like a crop and the stallion's flanks were lined with red and the creature's eyes rolled in frenzy. All the branches of the trees that vaulted the nave became the bows of violins and they were wailing one word: 'Lost! Lost! Lost!' Mr Grant was searching frantically among the trunks of trees for something. Peter did not know what, but he was convinced that unless he discovered it both he and Mr Grant would die, for Peter himself was in the dream too by now but transfigured into a creature of light, but his light was a black, dark light that fought to find vision but could not. Wherever the torches of the giant shone, his light shrivelled away and he could see nothing. Around him the thick ribbed bark of a monstrous oak began to grow and it pulled him up with its surging strength and held him rigid until he felt that all his light had been extinguished. He could just turn his head and around him sat other birds, all of which had heads of people he knew. He wanted to hide the loss of his beak, let the creeping power of the bark envelop his face lest they turned and threw him from the tree as an intruder, but then the great Firmani bird landed shudderingly on his head and screamed in his ear, 'Giuseppe didn't know what he was looking for and he found it. Giuseppe didn't know what was looking for him and it found him.'

Then the fringed black leaves of his winged gown flapped in his face and another bird was cheeping in his ear, bleating into his brain, but the words were gobbledegook and belonged to Mr Eldon. Eldon was a budgerigar and the other birds swooped upon him and he flew away protesting, but then he was his mother and she was flying away from the tree, leaving him to the great oak creature that wanted to stifle him and make him a wooden mask and she was shrieking, 'It's best not to know!'

The next moment Mr Grant began to hew the trunk of Peter's tree with his baton and the bark began to shred and then split. Peter knew he was doing it to help him, to rescue him, but the walls around him cried 'Murderer!' with every stroke of the fierce cutting edge. Inside the tree cowered a small naked creature, a pink little shell with the sheen of dew and tears upon it, but Peter knew it was his father. Mr Grant swept it into his purple arms, leaped back upon the stallion and rode away. The creature, folded in dark swathes, turned its head and stared at Peter accusingly. As it did so, it grew bigger and bigger until it seemed to swallow Mr Grant and fill the forest until he was a greater giant than the world had room to hold and he was riding a greater horse than could be supported by the earth so that the crust of the ground began to shake and fragment like a crumpled jigsaw and the tree which was Peter's began to sway. Peter knew all this was happening but he could also see that this giant was holding another creature in its turn and this time it was Keeping, but Keeping was wearing a dress with tiny pink strawberries on it like Claire's and a great mouth loomed over him and he was swallowed. Peter felt a harsh constriction in his throat as if he were having to gulp down the ball of Keeping's head. A massive hand was pulling back his hair so that the skin on his face was stretched to tearing and the monstrous creature was on him, in him, around him, blotting out all sensation but fear. Then the Firmani crow was hunched on his head again and his beak was pecking at his bowing hand, trying to win his attention because he was playing the music for the earth to dance beneath him, and beads of blood appeared on the back of his hand, pricked by the pecking beak. A word appeared, written in his blood, and suddenly Peter was cold and naked in the tree with a frost on him, being dragged inside the trunk. He shook and struggled but he could not free himself, only shrivel into a tiny shell.

'Wake up, Alan! Wake up!' Moonlight shone across Mrs Byers's face as she leaned over Alan's bed. 'Heaven help me, the lad is worse than feverish. Keep those blankets on you now. The doctor is here.'

Slowly Peter focused on matron. The light from the moon made her pale, but her face was frightened as well, her eyes sockets. She could not see the dark creature looming behind her, nor hear the roaring hatred of its presence and Peter could do nothing to save Alan for Peter was locked inside the great tree, a small defenceless naked creature sheltering from a storm. He watched the shape gather Alan up and carry him away. He heard her say, 'I've been run off my feet all day.' He saw her clutch the bowl of grapes and follow down the centre of the dormitory and then he slept.

Morning brought weak clarity to him. His body was still, his head so emptily clear again that it seemed as if each cell had been scrubbed clean by a scouring pad. As he opened his eyes, the shivering white window opposite shone brightly at him, making him wince. He closed his eyes, turned his head with great care away from the glare and opened them again. There was Alan's locker but the toothbrush glass was empty and the bowl of grapes had gone. They have taken him away and I know not where they have laid him. Mr Eldon said those words but he was telling lies because Peter knew where Alan was. He was dead. A cold heavy certainty lay like a huge quarry stone in the shivering ice of his brain. Why could he not regulate his power, the power of his father, so that Alan could be saved? It was because he had been an unloving son. He had not obeyed as he ought to have done and there was no good in him.

Mrs Byers arrived, her broad white face narrowed by the night's vigil. She was like his mother, mopping up and clearing away the mess of her life. It would be best if he could be swept away in the rusty blue dustpan and tumbled into the great bin outside the school kitchens with all the other rubbish. She leaned over the boy, her normally capable hands fumbling with the bedclothes.

'W-w-where's Alan?' he asked, but Mrs Byers placed her coarsened hand on his forehead and put a finger to her lips.

'Well you're on the mend. No tummy pain?'

Peter just stared up at her. He knew the answer to his question, but why had she not told him? It confirmed the certainty and made it absolute. She, in turn, gazed at the misshapen little blotched face beneath her and thought of the other boy, such a handsome lad. Peter saw pain cut her eyes into sorrow.

'Alan had to go into hospital,' she said uncertainly. 'He was taken ill in the night, very ill.'

All those grapes, thought Peter inconsequentially.

'I thought he was suffering from flu, like you and Anderson across the way. Anderson has been sick in the tum – it takes people like that sometimes.'

Matron patted the pillowcase absent-mindedly and straightened up.

Mr Grant came into the dormitory. He strode down the aisle, white hair and black suit like a consultant in a hospital ward. His voice rang out.

'Well, how are the little patients, ma'am?'

Peter, lying like a statue, observed his teacher and matron as if through a telescopic lens. All the outward details were magnified, so that the mole on matron's chin appeared enormous and the tiny wisp of hair from it a fearsome bristle. When she spoke it quivered. He saw the teacher sweep his hair from his eyes and place his nicotine-stained forefinger on his chin and he could also see Anderson, propped up opposite him, and he remembered how Keeping had talked about men who liked boys and sticking their things in boys' bottoms. He felt ashamed and guilty at the same time, hot and with slugs sweating clammily across his flesh because Anderson was looking at the teacher with the same sneer that used to cross Keeping's face when he looked at Peter. Then he believed with a frightening intensity that the figures in front of his eyes were deceitful, that they hid themselves in appearances. The shapes that weaved and acted inside his head were far more truthful and exact. His eyes kept watching, registering.

'On the mend . . . on the mend,' Mrs Byers said, trying to match the teacher's heartiness but failing. He looked round and Peter knew he would look at Alan's bed first.

'Alan Wright?' His voice held surprise or a new wariness and Mrs Byers looked at Peter quickly, but the boy seemed oblivious. She touched the teacher's arm and the two drifted away from the beds. Her voice became low, confidential, but Peter could hear – every syllable was supernaturally resonant. He would have heard if they had walked into matron's cubbyhole and closed the door. He had always been able to hear, but now he could also see how Mr Grant's face grew grey and lined, how his shoulders grew together and his high head dropped.

'Danger list, you say?' he asked, rubbing the side of his face and then looking at his palm as if he expected to see scales of skin scraped off his cheek.

'Peritonitis can be very dangerous.'

'Appendix?' Grant laughed, a high quick sound. 'They're whipping them out like first teeth nowadays.' Mrs Byers looked more

192

worried, rubbing her forefinger where one of the knuckles was aching.

Peter watched, and knew that he had brought the evil, but could not be to blame. There had to be another culprit, for although he recognized that Keeping's death showed his power, he did not want to hurt Alan. To agree to kill Alan, his only friend, was to become the shadow itself, the destroyer that tracked him down. Peter thought of the grapes, the teacher by the arches, the hand on the nape of Alan's neck, the word 'bender', Keeping's jeering voice, Alan's face so clear and open, his own twisted and dark, his own sudden change for the worse after eating a grape, the apple in Snow White: jealousy again. He felt lucid and rational in the midst of his fever. Mr Grant had poisoned Alan because Alan wanted Peter as his friend. The shapes in his head told him that this was so. He sat up in bed and screamed once, shattering the scene in front of him. Mrs Byers rushed to his side.

'It's all right, my lamb! What is it?' Peter tried to push her arms away, pointing down the ward at Mr Grant. He was shaking wildly.

'H-h-he d-d-d-did it M-m-miss,' he whispered. 'It w-w-was the g-grapes, in the g-g-grapes. H-h-he t-tried to p-put his thing in h-him Miss.' Then Peter screamed again as matron forced him back to the pillow. She slapped him across the face; the blow burned and he went silent, but the words kept ringing through his head as if they were being bellowed from every corner of the school. She slapped him again on the other side, then sat on the edge of the bed pushing her fingers through her hair and leaning over to touch Peter's forehead. The boy's temperature did not seem to be unduly high. She forced herself to turn and look down the ward to the teacher. Her face split into what was meant to be an apologetic and supportive smile, but he had eyes only for the boy in the bed.

'Feverish, very feverish,' explained Mrs Byers, 'and highly sensitive as you know.'

Mr Grant turned away, giving just a small nod. His face was crumpled like used plasticine. Of course the boy's accusation was ludicrous, the product of fever, but the man was shaken to the core, guilty of murder itself. He felt repulsed by the workings of Peter's strange eyes and bruised lip, his curiously deformed face. He felt deeply responsible, but for what?

He had always had this affection for boys, had never believed it to be strange or destructive. He loved to watch them in their shorts, legs scissoring by in races, or curled up under a mop of untidy hair and a thumb stuck in soft round lips. He enjoyed their unruly excitements and sudden invigorating enthusiasms. He liked to touch their finely boned shoulders and set their often grubby fingers into musical correctness. He had always been intensely careful and been satisfied with gentle caresses across the hair or playful smacks on the bottom. Beneath the leonine features, Grant was exceedingly gentle. Mrs Byers had been in the school long enough to see through him. She had observed his hopeless infatuation with boyhood and dealt with his gifts of fruit and comics to the boys in the dormitory with a little joke that made him feel foolish yet safe.

Yes, he liked Alan greatly. The more the good-looking arrogant lad had treated him and his practices with joyful indifference, the more he had yearned for a touch of the boy's hand or cheek, a smooth caress of the nape of his neck, a tiny sprouting of velvet brush just right for smoothing. He had never and would never hurt one of the boys, never molest one, yet this Peter, ugly and worshipping, was staring at him now with gleaming little eyes. Mr Grant slipped out of the sick-bay, his inward poise destroyed.

As the door closed behind him, Peter relaxed and the tension oozed out of him. Suddenly he was flung upright by Mrs Byers. She held both his shoulders and stared furiously into his eyes.

'That man loves these boys.' She waved an arm down the ward. 'And look at all the music he brings us.' Peter lolled unresistingly. 'Alan has severe appendicitis. That is all.'

Peter's mouth formed the word 'grapes' and a hiss dribbled from its corner. His chest started heaving and tears began to flow, but the matron could find no affection for the tortured body. She left him, her legs like rusty levers, and walked into her little study at the end of the ward. She looked at the grapes by her armchair before putting on the kettle and sinking down at last into the worn upholstery. She kicked off her working shoes and eased her shoulders. Then she reached over to the grapes, tore one quickly from the bunch and put it into her mouth. She chewed it mechanically, carefully removing the pips. The kettle was boiling and she deftly forked the teapot to her side with her left foot. She brewed the pot quickly and nodded gently in her chair while it stood. Her eyes had to close. She had been up all night. Her mouth dropped open, bottom lip full and flabby. Breath wheezed through her nose.

In the dormitory, Peter lay in a state of shock. He knew it to be true that Mr Grant loved Alan too much to harm him. The black creature of his nightmare, the stalking evil that had manifested itself so clearly, had not belonged to the music teacher. There was only one person who could be responsible. He had brought this terrible blight with him. The creature demanded the death of love, for Peter had not loved his father as he should. Tears formed on the edges of

Peter's eyelids. How could he fight against such a stern justice? Should he not just lie in his trance, pretend he had no responsibility for the dreadful wounds that the brooding darkness inflicted? No. He had to take away this evil from his friend. He was an outcast. Better that he should cast himself out, taking the shadow with him, than that he should stay, bringing death to Alan. He would slip away and take the revenge with him. He would have to renounce this world of Greelham in order to save his friend, and risk the anger of a creature robbed of its prey.

Peter slid from his bed and limped the length of the dormitory on cold bare feet, expecting one of the boys to stop him, but nobody spoke. They were watching the wall or their pillows, under the blankets or caught in sleep. He sidled through the door, down the stairs and into the silent 2 Rowe dormitory. The rest of the class was in lessons. It was still, bare and functional. He pulled clothes from his locker so that all his belongings sprawled across the floor, but he did not stop to clear them, just pulled on trousers and jerked on an old shirt, shoved his feet into a pair of grey socks and his shoes. His outdoor coat was hanging in the cloakroom along the corridor. He went to find it, padding between the rows of dark blue regulation mackintoshes until he reached his peg. The coat had been bought to last and it shrouded his thin shivering frame, its hem rubbing the top of his calves. Its belt was twisted inextricably and he threaded it through the buckle with difficulty.

At the end of the cloakroom was the doorway to the black ironwork fire escape at the side of the school. It was there for emergency only, but Peter was caught in an emergency, desperate to escape and take the evil with him. He forced the door outwards and found himself clinging to the creaking frame of the rusty and rickety stairway. From a distance the fire escapes looked strong and firm, but standing in the bitterly cold December wind and hearing it wail through the open railings was like teetering on top of a precipice. Peter clutched at the safety bar and forced his way down the ringing stairwell. The metal froze his palm and his feet skidded on the smooth steel treads. He reached the ground and immediately flinched to his right, away to the line of elms along the side of the playing field. His shoes squelched through the pock-marked mud where rugby boots had passed and then he was among the trees. He put his head down, grabbed his coat collar to shield his neck, and trudged through the slimy leaves down towards the grand entrance and out into the inhospitable grey lands of Norfolk. He did not look back. He did not look forward, but his feet carried him without effort and without instruction towards Dinsbury. The countryside

# CHAPTER
# TWENTY-TWO

It is nine o'clock in the morning. The luminous dial on the bedside clock is unnecessary at last. The night has shifted into grey just sufficient to find the details of morning in Mr Eldon's bedroom. An hour ago he needed to peer through the gloom, to twist his head round and back again before the heaving cough inside him could wake and tear his chest apart. At three o'clock in the night he knew the time, greeted it as a deep but well-known enemy, a customary tormentor. Now another December morning marks another small victory against the choking devil.

His pillows, stacked behind him, are pressed back and have slipped sideways, now propping him ineffectually so that his left side is lower than his right and all the poisonous juices in his body seem to have drained down to his heart and left lung to form a tightly bonded cramp around his ribcage. He cannot move. He feels paralysed, not for physical reasons, but because his mind is bound and holds his body numbly stiff while he is forced to traverse his life in hazy review, occasionally leaping on a vivid memory as if greeting a friend unseen for years. These memories serve as weapons against the inevitable arrival of the immediate second and the immediate racking pain.

Now I must not touch 'if only' today, thought Arnold. 'If only' is a severe critic and a wasted emotion. Everybody in the world who ever lived, lived by and for 'if only' far too often. Think rather of the precious deed and the fulfilment. Think of kindnesses wrought and friendships freely given. Is there not a hymn with words and sentiments of that ilk?

He sat for at least a minute trying to piece together a verse, but he did not succeed. The words he thought of disappeared with the arrival of the next possible line.

I need to speak aloud, to create verse and proper terms by listening to my own voice, but now I can hardly speak without spitting phlegm and gasping for breath for an hour. That makes me highly selective in my words, he thought, smiling wrily. If only I had

197

written down my verses and my tunes, the hymnbook might be richer for it.

Arnold caught his breath sharply in annoyance and the action convulsed his little chest. Between each spasm, his mind kept clutching for words.

His eyes ran and he collapsed further down to the left, wheezing and gasping, fighting the cough instead of trying to soothe it back to sleep. His chest slowed eventually and his breathing steadied.

Bronchial pneumonia and a weakened lung eventually mean death, but before that let me weigh and catalogue some of my life. Perhaps in the knowledge of death, St Peter enters the still-living soul and starts his catechism there, saving time later, for the pearly gates must be besieged by creatures. I cannot speak my deeds and there are few to acknowledge them, but I have tried to help and serve others. My peccadilloes are of selfishness I hope, not major omissions, dear God.

When, however, he tried to list his acts of kindness from the neat tablet of his memory, a veil obtruded.

I ministered to the wounded, shocked and dying in the bombed streets of Clapham, he thought, but then he remembered that there had never been a time when his heart had been pierced by somebody's plight. I built a shield around me to cope with disaster. To feel would have impaired efficiency, but no, there was a coldness in my heart as I offered my free and fluent words of love. Most learn personal love from their mother and, perhaps, their father. I was merely shown the shell of caring, the material security of possessions, and could only proffer that shell in the name of God, a cardboard vocation.

Then the image of Peter's face swam through the tears of his weakness and it was frightened, pinched and white.

I tried to give help from the depth of my reason, from the logic of my ministry and I have failed because my heart was not involved, only my vanity and my desire to show Joan my strength, my purpose and my compassion. Perhaps he will succeed in the life I have mapped out for him, but I have gambled when I should have treasured the gifts he had. I should have given him freedom.

Depression had begun to spread its disease through Arnold. He tried to fight it, tried to find another memory on which to build his justification.

I remember the girl, he realized, clutching at the memory. She was caught, legs under a beam and had been lying pinned like that for hours, unable to move. Oh the dirt of her clothes, her arm flung wide, fingers bloodied into the ground beside her and such short, stubby, rigid little fingers that had scrabbled their nails to the quick in trying to lever herself out from beneath the fallen beam. And then there were her eyes set deep in a white and grey face – a *papier mâché* mask – not wide lakes of eyes, those brown Italian eyes, but deep-set tiny flints sparking still on a tired old battery like old eyes, my eyes looking into hers, trapped. She could speak still, unlike me, for, for once, I had no words. I smoothed my linen handkerchief over her cheeks and then she spoke, but I could not hear the words above the sound of burning and the fall of rubble down at number 39. That noise startled my tongue, but when I brightly said, 'Speak up, my love. We'll soon have you out of here,' her eyes shone as if to forgive me and then they closed and her shuttered face fell away, disintegrated as the light of heaven was extinguished in her face. I thought to give comfort but I always blurted the wrong thing in a confident tone that fooled the living, fooled me too. I cried then and thought her look had touched me, but maybe my tears were for myself and not for her. The girl saw hypocrisy in the tune of my voice and left me for genuine consolation beyond the ruins.

And now I'm almost speechless, pinned inside this head, this bed. My thoughts are better left unspoken. I have only trotted out words and platitudes served on platters of sincerity, presentation being all. If I had held Joan to me as the greatest gift that God could frame for me, I would not have watched her leave me with hardly a pang of regret or concern. A wail of despair should have echoed after her, and it would not have been injured pride but fear for her future that would have sent me after her to plead. She was walking to her sacrificial death with Paul, and I was self-willed and thought her mother was exaggerating the boy's aggressiveness. I gave her my blessing when I should have urged her to test the substance of her love with a little time.

How many dying brothers and sisters have my consoling words sent into that last oblivion before the mighty rebirth of the soul into joy with uncharitable thoughts of me, a silly pompous little man? I won't know until I die, he thought. In fact, with each explosion in my chest, I feel closer to life and freedom. I am coughing out the bile of my past, each gobbet of secret poison implanted with every encounter, every hope I extinguished as I hid in dapper propriety and social conscience.

Arnold felt conscious of a huge and inescapable regret creeping up on his thoughts again. He lifted his eyes and pulled his little lips into his mouth as if gagging himself. Think of ministry. Think of service in God's name, he counselled himself. Do not think of me. When he tried, however, his mind refused and remained blank until unbidden thoughts continued.

I was cursed by God with a tongue that was silver in exposition and dross in content, for the more my congregation admired my eloquence, the less care I took with meaning. I let the polished surface blind the already darkened minds of my flock. I failed Peter, trying to graft upon a human soul the trappings of my speech. Oh Joan, Joan, how you must have wept to have your son dragged from you so soon after losing your husband, and what devious steps I took to win your agreement, offering you a reborn son, as if I had the power to mould another human being in the likeness of God. Is that why you actively seem to destroy all my protective cells of bachelor custom, little interests and fastidiousnesses, when you come to nurse me now?

Time has passed after all. It is ten o clock and she is here.

'Here's your tea. Come on – up you come. I don't know what you do with these pillows every night.'

He wanted to say 'Pillow fights in the dorm' and giggle, but he didn't, and then he felt pleased that he couldn't trust his chest because he had renounced such stupid, time-filling words.

Now Joan opened his mouth between finger and thumb and slipped his cold false teeth into place. They felt like strangers against his hot palate, uneasily making themselves at home. He used to hate Joan's handling of the plates and his indignity, but now he did not care. There were so many functions beyond his ability now that this was just a tiny service. The cup knocked against his lip and clicked against his teeth. Lukewarm liquid bubbled inside his mouth and he chewed the liquid slowly, ruminatingly, letting tiny droplets filter down his throat so that no sudden gulp would disturb the sleeping devil.

He could have held the cup himself, pushed his own false teeth in place and dared the raging cough, but he lay back and allowed Joan to minister to him. What power had finally brought him into these woman's hands? Was Martha so capable, strong-handed and apparently untouched by close emotion as this woman, moving him like a lump of meat and administering to him with monosyllabic care? Were there feelings hidden behind her functional face and movements as she lifted, plumped pillows, dealt with soiled sheets and soiled flesh with such clinical efficiency?

I like being treated this way, thought Arnold with a sudden warmth. I no longer resent the loss of pride for there is no greater humility and no greater sense of being flesh and bone than to give myself to the services of another, particularly a woman to whom I

200

owe service. But there is no room for sentiment or cerebral longings. The woman is following, willingly or not, the pattern of womanhood and I could have been lying in this bed alone with nobody to care for me.

Rarely in the history of old men have old women cried, their tears dried by the daily round of domestic servitude. Yet Joan has the mould and features of the experienced nurse as well as the housewife. Is there a genetic connection between female and nurse, or is it a role forced on them by us? When Joan bends from the waist to stuff linen into the laundry basket and then heaves herself up to look emptily out of the window for a brief moment before turning back to the bed, she looks as her daughter Claire does when she is playing with her dolls. Claire would probably hate to know she looked like her mother, hate to be told that a life of service was prefigured and predestined in her mother's womb. I would like to speak to my congregation about Martha, thought Arnold wistfully, not as the uncomplaining and righteous servant of men, but as the long-suffering, ill-treated but always loving creature of man's vanity.

'I'm going to the church now to help with the cleaning and then on to the shops. I should be back about midday to give you lunch. You'll be all right?'

Arnold nodded slowly.

'And don't take any notice of that telephone of yours if it starts ringing. They can always ring back, if it's that important.'

She smiled perfunctorily and left the room, the door clicking firmly behind her. She always said that as if he still had power to alter the world around him by his own volition. The telephone never rang for him now.

Time passed. The important moments of life proceeded without his aid or intervention. A thrush sounded outside the window and rain spattered occasionally. He heard the sound of a dog barking from across the green. In between times he looked across the room to the mantelpiece and the mass of cards displayed there – the outward and visible signs of his life of service – cards from the faithful, full of Christian hope and purpose. There were flowers and little pots of conserves and preserves, neat boxes of chocolates and amusing cards in which illness on the front was contradicted by a sickroom full of life and vigour inside. They are used to seeing out the incumbent, thought Arnold, and all my little improvements will not last beyond five years of neglect. There is not the money, nor perhaps the will, just the daily routine and custom. Down below in the hallway the telephone rang and rang and rang, but Mr Eldon stayed where he was, in his sheets.

They are my winding sheets, he thought, and the time is not yet come for me to leave them. I wonder who is ringing so patiently? The telephone bell trilled and silence returned. It was a relief because the sound had just begun to worry Arnold, to scratch the word duty on his mind.

Joan returned, prattling of the cold in the stone slabs at the church entrance and how she was not surprised Vera had arthritis of the knees and couldn't continue on the cleaning rota. She showed her thumb to Arnold where she had split it against the galvanized metal bucket and the soda had seeped in, turning it raw. She served him soup with squares of white bread, tucking them into his mouth with the practised ease of a mother with a small child. She wiped the corner of his mouth with his napkin and gave him warm weak tea through a straw. Then, with infinite care and minding his bedsores, she twisted him out of his cocoon and he fumbled to the commode a yard away from the bedside. He waited for the hacking cough to come, but it was kept at bay by Joan's arm at his back. He had no time to feel the embarrassment that used to flood him, caught as he was between the trembling fear of the bronchial cough and the shivering weakness of long bed-rest. His legs were pale and thin, with tiny etchings of blue veins traced on his shrunken shanks. They could scarcely hold him. He toppled back into bed and held his breath, for with the return into the newly folded and cooler linen, the cough often came.

'We'll soon be having you on your feet again,' said Joan, tucking in the side sheet firmly. Then she was gone and he had not told her of the telephone. She'd placed a book by C. S. Lewis in front of him — some of his radio talks — such eminent good sense and balanced judgements, Arnold had once thought, but now they read with the blind self-certainty of the unchallenged, untested thinker. I may only find Jesus through giving myself as he did, but such giving is not in my power, Arnold thought, and I must be satisfied with second best and second best is the worst of all gifts, turning to ashes in the mouth.

The afternoon wore on. He dozed fitfully. The telephone rang again. It woke him and the bell made him tremble lest the shock of its sound acted as an alarm for his chest, but still the devil waited. Arnold began to wonder about the phone, for everyone he knew knew of his illness, knew only to ring between nine and ten in the morning or between five and eight in the evening when Joan was there. It rang so long that Arnold began to believe that he could manage to reach the receiver in time. He had always been so active, so full of vim and bounce that to listen to the telephone only a flight of stairs away began to cause him stress. It pinged again into silence and Arnold began to listen for it, to wonder about it. It was obviously urgent. How urgent? What had happened to cause the caller to hold and hold and hold for so long? He turned his head to see the clock. It was three thirty – a very long time before Joan came back – too long for a matter of life or death.

If I start moving now, he thought, I shall be by the phone when next it rings, for it will ring again, I know. It has that desperate quality. I shall be able to take things slowly, wrap myself up warmly. It could be about Peter. The last thought seemed to arrive from nowhere, prompted by a faint recollection that he had given Greelham School his number in case of emergency. Before reason could restrain him, he inched his fingers under the sheet and tugged it, trying to use just his fingers, trying to prevent the action from jerking his body at all. The sheet slipped from its place and he trampled the covers down from his waist by little fumbling steps of his feet, pushing his toes into the folds and feebly working himself free. Finally he was able to swing his legs from the bed without having to bend them up and thus constrict his chest. His feet were like two white fish on the floor. He inched them into his carpet slippers and felt an enormous sense of achievement. His breathing was steady.

It is a question of faith, Arnold thought, shuffling his thin and painful buttocks to the bed edge. There has to come a moment in a life when action through faith alone is demanded. If the telephone call is merely routine, I have lost nothing because I am nothing stuck in my bedroom. If the telephone call is urgent, and faith affirms it must be, then I have gained everything for I have jeopardized my own life in the service of another. That is the sacrifice of faith.

He looked towards the door. It was only a couple of yards away, but seemed much further. He crumpled to his knees and shuffled forward keeping his body erect, his head still, focused on the door handle. Although perspiration was running down his back, it had been easy, he felt, much easier than he had envisaged. The handle, however, was at eye level and he had to raise his hand to bring the lever down. To do this required movement of the chest. He wondered about using his chin, but rejected the possibility. That would be even more strenuous. Inch by inch his hand crept to the handle and suddenly the door pushed open and his hand fell down so that he crouched on all fours looking out on to the landing and down the carpeted stairs. Once again it had been easier than he'd expected. Now he shuffled round so that his feet tucked themselves over the edge of the first step and he began to work himself down, exhilaration beginning to push one knee after the other. He was not done for yet. He was still able to move about, have a life of his own. He made himself stop after each step to allow his breathing ample time to retain its steadiness, but part of his mind said that he could leap to his feet if he wanted to and vault the stairs two at a time.

His toes touched the hall carpet. He knew that because when he scratched for the next tread, the surface stayed flat behind him. He would stay here, he decided, until the phone rang again, but first he would have to turn himself round to sit upon the stairs. Then all he would have to do was pull himself up on the banister and take the phone from the hook with his left hand before collapsing back to his seat. If then the coughing came, at least he would have the receiver rammed against his ear and he would hear the message. Meanwhile he would sit and rest, preparing himself for the mighty effort. He remembered sitting on the stairs when he was a child in London living in a draughty Victorian house in Southwark. He used to perch on the attic stairs and peer down the well right to the ground floor, watching the tops of heads and occasionally flicking tiny pellets of paper down, down, down out of sight. His eyes closed – he was more tired than he had realized – and he began to think of his childhood, the loneliness of it and the darkness of the creaking house.

When the telephone rang it almost took him unawares. His chest heaved and he had to wait to allow the coughing to subside, but it was not a violent attack and he was able to stagger up and take the telephone before sinking back gratefully.

'Mr Eldon . . .' The voice was very close, crackling and full of concern. 'It is Mr Salmon here, Greelham School. I am ringing about Peter Townsend.' The voice paused, waiting for acknowledgement.

He would have to speak. It was not enough to listen. Arnold swallowed hard and muttered into the mouthpiece,

'Yes. I have not been well.' The words caught on his throat, caused him to cough, but once again he managed to control it. Mr Salmon's words flowed on.

'I'm afraid he is missing at the moment. He discharged himself from the sick-bay and seems to have left the premises. We've been expecting him back for some time, have sent senior boys out to find him and, of course, notified the authorities, but matron is concerned lest he is feverish – a nasty bout of flu has been affecting the boys. I'm sure he is all right, but we wondered whether you had heard from him. Presumably he has your phone number?'

He would have to speak again. Perhaps it was like moving now – every step would make it easier.

'I have not heard,' he said.

'I do not wish to be alarmist about this,' continued Mr Salmon, 'but perhaps you could tell his mother. I'm sure he will turn up very soon. I'm told that he was upset by the illness of a friend. If he does happen to contact you, do tell him that Alan Wright is out of danger. His appendix was removed last night and all is well with him.'

'I will. Thank you.' The phone clicked dead at the other end and Mr Eldon released the receiver so that it dangled down, knocking gently against the wall. He felt utterly drained of energy. He would have to sit there until Joan arrived and then he would have to talk again, but he felt calm and happy. He had acted through faith. Of course he was worried about Peter, but at least he could tell Joan himself what the school had said. Boys did become upset from time to time. Every boy that ever was must have been tempted to run away from home or school at least once. That Peter had a touch of flu was the most worrying aspect. Matron was right to be concerned about that, but he could not have travelled far being ill. He would be found soon enough.

Slowly his eyes began to close again but then they sprang open, panic filling them, for the band on his chest was tightening. Racking sob-like coughs tore his chest, ripping and ripping as if each spasm was slitting a wound in his chest wall and removing a sheet of tissue from his lung. Eventually he collapsed back against the banister side, his small face purple and his lips white as pastry. His mind kept saying, I must pass my message to Joan and then I can die. I will not fail in this. I cannot fail in this.

# CHAPTER
# TWENTY-THREE

Rain – a great sluice of mist and soaking water – covered Norfolk from flat horizon to flat horizon, from hamlet to hamlet, from isolated tree to isolated tree. It seeped into every vein of the leaves, every tongue of grass, and filled pools with gurgling, sucking power. It smeared Peter's hair to his skull, sprayed every eyelash with pearls of water so that his face was awash with cold tears. The cascade fell down his gaberdine, turning it into a blackened cloak, and soaking his school shoes so that they squelched and oozed with every step. Wind scuffed up the wetness and drove it into his face; long reeds wrapped themselves around his legs and hedgerows leaned towards him as if to engulf him and yet he walked on, past Dinsbury and on towards Barham, another ten miles across the Sandringham Estate. There was an inner compass that directed him and a desperation that kept him moving. It was the work of the black creature to drag at his legs, to bring the wind against him, to torment his passage, and he dully fought against it, knowing that the creature had the power to whirl him into the shivering sky like a fearful pheasant and back to the school if it wished. Now, however, it sat at his shoulder, shrouded his head and dripped words of poison in his ears. It spoke in many voices.

'Death? Whose death? Your own death? Look your last on all things lovely for you have lost your right to be loved. Was that why Milton lost his eyes?' asked the Firmani crow. 'Was his love for Lucifer, the fallen angel, greater than his love for God? Was Hamlet's delay caused by kinship with the inadequate or a less than absolute filial duty?'

'You're the runt, but you'll have to do me. One's a little Mummy's girl and the other's a runt.'

'They like putting their things in boys' bottoms because their mothers hated them – sent them away, as like as not.'

'A sacrifice unto the Lord.'

There was no fever in the boy now. The rain had drained it from him and he limped forward cold and shivering, lugging the jewelled bird, his friend, along a dead path. He stared ahead into the greyness as if trying to see the figure of his father striding on, but there was nothing but darkness and the voice in his ear,

'Too late, too late – it's all very well coming and saying you're sorry now, but it's too late to make a difference.'

He was being sucked back to a nature that should have been compassion but was cruelty, and he was the fugitive in a hostile country. His only hope was to drag the musk of evil away with him and hide it within himself, becoming ferret, hunter and hunted, fear and fight in one. All else was artifice and would be brushed aside by the impatient hand of a shadow. A great arm seemed to drag him round and he had to stagger along backwards, but he could see Alan running away from him towards Greelham, leaping the puddles, throwing back his face and catching the rain in his mouth, shaking his hair so that a rainbow sprang from his head.

'Alan!' He screamed, but the wind flicked the words away and the creature dragged him on and all he could see were the stricken trunks of beeches stripped of their summer gold and reduced to sodden skeletons, skirting a metalled road awash with scummy debris. His leather shoes hopped and then swivelled round towards Barham, the water pluming around his toes like miniature rowing boats cutting through spray.

Night crushed down upon him and his feet stumbled on the verges, through ditches and squelching mud. Branches cut across his face and paths disappeared before his feet could find them. His fingers continually grabbed at his eyes as if to pull away the blindfold that had been tied by his dark torturer, but they came away empty until quite suddenly a hole was blasted in the sky's covering and a moon sailed out over a shimmering sea.

'A lunatic is one governed by the moon,' said the Firmani crow, flapping his sleeved wing gently against his face, 'but I fancy that Shakespeare took that with a pinch of salt, and could see other reasons for insanity. It is a brave man who can portray madness so that others may recognize its presence without himself being tainted by it. Is Hamlet mad as Ophelia is mad?'

The road shone ahead of Peter like a line of ice, a glacier mint of a surface, and the rain ceased. The moon brought its chill with it, however, and the watery surface quickly began to congeal so that his feet slithered along. He fell once, landing awkwardly on his knees, and he squealed like a crushed dog. He scrabbled up whimpering, moving on before Slater said 'bender' in his ear and kicked him 'just the once'.

He stood above Barham village on top of the small incline along the old Priory Whelk road. There was mist in the tiny dip where the houses clustered, but he recognized it well enough. Away to the right a silhouetted spire floated and through the darkness came the sound of the trees around the green sighing and moaning. He crossed to the five-barred gate and pulled himself over it wearily. He would not risk going through the village. He was now dragging his lame foot behind him and his shoulders were rigid with tension and ice, but he struggled on, reminding himself that there was only a mile to go and then warmth and shelter. He pictured the old range as he remembered it, the close friendly smell of it, the crackle and hiss as his mother threw on fuel and then battened down the lid. He would sit in the corner and steam would rise from his clothes. He would sleep and maybe his mother would give him food.

'You have come for vengeance not for comfort,' said the hateful voice in his ear, but he ignored the creature now. It had become stupid with its continual shrieking and it could not compete with the exhaustion, exposure and cold that numbed him. As he stumbled over the back field, the presence seemed to shrivel away. Peter moved by instinct like a badly beaten animal, its flame dying, its limbs stiffly returning to its only resting place.

The dark house was blinkered, locked and empty. His heart ached for the light in the kitchen, the velvet curtain at the door. He was so wet, so cold and so tired that he could hardly fumble his way to the back door. He put his water-wrinkled hand round the knob and pushed, but the streaming boards did not shift against their bolts. His knees almost gave then. He could easily have buckled on to the doorstep, but he managed to push himself to the house front where the large sash windows were. A cord was broken and the window could be forced up on one side, making just room enough to flick the catch. If the rain had caused the wood to swell, he would have to break the pane, but he would try the sashless window first.

He scrabbled on the ground and found a rusty strip of metal. It was what he'd used before if he'd wanted to slip into the house unobserved. It gave him a small knot of warmth to find it still there ready for his fingers. The window gave when he forced it up and he managed to slip inside, belly down and head first. He had come home.

He lay for a few moments beneath the window and the turmoil of wind and mind receded. The musty arms of the house embraced him. Another voice came to him, but it did not belong to the evil. 'Don't go walking your mess over the carpet.' He slipped his hand down to the sodden mass of shoelaces, squeezing the threads until they reluctantly parted and he could twist a thumb into the knots.

'Put them in the kitchen filled with old newspaper from the cupboard – but not too close to the range – don't want the leather stiffening!'

He held the dripping shoes by the heels and padded damply past the shrouded chairs of the best room. He pulled open the door, making sure he pushed the handle down well to prevent it sticking, and made his way into the kitchen. His feet made little wet squeaking noises on the black hardwood of the corridor but he was walking blind until he opened the kitchen door and met the moon full on as it shone through the window on to the stone-clad floor.

'Hang up your coat to dry. You'll catch your death with it sitting on your shoulders.'

He put his coat over the peg by the back door and walked over to the range, to the small hole in the wall where Mum always kept the matches and sticks of wood. He pushed his fingers into the fissure, but it was empty, all except for two slivers of wood tucked into the brick join. He fumbled them out into the open, peering at them in the deceitful light. They looked like matches. He opened the fire door in the range. The old grate gaped its rusted teeth at him and so he limped to the coal cupboard to find newspapers and coal. He could not see inside and had to feel forward in the darkness, but there was fuel there, lumps of scratchy cold coal and chunks of wood mixed together. There were damp old newspapers too and Peter hastily crammed the paper into the range, threw on wood and a few lumps of coal and turned the ventilator round to create a draught.

He jerked the first sliver of wood across the wall. Nothing happened and he tried again, but all he succeeded in doing was to catch his knuckle against a jutting brick. He held the match up in the moonlight again but couldn't tell whether it was a red or black top and so he tried the second match. It glowed across the wall and flared immediately. Peter cupped the precious flame in his hands, fearful of losing its promise, then edged it against the newspaper. For a moment the fringe of paper singed and blackened but did not burn, but then a spurt of purply light sprouted and orange flickered through the newspaper, crackling like crumpled dried leaves against the wood. Peter continued to hold the match until the flames burned his fingers and then he held his frozen hands to the blaze, feeling its warmth as from a distance, before slamming shut the door to intensify the draught.

'If the wind's right, the fire's right,' said Mum in his head and he prayed that the knife of the easterly outside would kindle a fine fire. The range muttered in front of him and a muffled roar sounded as the wood caught and the coal began to glow. Huge relief weakened Peter still further and he tumbled into the alcove corner by the range – his old accustomed spot – and hugged his knees up into his chest, rocking from side to side, willing the heat into his body. He began to giggle, his head light with fatigue, his stomach empty of food. He rocked on the floor and giggled because he had freed himself from the asphyxiating band and reached home.

There were a few tins of beans in the old pantry, emergency rations. 'It's important to have a few things put away for times of need. That's what my mother always said and she was a grocer's wife.' There were old clothes up in the wardrobes, but for the moment he would sit and glory in his escape and in his return. It was his farm, given him by his father and here he would live for ever.

Clouds chased across the moon like a dead man's hand, blotting out the room, filling it with shadows. Peter stopped rocking and tried to cover his face from the presence that had been conjured from his mind again. The attempt was futile because it had arrived solely because of his jeering belief that he had won his freedom. The creature was a tangible force of anger. Its tattooed arms were spread across the room, strong and sinewy, and its voice was raised in a howling cry. It sounded as if he were calling out his sister's name.

'Claire! Claire! Claire!'

Every room in the house shouted back in mocking echoes, 'Where? Where? Where?'

Peter could not remain curled up, protecting his injured pup. He peered through his fingers into the red eyes of his father who was also a beast caged by fury beyond himself, which in turn was haunted by a greater monster until the howling wind outside was also the howling creature battering at the door, trying to invade the sanctuary of his home, his resting place, the farm his father gave him in return for his allegiance that he had not given yet.

'Don't open the door, Dad! Not this time! You mustn't open the door!' He clutched the sleeve of the great blue coat but he was flung backwards.

'You don't have to go this time, Dad. Stay here! Stay here!'

He could smell the animal outside, the points of its fangs – trying to flush the rat from its hole, the rabbit from its burrow, his father from home. Peter launched himself again from the alcove and Nipper squealed in distress but he did not care because Westby was there with a shotgun ready, waiting to take him out into the snow, waiting to stain the cold snow red. Once again he could feel the old coat stiffen in his hands and then he was holding nothing for he was inside the coat itself, burning with anger and fear.

210

'You won't get me twice, Westby!' He screamed at the banging door. 'Once caught, twice shy. I won't die because of my son's pup. I won't die because of my daughter's wanderings.'

He backed away through the kitchen door, along the corridor and doubled up the stairs. He forced his way into Claire's room. She was not in her bed. There was a shape but it wasn't her. He barged into the big bedroom and across to the wardrobe.

'You won't find me in here!' he screamed. 'You won't find me in here!'

It was dark in the wardrobe and Joan's old clothes hung about him like veils of security and secrecy. He burrowed down into the corner, pushing under folded curtains and blankets, and there he found an old oilskin-covered packet, heavy and slimy cool to the touch. He put it to his forehead and it smelt of grease like the shotgun after cleaning. He knew what it was, how it came to be there, why he needed it now. He undid the package and felt the squat pistol butt firm in his palm.

He walked downstairs steadily, the gun held forward, its barrel as dark as the leaden sky through the landing window. The knocking on the door continued and he would stop it once and for all. He entered the kitchen and the moon was out again, bleaching the room to bones. It was like the reflected light from deep snow. The knocking seemed to stop and an absolute hush surrounded him. He looked down at the gun and did not know how it came to be in his hand.

'Peter! Peter! Is that you? Open the door, there's a good lad.'

There was a scratching at the window and his mother's voice. She shouldn't have been outside the house. She belonged inside with him, away from Mr Eldon, staying with him, looking after him. He brought his face round to the window. Yes, there was his mother staring in with the moon behind her. He brought up his hand to shade his eyes, to see her more clearly and the gun was heavy in his palm. His mother had deserted him, cast him away and thrown him from his home. It was right that she should be beyond him now, but the voice of his future said that his mother was needed, that she should serve him like a woman. The gun tumbled to the floor and he went over to the door, pulled across the bottom bolt, and wondered what he could stand on to reach the top one. He lifted his hand, thinking it would be too high for him, and he found he could reach it and it wasn't that stiff after all.

Next moment he was pulled by his mother into her coat and held so tightly that the bonds of her womb seemed to take him in again.

'Whatever have you been up to?' she muttered and her voice

sounded from her heart straight into his head. He buried his head deep into her front and held her with every ounce of his remaining strength. She needed him, his heart sang. She was his mother and she needed him. He felt her hands on his chin and, reluctantly, he brought his head up to look at her pale unhappy face.

'Mr Eldon told me,' she said. 'He took the phone message – he had a stroke in the doing of it. They've taken him to hospital, but he'll not live, the doctor says. I don't know what made him do it. He shouldn't have got out of bed.'

That's right, thought Peter.

'He said something about Alan Wright – difficult to make out the words though. He's all right, recovering in hospital.'

Peter sighed deeply. He had been right to take the creature away from the school, away from Alan. His journey had transferred the vengeance to the minister and his friend was safe.

Joan looked across the floor to where the gun lay. She had seen it in Peter's hand when she'd looked through the window. For a moment she had feared for their lives. Now she prised herself from her son's grasp and picked it up.

'And what was this for, may I ask?'

Peter did not know and shook his head.

'It was your father's,' said Joan, holding it gingerly by the barrel end. 'He stole it from a dead man, but it didn't bring him much luck.'

She looked round the room as if expecting a hole to materialize into which she could fling it. She stuffed it into a drawer.

'Out of sight for now – out of mind. Shall we go then?'

Peter looked at her. He was home. He would not leave this place again. Joan noticed that the range was roaring. Already the old room was warming up. She smiled briefly. It would be nice, she thought, to stay here for a while. There was nothing to stop her, and Claire was with the Luffmans again.

'Some beans for you, my lad,' she said, and went to the pantry. She found the tin opener in her hand before she had to think where it might be.

'Fetch some sheeting from the front, Peter. We'll make a pile on the floor by the range.'

Peter did not move. He was happy watching her bustle round him, making him comfortable by her presence. She whisked some sheets into the alcove. Within minutes they were sitting together, forking baked beans from a shared tin.

When they'd finished, Peter snuggled into his mother, sleep weighing quickly down upon him. He was happy now, protected from the nightmares that surrounded him outside. As he lay there, his eyes closing, fluttering open like a dozy butterfly's wings and then shutting again, Joan found herself talking, explaining to the night, to the moonlight around her and to Peter, if he would hear, something of her unhappiness. She had never spoken of it before, had repressed her thoughts and feelings under the snow, and then could find no way of communicating with her children. But something in the warmth of the range, the return of Peter, prompted her. 'I didn't want you to go away, Peter, but I didn't think that I could help you any more. Perhaps it's all wrapped up in your father's death, what happened on the night he died. You only have to hear a door knock and you're all of a twitch and a bother.' Joan smoothed a damp strand of Peter's hair away from his eyes. 'Arnold should never have told you how wonderful your father was, how he was a brave soldier and a good man fighting tremendous odds. Not that there wasn't good in him, you understand, there was, but his life here was wrong for the man he was, bottled him up. He knew he'd made a mistake but he was obstinate, your Dad, and so he went from bad to worse.'

Peter's breathing was steady, the sleep deep upon him. 'I killed him, you know. I pushed him over the lip of the quarry and I knew I was doing it. It was not just a little slip. There were his eyes staring at me and I hated him.' She gently passed her roughened fingers over the boy's cheek and looked beyond him, through the walls and out along the quarry path.

'You're far too young to know what it is like to kill a man. I've suffered for it and I've brought you suffering as well. When Arnold offered you rescue, who was I to deny it to you?' She paused, looking round at the old warped cupboards, the dirty window and the clean moon shining through it.

'The night he died, he'd driven me out of the house into a blizzard and destroyed the washing and the table. Perhaps you know better than I what happened earlier that day with Westby. There were all sorts of rumours in the village about a fight. I came back that night to protect you and Claire. You have taken Arnold's words and weaved another image of your father, made him into a great god. You see, Peter, if you grow up like him, you'll end up like him. You have to learn to be your own person in this world.'

She trembled a little now the words were spoken and inspected her son again, closely. There were streaks of mud across his cheeks, congealed blood was stuck in his hair where he'd collided with a tree in his flight. His legs were scratched raw by brambles and his fine Greelham's tie was twisted into a knot over his shoulder. His face, however, seemed smooth, the colour even and his mouth, in repose,

# Postscript

Peter now lives with his mother at Townsend Farm, Barham. The Christmas Concert at Greelham School was cancelled because of illness among the boys and Peter did not return after Christmas, the terms of his scholarship being revised and then rescinded. There was no financial hardship because Mr Eldon's will provided an ample allowance for Joan and, when Claire left home and married Dan Westby years later, Peter and his mother were truly alone.

Townsend Farm is a successful battery unit for poultry and eggs, highly mechanized and self-sufficient. Joan never enters the white concrete block where the automatic feeders and collectors of eggs whine all day and night, extending laying times and improving profits. In the summer she suffers marginal discomfort caused by blow flies and the inevitable smell of chicken manure heated by the sun, but Peter does not notice these things. He inspects the rows of caged birds every day, pleased that his plans are prospering, keeping a tight hold on the fury that still occasionally burns through him, conscious that the hens he breeds are descendants of the poultry run ravaged by Josie and that his cages are clinically clean and efficient. He remembers the dung and smell of old rabbit hutches in a leaking outhouse.

Sometimes, rarely, he worries about his mother – how she sits all day doing little except cook his meals and tidy the house – but she keeps in good health and her thoughts remain her own as she watches the tall figure of her son, swathed in a dark blue coat, climb into his new Volvo estate and drive to the hypermarket in Thurriton where his eggs sit in light blue plastic trays and are sold in hundreds every week.

The gun lies wrapped in its oilskin in the bottom of the wardrobe in the room where she sleeps.

215